ORIGINALLY PUBLISHED BY BIG SKY PRESS

New Cover illustration:
Desiree Dixon
www.desireedixonart.com

Book design:
Angie Underwood
www.brandingbyangie.com

New Publisher
James Milward

REPUBLISHED BY JAMES MILWARD
2017
SECOND ADDITION

ISBN: 9780998175645

Printed in the United States of America

PREFACE

"There is nothing to writing. All you do is sit down at a typewriter and bleed."

\- Ernest Hemingway

I introduced the character of *Sammy Shovel* in my P.I. mystery fiction, *An Adventurous Night.* The love and encouragement I received for this character was more than I could ever imagine. And so, it wasn't with much struggle that I decided to do follow up stories involving this character who had quickly made a place in readers' hearts. While writing this novel there were a couple of changes I wanted to see in his character from the earlier version. For starters, I wanted to show some personal growth in *Sammy.* After losing both his parents and his P.I. partner within six months of each other, I didn't want him to turn into a dark, broody character wallowing in self-pity. I of course didn't want him to turn into a happy, chirpy bird overnight either. I wanted a man who is able to look at the world in a more positive light. I also felt that he needed a new partner in his life. I made this happen by introducing a woman character, *Zondair* towards the end of the book. She is mysterious and he is completely intrigued by her.

Sammy Shovel, the super P.I. makes his second appearance in the novel *'Too Beautiful For Words.'* The CEO of a big corporation with a squeaky clean image gets murdered, but he leaves behind a set of clues - almost as if he's pointing towards his murderer. The local police department is stumped and can't make heads or tails of this case. *Sammy* is hired by the corporation to find their boss's murderer. He quickly delves into the case and unearths explosive and controversial information, including an international assassination ring. And *Sammy* has to depend on his super sleuthing skills and gun slinging ways to find a way out of the latest muddle he has found himself in.

I would like to acknowledge and thank the work, research and support of many who helped me write this book.

PRAISE FOR *TOO BEAUTIFUL FOR WORDS*

"James rewards his fans and mystery readers with *Too Beautiful For Words*."

– Publisher's Weekly

"The narrative in this detective story is a mix of classic whodunit style and character driven plotting."

– Moterwriter.Com

"James' second book featuring P.I. Sammy Shovel has a tight, clean prose that is perfect for this genre."

– J.L

"A great book – even better than the first one."

– Patricia

"It is an engrossing whodunit with an interesting lead character."

– Jeffrey

"A thought-provoking mystery that provided a little action and a lot of surprises."

– Sandi

DEDICATION

This book is dedicated to Margery, my loving wife for fifty years. "I miss you my darling!" and all my children, grandchildren, and great-grandchild.

Other books by the author

The Two Jacks (Adult)
Harrington Manor
An Adventurous Night

TOO **BEAUTIFUL** FOR WORDS

By

RONALD M. JAMES

CHAPTER ONE

When you need a friend,
He might find you.

April 28, 1993—10:16 PM

"Joel! Working late again tonight?" Donald Anderson asked happily; he wore an Armani suit that oozed success. Joel, was the founding father of Golden Opportunities, and insisted that every employee display the habiliments of a thriving corporate business.

"You know how it is, no rest for the wicked—or the CEO's." Joel replied, glancing up and grinned. "Have a safe trip home, and give that bride of yours my love. She's a real sweetheart." He felt a frown coming on and successfully hid his fears that ominous international congeries may try to annihilate him and take over his company any second, simply because he might have unwittingly cautioned his gym's new workout partner a week ago about changing employers.

"I will, sir, but we've been married for six years." Donald said with a chuckle. "She's hardly my bride."

Donald graduated from the University of Santa Clara and had been winding his way through a tiered corporate structure. Joel dubbed him with the dubious title of vise president, as he assigned to all executive caliber employees after one year of employment.

    TOO BEAUTIFUL FOR WORDS

"Son, they're all brides to me. Go home. I'll see you tomorrow." Joel said. He pushed back from his desk as Donald left. Rotated his chair and faced the window, a smile flashed across his face as he clasped his hands behind his head.

San Francisco had a special charm after warm days and Joel wanted to soak up every moment of such incredible morphing allure.

When the sun's red glair disappeared, office lights took over. The city initiated its mysterious life, especially on crisp nights. Illumination clearly identified each building, but gradually, and without warning, fingers of dense mist slipped between tall buildings, blurring their edges and engulfed them.

Garbled images immersed throughout his senses as streetlights blinked eerily through the damp, hovering fog. Entranced, he watched automobiles plunge in and dash out of the milky soup, while garish neon signs, perpetually beckoning customers, melded together into a wild, spasmodic glimmer, until disappearing without a trace.

A tingle shot up his spine when his phone blasted out on his credenza top. He frowned before apprehensible picking up the receiver. "This is Joel; how may I help you?" He heard a familiar voice; he stiffened in anticipation of a ferine firefight. "Yes, I've—I've been expecting your call. Same place? What time?" He glanced at his Rolex. "The usual then. I understand." He replaced the receiver and continued gazing out of his revered window. He checked his watch again, then he turned abruptly back to the documents he had been laboring over on his desk. He paused for a second, now a man with destiny, he furiously re-sorted the various papers into three neat piles. He opened his desk drawer, pulled out a pad of Post-it notes and scribbled information on three of them. He stuck one note on each of the piles, and tossed the pad back into the drawer. He placed his pen back into its holder. Then arranged the three piles of papers in a consecutive row. He picked up his antique stone pyramid-shaped paperweight and rolled it over and over in one hand as a magician about to execute a sleight-of-hand trick. He gazed back toward the window, a distorted face reflected back to him, anger written around his mouth. He turned back to his desk, frowned at the hieroglyphic with symbols hewed in its surfaces, grumbled slightly, gave his wastebasket quick look, but instead slammed it down exactly where it had been.

Joel sighed. He got up and glanced out of his mystic window one more time, then went to a closet, reached in for his suit jacket and glided the left sleeve over his slight frame being carful not to damage the silk lining by his diamond pinky ring, jewel studded Rolex watch, or perhaps a hangnail his manicurist might have missed.

His haberdasher had carefully selected and coordinated Joel's silk tie and hanky to complete the CEO image. Posh could hardly describe his everyday tailor-made wardrobe.

He gazed around his office, and spotted an old dirty hat in a handcrafted trophy case. He removed it. His eyes water as he held a childhood memento. Joel checked his watch again, then carefully put the hat back where it belonged, closed the case, and walked to the office wall safe. It was open, precisely as his office, files, desk and everything else he owned or used. Joel didn't believe in keeping secrets.

Everything was shared in the firm; he wanted an open-door policy, similar to Hewlett-Packard management concept. Any and all ideas were welcomed, and were never swept under a rug where no one could build on a crazy, but perfectly logical idea. All employees were encouraged to put forth their most outrageous whimsies, for Joel embraced them all in various stages of enthusiasm.

At the safe, Joel reached in and retrieved a small revolver sitting on top of a large envelope. It was a snub-nosed 38. In one motion, he exposed the chamber and checked for ammunition. His wrist jerked the barrel back and he heard it slap home. His action smacked experience with firearms. He grabbed the box of ammo.

He tucked the revolver snugly into a familiar location behind his waist belt, then slipped an ammo box into his left pants pocket. He took the elevator down to the parking garage, where he located his black Ferrari. He wheeled it out onto Pine Street and disappeared into light fog.

*H*e stopped the car three blocks from the agreed rendezvous location; Joel carefully surveyed the immediate area before parking. It seemed as though he was standing next to a broken steam line, and the impenetrable fog obscured his sight fifty-feet in any direction. He scanned the perimeter mist for signs of trouble; Instinct told him—*something was wrong; the murky night reinforced his caution.*

Joel scanned the fog again before getting out of the car, but it was rapidly thickening. Once out, he ducked down and quickly extracted his revolver. He crouched, then moved away from his car and advanced up the streets toward the meet. He knew any sneaking enemy could see no further than he could, but dreaded more than three assassins. With that in mind, he checked each building's entrance before moving to the next. He expected an enemy to open fire at any moment.

Finally, he reached the designated intersection, noted a low stonewall where he could retreat, then quickly shielded himself behind the street corner's telephone pole.

Through the dense fog, Joel spotted the outline of a large figure in a doorway across the street. The man moved toward the curb, waved, and softly called, "*Ho'el—Ho'el*, 's that you?"

Surprised, Joel muttered slightly above a whisper, "Manny?"

"*Si, Ho'el*, 's me, Manny." The figure waved his right arm again.

"I'll be damned," Joel murmured to himself, "I thought I was going to be ambushed."

He crossed the intersection. The thickening night soup still made his first steps cautious. When he identified Manny, he tucked his revolver back into its hiding place.

Childhood images flashed across Joel's mind; Manny in their Mexican village. The big lummox still had a chubby round face.

*S*houts of laughter are common in any village, town or city where children play. It's the same in poor Mexican villages, but childhood is brutal when they awaken to the significance of poverty. Gaunt, barefoot children in tattered clothes learn the meaning of despair through the senses. The children's savior was usually the village priest, teaching all, who were willing, to read and write. Joel was eager for knowledge, while Manny, being somewhat illiterate, only thought of a heaping helping of refried beans wrapped in a tortilla—sometimes it was accompanied with pickled cactus and a scant amount of chicken. A bedazzled mind enjoyed simplicity.

     TOO BEAUTIFUL FOR WORDS

Joel and Manny's parents, like others in the village, made them beg for money at the town's crossroad. The two didn't even know what shoes were. They wore ragged clothing, but both proudly sported new hats, gifts from an American welfare agency. If Joel and Manny came back empty handed after a day of panhandling each got a whipping. Oh, they got supper, a plate of tortillas and a half portion of beans rather than the full bowl. The food was meager, but it was food. It was all anyone expected in their village.

One day Joel hid on the back of a truck going to Mexico City. He found his way out of hell. In three years, he made it to America. Years later, he discovered his old playmate, Manny, now a loveable half-witted lumbering oaf, still hustling in the same village, and sent for him. The two have been inseparable friends ever since. Because Manny was slow, Joel has had him doing odd jobs. He paid for Manny's gold front teeth, his house, car and nearly anything Manny wanted, which wasn't much. Neither had married; friends said they had each other for strength.

*M*anny's familiar big grin eased Joel's trepidations.

"*Amigo*," Manny said as he reached for his friend's right hand. Manny grasped Joel's hand tightly. As the two come closer, Manny pulled a gun out with his left hand and pumped two slugs into Joel. The voltaic action ripped apart their handshake and hurled Joel to the sidewalk.

Mortally wounded, Joel gazed up at his still grinning friend and gasped, "Why—why you?"

Manny forced his grin wider exposing his two upper front gold teeth, but it quickly faded. He became a grim faced officer speaking after taps. "Because, amigo, because of the code." With that, he blasted Joel in the heart, a sort of coup de grace. "*Adios, mi viejo amigo*," he muttered, and expeditiously dissolved into the fog.

CHAPTER TWO

Welcome to this corporate world.
It has its head in the clouds.

April 29, 1993—8:30 AM

---

*M*etal tipped high heel shoes clattered along the outskirts of the financial district until dawn. Now they were silent. Cable cars clanked up California Street while their conductors gleefully rang tunes on the trolley bells replacing San Francisco's Nightlife. Plebeians, intent on grinding out daily business transactions, avoided clustered raindrops that formed into shallow ponds making the evening's debris treacherous. A steady stream of semi-wet bourgeoisie flooded the building where Golden Opportunities' were headquartered. The corporate offices occupied the entire fifteenth floor. Opulence greeted visitors as they exited the elevator.

At the far end of the lobby, massive carved double doors led to the executive suite. They stood nine feet tall, sturdy talismans beckoning clients to a lavish lifestyle. Superbly shaped maple trim broke up multi-hued red faux-finished walls. Mahogany panels above each elevator doors dazzled onlookers with bronze inlay, and were meticulously crafted in Mayan motifs. Ancient Mexican pottery tubs constrained lofty ficus trees at the other end of the lobby.

A Mayan image made of strands of gold and black granite was fused into the company's logo and centered in the lobby's polished black-flecked red granite floor. All these trapping were created to impress potential clients—we know how to make you successful.

The twelve-foot high, bronzed ceiling grid of squared mirrors reflected wavering images of pandemonium below. The police had invaded the sanctity of Golden Opportunities. When employees arrived, uniformed officers greeted them with clipboards, noting their names, time of arrival, and employment title. Other officers, standing at attention, were stationed around the lobby perimeter prepared for mayhem.

Some employees milled around in shock; confused others pounce on anyone exiting elevators for answers why the police presence.

Sergeant Tom Ryan, out of Central, asked if there was a chair he could stand on, and grumbled under his breath. "Why me? Why doesn't Homicide do this? It's their case."

A young man, holding a wooden stool above his head, weaved through the commotion. He approached Sergeant Ryan and placed the stool beside him.

The sergeant stepped up onto the stool and stood as if he were a steel beam projected out of a concrete base. He epitomized a police—*I want you* poster. He waved his chevron-adorned arms up and down, trying to hush the crowd. "Please—please. May I have your attention—please, your attention?"

He surveyed a hoard of dark business suits scurrying around like a band of confused cockroaches after a spritz of Raid. His mind flashed back to his high school literature classes: Mark Anthony on the steps of the Forum about to deliver his rousing oration. "Damn, they won't listen," he mumbled, "I wish that Roman were here," he then boomed out. "Quiet!... Quiet!... I must have your attention!"

Startled, the throng stopped and gazed up at Sergeant Ryan's officious manner. "I've come to—to—ah—to explain why we're here today. I'm Sergeant Tom Ryan from Central Station." He spoke with the usual finesse of a career cop, who was never taught suave confabulations when interacting with the public. He continued, "First, let me say Lieutenant Braque from Homicide will head up this investigation."

"Investigation?" A few immediately asked.

"What on earth is he talking about?" another commented.

"Homicide?" Others frowned.

"Did he say homicide?"

"He will want to ask you a few questions." Ryan continued. "We don't want to disrupt your regular office routine, so you'll be called individually, and we'll try to keep you for as short a time as necessary."

Employees shrugged, frowned, a few turned to each other, and asked, "What the heck is going on? Why isn't Joel here? Where's Mister Ballard?"

The sergeant, who climbed from a beat cop, showed a totally lack of crafty enlightenment skills and immediately strafed the throng. "Although we've been through many homicide investigations before, I'm sure it's a shock for you to learn your employer was murdered last night, sometime after eleven."

Some women gasped, others gazed around in bewilderment, and other's started to weep.

"Oh no!" one cried.

"He was like an angel." A woman said, frozen to the spot,

"Why—why? Why him?" A man standing close to the sergeant sputtered.

"No—no! We don't believe you!" Two other men said over each other.

"You must be kidding. This can't be!" an older gent leaning on the rear wall shouted out.

"Who was murdered?" Someone asked.

Maria Hernadez, Joel's personal secretary, screamed and fainted.

Peter Ballard and Donald Anderson picked her up and rushed her to a chair.

The sergeant waved his hands again to quiet the mustered employees.

A tall, burly figure, who looked like a hatted bear, complete with brown coat, exited the elevator and pushed through the crowd. He maneuvered, with a few quiet, "Excuse me's," until he reached the executive doors. He motioned to the sergeant to get off the stool, then he climbed up.

"Thank you, Sergeant Ryan." The grizzly stood tall, and said in a commanding voice, "I'm Lieutenant Bracque with Homicide. Spelled B-R-A-C-Q-U-E. It rhymes with rock; get the picture? We've been up all night dealing with your boss's corpse at the crime scene and searching for clues that might lead us to the murderer."

Every time Joel's death was implied whimpers began.

"This morning we're here to question you for information to direct us to the person or persons who might've murdered your former employer, Joel Che Ja."

Again commotion burst forth, but someone yelled, "It's pronounced Che Ha."

"Now—now." As if yelling through a megaphone, Bracque shouted, "Hey, calm down! I know it's a shock to you, but we need to continue our investigation." The Lieutenant's

     TOO BEAUTIFUL FOR WORDS

brambly dirty blond eyebrows half-hid deep blue pools of furious eyes, that could worm facts and figures out of a dead fish, so his demeanor demanded attention. A square jaw completed his bulldog façade, framing heavy lips that began moving rapidly. "We're starting with you, his employees. Later, we'll be interviewing his friends, acquaintances and business associates. The way we conduct large interviews is to start with management and work our way down the ranks. I suggest you all return to your workstations and wait for our call. In the meantime, please jog your memories to recall if you noticed anything out of the ordinary."

"Out of the ordinary? Like what?" Someone called out.

"Anything. It could be your work routines, phone calls, a new account, a new salesman—oops—err, sorry—ah, salesperson. No matter how trivial, please write it down and bring it with you when you're called."

The staff began to disperse, some alone, others in groups. Men appeared bewildered and numb; women wandered about with tear swollen eyes.

Lieutenant Bracque stepped off the stool, took his wet hat off, wiped his eyebrows, turned, and asked the sergeant, "Ryan, has forensics finished in the deceased's office?"

"Yeah, I think so."

"What do you mean think so? Have they or not?"

"I saw Reinhourse and some inspectors enter his office before you instructed me to break the news about the owner's death, so I assumed—"

"God dammit, Sergeant, never assume anything. Gather up the controller, Joel's successor and secretary and—and the personnel manager and bring them into his office."

The sergeant just looked at him, then Bracque, admit a bit sheepish, said, "Look, I've been up all night, it started to drizzle around four, I'm wet, cold, and I'm tired so don't get on my case."

*T*he lieutenant entered Joel Ceja's corner office, which looked like a setting arranged for Interiors magazine. He thought, how could anyone run a company and keep his office so clean? He watched inspector Reinhourse gabbing with Kohler and Deaux about last nights Giants game and asked, "Are the lab guys finished in here?"

"It's been dusted, photographed and cataloged over an hour ago."

Bracque noticed officer Susan Jeffery standing by a bay window. "Thanks for coming, Jeffery, I know my call was on short notice, but this murder already is creating political rumblings and I need all the bodies I can muster up while leads are fresh." The lieutenant removed his wet coat and together with his corduroy hat, then carelessly threw them on a leather couch. Drawn to the large window, he joined Susan standing behind Joel's desk and also gazed out at Coit Tower and Nob Hill. "Nice view."

He moved toward built-in museum-quality trophy cases. One exhibited ancient Mexican pottery of all sizes and shapes. Some of the items were broken. The Lieutenant was puzzled, why anyone would keep, let alone exhibit, cracked vases. He then spotted an old dirty hat among the relics and immediately thought this guy had strange tastes. Another case contained silver jewelry and sculptures shaped into strange animals. Many of the pieces were set with turquoise stones. *That's more like it*, he thought.

                    TOO BEAUTIFUL FOR WORDS

"You haven't touched anything have you?"

Inspector Reinhourse, the proverbial clown, responded, "No, Lieutenant, we're just looking for clues. Besides, forensics spent two hours in here. You ask that at every crime scene and the answer's always the same. We're not kids—"

"Knock it off," he said glaring at Reinhourse. "The guy who ran this firm has been murdered. The mayor knew this man as a friend and he was an asset to the City. He told our chief he wants quick answers. I'm tired of trying to explain, in court, why didn't we do this or do that or have some smart ass detective find out things that were never checked. We're going by the book, and be especially thorough on this one."

Reinhourse, a dangling string bean, with a bloodhound face complete with perpetual drooping eyelids, pulled both cheeks and mouth back to speak. "I just—"

"Didn't I make myself clear? In a few minutes the personnel manager is going to be in here. I want inspectors Deaux and Jeffery to go with him and check out all of the personnel records. You know who's been recently fired or hired. Get their addresses and run a check on them. I want a preliminary status check by this afternoon."

"Check!" inspector Susan Jeffery answered.

"Wait! Hold up, Susan. I believe you might be better interrogating Joel's secretary. I heard she's distraught. I'm sure she'll need a kind face to look at when we interview her."

"Hey, does that imply the rest of us look grumpy?" Reinhourse quipped.

The comment brought about a few guffaws from Deaux and Kohler.

"You're not funny, Reinhourse," Bracque said. Reinhourse turned away in disgust. "Kohler, you go with Deaux and be very thorough."

Reinhourse tried to irk Bracque more. "How come Jeffery sometimes gets addressed by her first name?"

"Because, Inspector, I'm not the insensitive oaf everyone thinks I am. I show respect for women. Reinhourse, I want you to go with the controller. If anyone can find a bean missing from a pot it's you. If anything seems out of the ordinary, arrange with the chief to have Ernst & Young's guys do an audit."

"Before anyone arrives you better glance at the victim's desk," Reinhourse said.

The lieutenant gazed down at the top of a pristine desk, wondering how anyone could work and not clutter. "I see papers," Bracque snapped.

Inspector Reinhourse quickly replied. "Papers? There are three neatly formed stacks with Post-it notes on each pile."

Sounds were heard from the hall. "We'll check it out later. Sergeant Ryan has arrived. We'll start debriefing the staff and let them return to work. Stay here Sergeant."

The lieutenant turned to face two men, in their early forties, a woman in her late twenties, and an older lady with red, teary eyes. All appeared bewildered, and stood acquiescent and looked flogged, as if they were waiting for the executioner's noose. Bracque moved away from the desk, and barked, "Sergeant, close the door."

The older lady, Maria Hernandez, Joel's personal secretary, feebly cried out, "Oh no! Not the door!" She started to sob uncontrollably again, which startled the lieutenant.

"Ma'am, what's the matter?" He asked in a lower voice.

"It—it's the first time that door will be shut since I've been here."

"How long have you been employed here?" The lieutenant inquired, still speaking softly.

"Twelve years—twelve wonderful years. Now—now it's gone." The secretary turned away to hide her stream of tears.

"You mean in the twelve years you've been here this door has never been closed?" The lieutenant blurted out in disbelief.

Still sobbing, the secretary headed for a chair to sit. Officer Jeffery rushed to her, leaned over with words of comfort, and placed her hand on Maria's shoulder.

"Please, may I answer that, sir," one of the men said.

The lieutenant tried to size up an overweight balding man with two chins and heavy jowls that wobbled when he spoke. "The name's Lieutenant Bracque. And you are?"

"Peter Ballard. I am, or was, Joel's executive president."

"I see. Just what does, ahhhh—"

"Maria—Maria Hernandez," Peter helped the lieutenant.

"Ah, yes…yes. Uh—what does Maria mean, the door to this office has never been closed?"

"Tis true. The years I have been engaged with this company not only his, but also all the office doors have never been shut."

"What about discipline meetings, conferences and such?" Bracque asked in astonishment.

"As far as I know, Joel never had to discipline an employee. He had no reason to do so. When hired, Joel made it clear, work and be morally straight or, as he put it, there's the door. As for meetings, nothing in the company was a secret.

Everyone knew what was going on and in what the direction the firm was headed."

The lieutenant eyed the other investigators. They all had blank stares, even Reinhourse. "I mentioned my name is Lieutenant Bracque." He nodded to Reinhourse. "Inspector Reinhourse was the lead investigator last night until the department identified the importance of the victim. The chief roused me out of a comfy-bed at four this morning to take charge. I am irked, I am wet, so don't cross me."

Through the open door, Donald Anderson wandered in and headed for Peter Ballard. Bracque glanced up and tersely said, "This is a closed meeting—police business."

"Lieutenant, Donald was the last known employee to see Joel alive. I suggested he be here," Ballard intervened.

"Smart thinking." The lieutenant turned to officer Jeffery, who was gently rubbing Maria's shoulders. "Ah—Susan, would you accompany Maria to her office and ask what she can tell us about yesterday?"

"Yes, Lieutenant." Jeffery guided Maria to her feet.

"Susan."

"Sir?"

"Ask—don't pump."

"Understood."

As the secretary left with officer Susan Jeffery, the lieutenant added in a soft voice, "Leave the door open as you go out—please."

He addressed the remaining four. "Mister—ah—Ballard. Is that right?" Bracque took note that Peter was about five nine, beefy and had all the hallmarks of success: A tailor-made double-breasted dark-blue suit, red and blue tie, matching silk pocket hanky and a monogrammed white shirt clung to his roly-poly stomach perfectly, without a hint of stress. Most people didn't earn in a day what Ballard's patent leather shoes cost.

"Yes. Peter Ballard."

Bracque's gaze turned to the young woman and beheld more glitter adoring her fingers than Tiffany exhibited in their display windows. "You are?" He observed bouncy honey hair atop a doll face that sat on a swan-like neck, making her appear taller than her petite figure.

"Why Lieutenant, I'm Nancy Foster, personnel manager." Turning, she flashed her rings when she grabbed the man standing next to her and pushed him to the front. "May I introduce Mack Diverson? He's our Mister Moneybags."

Bracque detected a slight southern drawl that complimented her natural teasing nature. "Run that by me again."

"Controller. He's our controller," Donald said.

"We're asking you key employees to join with us in finding your boss's killer. We know he was murdered around 11:30 PM last night. It appeared at first glance to be a robbery. However, while his wallet was missing, an expensive watch and ring were left behind. A mugger normally wouldn't leave them. This always makes us suspicious. It suggests the victim wasn't killed during a robbery." Bracque glanced at Donald. "You were the last employee to see him alive?"

"I believe so," Donald answered.

"What do you mean you believe so? Did you or not? Who else was here?"

"I left at 10:15. The janitors finish before 10:00, so when I left all the office lights were out except Joel's and the lobby's night-lights. I stopped, said goodnight and went home."

"What did he say?"

<hr>

"He asked about my wife."

"Why?"

"He—he just did—he always asked about our families."

"So, he was interested in your wife and you suspecting him of having an affair with her. He left; you followed; you killed him out of rage. It's an old story that's repeated daily or did you have some other grudge? "

"You have quite an imagination, Lieutenant," Peter said.

"Stay out of this!" Turning back to Donald, Bracque continued to grill. "Well, were did you toss your gun or is it still in your car?"

"I don't own firearms of any kind. I went directly home, tucked my kids in bed and ate a late supper with my wife. I wouldn't think of hurting Joel. When you said he was shot I was driving up my driveway."

"Where do you live?"

"San Carlos; about an hour from here. Call her," Donald said, looking at the phone on Joel's credenza.

"It was a quick shot, but we will check your alibi—thoroughly. I'm positive Mr. Ceja wasn't killed during a robbery."

"You mean he was murdered for some other reason?" Nancy asked, while constantly flashing her dazzling rings. She did this by constantly moving her hand to her mouth, then she fluffed her hair around her ear.

"Exactly. Most muggers remove the wallet's contents then toss the billfold into the nearest garbage container," the lieutenant said. "We couldn't find the wallet anywhere in a ten-block area. In fact, the only reason we had a lead on the victim's identity so early was his car was parked about three blocks away. It was noticed because it was a Ferrari."

"Why would that make a distinction?" Peter interrupted.

"It was out of place for the neighborhood. We might have had a John Doe on our hands for days."

"I never thought about that," Peter said. "Lieutenant, I think I can speak for everyone here. We'll do everything possible to help you catch Joel's killer."

"It could be killers. Who's the controller again?"

"That would be me. The name is Mack, Mack Diverson," Mack donned a lean built, sun-bleached blond haired man. He sported a loose cardigan sweater over a Hawaiian shirt, no tie, faded jeans, open sandals, and a two-foot long heavy gold necklace draped around his neck, defying Golden Opportunities' consummate image.

"Mister Diverson, will you accompany inspector Reinhourse back to your office? And try to be as cooperative as possible."

"Of course. Follow me, Inspector."

"Wait," interrupted the lieutenant, "I want all of you to look at Mister Ce'-ja's desk."

"'Joel', Lieutenant, everyone addressed him as 'Joel,' but his last name is pronounced Ce'-ha," Ballard said.

Bracque gave a disdainful stare. "I'll try to remember."

Peter Ballard, Mack Diverson, Donald Anderson and Nancy Foster gathered around Joel's desk and glanced down at the three piles of papers. Peter frowned.

The lieutenant picked up on his expression. "Ah, Mister Ballard, this isn't what you'd expect to find on Mister Ceja's— Joel's desk?"

"Quite frankly, no. Joel was remarkably tidy. I've never seen his desk like this with papers on it. Don't you agree, Mack?"

Bracque scowled, for he already thought Ceja's desk was too clean.

"I certainly do. Something's strange. And there's a Post-it note on each pile."

"He didn't use Post-it notes?" Bracque asked.

"Oh, he used them all right," Mack responded, "but...well, not this way."

"What do you mean, 'not this way?'" Inspector Kohler asked.

"What Mack means is, the only time Joel ever used sticky notes was to favor the employees. He never said a beastly word about anyone," Ballard said. "We all knew we weren't perfect, but Joel kept it to himself and only embraced tiptop results."

"Hmmm, before you leave with an inspector, look around and see if there's anything else out of the ordinary," Bracque suggested.

Each of the employees examined the room. After three minutes they looked at each other. Peter shrugged. "I can't recollect anything out of order."

Reinhourse wanted to shake up the Golden execs. "What about the safe? We noticed it's open."

Peter went over and looked in. "The bloody gun's missing!"

"Gun! What gun?" Bracque asked.

"A small 38 revolver has been tucked in here for years!" Peter said surprising the police.

"Wow! You mean the safe isn't kept locked?" Reinhourse said.

"Except for an after hours lockout on the elevator doors, nothing is locked," Donald answered.

Lieutenant Bracque shook his head. "Amazing." He threw his hands over his head as he faced the other inspectors. "Did anyone find or report a revolver on the body last night?"

"No report of a revolver, Lieutenant," Reinhourse said.

"What else should be in that safe?"

Peter pulled out some papers and inspected them. "A copy of Joel's will. The original is gone." He peered inside the safe again. "The ammunition box is gone and I see black dust littered around. Where did that come from?"

"Reinhourse, check with the crime lab and ask what they found and confiscated." Bracque noticed Reinhourse didn't jump, and he yelled, "Now and ask about the missing revolver!"

Reinhourse glared at Bracque, and desperately restrained thrusting his middle finger for an appropriate salute. Deflated, he slinked toward a phone-table cuddled between two leather chairs.

Donald eyed Ballard. "May I leave now?" He turned to Bracque, The lieutenant nodded. Donald left the office.

"Okay, let's go over to the desk and look at the papers again. I see three piles of papers on the desk. There's a pen and pencil set, and a paperweight. What I don't see are pictures of his wife and kids or family. Where are they?"

"Lieutenant, Joel wasn't married." Peter noticed Bracque's right eyebrow rise. "Also, he didn't associate with the chaps."

"Where were you born?"

Peter turned, frowned, narrowed his eyes and gave Bracque an *I beg your pardon* glance.

"Why, Lieutenant, our Peter is all American," Nancy spoke up. "However, he was born in England when his parents were stationed at the London embassy. He's not a foreigner."

"I never suggested he was."

Nancy giggled slightly, then evoked the reasoning behind the lieutenant question. "Peter received a Fulbright and returned to Oxford."

Bracque gazed in obliviousness.

Aware of the lieutenant's remark, Peter directed his attention to the situation at hand. "Getting back to the desk, those items you cited are always on his desk top. What is unusual are the piles of papers. They are regularly placed behind him on his credenza, next to the phone and computer. If there was no room on the credenza top he would place them within it, but never on his desk."

The lieutenant gestured to Kohler, who went over and opened the credenza doors. Inside were some stacks of papers, confirming Peter's statement.

"Okay," the lieutenant said, as he stood over the paper stacks, "what about the sticky notes? The first one from the left where Mister—Joel would have been seated reads, *HOLD THIS PILE FOR FUTURE STUDY*, the second, *IN THIS PILE ARE PAPERS TO BE FILED*, and the last, *THIS IS THE PILE THAT NEEDS IMMEDIATE ATTENTION*. Since you indicated this wasn't normal, does anyone know what Joel was trying to tell us?"

"May we examine the papers?" Peter asked.

Seeing the forensic team left minute traces of black powder everywhere, Bracque said, "Sure, go ahead, please, and take your time." His gaze turned to see if Reinhourse was still on the phone.

"Inspector Kohler, place a number and a stack identification on the back of each sheet so we can keep the piles exactly in the order we found them. There may be a hidden clue that we don't want to overlook."

Bracque stepped toward Joel's enchanted window. He thought about his own eight-foot-square inside office, cluttered with stuffed file cabinets that had spilled their guts onto every available flat space. Bracque had to wiggle between cardboard file boxes and the keen edge of a steel worktop to sit at his desk. In order to shut the office's door, he was required to move either one of two side chairs. He knew these people work in opulence, while he waddled around in the city's ugliest excrements to enforce law and order.

Bracque turned to check the progress, and watched three Golden Opportunities' executives fashionably attired. Even Mack's casual appearance smacked excellent tailoring. The golden clan was adorned with exquisite jewelry and two wore Rolexes, Ballard a Patek Phillippe. He scrutinized them sifting through the paper piles, scowled and returned to gazing out onto the cityscape.

Classmates compared him to an oafish bully, but he wasn't. Teachers constantly scolded him, his peers avoided him, and parents feared for their children. If they only knew he was a gentle ox, not a raging bull. Bracque never was assertive, didn't know how to approach women, craved love, but being shy couldn't express affection the few times opportunity knocked. His façade remained gruff. As a result, he became a loner; never had a girl friend; never married and as time marched on became less than amicable—brusque would fit the bill.

His mind was flooded with what-ifs. Doubt took over. What happened, he asked himself. He lived and slept alone; he'd eat out; he had no friends. He rationalized he has no choice unless he can change, but didn't know how. He envisioned a large office with a similar window of dreams. Bracque craved embracing a glorious such as this each day—beautiful people, beautiful office, beautiful job, beautiful—.

While the lieutenant stared out Joel's window, Golden Opportunities' executives searched through each pile carefully. For almost five minutes, they discussed among themselves the order of the papers and what is in each pile. At the conclusion, Peter announced, "Lieutenant, we have no clue what is going on here."

Peter interrupted Bracque's fantasy.

Startled, the lieutenant turned and said, "Eh?" Sharply raising his voice. "What do you mean?"

"Each pile has no importance to its attached note and the papers in each pile are disseminated with a mix of subjects in all three," Peter announced.

Bracque moved toward the desk, and raised his voice. "Run that past me again."

"What we're trying to say, Lieutenant," Ballard said remaining calm, "it appears groups of papers were tossed together into three piles and a different sticky note placed on all three. But the notes have no pertinence to the piles of papers."

Reinhourse turned from the conference table phone. "Lieutenant, the lab boys have the original Will and never found a revolver." While still holding the phone, he turned to Peter. "Mister Ballard, may I ask just what does this company do? I noticed on the lobby wall opposite the elevators a sign that says, Golden Opportunities. What opportunities?"

"Sir, we provide businesses with decisive knowledgeable projections so they can make informed management policy options." Peter said smiling.

"Can you explain that in simpler terms?" Bracque asked.

"Simple it is: We do marketing. If you have a product, a service, a potential business opportunity or location, we will make a comprehensive survey for you to predict your chances of success," Ballard answered. "That's why we call it Golden Opportunities, because if you heed us, you will have gold in your pocket. We have a phenomenal success rate, and as a result we've done remarkably well in a tough, competitive field."

"Do you know where Mister Ceja parked his Ferrari?" Bracque inquired.

"Why, in our basement garage," Nancy answered in her sultry southern voice.

The lieutenant frowned, still trying to get a read on Nancy. He observed a simple narrow gold wedding ring almost hidden amongst the rest of her finger hardware.

"Lieutenant, the entrance is from Pine Street, and it's Joel. That's the way he wanted to be greeted and remembered," Nancy informed.

Bracque nodded and cracked his first smile of the day, maybe even the week or month. "Of course, I wasn't thinking. Thank you, it's been a long night for most of the inspectors and a tough morning for me. I want to thank all of you for your efforts. If you'll join with our inspectors for some more questioning at your respective offices, we'll finish up shortly. Tomorrow we'll question the other employees. I appreciate your cooperation. By the way, we will want to know what each of you was doing last night and where you were. It's just routine procedures, but I believe you understand that we must ask that question of every employee, past or present. We will check out each of your stories, so don't lie or you'll be considered a suspect."

The inspectors and executives left the room. Bracque sat down in Joel's chair, picked up the pyramid-like paperweight, and instructed Sergeant Ryan, "I want forensics to examine this paperweight again. Get copies of all these papers in the order we found them, including the attached notes, and leave them here. Have the originals brought to Homicide. I want the computer guys to run them through an encoding program. Ceja may have been trying to tell us something. We owe him that look. I didn't care for Ballard's comment about the Ferrari either."

"What was that?"

"The crack he made, 'I never thought about that.' I'm going to check him out real carefully. You know how the story goes: president takes over firm and runs it into the ground. In fact that Nancy and Mack seem too slick for me."

"Good idea." The sergeant said. He hastened to the door to locate file boxes, stopped and asked, "Did you know you could have people check to see if you're going to be a success or not?"

Bracque leaned back in Joel's chair, rolled his eyes and sighed. "No—no I didn't, but it tells me why there are so many people with big bucks, and the inevitable crime that goes with those inflated bankrolls."

"I guess that's what keep us busy, huh?"

"I guess so," The lieutenant said. He kept fondling the paperweight. He was fascinated by the strange markings engraved into the surfaces. "When the crime lab returns this afternoon have them take a real good look at this. I find it strange the way Mister Ceja arranged his desk."

"It's Joel, Lieutenant."

"God dammit. Who's running this investigation?"

CHAPTER THREE

In the P.I. game you're always praying
For deep-pocket clients.

August 10, 1993—9:25 AM

Sammy Shovel's office was one flight up in an old four-story brick building within walking vicinity of the Financial District. The building straddled the line between major downtown stores, hotels, and Chinatown. A little further north was North Beach, the Italian district, and Broadway's sleazy nightclubs. Location, location—it was San Francisco's snooping dick's address extraordinaire.

Samuel Shovel Investigations was painted in gold leaf on a frosted glass door. Sammy's reception area was a tomb. Egyptian burial chambers exhibited more charm and their wall shown colorful hieroglyphics. Window frames and wood wainscots flashed curdling streaks of almost black 1920's varnish. Lusterless patina was incrusted on an old heavy mahogany desk. Behind it were different colored odd-shaped file cabinets. Ancient and now dark wallpaper needed stripping, but a new coat of paint would be cheaper—preferably something on the light side. Three unmatched chairs and a couch, probably salvaged from some doctor or dentist's office, were strewed on a severely coffee-stained carpet. A table stacked with paper sat directly below a window. On those few hot days when the city's sweltered in heat, San Francisco's old air conditioning system

---

kicked into gear—open the window. Immediately, wind scattered paper everywhere. A severely stained Mr. Coffee machine sat on a dilapidated counter likely rescued from a nearby dumpster, but it did have a small sink. Above it was a sagging shelf that supported a microwave. Drooping potted plants lined up against a frosted-glass corridor wall, pleaded for water. A basket of dumped trash made the sloppy décor ready for an organized bonfire.

A brand new ergonomic secretarial chair, and matching desk wore heavy coats of dust, was out of place. One afternoon at Kantor's Office Furniture, Sammy envisioned a secretary bringing him coffee and answering the phone. His judgment was swayed by a smart display. He bought the chair and desk. When Sammy read secretarial want ads, he knew he could never afford to feed anyone else on his income, but repeatedly denied he'd stoop to hated repo work.

He had dealt with enough blond bimbos in other firms not to hire one himself. He kept the chair, year after year, hoping to find that one flush client, willing to pay, who could guide him to a new successful course.

Bored, Sammy straightened up his office desk, if you called rearranging the same clutter into new positions a cleanup. For a private eye, Sammy was comical and rather short: a buffalo would've had seemed an appropriate disguised as a man. At forty-two, he was getting bald. He called it a receding hairline. His attire steadily deteriorated after he was mustered out of the military. He now dressed one rank above vagrant. His clothes were a means to avoid running around naked.

Actually, he was lonely, and unfortunately loneliness had the nasty habit of torturing one's mind. All the better days

     TOO BEAUTIFUL FOR WORDS

reminiscing about his partner turned frightful. Harry's death constantly crept back into his reflections.

Harry Hart was Sammy's mentor. Five lonely tormenting years of asking why, Sammy still tried to live up to Harry's expectations.

They worked together, at the David L. Schwartz agency in Los Angeles. Harry was amazed at Sammy's grit in solving riddles. When Harry opened his own agency in San Francisco, he asked Sammy to join him. Harry had said illusions never befuddled Sammy, for his mind was always thinking of thousands of solutions, discarding most, faster than computers.

Yeah, Sammy thought, burying his head into his hands. He glanced up, and tried to catch something to take his mind off Harry. Out the window he saw the morning fog had disappeared, then he started to shuffle papers around to shake off this constant nightmare—it didn't work.

He remembered all too vividly that evening, when gumshoe Harry became a local hero to his drinking buddies, mostly cops, when he dove in front of his young partner during a stakeout that went sour. For in that instant of instinct or compassion, Harry took a cluster of fiery lead meant for Sammy and saved his emerging sleuth's life. He knew Sammy's decisive intuitions would impress good clients and dismay ugly punks. He traded his long teeth so Sammy would carry on.

Sammy knew he was part of a cast of tens of millions. Ten thousand or more loved ones were killed every minute in this world. The surviving loved ones had to live with death just as he did. He wondered how they accomplished it. What he didn't understand was all survivors went through the same thing, and only time could weaken grieving—even though as years pass, a comment or perhaps a seemingly innocent event would stir misty eyes.

Sammy believed Harry wanted to give him the chance to blossom out on his own. But, when facing clients, Sammy tried presenting a facetious façade so they would perceive a gregarious persona. He thought this would seduce them into giving him reasonable fees; it never worked. Unlike Harry, he could never close a pecuniary deal and gave the farm away.

However Harry, be it friend or foe, was glib and knew when to suggest a libation during contract negotiations. Harry liked to walk and talk money, so when passing a local watering-hole, he'd say, "Come-on folks, let's go in and have a smile at Lefty's, and they'd agree on a contract price."

On dull, drab days like this, Sammy missed Harry's wisecracks, womanizing adventures and crazy weird way around clients. Ladies adored him, for Harry delivered what women wanted to hear without patronizing them. Men couldn't get enough of Harry's antics. He'd swear, embellish any story to the delight of gathered listeners and called men, bastiers, telling them it was French for playboy. He was a fun guy; he was exciting; he was a man's man.

Sammy stood up, headed for the reception area. He asked himself why he couldn't loosen up around clients, then he sadly remembered. Harry never ceased to remind everyone that his partner was a Sam Spade sequel. Sammy felt even more inferior. Now though, Sammy would welcome thousands of ribbings just to hear Harry's gravel voice again, especially the "Well, me boy, this is another fine mess we're in." Raised in Los Angeles during the Depression, Harry loved Laurel and Hardy.

Sammy shook his head, still trying to release Harry's memory. He poured a mug of coffee and sat on the receptionist

     TOO BEAUTIFUL FOR WORDS

desk. He listened to his answering machine. One call, from a Barry Grossnell about warehouse thefts, immediately perked Sammy's attention. It was a return call supplied by the chief of burglary police. He realized the owner's insurance company would hint at a liberal payday to catch burglars. However, he always stumbled around during negotiations when his stomach cramped into a knot. Before his proposed fee slipped through dry trepidation lips, the insurance company offered him half of what he was worth. What was worse, Sammy came to realize squeezing his earned money out of insurance companies was an adventure in futility. He copied down the particulars anyway and returned to his office.

His private office resembled the reception area. The walls and ceiling were coated in dead smoke film from previous tenants. It made the 1940's hospital yellow appear brownish and the whole room smelled stale. An old empty cobwebbed dry Airwick bottle lurked in a corner—it was there when he and Harry moved in six years ago.

A deliveryman knocked on the corridor open door frame. "Package. Anybody here?"

"Hold up, I'll be right out." Sammy yelled. A Modern Mail man entered the reception room with a package from MacMall. Sammy shook away all thoughts of Harry, trotted in and gleefully signed for the package, saying, "Thanks, pal." His gloomy demeanor quickly evaporated as he attacked the wrapping tape. Ah ha, he surmised, now I've got a new toy. He took his new software program, Dramatica, from the box and turned to rush back into his office when his fax machine hailed.

I don't believe it, thought Sammy, *don't twisted minds ever rest?*

The incoming fax read:

Mr. Shovel,

You don't know me, but I'm a friend of your sister's husband. Please call. Our CEO has been murdered. We're willing to pay.

Donald

"I don't have a sister. What the hell's this? A prank?" Sammy grumbled under his breath. "Of all the dumb, jack-assed, lame brained, waste of time crap…and my paper too! Is this a stupid trick?"

Sammy balled the fax up and threw it to the floor, but his initial reaction suddenly faded. Frowning, he picked up the paper ball and unfolded it. The fax had a company name, logo and address. Golden Opportunities—the name seemed familiar. Sammy's nose and eyebrows pointed down at the paper as he attempted to straiten it. He sat down on a corner of the reception desk. He stared at the message, speculating when he last saw that name. He remembered it struck him as rather clever. Was the name on a billboard? Perhaps it was in a magazine ad? Getting up, he pranced about racking his brain and said out loud, "Come on, guy, you can do it."

Finally, it gushed out of his mouth. "The Chronicle! It was headline news! Of course," he congratulated himself with a sense of satisfaction. Yeah, he thought, I remember now, an owner or president got bumped off. Jeez, that was nearly two weeks ago—no—no, over three weeks. Get real, master sleuth, it has been over two months, maybe three.

His pulse quickened. I guess the cops haven't nabbed the slayer. "Well, guy," Sammy said to himself, "do you make the phone call?" He grinned at the last line, willing to pay. The grin turned to a smirk when he thought, don't screw up, this time act tough, maybe I've found my money tree.

Shovel picked up the phone and punched the seven numbers that, in his mind, spelled money, and for a man who rarely had more than twenty dollars his wallet this could be a real payday.

"Golden Opportunities. How may I direct your call?" A pleasant voice answered.

"Sammy Shovel, here, calling for someone named Donald. Anyone employed there by that name?"

"Yes, Donald Anderson. May I tell him who's calling?" The receptionist asked politely.

"Sammy Shovel."

"Please wait; I'll page him."

"Sure! Sure, I'll wait."

After a minute, a weak, but well-bred voice came on the line, "Is this Mister Shovel?"

"Maybe. Is this the Donald who claims to know my sister?"

"Well—Yes, I guess so."

"I hate to tell you this, pal, but I ain't got a sister."

"I meant your brother."

"You're batting zero. Forget all the weird relations shit, pal, and tell me why you sent me the fax?"

"Was—was I that obvious?" Donald said hesitantly.

"Very. What's this all about?"

"I didn't how to approach you. No one here at Golden Opportunities has ever dealt with detectives before and we were all afraid to call you. Will you help us?"

"Look, I've got other things to do than listen to a corporate con. Are you rotating family relations or playing twenty questions?"

"Our boss's been murdered!" Donald blurted out. "It's been over three months and the police haven't a clue who killed him. We've—well, we've all chipped in to hire you. Please, can you help us, Mister Shovel?"

"You've all chipped in? How quaint," Sammy said deflated, thinking no nest egg here. "Just how much chipping is your bottom line? Or, should I dare ask?"

"Well, so far we've collected over twenty-two thousand," Donald divulged then continued, "but that was only yesterday afternoon when we started. I'm sure our retainer could go higher. Do you need more to start?"

Sammy reached for the desk to steady himself, then leaned on it so he wouldn't collapse. His head felt as if it was in the spin cycle of a washing machine—confused, light headed, and he wasn't sure if the North Star ever existed. His pulse raced, and he wondered, Harry, you old dog, you found the money fairy and sent her to me. "How much did you say?"

"Twenty-two thousand."

Bingo, he was paralyzed by a brain short-circuit. "Is...is this the offices of Golden Opportunities?"

"Yes," Donald replied bewildered.

Sammy recovered. "I was just...just testing you."

"Did I pass?"

"Sure. Oh yeah—indeed pal, you passed all right. Now, when can we meet? Let's say—oh—ah, how about fifteen

          TOO BEAUTIFUL FOR WORDS

minutes at your offices? I'm on my way out the door, Donald. No need to call anyone else. You've hired your detective!"

CHAPTER FOUR

August 10, 1993—10:35 AM

*S*ammy stepped from the elevator into Golden Opportunities' lobby. He was overwhelmed by an unfamiliar world that was drenched in obvious wealth. He stood in awe, his mind unable to comprehend the resplendent abundance that adorned every wall, ceiling and floor. But he recognized money—lots of money— piles upon piles of green, and reckoned some could become his. He quickly realized he didn't belong here—he conjectured probably a $4,000 tailor made suite would have been better. He recoiled, sure, who has the four grand?

His stupor was broken when a receptionist opposite the elevators asked, "Sir—may I help you?" Her custom made desk was in a curved marble alcove below the gold-leaf Golden Opportunities sign. Inlaid gold embellished the front counter.

Still discomposed, Sammy moved toward the voice. "I'm Sammy, and I'm looking—

"The janitorial services are controlled by the building's owners," the receptionist said, noting how he was dressed and presumed he was searching for a job. "Hiring is done through their Human Resources Division on the first floor."

"No. I'm here to see Donald, Donald Anderson."

"Is he expecting you?" She asked inquisitively, then studied him up and down in a bewildered gaze.

"I told Donald I would see him shortly," he said, still gawking at the lavish surroundings.

"I'll check. Your name again?"

"Shovel, Sammy Shovel."

The receptionist asked Sammy to take a seat, contacted Donald, and told him his appointment had arrived. In a few minutes Donald greeted Sammy and they retired into one of the conference rooms.

"Wow," Sammy said, "I thought the lobby was elegant, but this conference room is even more impressive."

"Here at Golden Opportunities we try to ingrain success into the minds of our clients. However, it's in the executive suite where real money is splashed around. Have a seat. Peter Ballard, our acting CEO, will be joining us shortly. Would you mind if we ordered lunch? We can send a runner over to Belden Street. The whole alleyway is teeming with outdoor restaurants. My favorite is the Moroccan."

The word money didn't go unnoticed. Sammy tried to sizes up Donald, Probably a college grad, who wore a high-end-off-the-rack dark-blue suit, likely an Armani, surpassing the IBM look. He was around five-eleven and sported a beautiful tan.

"I know the street, but hold the lunch. Have you been working here long?" Sammy asked. He guessed Donald's age at somewhere around twenty-nine.

"Five years. None other than Joel himself recruited me right out of Santa Clara. I was lucky because my wife was expecting."

"You're married then."

"Yes, for six years. My wife's name is—."

Another man entered and Donald rose. "Mister Ballard, this is the detective I contacted. His name is Sammy Shovel."

"Mister Shovel, Donald has told me super things about you. I'm bowled over, you must be working on a case undercover—great disguise."

"All good, I hope." Sammy replied, sized up Peter Ballard: heavy sagging jowls with worry lines on his forehead that meant all business. The sun's rays were hitting him straight on, his brain caught the signal, if I want better work I need to change my image from vagrant to at least presentable.

"Absolute crackers."

"Don't you want to shut the door? I figure this is a private matter," Sammy suggested.

"Heavens no; there are no secrets here. Let me give you some background. Our employees gathered together last week, because they felt the police investigation is floundering. Our founder, Joel Ceja, started Golden Opportunities. He was loved and admired by everyone employed here. I can't begin to tell you how much we miss him. They all want action and I want action."

"Maybe we should ask Mack and Nancy to join us?" Donald suggested.

"Good idea." Peter reached for the phone. "Helen, ask Mister Diverson and Ms. Foster to come into conference room two." Turning back to Sammy, and said, "We decided that the firm would hire our own private investigator to assist the police in finding who killed our beloved Joel and why. We've never been involved in criminal work so we asked around. Donald remembered talking to one of his—ah, Nancy, Mack, come in and meet the detective we're going to engage. He has a ginger name."

     TOO BEAUTIFUL FOR WORDS

Sammy watched the young woman place her hand near her mouth, flashing her rings at him by moving the fingers below the index. "What could that be? I'm Nancy, and you are?" She spoke slowly and softly in a Southern accent—Georgia was Sammy's guess.

He started to rise, but Nancy pushed her gem-laden hand down, fingers spread, in a stay gesture, like she was disciplining a dog. Sammy noticed delicate fingers that almost glowed surrounded by enough rubies, pearls and sapphires to open a gem shop. Didn't she ever hear the song, Diamonds Are A Girls Best Friend?

"Shovel, Sammy Shovel."

"I like it—it sounds—so—so earthy. My, you certainly have massive shoulders. Where do you find clothes like that? You look just like the street people. My goodness, I'd have never known you were a detective!"

Sammy quickly suspected he was now in Oz and soon would be with Dorothy wandering down the yellow brick road. What's going on here? He asked himself. They think I'm in disguise, yet glancing at the man smiling next to her, who's dressed like a rogue vice cop, is strictly out of place with the surroundings. Sammy studied his clothing further. Where does this guy shop, the flower children parted the San Francisco scene thirty years ago? Then it hit him, the guy must be Tiny Tim's protégée. At his closer inspection it appeared all his clothes were tailored, harmonizing with mother earth. Damn, tomorrow I must buy some better duds at the Thrift Store.

"Mack, meet Sammy Shovel." Peter introduced Diverson.

"Pleased to meet you. Donald says you're good."

"Thanks."

"Peter, did you tell him we don't like the way the police are handling Joel's murder?"

"We were going into it when you came in."

"Mister Shovel, I mentioned we don't get involved with criminal activity and didn't know who to call. Oh, Donald, you tell him," Mack said.

"You see, my cousin, Lydia has a rather disreputable uncle. She said her uncle cursed you when they hauled him away to jail. He blamed you for being caught."

"How do you know it was me?" Sammy asked. "There are plenty of P.I.'s around this city."

"She remembered your name. It reminded her of the Maltese—"

"Please! Don't go there. I've heard it a thousand times. How did you manage to collect so much money?"

"We have one-hundred-thirty-two employees," Donald explained. "They donated from their heart and to my surprise it came to thirteen thousand four hundred and fifty-three dollars in only two hours."

"I was told the dollar figure would be more in the twenty thousand range." Sammy replied disappointed at the amount.

"It is," Peter interrupted. "At Golden Opportunities all management employees have key-man insurance policies in case of death or debilitating injuries. Joel's policy was worth—let me say, a very substantial sum. We're not concerned with haggling, negotiating or interviews. We want tip-top results and we're willing to pay. So, I added another ten thousand to the employee's contributions as a start. More donations will be forthcoming. Donald, give Mister Shovel the retainer."

Damn, I don't believe it. I've finally hit the jackpot, Sammy reckoned. He hoped they wouldn't ask his hourly rate.

     TOO BEAUTIFUL FOR WORDS

While his heart pounded, he tried to remain calm and wondered what Harry would do.

Donald handed Sammy an envelope containing a check for twenty-three thousand four hundred fifty-three dollars.

Sammy raised one eyebrow and pocketed the check in a matter-of-fact motion. He hoped his action would convince to Peter and the rest that he often received big paydays.

"Donald is the liaison regarding the investigation of Joel's murder. All dispatches should go through him," Peter explained further.

Donald passed his business card to Sammy.

"I understand, strictly hush-hush."

"We want you to know, Mister Shovel, the check is a retainer. We will pay liberally to get to the bottom of our beloved Joel's murder. Money's not an issue. We want answers, not stonewalling, like a certain police department is giving us. Our loyal employees are having difficulty with Joel's death. We all want closure," Peter said.

"Okay, fair enough."

"By the way, what's your hourly rate?" Peter asked.

Oh shit, Sammy guessed, do I say my usual hundred-twenty and have to give back most of the retainer? Come on, Harry, help me out here. He held his breath for a second and blurted out, "Five hundred plus expenses."

"That is hourly, isn't it?" Mack, the controller, said.

"I'd say, quite reasonable," Peter remarked.

"I bill weekly." Sammy quickly added, smiled, and correctly surmised the corporate world does indeed own money trees. "Now, tell me what you know about the murder, and are there any photos of Joel Ceja I can take?"

"Maria, this is Peter. Go through our publicity photos of Joel and bring them to conference room two." Peter Ballard said into the intercom.

"Who was the last person to see Joel Ceja alive?" Sammy took note of the quick response.

"Why Mister Shovel, dead or alive, our founder only wanted to be called Joel," Nancy corrected.

"Very good Nancy," Peter added.

"That would be me. I worked late one night and...." Donald spoke up.

They filled Sammy in on what they knew. It was the same information they gave to the police. Nancy and Mack described how the police scrutinized the accounting books and searched the personal files for the background of every employee who worked there, both past and present.

As he listened, Sammy began to worry about Nancy. She appears to be barely thirty, with light brown hair, large round-eyes set in an egg-shaped face. She was petite, but extremely well proportioned, and endowed enough to make men stare.

Sammy observed an excessive life style that was being fed by money—lots of money. He tried to understand how could she afford all the jewelry? Her rings glittered like sun hitting gold flakes in a miner's pan. She wore wide gold bracelets encrusted with jade and pearls, which match the gems on the necklace dangling around her neck. He decided to check her out very carefully, unless—he didn't want to think that someone so young could actually be earning that kind of wealth. He remembered, though, the golden gang never questioned his hourly rate. "I'll be back tomorrow morning to look over mister—ah Joel's office and the rest of the offices. I want to talk to the homicide detectives first."

"I believe that would be Lieutenant Bracque." Peter informed.

"Of all the homicide detectives," Sammy bit his tongue, but wanted to shout, "Why him?"

On Bryant Street, Sammy climbed the steps of a cold gray box, employment for some, safety for others, and a timely incarceration for a select few. It had all the charm of a no-nonsense, turn of the century, East Coast prison. Sammy envisioned the nice one in Oakland.

He was muttering an opening line to break the tension he knew existed between Bracque and himself. In the crowded lobby, he started for the bank of elevators when he heard that irritating, bellowing voice, demanding— "Shovel... why are you here?"

"Why, Lieutenant, I came to see you," Sammy replied, feeling cornered, he turned and smiled at Bracque.

"Oh, really—I'm thrilled," Bracque said scowling.

"It's a fact."

"I'm going to my office—follow me, but make it snappy. I've got real work to do."

Sammy and the lieutenant remained silent as the elevator cab ascended to the fourth floor.

Sammy kept his eyes straight ahead, and reviewed the events that took place six months ago.

That's gratitude for you, he concluded. On my first encounter with Bracque, I accidentally stumbled on a local gun-for-hire killing and exposed a drug operation that eluded the SFPD for over forty years. Because of that bust, Inspector Bracque was made a Lieutenant and the bugger's never thanked me. Okay, he bought me dinner that night, if you want to call a plate of cold linguine dinner, scattered with strips of some tough chicken. I don't care who got credit. I'm just like any other city gumshoe—give me cash. I learned an important lesson that night. I'll direct my snooping nose away from phantom clients.

He was still fuming when the elevator door opened. He and Bracque entered the Homicide Division and passed through a tiny, but long, lobby, with two reception desks. In all the years coming to homicide, Sammy had never observed anyone manning the desks; however, each of the two stations always contained a computer, piles of papers, pens and the usual stationery-store trappings. Sammy followed the lieutenant into his office and watched him squirm to get around to his desk. "Should I close the door?"

"Leave it open," Bracque said curtly as he plopped down. "After that big drug bust some months ago, a few of my men are getting the idea we're buddies. Now, you know and I know we're not. I want to keep it that way. You can snoop around for informants when asked, but stay out of this division unless invited."

"Of course. I wouldn't have it any other way and the drug bust was around Christmas," Sammy responded, then brooded for a moment. The bastard will never own up that I cracked the case.

"Gosh—by golly, that's right. I bought you a Christmas dinner, didn't I. Tell me, why you're here or get out."

"By the way, Chandler had nothing to do with Casablanca."

"What the hell are you talking about?"

"That night, when we busted the day to day drug ring, before the dinner you bought me, you said, 'I hope this doesn't turn into a beautiful friendship.'"

   TOO BEAUTIFUL FOR WORDS

"Did I? I don't remember, but it's a famous line. You try to act like you're Bogart's character, Sam Spade, and, quite frankly, it's getting on my nerves."

"Do you read much?"

"Rarely. I watch TV while eating."

Sammy figured Bracque mixed up Bogart, the man, for Bogart's characters, jumbling the actor's roles from novels by Raymond Chandler and Dashiell Hammett, with whom neither were involved with the Casablanca movie. Sammy decided to drop the subject before he alienated the Lieutenant further. He glanced around and knew Mister Clean would probably turn, throw his arms high and quickly flee rather than face Bracque's inner office. Paper bulletins hung on the partition wall windows; the new file cabinet drawers Sammy witnessed back in December were so stuffed with papers now they can't be shut. Sadly, however, Sammy felt comfortable, because his office looked similar.

Lieutenant Bracque began sorting papers on his desk, ignoring Sammy. Finally he squinted up. "Come on Shovel, what's on your mind? Can't you see I've got a lot of work to do, so keep it simple."

"Simple it is. Do you know of Golden Opportunities and one late CEO by the name of Joel Ceja?"

The lieutenant froze, then said, "Shut the door." He stared right at Sammy, scowled, and didn't blink.

Sammy stood, moved his chair, shut the door and retook his seat. He sensed Bracque was about to lecture him.

The lieutenant leaned forward showing his best repulsion. His tangled eyebrows frame his narrow fierce eyes and his big lips parted. "You know you can't get involved with murder cases in San Francisco. The department, frown's on P.I.'s investigating

high profile homicides. This is police business—stay out of it....
But, if you know something about this murder, what is it?"

"Nothing."

"Nothing?"

"Like I said, nothing."

"How dare you come in here, ask about Golden Opportunities, and then say you know nothing?"

"I'm not investigating. I know nothing. I received a fax from Golden Opportunities asking me to help the police find their boss's killer. I called a Donald Anderson and he said you were heading up the investigation.... Here I am. So—may I help? And my license says I can investigate anything."

"Who asked you again?

"The executives at Golden Opportunities. They contacted Mayor Bertolucci, and he made the call to the police Chief."

Bracque's face relaxed. He remembered the call, but expected a quality firm like Jack Palladino, not the contently broke flatfoot before him who takes on repo work. He turned and rooted through some folders, picked out a fat one and opened it. He leaned back and tilts his chair and immediately hit the file cabinet—it jerked him unpleasantly.

"This is a tough one, Shovel. I've got the mayor, the Mexican American League and the business community up my ass. Sometimes, I believe the Chief thinks I'm the murderer."

Sammy realized the lieutenant had no clue about who killed Joel or why he was murdered. However, he was being harassed because everyone wanted to know where his investigation was headed.

"Again, what can I do to help?"

"Help? Yes, you can help, but you know the rules regarding homicides in San Francisco."

"Yeah, I know the rules, the silly department rules, but you know I can legally—anyone can, even without a license. Look—I don't want to fight. Will you allow me to help?"

"Didn't I just say yes? Let me fill you in on what we know." The lieutenant glanced at the open file. "Joel Ceja founded and headed up a marketing firm named Golden Opportunities. He did very well and was well liked, especially by his employees. We couldn't find anyone in his employ that didn't like him. In the beginning, we were suspicious of his Executive President, because of a comment he made."

"Who's that?"

"Ballard, Peter Ballard."

"Let's have it—why did you suspect him?"

"When we were discussing finding Ceja's car in the surrounding neighborhood he seemed surprised, and made some kind of a comment about us finding it. It didn't sound right then and still doesn't, but he's a clean Arlene as far as we can ascertain."

"But you're not sure?"

Bracque shrugged. "Joel was generous with salaries. At the present time, no one's a suspect. All his employees' alibis check out. And why wouldn't they. The company is a closed corporation with the employees owning seventy-five percent of the stock. Everyone who works there gets one-hundred shares after one year."

"What about his will?

"We found it right in his open safe. We verified it with the company's attorney, signatures and dates match. Everything he owned went to a charity trust fund, including his twenty-five percent of the company's stock, except modest amounts he bequeathed to Manny Soto and some relatives who live in Los Angeles. The relatives were contacted by Ceja's attorney."

"Who's Manny Soto and why him?"

"He was Ceja's best friend. It seems Joel was born in Mexico. Manny Soto, was his childhood chum, so when Ceja came to America and established his marketing firm he sent for him."

"So Manny Soto was special. Have you talked to this guy?"

"We located his house, but no one has seen him for months. Ceja's attorney has sent notices and made phone calls, all with the same result. However, his neighbors told us this is normal for Soto. They say he's got relatives in Mexico and goes there on a regular basis, stays for months. We've posted notes at his home to call as soon as he arrives, but I doubt it will do any good."

"Why's that?"

"He's a little dense. Everyone we talked to said his I.Q. was less than swift. One smart-ass said he could barely read Spanish, let alone any English."

"What about Joel's wife and family?"

"Never married, but business associates all report he was an asset to San Francisco. Everyone who knew him spoke accolades."

"I assume you did a background check on Ceja?"

Bracque became irritated. "Of course. Listen, Shovel, contrary to what you believe we aren't amateurs." Fumbling through the file. "Since we've had trouble finding suspects, LAPD did some extra work and sent us a complete chronicle of what they know about the family. Ceja came to America as an immigrant. A family, the relatives I mentioned, came to love Joel

---

                    TOO BEAUTIFUL FOR WORDS

and sponsored him, when they saw the kid begging in Mexico City. After a couple of trips they adopted him in 1964. He was eleven at the time."

"What else? And has the sponsor got a name?"

"Sure, the family name is Perez, Dorlisa and Francisco Perez," Bracque said as he skipped through the report. According to the L.A.P.D. the family brought Joel to Los Angeles as an abandoned child, adopted him because all they had were two girls, Elsa and Jane P, and a boy, Julian. Francisco came from a large family in Spain. Joel grew up working in the family laundry business. We understand Joel was a fast learner. He suggested they add dry-cleaning and change the business name to Franko's Ultra Cleaners. They've now have expanded to over twenty locations in the L.A. basin."

"Smart then."

"Very. They sent him to USC, and after graduating he worked in the New York garment industry as a sales rep for two years. He journeyed all over the States. Did very well according to our sources. Came to San Francisco in seventy-nine and set up Golden Opportunities. He's been here ever since. We noticed he traveled frequently to Mazatlan, but we understand the company owns a condo or house there."

Sammy remained motionless and stared at Bracque.

"According to the report, Perez retired...." Sammy continued to stare, so the lieutenant said, "For Christ sake, he's in his eighties. His wife died about ten years ago. In fact, he attended Ceja's memorial service. Reinhourse talked to him after the observance asking about any enemies his son might have had. Reinhourse said the old gent was so wrought with grieving he was visibly shaken and could barely stand. He must have truly loved his boy. He told Reinhourse, his Gods would avenge the killing."

"His Gods?"

"Reinhourse thought that was strange so he added it in his report," Bracque remarked, as he shuffled through the folder looking for the interview.

"Who showed up, and does that mean he was cremated?"

"Besides his employees, hundreds including the mayor. It was like a herd of buffaloes joshing for position to see and be seen, but they remained orderly and quiet. Ceja's body was shipped down to Los Angeles, where the family priest conducted a private funeral service. He was buried next to his adopted mother in their mausoleum."

Sammy glanced down for a few seconds, reckoning that cemeteries charge a lot of money for family mausoleums. "What about the piles of papers Donald was trying to explain to me?"

"Damnedest thing," the Lieutenant responded. "We found three piles of papers on his desk, which he supposedly kept totally clean. I mean not even the phone is located there. The only thing he usually kept on his desk were a trophy pen and pencil set, given to him by the Chamber of Commerce as an outgoing presidential gift, and an antique stone paperweight. We were told the stone's some kind of nostalgia thing. We had the lab check it out and gave it back. His employees, and I mean all of his employees, said the paper piles had no relation to each other, nor did the papers in each pile belong together. Most significantly they didn't belong on his desk."

"That's all there was? Just three piles of papers?" Sammy questioned.

"Well yeah, except they each had a sticky note on them."

"Well?"

   TOO BEAUTIFUL FOR WORDS

"You want to see the notes? Hell, I've had our computer guys trying to figure out the notes and papers for weeks. We just don't know what they mean!"

Sammy leaned back, folded his arms and in silence stared at the Lieutenant.

"You know, Mister Shovel, you can be very aggravating. If I didn't know the Chief said a private detective may be asked to help, I'd throw you right out of here long ago." Bracque picked up the phone and said, "Reinhourse, on the Joel Ceja case, bring in the papers with the sticky notes."

"I appreciate this Lieutenant," Sammy said, realizing the Lieutenant was upset, then wondered, what else he was not being told.

"Well, you won't find a thing. I even had two other computer encrypting firms have a go at this and they didn't find anything either. Oh, by the way, did I tell you there was a company gun missing?"

"Donald mentioned it."

"Say! I thought you said you didn't know what was going on!"

"Trust me, I don't. I was told a lot of things, but they didn't make sense because everyone was talking at once. That's why I'm here."

"You told me you talked to Donald over the phone!"

"Wait a minute, Lieutenant!" Sammy exclaimed, totally exasperated. "I'm not the suspect. Christ, yeah, I went over to Golden Opportunities. Hell, they're paying me to help find Joel's killer. They're entitled to see what I look like."

"You look like shit. And who told you to call him Joel?"

"They all did—is there something wrong with that?"

The door opened. Sammy moved his chair so the tall thin Reinhourse could squeeze in. He laid a file on Bracque's desk, and didn't look at Sammy, but brought both hands up to his waist in a defiant motion.

"Thanks, Inspector," Bracque responded. "You know Samuel Shovel?"

"I believe we've met," Reinhourse answered coolly.

"Well, Mister Shovel, here, has been hired by Golden Opportunities to find their boss's killer."

"I thought that was our job."

"I was asked to assist the police in finding Joel's killer," Sammy said quickly.

Sammy's earlier comment, 'paying me to find Joel's killer', didn't escape Bracque's attention.

"Sure you were," Bracque snapped back.

"Really. Good luck, you'll need it," Reinhourse retorted.

"Okay—Mister Shovel—here are the papers and three sticky notes," Bracque said.

"Is this in the order they were found?"

"Wait. Let me turn them and put 'm in the order we found them from your side of the chair." He and Reinhourse glanced at each other and traded grins.

Sammy inspected the piles of papers. He stared intently at three sticky notes trying to make sense of the messages scrawled on them, wondering what Joel was trying to tell the authorities.

He read the first note, HOLD THIS PILE FOR FUTURE STUDY.

The second note, IN THIS PILE ARE PAPERS TO BE FILED.

The last note, THIS IS THE PILE THAT NEEDS IMMEDIATE ATTENTION.

He surmised that Joel had to write the notes quickly and they were probably put in this order for some obvious reason. Suddenly, his frown faded and the right side of his upper lip rose.

"What—What's going on? What did you find?" Bracque asked picking up on Sammy's facial expression.

"He didn't find dick shit," Reinhourse snapped.

"Come on, Shovel—don't hold out on us! Remember, I can pull your any time I want," the lieutenant roared, leaning forward like Leo the Lion.

"Less not go through this again, you can't. Mine is issued by the state, but anyone can call themselves a P.I." Sammy eased back in his chair. Now smiling, and began the lecture, "The trouble is you were looking for some grand scheme that would wrap up Joel's killer in a nice neat package. Think about Joel's last few hours. He was at his desk, working late. He probably received a phone call—"

"Yeah," the lieutenant broke in, "a call came in less than an hour before he took the slugs. We traced it to a phone booth in North Beach."

"Any Prints?"

"Yeah, all smudged or overlapped."

"As I was saying, he receives a phone call, as it turns out, a lethal phone call, to meet someone quickly. He had no time to plan. If something should happen to him, he wanted the police to know what may have happened, but not his loyal employees who think he's a God. So he took the papers he was working on and put them into three piles, deliberately making sure they had no relationship to each of the other pile, hurriedly scribbled a note on each pile, leaving a simple clue.

"Damn you Shovel, quit lecturing us," Bracque said completely exasperated.

"He goes to the safe, picks up the company revolver, which I don't believe was the company's at all, and made his deadly meet."

"How in the hell do you know all this by just looking at three scraps of paper!" Reinhourse yelled furiously.

"Lieutenant, read the first letter on each note."

Bracque turned the papers around and said, "H-I-T. A hit! Son of a bitch.... He—was he a goddamn gangster?"

"Wow—wait a minute," Reinhourse interrupted, "how do we know he wasn't working for—let's say, the CIA?"

Sammy and the lieutenant glanced at each other and said in unison, "Naaaah!"

"A hood, maybe, but unobtrusive," Sammy surmised. "To find his killer we've got to presume he's more complex than his ordinary appearance. The good news is, we can now begin. Lieutenant, can you check if there have been other prominent businessmen murdered in, say, the last ten years? No, make that the last fifteen years."

"I fail to see the connection," Bracque said.

"I don't know of any connection, but who knows what you may find."

"Hey, Shovel, that's a lot of work," Reinhourse snapped back.

"The assignment's yours, Reinhourse," Bracque announced calmly.

"You bastard, Shovel," Reinhourse said. "Now see what you've done."

"Lieutenant, I think your inspector feels you're punishing him!"

"Back off, Shovel. Reinhourse can be a pain, but he knows how to dig. He's our best man for the assignment."

                    TOO BEAUTIFUL FOR WORDS

"May I ask one more question?"

"I'm listening."

"Did you find where Joel lived and if so did you—"

"Dammit, Shovel, now I'm really upset!" Bracque retorted. "How many times must I tell you we're not children. Of course we did. He lived in Laguna Heights. We went there looking for anything to tie in Ceja's killer. You know, maybe a jealous girlfriend, past lovers, maybe some gambling debts."

"And?"

"Nothing. Absolutely nothing. Just like his office. This guy should have been riding a white horse rather than steering a black Ferrari, based on what we found."

"What Ferrari?"

"If you took notes, you'd remember I mentioned Ballard's comment about a car. It was a black Ferrari. We found it three blocks from the killing. And yes, we went through it and it's clean. I had a special team on the car and house for a week to check and double check. We talked to neighbors, grocery stores, his mechanic and anybody who might have contact with him. Like I said, nothing—everyone thought he was angelic. It appeared he was robbed, for his wallet was missing, but we're sure it was deliberate out of a moment of rage. We never expected it was an organized murder."

"Okay, you do your checking and I'll do mine. It seems Joel's halo has been slightly tarnished. We will share information, won't we?"

"Of course. But if you're really going to help us, you better start writing down what you've discovered and pass on that information to us. Otherwise you'll be worthless to us and Golden Opportunities."

"Ballard never mentioned the car. Most of the other stuff you also told me." Sammy said pointing to his head, "I have made mental notes right here."

"I bet you have. Remember this is police business."

"I will honor the department's directive and not interfere—unless I…ask permission. Now, may I look at the Ferrari?"

"Again, of course, I'll call the impound garage."

"Now that we know Joel was more than a generous businessman, I'd be very careful with his pal Manny. As close as they were, it could be they were mired in muck up to their armpits. The question of the hour is, whose muck?"

"Damn you, Shovel, quit putting us down. You just don't get it do you. If you lecture me one more time, I'm shutting you out. Do you hear me? We know what we're doing. This is why the department doesn't want P.I.s snooping around and screwing up the works. I'm going to tell you right now you're no different than most of the rest, and more of a pain in the ass."

"Well thanks." Sammy rose from his chair. "As agreed, we'll stay in touch, if that meets the department's P.I. etiquette."

*R*einhourse watched him leave and couldn't contain himself. He threw a punch at the file cabinets, and said. "That dumpy little bastard comes in here and in less than five minutes, figures out the meaning of the sticky notes and determines our Goody Two-shoes is nothing more than a common hood. Goddammit, it—it isn't fair. I'm going to get that short shit and when I do I'll—"

"Reinhourse! Sit down! You know I've never—how shall I say it, been fond of our nemesis, Mister Shovel. But, to be fair, he has helped the department, and while he didn't ask, he got me promoted. I don't care for his style, his constant lecturing, or his

   TOO BEAUTIFUL FOR WORDS

dress code for that matter. I mean, the man has no sense of color, he throws on clothes to keep warm, and he smeared breakfast jelly on those battered garments he was wearing today. In fact they looked like a peasant's costume for a twelfth century harvest pageant, when the last hay was stacked, and the laborers were still sweaty and grimy, but they still enough energy to brake out the wine barrels and party."

"I don't need to hear this dribble." Reinhourse straightened up and brought his fists to each side of his face.

"What I'm really trying to tell you, Inspector," Bracque said meeting Reinhourse directly in his eyes, "I don't like private dicks digging around in my sandbox, but Sergeant Ryan informed me that Shovel has an intuitive nature when it come to nosing around for leads. Shovel's demeanor's one thing, but I will admit, his nose is strictly pedigree and smells out trouble. I mean, discovering that aged bootlegger, Knuckles Malloy, in San Francisco was brilliant."

He leaned back in his chair and grinned, the chair's back hit the file cabinet again and gave his head another quick blow. "Damn," he snapped, trying to regain his composure.

"As of right now, Mister Shovel knows no more than we do. He has no more idea who killed Joel Ceja than we do. He has less information than we do. However, I can now report to our Chief that progress has taken place and we're developing new leads. I don't believe we need to mention Mister Shovel's involvement. Do you get the picture?"

CHAPTER FIVE

The best part about public records
Is they're free, well almost.

August 10, 1993—1:10 PM

Sammy left the Hall, knowing the lieutenant was not going to completely share. He reckoned two could play that game. He hailed a cab and barked, "Assessor's Office, City Hall." Sammy knew public records were open for all to scrutinize.

Sammy's head was spinning, a fax, money and a murder mystery in less than two hours made him dizzy, but he stayed focused, and suspected that a complex man like Joel might have had two residences.

Joel's house in Laguna Heights was where he gave social parties, discussed politics with the city's bureaucrats over a glass of port, and shared delicately prepared canapé's of foi-gra. Joel parked his Ferrari and slept alone at this engaging home. He made sure nothing there could ever tarnish his image.

Sammy deducted Lieutenant Bracque's men scrutinized that one and found nothing. When the late Mister Perfect revealed a tarnished image, Sammy speculated Joel must have had a hideout, an obscure location where he could flop and scheme, probably within walking distance of his office. He was sure the lieutenant had checked on everything Joel and Golden Opportunities owned, but maybe—just maybe Bracque didn't

---

　　　　TOO BEAUTIFUL FOR WORDS

have the right resources to check thoroughly. Sammy figured if it existed, will I find it?

At the Assessor's office, Sammy went from one section of books to another. Acting as if lost, he scratched his head, drifted around, and stomped toward the microfiche file. With each heavy step, he released deep guttural sighs.

A black woman clerk, who'd been watching his erratic actions, determined Sammy could be a homeless drifter, so she decided to confront him and then call security.

A velvety voice asked, "Ah, sir—ah—sir—over here—you. Yes you. You seem to be having difficulty and need help. What are you looking for?" She asked from behind the counter.

The clerk appeared to be medium height, with a lissome figure, but Sammy couldn't see if she's wearing spiked heels. While not a raving beauty, she was cute—light skinned, protruding lips, with short black hair surrounding a perfect moon face.

"Oh, you're a beautiful angel," he said. "Can—will you help me find some properties?"

"I'll try," she said, smiling at the compliment. "What are you trying to find?" The clerk realized he was not a bum.

"Well, you see the out-of-state bank I represent asked me to check on the real ownership of some properties listed by Golden Opportunities. They've applied for a rather substantial loan and listed capital holdings in San Francisco as collateral. They asked me to find out what the company actually owns and the indebtedness on each."

"You are?"

"Sammy Shovel."

"You're not related to Mickey Rooney are you?" She said coming closer to the counter, and then surveyed the top of his head.

"Distant cousin—how about that help you promised?"

"It's easy. You just go the—"

Take it slow, he cautioned himself. The clerk was trying to help him and was dressed nice, too.

"Of course, it would be easy, but you see I've lost the list of the properties, and, well, if I ask them to send me another list, they'll probably fire me. You see, I'm just a temp. This job, it—it means a lot to me and my family."

Glancing at the hapless man before her, she said, "I understand perfectly. Come with me. I think we can find that information. In fact, how would a printout do?"

"Perfect." Sammy said graciously.

The clerk stopped for a second because she noticed Sammy's rumpled attire and food stains on his mismatched tie. She informed him, "However, there's a dollar-fifty per page charge."

"Please, print it."

"Did you say the name is Golden Opportunities?"

"Yeah, on California."

The clerk retreated to her computer. Shortly, she walked to a printer, returned with some printouts and handed Sammy the lists. "They have a lot of property; four pages worth. That comes to six dollars."

Excited, he ignored the clerk and started studying the pages. He discovered a mixture of office buildings, apartments, warehouses and even a church. Sammy felt he could cross most all of them out, except the apartments. He eliminated three of the apartment buildings in a high-rent district because by living there, Joel could easily be recognized. The two remaining apartment buildings were in blighted neighborhoods. The closest one to Joel's office turned out to be an old converted hotel on

Eddy Street. The other was an apartment building on Geary, near Japan Town.

"I noticed there is a hotel on Eddy Street. Is there more information as to it's value and any notes that might be on the actual property books?"

"I don't know. Let me get the original book."

Sammy thanked the clerk profusely for retrieving the book, and peeked at her white snickers with rolled down white cotton socks over nylons, as she walked over to bin that contains the right book. He figured she had a hot date later, since he didn't detect a wedding ring.

The clerk carried the book to the counter, opened to the property's page, so Sammy could scrutinize what was on it. She casually mentioned, "Funny, Sergeant Marge Fellows, was in here some months ago, also looking for information from this book."

Sammy pulled out his wallet and found a scrap of paper, while the clerk tried to hand him notepaper and ballpoint. "What a coincidence. Does she come here often?" He noticed Golden Opportunities bought the property shortly after Golden Opportunities opened up for business.

"Not really. Small world isn't it?" The clerk said slyly.

Sammy peeled off a ten-spot from a large roll of bills.

The clerk looked down at the money roll, raised her eyebrows, stared at Sammy, then started to make change.

"Keep the rest as a tip," Sammy said with a toothy grin.

"I can't do that. We don't accept tips. We work for a salary, not gratuities."

She opened a cash drawer, put in the ten dollars and quickly snatched out four one-dollar bills. "Here's your change... I'll make a receipt." She grabbed a pad of duplicate receipt forms. "I must give you a copy for tax expenditures. Would you spell your name again?"

CHAPTER SIX

The stuff they teach kids nowadays.

August 10, 1993—3:46 PM

Sammy called the Kristy Lipp Agency.

"Kristy, sweetheart, Sammy here. I've got a job tailored for your operatives. I need one of your pregnant thespians."

Kristy hired women investigators who can act. Her gals normally did domestic grunt work, like skip tracing, adoption searches, unfaithful husband and wives mixed with some surveillance; they always delivered.

"Sammy, when you embellish your opening volley with the term 'sweetheart,' I feel you're about to snatch my purse. What pregnant employee are you talking about?"

"No—no. I want them to act pregnant and check out a couple of apartment houses for me." He said, lying, but it didn't bother him at all. "I'm looking for a missing person. They just have to ask the same question at each apartment."

After further conversation, Kristy agreed to take the assignment. She insisted Sammy sign a contract for she had already experienced he would change the terms of a verbal agreement. "Why don't you come here, sign the contract and meet my investigators."

"I'll be there in about an hour."

Sammy arrived at the Lipp Agency about two hours later. "Kristy, please," he said to the woman seated next to the reception counter, almost ignoring her. "Where's your coffee?"

"Does she know you?" The woman asked thinking another vagrant wanted a place to rest from the heat.

"Yeah—yeah, we go way back."

"I'll get it. Cream or sugar?"

He brought up his hands. "Just direct me."

She did and Sammy returned with a paper napkin wrapped around a waxed paper cup. He observed Kristy waiting at the counter with distain on her face.

"Kristy, I haven't a lot of time." Sammy fumbled, trying to put the cup down without burning his fingers. "Show me the contract."

Seeing clear wax dots floating on black liquid, Kristy scolded. "We have Styrofoam cups. Don't you realize you're drinking paraffin?"

"I'll live with it. Where's the contract?"

Kristy reached toward the suspense tray, grabbed two copies of her standard contract, and handed them to Sammy. "I thought you said you'd be here within an hour." She held out a pen. "Just sign these, date them and then I'll sign. We will get you on your way quickly."

"I had a lot to do and I don't sign any contract without looking at it."

"Then glance it over," Kristy said irritated and slapped down her pen.

"Kristy, are you crazy?" Sammy read over the contract terms. "I won't sign anything that contains time and material phrases. Remove it. I want a not-to-exceed amount. I can barely make ends meet."

     TOO BEAUTIFUL FOR WORDS

"How can you expect me to estimate this assignment with such little information? If you're so poor, how come you live in a guarded building?"

"I saved a client's ass, that's how. He signed over the balance for his condo as a fee and left town quickly. Look, I don't have steady clients like you do. I live from day to day, week to week. My overhead kills me." He grappled with his paper cup and took a *schluck* of coffee.

"Overhead! That's a laugh. You don't even have a secretary."

"See, that's what I mean. I want one of your girls to nose around the two apartment buildings I mentioned and ask some questions about the whereabouts of a guy. If you can't figure out how long it will take to do that, then I will."

"I want a signed contract before you leave here," Kristy fumed. "Come into my office and we'll thrash this out right now." she said, then turned to the woman at the reception desk. "Deborah, throw out that coffee mess on the counter and bring a mug into my office for our pest—guest."

Inside her office, Sammy held tough, demanding that the rate be tied to a maximum number of hours. If it took longer, then it was Kristy's problem. They kept clashing about the final cost. He wouldn't budge, but decides to allow travel time, then throws in a bone to ease Kristy's frustration. "Check out a Nancy Foster and Mack Diverson with background and surveillance checks." Reluctantly he mentioned they work for Golden Opportunities. He especially wanted to know of Nancy's total wealth and spending habits.

"Sammy, you were sired by that infamous stubborn mule. At times, I hate you," Kristy grumbled.

Finally they agreed to the terms of the contract, and it was printed and signed. As he tucked away his copy, Sammy displayed his happy I-won-again-face, then realized he did the same thing that his clients do to him. He recalled his father quoting the Elks: *To do unto others as we would they should do onto us.* Sheepishly he said, "Good. May I interview your girls?"

"Sammy, for God's sake, they're women, not girls."

He picked out one of Kristy's top operatives, diminutive Paolina Peralta, who swore her great grandmother was a contessa. Sammy believed she could be some count's bride.

She answered to Papi, a nickname bestowed by her baby brother who couldn't manage all the syllables in her full name. Though compact, she appeared big boned, athletic and wiry. She had chiseled cheeks, bantam chin, long coal black hair, bronze eyes the size of quarters, a short upturned nose and olive complexion.

"For your information, Papi's a black belt. She competes internationally." Kristy said.

"You're a black belt?" Sammy said surprised, then gazed at Papi from head to toe.

"Yes."

"How long?"

"Since I was fourteen," Papi grinned. "I had my first lesson at seven, because the school bullies were picking on me. When my mother found out they took my lunch money every day she dragged me to the nearest karate studio. I loved it, and now have a hundred eighty-five trophies. At first glance I may appear puny, but I can kick ass big time."

Kristy sat quietly and beamed at her operative.

   TOO BEAUTIFUL FOR WORDS

Doubtfully, Sammy handed Papi some papers. "Here are the locations of two apartment buildings. I want you to check everyone in both."

Kristy glared at him.

"Okay, as many as you can catch from ten to six. Papi, you must look homeless, act pregnant and find someone who might have seen this elusive person at either location." He handed Papi a photo of Joel.

"Who's the guy in the picture?" Kristy asked.

"Right now consider it hush hush."

"Papi, Why don't you call that theatrical outfitter, what's their name—er—ah—Costumes and Props. Check them out. They might have a seven-or eight-month pregnancy pouch. That should gain scads of pity."

"Great suggestion," Sammy concurred. "Show this picture and sob that you're homeless and when your boyfriend impregnated you, he vanished. Never mention any name. If the residents are reluctant to squeal, give them this phone number. Memorize it. It's my secure answering machine. Don't say anything else."

"What if I complain we were lovers? I could tell them using a sensuous voice, oh—like, 'For six months my man and I were like one. He'd bring us to heaven two or three times a day, but when I became pregnant he threw me out like old dried dog turds."

"I like it. Very colorful, but tone it down a tad, especially the two or three time a day stuff. Let's work on it."

"So, we're lacking in stud attributes?" Kristy chided Sammy.

"Kristy, I'm forty-two."

Before he left, Sammy turned to Papi, and said, "Remember, you're eight months pregnant, so don't threaten anyone with that judo stuff."

"It's karate."

*T*he next day, a very pregnant homeless-looking woman waddled up the Geary apartment complex stairs, wearing dirty gray jogging pants, tattered blouse, torn knitted sweater and army boots. Duct tape was wrapped around the arch on the left boot. A brown skullcap framed a dirty face. She dragged a large plastic shopping bag half full of aluminum cans in one hand while holding a photo in the other. Her recipe for sympathy complete, Papi went through the building door to door. She received an abundance of kindness and well wishes, but no hints about Joel.

She arrived at the Hotel Harald around 2:30 PM, she gazed up at the sign on Eddy Street and mumbled, "My goodness sake, it is spelled H-A-R-A-L-D. I thought Sammy was just mispronouncing it." She was about to go in when she noticed three young toughs on motorcycles watching her. An older couple exited the hotel, so she went into her routine, crying, showing the photo and making them write down Sammy's phone number. Before going into the building she glanced back toward the would-be desperados. The bikes were still there, with two Nazi-type helmets sitting on the handlebars, but the punks were gone.

On each floor, Papi moaned about her lost love, and cried for compassion. She made sure they got a good look at her pregnancy and showed them the photo. But the tenants shook their heads. Some wished her well. On the fourth floor one man hesitated before saying he never saw the man before. She watched his eyes, and figured he knew something. Taking a piece of paper, she jotted down Sammy's phone number and shoved it into the man's shirt pocket, begging, "Please, mister, my baby needs a father."

On the top floor, she spotted the motorcycle goon gang huddled at the end of the corridor. She figured they must have snuck up the back stairway and wondered whose apartment they planned to rob. She heard one of them refer to the shank of something, but couldn't make out the words clearly.

Papi knocked on the first door. When no one responded, she knocked louder and longer. After three minutes she went to the next door, and knocked, moving away from the motorcycle vermin. As she waited at the door, her peripheral vision detected movement. The goons were creeping slowly toward her.

The door opened, revealed a big man holding a drink, dressed only in his skivvies, with a huge bulge. He yelled in a deep gravel voice, "What the hell do you want?" Papi was about to speak when she heard a shrilling woman. "Honey, get your butt back in here and finish what you started." The door slammed shut.

Startled, Papi stepped back and mumbled, "Have fun." Then she continued knocking on all of the doors except the ones at the end a short corridor.

She looked for the toughs, but they were gone. The corridor appeared darker where it turned into the last corridor. She concluded the three sinister cyclists were impeding the light as they attempted to break into an apartment. She decided to creep along the corridor and catch them in the act. Using her surveillance skills, she didn't make a sound. About two feet from the corner, she was about to put her hands on the wall, to steady herself, and then peer around the corner. The biggest tough, a fallen angel straight from hell, jumped out with his arms stretched out.

"Surprise!" He wore an old-fashioned aviator's leather cap with the words *Fuck You* written across the front. "Hey, little bitch, whacha looking for?" When he spoke, decayed and missing teeth gaps were visible through a thick unkempt reddish beard.

Papi was surprised, backed away, and couldn't help notice his chest girth and huge hands. He had on some tattered baggy black Frisco jeans salvaged from the fifties.

"Mister, I'm not a dog. Please. I'm looking for my husband."

"Well, you smell like one."

First one and then the other gang member peeked around the corner. Papi noticed each wore the same leather jackets, with some kind of club monogramed on the rear. The name wasn't familiar, but the other two had faded holey Levies that were left in bleach too long. They all had the odor of oil, gas and body excrements.

"Looky here, boys, I think we've got a live one."

"Leave me alone."

"Hey, Shank, under all that crud she's not bad looking."

"If you don't leave me alone, I'll scream." Papi started to run.

"Grab that bitch!," the big bully yelled. The two other bullies gave chase. Down the corridor one grabbed her left arm and pinned her against the corridor wall.

The leader observed she was holding a photo. "Give me that, you piece of shit. If you scream, I'll take this fist, smash your jaw and knock your teeth out." He waved his flesh-colored cantaloupe in her face. "Hey, will you look at this. He's a twerp

　　　　TOO BEAUTIFUL FOR WORDS

too." He got into her face. His breath was so foul that Papi almost gagged. Trying to hold her breath, she noticed a dead fly in his beard. "You're getting me all excited," he said. "We're going to give you the best screwing of your life."

Papi noticed the two other goons were quite thin. One had a well-trimmed beard, the other long sideburns. One of the cyclists stepped forward. "Hey, bitch, how about a blow job?"

"Will you leave me alone?"

"Come on, we're going to show you what real men can do," the third vile goon said.

"Please, mister, leave me alone. I never did anything to you."

"Didn't I tell you to shut up?" The leader growled and searched around for others who might interfere. Sex was on his mind.

"Hey, Shank, she's too far pregnant. We might kill her or the kid."

"Who cares? It won't be the first time I killed some babe. I want her. Drag her down to the back of the building."

*T*he three pushed, shoved and dragged Papi to the back of the hotel and found a holding area for Dumpsters. It was hidden enough to rape in seclusion. Two of the motorcycle's goons each grabbed a hold of one of Papi's arms, pinning her against a wall between two Dumpsters.

"Mister Shank, I beg you, don't do this. Let me go. Please."

"Will you listen to that," Shank said. "She's begging. I love it. You're really turning me on. Okay, boys, hold the bitch tight, I'm going to be first." Shank looked at Papi and scowled. "Remember, one scream out of you and I'll break your jaw."

With the two bullies on each side, Shank said, "Come on, you worthless bitch. My buddies and me are going to screw your brains out." He unbuttoned his pants, wiggled down the Frisco's exposing his urine-infested underwear, a bulge, then he started to approach Papi with both arms stretched out to tear off her clothes.

In his excited sexual flutter, Shank failed to observe Papi had placed her left boot against the wall behind her. His trousers were now dropped to his knees making him unsteady.

In one motion, using the ringleader's buddies as a fulcrum and the wall as a boost, Papi's two army boots come out of nowhere and struck Shank's bearded chin with such force his jaw fractured. His chain ganged Frisco's had so shackled his ankles his body stumble back eight feet in a sort of pirouette, then he crashed onto the concrete surface, sprawled out face down, yelling, "Ma shaw, ma shaw." Meanwhile, Papi's legs carried over, and like a circus acrobat, she touched the wall, as her arms gained release from her capturers. She twisted her body and stomped her boots down onto each of two-startled wannabe thug's shoulders. Landing, Papi assumed a Karate fight posture—her left arm out, right arm cocked tight against her side terminating in a fisted hand.

She spitted out a shrilled, "Kiyai." Bending her right arm at the elbow she lashed it out in a lightning strike to the closes thug. The startled goon received a blow to his Adam's apple. He dropped to the ground, grabbed his throat with both hands and gasped for air, gurgling, "eaaah—eaaah." As she turned to face the second goon, Papi twirled jumping forward into the air, and applied boot blows to his body, sending him reeling against a Dumpster.

  TOO BEAUTIFUL FOR WORDS

She noticed the leader, who was still dazed, but tried to tug up his pants so he could stand. With one knee down and one foot planted, Shank peered up to see Papi over him. He lost his balance. She grabbed his leather hat with her left hand and pulled his head back. Two right hand steel like fingers plunged into his eyes. He tried to scream through his broken jaw, "Eaaaar." She crashed her right elbow across his face, breaking his nose and further jarring the cracked jaw. He shrieked again with even more pain.

The second goon had recovered and came after her with a knife. She feinted a kick, twisted to the right, dropped to the ground, delivering a left round kick to his gut, then made a scissor kick with her left leg swirling over head, to catch behind his knees while her right leg trapped his ankles, throwing him face down on the concrete. In one acrobatic move she instantly jumped up, and saw the goon had pushed himself up onto his hands and knees searching for his knife. His rear end was a prime target, so Papi attacked the disoriented thug again. She buried her left boot into his exposed groin.

The thug shouted, "Aaaah!" He grabbed his manhood area, then kept yelling, "Ow—ow—ow, unable to move.

Going to the first kneeling thug, who was still grasping his throat, she said, "Want to play rough?" She grabbed his head between her hands and brought her left knee up, like a fullback plunging through the scrimmage line. He reeled backward, his face bloody. He was out beyond the count.

Papi decided the ugly leader needed to be taught a serious lesson in manners. She strolled over to the moaning deviate. He was on his knees this time, holding his eyes. "So you like to threaten little girls with your big fist."

"Shay-awa o-m e," he tried to shout, but the broken jaw prevented it. "Me eyes an shaw. An's see."

Shank dropped his right paw to the ground to steady himself.

Papi jumped up and brought her whole body weight down, aiming her left leg toward the fleshy target and crashed her boot onto his knuckles. The heel hit with such force, bones pulverized. Hideous gargled sounds sprung forth from a nasty hairy orifice. A once proud bully, brought down by his victim, cowered like a wimp. He rolled over in pain as he tried to speak, "Hur-han, ma-han. Ya hur ma-han, me eyes an shaw." He collapsed still moaning.

Papi stood straight, took both of her hands, grabbed her pregnancy pouch and straightened it back into position. She adjusted her jogging pants, sweater and skullcap. Then glanced at her assailant writhed in pain, and Shank kept screaming.

"Did I hurt your big old threatening fist?" Papi scolded. "Mister, I begged you and your buddies to leave me alone. Maybe next time you'll think twice about picking on someone smaller than you.

"Boy oh boy. Was that a great tune up or wasn't it. I can hardly wait for the Internationals next month in New York," She said, without turning back. She walked away from three strewn, yowling bodies.

CHAPTER SEVEN

> *I'll do work for a corporate client.*
> *I just wish they paid in a timely manner.*

August 12, 1993—10:46 AM

---

*I*t was late morning and Sammy sat at his desk in his office reading the *Examiner's* second morning edition. He shook his head at an inside headline: THREE MEN FOUND BEATEN.

Three men were rushed to the hospital with multiple injuries from a fight with a rival motorcycle gang. Police said the scuffle started at the rear of the Hotel Harald, at the corner of Eddy and Jones. Claiming unknown assailants attacked them; the three victims are in serious but stable condition at San Francisco General. The men, whose names are being withheld, claimed a rival gang armed with baseball bats jumped them.

Officer Mark Telleal, arriving on the scene before the ambulance, said it appeared one person beat them.

"He must have been a giant for the kind of damages inflicted," said Telleal.

A hospital spokesman said one man had his larynx damaged by a broken thyroid cartilage that mutilated his vocal cords leaving a permanent speech impediment. Another man's testicles had to be surgically removed.

The most seriously injured of the three may lose sight in both eyes. His jaw had to be wired shut, but his nose was successfully reset. Almost every bone in his right hand was broken. An orthopedic surgeon said the prognosis for the hand was poor. Many bones were shattered; he may lose the use of it.

Sammy reread the article and wondered, no—Papi couldn't have—she's too small—then again, didn't Kristy intimate she likes to kick butt. No way—could she? I'm not going to call Kristy about this. I don't want to know.

The phone rang. "Shovel here."

"Mister Shovel, George Stanton from Defender Mutual."

"George, good to hear from you again," Sammy lied knowing Stanton was a company man deluxe. He liked big bonuses and always shook down outside consultants to increase his budget. It was an old Navy trick, save money allotted for enlisted men, and you received quicker advancements in rank.

     TOO BEAUTIFUL FOR WORDS

"Because of the quick job you did exposing the fraud injury case we sent you, we have another assignment. Are you available?"

"I'm always ready. What can I do for Defender Mutual? Oh, by the way, thanks for that last check." He thought I got the check all right, only after nine months of follow-up invoices and numerous phone calls. Corporate red tape wasn't amusing.

"Missing person. We did an in-house check for a preliminary claim on one Toll Washington. We have copies of the police file and ours. The police missing person's report states that there was no reason for his disappearance, however they couldn't detect foul play either. All his friends and relatives checked out. We'll have to pay off on this if we can't find him in a year. Our investigators have been looking under stones of all sizes and shapes, but when they turn them over they're staring at dirt."

"You mean they've struck out."

"To a point—yes."

"Do I dare ask the face amount of the policy?"

"A mil."

"No wonder you want to find him! How much for me?"

"How about half a percent?"

He weighed the insurance corporations' slow pay and his current client. Feeling it worked with Golden Opportunities, he started high, and answered right back, "How about ten percent, pal?"

"Hey, that's too high. I'm going to be generous and say two."

"No, eight."

"I can't authorize that."

"You've wasted more than that on this case already. How long has the guy been gone?"

"Our insured has been missing for ten months."

"That means I only have two months? I want ten percent."

"I'll more than generous with you, five and a half."

"Well."

"Take it, for Christ's sake."

"Okay—but only for eight." I hope I don't regret this, Sammy thought.

"Good, five it is."

"Your ears are waxed. It's eight or no deal."

"You win. I'll send the contract and the file info by Fed Ex overnight. Why don't you give Mrs. Washington a call and let her know you're on the case?"

"George, you old dog, you've been stonewalling her."

"Here's her number, 4-1-5-5-5-5-8-3-4-7.... Make the call—please?"

"What if he's dead?"

"We pay, but I figure it's a scam. You know, when you find this guy, Defender Mutual is really going to be impressed. It could mean a lot more work for you."

"George, I'm always eager to serve. All I ask is more wiggle room." Sammy hit the off button, then glanced down at the phone number and mumbled, "*Mañana.*"

*S*ammy puttered around still waiting for the phone call that would prove there was another lair for Joel. It's been almost two days and still no results. He thought he might have to ask Kristy to send her operative back out for another try. He shuttered just thinking about it.

                    TOO BEAUTIFUL FOR WORDS

Turning his attention to his new software program, Dramatica, he read the operating instructions. He wanted to take this writer's tool, which kept track of story characters, their gender, sexual preferences, physical description, work ethics, likes and dislikes, habits, and use it to organize suspects in his cases. Sammy saw an opportunity to begin with the crime, add the characters as they're discovered, thereby working the program backwards. He believed this approach would make it clearer who's doing what to whom and why.

After two hours, he decided to go out for an early dinner. He returned at seven and noticed his secure answering machine blinking. Sammy's pulse quickens while he pushed the button and shut his eyes. A strong male voice announced, "Your boyfriend resides at the Hotel Harald on Eddy, fourth floor, apartment 403."

"I knew it, I just knew it." Sammy bellowed ecstatically.

He figured the best course would be to go early in the morning, no sand traps; most of the building's occupants would be asleep or, better yet, passed out.

"Clothes, I must have clothes to play the part," he muttered and dashed out to find the nearest open thrift store. He discovered his present attire was shoddier than anything the local Thrift Store had on the men's clothing racks. He picked up a sports jacket and examined it closely. Then he picked out some slacks, shirts and accessories. "Damn, there's lots of neat stuff here and at five-hundred an hour I can finally afford it." Sammy rummaged around for tomorrow's planned hotel exploit and found some shabby brown slacks, a brown shirt and a brown coat. Before leaving, he discovered a large black scarf that could be use to shield his face. He rounded out the ensemble with a cloth shopping bag and floppy brown hat. Back in his apartment's garage, he wiped sections of the pants and coat on the garage concrete floor's oil and dirt stains. He thought he was ready to hob-nob with the homeless; actually it was a grade above his usual attire.

CHAPTER EIGHT

What did mother say to stay out of?

August 13, 1993—6:30 AM

---

*A*t six-thirty the next morning, Sammy set out for Eddy Street to find out if there was really another side to the *White Knight* image Joel portrayed. He staggered along, like a wino, until he reached the Hotel Harald. He climbed to the fourth floor. Whoa, he witnessed an alarm system; breaking in could be another matter, but he brought the right tools along for a "just–in-case."

The door was equipped with the best hardware money can buy, an alarm key switch below a metal sign announcing in three lines: WARNING - THESE PREMISES HAVE A - BURGLAR ALARM.

Sammy opened his bag, pulled out an electronic carpenter's nail finder. He moved it along the top of the door's edge. Nothing. Then he started from the top and slowly ran the finder down. When light signaled a solid presence of metal he carefully marked the spot with caulk. He knew a magnet was holding the door alarm detector closed. He rummaged through his bag, grabbed a large magnet, attached it to the doorframe opposite the spot on the door, and mumbled, "That should hold the switch closed. Whatever's on the other side of this door must be important." He worked on the lock until he heard a click.

He twisted the knob and opened the door.

"Jeez!" Sammy muttered as he pinched his nose, the foul odor from within swept over him. He stuck his head through the doorframe and looked inside. He viewed beer and liquor bottles scattered about, some contained dried powder. There on a coffee table were wineglasses smeared with caked-up contents. Near the glasses he spotted various colored pills that had spilled from plastic containers. Moldy food spores drifted about due to the rush of fresh air. Sammy retched, pulled out a hanky and held it to his nose to repel an unpleasant stench. However the rank odors were too overpowering for a mire hanky. He discarded it into his bag and decided to tough it out.

"So, this is the dark side of one Joel Ceja," Sammy said rattled.

It was still early, so he took his time. Before starting the search, he pulled a pair of surgical gloves from his coat. He always brought a few along so he didn't leave prints. After seeing the place, he was thankful he had the protection for his own personal safety. He also understood how thorough Lieutenant Bracque could be. Even if nothing appeared disturbed, he would have forensics double check to determine if evidence had been sifted through.

Opening drawers and cabinets, he discovered porn tapes, girly magazines, assorted whips, cuffs and leather paraphernalia. What the hell was this guy doing with all this stuff? Joel had enough material strewn about his apartment to open his own adult toy store. He observed a dildo on the unmade king size bed, then eyed the stains on the bedding, probably left by body fluids discharged in moments of passion.

He picked up a glass from the nightstand. A dark syrupy substance clung to the bottom. It contrasted with the rim's bright red lipstick. He mumbled, "Women have been here too, yet I

     TOO BEAUTIFUL FOR WORDS

don't see any spent condoms scattered about. Didn't this guy ever hear of AIDS?"

The apartment was a studio unit, only bigger. A roll down desk in the living area revealed nothing significant, nor did the bedside dresser. Sammy discovered a Polaroid camera lying on the foot of the bed, and a spent photo on the floor, almost covered by a comforter. He picked it up.

"Oh Christ, two women engaging in oral sex! This guy was a sicko," Then he frowned. One of the girls, with long black hair, had a familiar face, but he wasn't sure where he had seen her before. Maybe this gal's boyfriend whacked Joel. He pocketed the photo for future reference. He imagined women being dragged into this den, gagged, then tortured. He checked out the closets and the bathroom, and peeked behind wall pictures. Nothing unusual. He returned to the bed and inspected a pair of cuffs he spotted earlier. Seeing they're covered with black foam padding and easy to open, he dismissed the sexual torture theory and moved to the kitchen.

It was obvious to Sammy, who did cook from time to time, that Joel wasn't a chef. The fridge contained nothing but imported beer, various labels of chardonnay, eight bottles of Dom Perignon, imported Brie cheese, molding limes, and an open tin of Beluga Caviar that was beginning to reek with age.

The upper cupboards were almost bare, except for fancy canned goods, Bremner crackers, and expensive crystal sets for cocktail, wine and highballs. A few plates, mugs, water glasses and items of silverware were scattered in and around the sink. He opened the lower cabinets to reveal bottles of red wine, vodka, tequila, and gin, representing the whose-who of liquor. Sammy had never seen these brands before—in the stores where he shopped, they're kept locked up.

He was about to give up when he noticed in a shadowed corner, behind paper bags, a toaster, coffee maker and other kitchen gadgets, the proverbial cookie jar. It was more than half-hidden and very plain looking, but it was a cookie jar. I've looked everywhere else, he thought, why not there.

He opened the lid, peeked inside, and pulled out newspaper clippings. They all were reports of worldwide assassinations covering a period of over twenty-years. He started to read a few. He noted these victims weren't your ordinary citizens, but some of the best world leaders in a host of fields. Nuclear scientist found dead in London. Brilliant linguist shot to death in Peru. Why would anyone keep these - unless?

Holy shit! What on earth have I discovered in this dump. Could—am I holding his souvenirs? Damn, this can't be. Joel, a big-time hit man? Naw, he may be shady and a closet pervert, but an international assassin? The thought rocked Sammy back on his heels and gave him a whole new respect towards Joel.

But if this guy was an assassin, where were his special artillery? None were here, and why these men? To Sammy, Joel appeared more than Golden Opportunities' CEO.

He frowned and scratched his head as he tried to figure out a common denominator for the killings, but on the surface there was no apparent relationship. That will take time. He grabbed all of the clippings and stuffed them into his bag. Enough is enough, for one morning.

Before Sammy left, he scrutinized the main room one more time. He searched over and around the desk and went down on his knees to look under the bed. That was when he espied a crumpled paper behind a wastebasket. He crawled over and picked it up. Flattening it out, there were all kinds of symbols on it. Hummm, they look Chinese. No, maybe Egyptian or like

   TOO BEAUTIFUL FOR WORDS

those on Inca or Mayan Temples. Sammy decided to pocket the note too.

He checked his watch and heard voices in the hall. He crept toward the door. He conjured maybe his magnet attracted nosy tenants. He listened for faint words.

"I guess it's that gal he knocked up. I told her he lived here. Serves the bastard right. Always pussyfooting around, but never sharing his nookie with us."

He glanced up and viewed a horn above the door that will wail if the alarm switch opens. His heart starts to pound faster because if they pull off his magnet it will bring big trouble.

He strained to listen for more, but the voices faded, stopped, and then herd a loud slam. He gently opened the apartment door, ready to dash if the horn blew. Nothing but quiet. He sighed in relief and peered around. The corridor was vacant. Taking the scarf, he slipped out, reactivated the alarm, wiped the door, frame and knob. He raised his scarf to hide his face, adjusted his hat, grabbed his sack and bolted down the stairs.

Pausing at the entrance, Sammy looked both ways, darted across Eddy and headed up the street. When he turned back to look at the apartment building one last time, Sammy spotted a brown Caddy drive up and double park. Two men jumped out and ran inside.

Sammy thought about the apartment, but couldn't remember noticing a motion detector or infrared beam. It came to him, the carpet, dammit all, the unit must have a proximity device below the carpet. He touched his cell phone, but decided to use a local phone booth so the police couldn't trace his number. He raced to the corner, went into a donut shop and called 911. "Hey, there's a burglary taking place in a fourth-floor apartment at the Hotel Harald. It's on the corner of Eddy and Jones. Hurry before they get away." Sammy slapped down the receiver before he could be questioned, and bought a dozen donuts. He went back outside and copied down the Caddy's license number on the back of the picture he lifted from the apartment.

In less than two minutes three squad cars reached the corner. Three uniforms went inside, two searched for other exits and the sixth officer stationed himself to guard the entrance. Shortly the officers returned with the two men, cuffed and cursing.

"Call an inspector over here and find out what's going on." One of the officers said. "You should see the place these hoods were ransacking, you won't believe it."

He guessed the lieutenant would find Joel's hideout after all and without my help. Sammy turned, and melted into the gathering crowd.

"I wonder how long Burglary will sit on this before Bracque can make the connection? I'm betting three to five days."

CHAPTER NINE

Nice man, nice family,
So where did he go?

August 14, 1993—10:36 AM

*O*n Saturday morning, Sammy located Toll Washington's modest home. It was located in a part of San Francisco that was called the Avenues, about four blocks from Ocean Beach. Residents enjoyed a full sun about ninety days a year, even though it was mid August, Sammy tugged at his jacket collar, and held the front lapels as if he were in a violent snowstorm. Bundled up, he approached a stucco two-story residence that showed aging faded yellow paint, the result of ocean salt. It was part of typical middle-class row housing built on sand dunes in the twenties for San Francisco's growing population.

He wondered if the family was expecting him to bring the insurance check. He pressed the doorbell and took a deep breath. He heard the fumbling of a dead bolt, but couldn't see who was at the door. The owner had installed one of those new iron security screen doors painted white. It kept nosy solicitors from peeking inside. Finally the screen door swung out and before him stood a big grinning woman wearing a low-cut dress revealing bosomy breasts.

"Why, you must be that new detective, Mist'r Shovel, the insurance company sent. My-oh-my, you's right on time. Come on in. Careful now, don't let that heavy screen door hit you. I've fixed you some cobbler made from fresh peaches. I used ta own a soul food restaurant in Oakland. Everyone loved Haddie's peach cobbler—yessir—they did—just loved it."

Sammy figured this lady ate too much of her own cooking. He followed her inside and watched in amazement as she glided along, without waddling, by taking small steps. He guessed she must weigh between three hundred to three-fifty pounds and noticed that her head was too small for her body. Trying to be sociable, he replied, "Mrs. Washington, I'd love a piece of your cobbler."

"For a detective, you sure is short—not like the others."

"I hope I'm not like the others." Damn that George, he said he sent one. "How many have there been?"

"Actually, three that we knows of.... Well, don't stand there set a spell. I'll gets some coffee too. You must be famished coming all the way out here."

He observed a happy face marred by vitiligo; honest words flowing from full lips and dancing ebony eyes, an extraordinary gift. Sammy could visualize delighted customers lining up and making her soul food restaurant prosper.

When he finished the first helping of cobbler, Mrs. Haddie Washington scooped another helping onto his plate, before he could hold up his hand. Haddie said, "Now don't be bashful. A young man like you needs meat on his bones."

"Thanks for the young man compliment. When I called, I explained Defender Mutual hired me to assist them in finding your husband. Why don't you tell me about him, like how you met, his hobbies, and work habits? You know, things like that."

"Don't you want to know where he came from? That's what all the police and other detective ever asked?"

"Okay, where was he born?"

                    TOO BEAUTIFUL FOR WORDS

"Detroit. We visited his family after were married. Nice folks. I got their address if you need it. They're worried about him too."

Sammy quickly surmised the San Francisco Police figured a person trying to hide would return to his roots. That's why their investigation consisted of asking the Detroit Police and other law-enforcement locals to put out an APB including the surrounding areas. "Mrs. Washington, I want to know more about the man. Tell me how you met and everything about your husband."

Haddie began her story with how she and her husband bought their home twenty-one years ago.

"My father came to California during WWII to cash in on some of the War Bond money and ended up in Kaiser's Richmond shipyard. He returned to Alabama after the war. He was thirty-six and married my momma, a seventeen-year-old bride. I was their firstborn child; popped out on the morning of February 13. My momma told me the heavens open up to let rain wash away all earthly sins so I could be raised pure. She was a strict Southern Baptist." She glanced at him, folded her hands in contentment, and smiled, then went on with her tale. "As I was growing up, I hated Alabama. The living conditions, heat and humidity were too much, and my mother was a baby factory. I remembered all of the stories my father told about California. At eighteen, I packed up an old suitcase and headed west.

"I worked in Mel's diner in Oakland, and met my soul mate, Toll, when he delivered UPS packages to the place. I always gave him a cup of coffee and pie. Now, I paid, don't think I didn't. I never stole nothing in my whole life, no sir. Toll was a strapping young man, and so handsome in his uniform. I'd 'f paid for his lunch and dinner every day just to get his attention." Her eyes sparkled at the memory. "Well, it worked. In a year we got married. After Toll was hired by the San Francisco Muni transportation system, we had more than enough for the down payment for our present home. I wanted to live in a cool climate, so we selected this house, out here in the Sunset District." She glanced around her living room. "Then I gets restless, Mist'r Shovel, and decided to open a restaurant to earn extra money. At first it was slow, but when I introduced soul food in the seventies the heavens opened up showered me with lots of green paper. Why, we paid off this house within five years." Her grin was infectious as she laid it on him. "Toll and I have been married for twenty-five years. We have three children. Charles, the oldest, is married and start'n his own family. Leroy and Celina live here. My Toll disappeared 'bout ten months ago. Can you help us Mist'r Shovel?"

"That's why I'm here. How are you doing financially?"

"I's having a hard time making bill payments if that's what you mean. The creditors won't wait much longer."

"What about your restaurant?"

"I gave that up years ago. My legs, well—they gave out you know."

At this point, Sammy was sure Haddie would request the million-dollar check.

"Mist'r Shovel, I knows you's our man, for you don't put on airs, came right away to see us and asked real questions about my Toll. Can you find him for us? I don't know what's gotten into Toll. Heavens sakes, he never done this b'fore."

"Haddie, er—may I call you Haddie?"

She was a big woman and when she laughed her whole body wobbled, shaking anything within ten feet of her. "Mist'r

Shovel," She said, "I won't let you call me Mrs. Washington. Haddie 'll do just fine—just fine."

Sammy stared into her eyes. He could tell she was genuinely happy the insurance company had sent another detective to find her husband.

"Good, Haddie it is. Now Haddie, will you explain when your husband disappeared?"

"Don't you know?"

"Only what I've read in the police and insurance company reports. But I want to hear it from you, word for word."

Sammy saw a flash from the corner of his eye, her two children were listening from the kitchen. One, a dainty girl, neatly dressed, appeared about fourteen. The other, was a big scraggy boy with a scowl on his beefy face. He appeared like a boat in a storm with a fatherless rudder, ready to capsize if a rouge wave hit him broadside.

He wore Levis, Nikes and a faded wide banded polo shirt. Thick gold chains hung from his neck, but his expression was full of pain and appeared uncomfortable. He could play pulling guard on any high school football team.

"Why don't you ask your children to join us? Maybe they can shed light on Toll's disappearance, too." Sammy said, smiling at Haddie. He figured it would be wise if he confronted the boy now rather than wait for a situation that could fester into confrontation.

"Come on in, Celina. You too, Leroy." Haddie motioned to the children.

"It's Nazr." Leroy retorted as he walked in scowling. "You knows I hates the name Leroy." His anger flared as Sammy checked him out. "What's the matter with you, whitey."

"Nothing, Nazr." Sammy said, then carefully phrased his next words. "I thought you and your sister might have information relative to your father's disappearance. Perhaps you could sit with your sister."

"I'll stand."

"By the way, the name Leroy has a French origin. It means *The King*."

"I guess you being white, you'd know all about that."

"Leroy, stop talking to Mist'r Shovel that way. He's here to help us."

"Mama, he's just another white detective, you know what I'm saying. All they do is come here and give us lippo mumbo jumbo. Where are the real P.I.'s, like Shaft? He'd get down to business with plenty of action and find Dad." Nazr said defiantly. His nose squinted and his mouth pulled down on one side. He stepped behind his mother.

"Leroy!"

Glancing at Mrs. Washington, "No—no, Haddie. This is good. The young man's flustered and wants, as he so eloquently put it, *action*." He said gazing at Nazr. "I can't guarantee I'll find your father, but I will try the same as if he were that French King I mentioned." He turned his attention to Nazr's mother. "Now, Haddie, can you tell me about the week before your husband—er, Toll disappeared?"

"Well, there's not much to tell. My Toll was a man of habits. He got up, went to work, came home, watched television and went to bed. On Sundays we all went t' church. My Celina's in the church choir."

"That's wonderful, Celina. Do you like to sing?"

"Yes, sir. I sure do." Celina sat up straight and glowed.

Sammy heard her velvety voice, smiled and visualized Celina singing celestial hymns to her church's congregation while clustered angels gazed on with approval.

"She's the lead singer, and Pastor Harris says Celina sings real fine, lifting the parishioners' spirits to embrace God with her soothing nightingale voice. He has her do a solo each week—he does." Haddie said quite proudly.

"Mama," Nazr interrupted, "Why do you keep wearing dresses that have low tops? You're too big for that kind of outfit."

"Leroy, if they didn't want me to wear it they wouldn't have made it in my size."

"Quit calling me Leroy."

"I'm gona whop you on the head, boy."

Sammy caught onto Nazr's cry for attention and missed his father. He wanted to help the boy, and Haddie too.

Tiny beads of sweat formed on Haddie's brow. She needed Toll too, for Haddie wasn't used to stress. Sammy's mission; find Toll. He tried to open up the discussion by pressing for forgotten information.

"You said Toll was a Muni driver?"

"My Toll worked his way up to become a supervisor." Her eyes opened wide. Haddie loved talking about Toll.

"My daddy work there for twenty-three years," Celina added.

"That's right. Shortly after we got married, Toll applied with Muni. Good-paying jobs back then was hard to get for a black man. It took two years before Muni hired him. He savors driving those dang buses."

"The Geary run is his favorite root. He races that tandem rig up Market, through downtown, up Geary and all the way out to the ocean and back. He done drive the Geary Street line for years." Haddie informed, now on a roll.

Sammy didn't dare correct her mispronunciation of savored.

"How does he get along with the other drivers?"

"Why, he gets along just fine. Around the Flynn Division, my Toll was known as the toasted Scotsman, because when it comes to money, he always answered, 'I's just thrifty.'"

"The Flynn Division. What do you mean by that? Is that a bus barn?"

"I don't know about any barn. The buses are stored in bus and repair buildings." Seeing Sammy's puzzled, Haddie added, "Toll said it's to keep off the graffiti."

"Clever. You mentioned buildings. Does that mean more than one?"

"They's seven Muni locations. I thought you'd've known that. My Toll works out'a the one on Harrison and Sixteenth Street. They have streetcar and electric bus divisions all over the city."

"Did Toll work at other divisions?" Sammy asked, wondering why the insurance company didn't tell him about the different Muni divisions.

"He sure did, Mist'r Shovel. Over near Pier Thirty-nine, there's Kirkland. That's where he started. Spent some years there. I believe he was at the Woods Division less than a year. But when them dang tandem buses came, he couldn't wait to pilot what Toll called human boxcars." Haddie laughed. "He used to pretend they were sports cars. He tried to juggle the standing passengers when he screeched at stops."

"Yeah. All the drivers did; I remember all too well." Sammy said frowning.

     TOO BEAUTIFUL FOR WORDS

He turned when the front door started to open. He glanced at Celina, while his peripheral vision's stayed fixed on the door.

"Say, did your father wear a white poppy in his cap every day?"

"Yes sir, my Daddy did. I made a new one for him every week, since I was nine."

"Celina learned how to make paper flowers in a local Brownie troop," Haddie said proudly.

"So that was Toll. Heck, he was a fixture on Geary. I rode with him many times." Sammy said, then peeked at Nazr and noticed that he had lost his scowl. The door opened wide and a well-dressed young man entered, complete with matching tie and hanky.

"Charles, I's glad you's here" Haddie greeted him. "The insurance company has hired Mist'r Shovel to find our Toll."

"Hi Mom, Celina and Nazr. I got caught up in traffic going through the park." he said, then turned to Sammy. "Pleased to meet you. I hope you can find our father. When mother called she was so excited that I didn't cached your name."

"Samuel D. Shovel," Sammy said, opening his wallet and taking out a business card. " I go by Sammy," He sized up Charles, and figured Charles was a combination of his brother and sister, lean, yet iron-muscled.

"Did you say that you came through Golden Gate Park?" Sammy asked.

"I'm a curator in training at the Palace of the Legion of Honor."

"I've always wanted to visit that museum." Sammy said, knowing he was talking to a college-educated man.

"Mister Shovel, call me anytime and I'll take you on a personal tour. It will be my pleasure."

"I just might take you up on your offer. But why don't we all drop the *Mister Shovel* crap and call me Sammy."

"Is you sure?" Haddie laughed, shaking the couch and floor.

"Very sure, Haddie. I'm curious, can you explain how your husband received the name of Toll?"

"Tee—hee. Why Mist'r Shov—Mist'r Sammy, yous' the first detective to ask that question. His Christian name is Thomas. His mama said he couldn't stop eating her homemade tollhouse cookies. As a child, he didn't care much for cake or ice cream, just them tollhouse cookies. My, how he loved dem cookies. Eventually the school kids called him Toll. The name done stuck. He still likes tollhouse cookies. He sent for his mother's recipe and I still make em. They sure were a hit at my restaurant. If we had a pile of money, them cookie stores would be Mrs. Haddie's instead of Mrs. Fields."

"Amazing—That's a great story, Haddie…. Let's get back to the week before he disappeared. Was there anything out of the ordinary? Did he break his routine? Did he receive strange phone calls? Anything like that?"

"No Mist'r—ah…does you mind if we calls you Mist'r Shovel?"

"No—not at all, Haddie," Sammy said grinning.

"I never notice any difference. Children?"

"How about it, Celina, Nazr. You too, Charles. What do you remember?" Sammy asked gazing at them.

"Mister Shovel, sir," Celina said, "I remember Daddy getting phone calls cause Nazr got mad because he couldn't use the phone. But on the phone, Daddy was happy and excited, like he got another promotion—of some kind."

Nazr's eyes open wide and his face changes to a bland expression.

"Is that true?" Sammy asked, turning to him.

"Well?" Haddie demanded.

"I'm thinking…. Celina's right. I was pissed those nights before he disappeared; you know what I'm saying, cause my homeboys couldn't reach me. I forgot all about it."

"How long, or I should say, how many nights did this go on?"

"Think hard, brother." Charles said. "This may be important."

"Dad left home early Monday morning, and we never seen'm again. Working back, let's see. Dad received a few calls on Saturday, less on Sunday, but a lot on Friday night and maybe one or two very late on Thursday," Nazr reported.

"No others?"

"No, except some marketing calls, you know what I'm saying. You'd always know if they came in because Dad would yell, 'I'm doing just fine thank you' and slam the phone down," Nasr remarked.

"Nazr, you said your father left home early on Monday morning like that wasn't his normal routine."

"Yeah. He usually ate breakfast before he left."

"Mister Shovel, my father didn't spend money foolishly by buying something he could get at home," Charles explained. "He never bought lunch. His beat-up lunch pail looked like it survived World War One trench warfare. But he'd treat the family to dinner once a month, sometimes at the wharf, but normally at local spots, usually Chinese."

"So, leaving early was unusual?"

"If someone offered to buy breakfast, Toll always accepted." Haddie jumped in adding to the information being bandying around.

"Is it possible Toll had a rendezvous that morning?" Sammy said thinking the worst.

"Why, my Toll always was very regular. Why does you ask?"

"No, mom," Charles interrupted, "Sammy wasn't talking about bowel movements. He wanted to know if father planned to meet someone that morning."

Sammy's fists stiffened, body tensed like a fighter hearing a round one bell ring, then he clamped down on his jaw straining to keep from laughing. He didn't wanting to embarrass this wonderful woman.

"He never said nothing to me," Haddie said. "Leroy? Celina?" Both shrugged and shook their heads.

Sammy stared still trying hold back laughter. When he saw everyone looking at him, his levity faded.

"Haddie, I have to ask this question. Why did you take out a million-dollar term insurance policy on your husband?"

"I didn't. Toll took the policy out his self. He said some pretty girl made it simple."

"Money, that's all you whiteys can think of like we're trying to steal your mother grabbing institutions?" Nazr growled again.

"Leroy! You keeps this up and I's going to whip you, boy," Haddie said sternly,

"Mom, Nazr, you're riled up. Sammy's asking questions. Let him finish," Charles intervened.

"If you had your choice, would you take the million or Toll?" Sammy asked and observed Haddie for any sign of hesitation.

"I want my Toll back."

"I don't need money, I want my daddy!" Celina said.

"Mister Shovel, my father was special to me and our family. They can keep their money," Charles said.

"What's your take on all this?" Sammy asked Nazr.

"My dad and I got into a lot of arguments, you know what I'm saying, especially the days before he disappeared. He didn't like my new friends, my homeboys, and because of the phone calls I yelled at him." Nazr moved around while his eyes searched for something lost. "But my Dad, is my Dad. Now that he's gone, I realize I miss him and maybe he was right. He provided good for our family and—and whipped us when we deserved it. He hated drugs...." He peered down, then continued. "I should have shown more respect. He—he deserved it—I know it now. Money, you know, isn't a substitute for discipline—yeah, I need my Dad to keep me—ah." Standing motionless, his misty stare revealed remorse. "Ah—I want him back in my life."

Sammy knew the young man was still a boy and was about to crack. Sammy didn't want to see tears flow from the eyes of one so prominently named Nazr.

"Thanks for that information, Nazr, I'm sure it's going to help," he said, then complimented him. "I see a great future ahead for you."

"Haddie," he said turning to her. "We've made a good start. I'll keep in touch—perhaps more questions; maybe some answers."

"Mr. Shovel, you've asked questions no one else has ever asked. Isn't that right, Mom?" Charles quickly noted.

"I told you, you's our man."

"We'll see—won't we," Nazr snarled defiantly when Sammy took his leave.

CHAPTER TEN

Conversations with dead men
Usually are one sided, unless.

August 14, 1993—2:28 PM

"Shovel? Bracque here. I've got some good news and bad news. The good news, we found Joel Ceja's buddy, Manny Soto. The bad news, he's been shot to death. The body's at the old container yard near Pier Twenty Four where they're doing some new construction. If you want to be part of this, you better get over here pronto. We're about to remove the corpse."

"I'll be right there."

While cabbing over to Pier Twenty Four, Sammy thought about Joel's death, his secret lair, the souvenir clippings and the sudden appearance of Manny's body. The events had all the trappings of a syndicate operation, but how did an honored business leader, like Joel, remain incognito? He now suspected Joel and Manny were just pawns, and something else is going on. Maybe it was big, maybe small; maybe it was organized, maybe not; then again judging by the news clippings, it must be worldwide.

He rationalized the last thought. *I was hired to find Joel's murderer, not to save the world from sinister killers. To poke that deep, I could become the next target. My life's worth more than twenty thousand, thank you. Oh hell, I'll see where this goes, before I back off.*

---

*S*ammy arrived across from the pier and made his way through a small crowd of nosey tourists until he came to a police officer. "I'm Sammy Shovel, Lieutenant Bracque is expecting me."

The officer glanced over to Sergeant Ryan, and received an okay nod, and then let Sammy through the yellow crime scene tape. Sammy spotted Lieutenant Bracque standing on top of a stack of lumber at the construction site with some forensic personnel.

Bracque recognized Sammy and waved while shouting, "Hey, Shovel, over here." "By the way, where did you get the sports coat? You're out of character," Bracque asked, eyeing Sammy as he approached a pile of stacked 2x4s.

"Needed it for a case I'm working on."

"I don't want to seem critical, but stay away from the Thrift Stores if you want to impress."

"Now what's wrong?"

"The pants are baggy and dragging; one coat sleeve is shorter than the other. Thrift Stores don't do tailoring in case you're wondering. You'd have to start shopping at real retailers for those kind of services."

"I thought you were a cop, not a fashion editor."

"Cute."

Sammy spine straightened defiantly, and his anger burned while he watched Bracque bark out orders like a seasoned Roman General positioning his troops before an attack on unwitting Hunnish hoards. The pathologists and crime scene investigators, who were carefully attending to the corps in order to keep themselves from falling off the lumber pile, all wore medical masks. One was taking photos.

 TOO BEAUTIFUL FOR WORDS

"Do you want to see this guy before they put him into a body bag and take him down to the morgue or not?" The lieutenant hollered down.

Sammy climbed onto the neatly stacked lumber pile.

"The way I see it," Bracque said, "Soto was here for a meet. He was eating a Chorizo burrito when, apparently, he had a stomachache. Part of the burrito is still in its wrapping laying on top of a box of nails below, and yes, mister know-it-all, we'll check it for fingerprints. Not wanting to be seen, he climbs up here to take a dump, and took a bullet right in his head. It caught him just as he was squeezing out—"

"Stop. I don't need to hear this." Sammy said trying to blot out the full mental picture that flashed through his mind.

"Okay, but it's not a pretty picture. His face has been pulverized." Bracque said.

"I've seen many mutilated bodies, what's one more?" Sammy said nearing the body,

"Careful, don't step in the vomit, urine, or feces excrement."

"What? Who?" Sammy asked as he closed in on Manny's body. The wind suddenly forged and his nose was assaulted with a disagreeable whiff of the funk. "Whew, the stench is overwhelming." Now we understood the need for the forensic unit's masks.

"One of the workmen, who takes a siesta up here after lunch, lost his burger and fries when he saw this." Bracque said, turning to face an officer. "Pull back the sheet."

Sammy beheld the corpse and he recoiled in horror. Manny's nose and lower jaw resembled meat lying on the local butcher's block ready to be ground into hamburger.

"Jeez!" Sammy exclaimed. "I haven't seen teeth knocked out like this since studying holocaust photos."

"What?"

"You know, when the German guards smashed out gold fillings from the corpses before they burned their carcasses." Sammy watched as a weird look came over Bracque's face. "World War Two and the death camps."

"Oh—that. Shovel, that was horrible. Why would you want to remember something like that anyway? It was sickening."

"Because it happened, but, why Manny? Who would smash out his teeth?"

The lieutenant removed his floppy wide-brim hat to wipe his brow, exposing his bushy eyebrows.

"Well, I heard that Manny's front teeth were gold. And if you look around, other teeth are laying about. If there were any gold ones, they got up and ran away."

"Gold, smolled. Who would do this for two gold teeth? They're almost worthless. They're made from low carat gold. There's got to be more to this than just a random killing."

"That's what I like about you, Shovel, you never accept the obvious, but I believe that could be a reasonable conclusion. Now, what if I told you our lifeless corpse, had an empty shoulder holster?"

"So?"

"And guess what the pathologist found when they patted down the corpse?"

"Is this a guessing game? I have no idea, but I'm sure you're going to tell me."

"This Soto guy was a pro. He had another gun taped to the inside of his thigh. I believe the killer missed it because he was frightened away."

"I'll be damned."

"It's the same caliber, nine millimeter, that killed Joel Ceja." Lieutenant Bracque said coyly.

"Oh! Makes sense."

"Makes sense? Killed his best friend?"

"Give you odds it's the same gun."

"What kind of odds? And for how much?"

"Four to one, and for a hundred."

"In spite of what you believe, I'm not the corrupt cop you want to make me out to be. So let's make it fifty bucks."

"You're on." Sammy noticed Ryan getting closer to the woodpile and looked down at him. "What about you, sergeant? I know you were listening."

"Oh, come on, Sammy, you know I don't gamble." Ryan said. Everyone knew he was a straight-laced cop.

"Who said anything about gambling? Call it a friendly wager. We're not in Vegas."

"I don't make bets either. But I do believe you're both right about the mystery of the missing gold teeth. Remember, Lieutenant, he still had his wallet."

"I'm well aware, sergeant. However, I can't rule out the possibility that some hothead who needed quick cash iced Soto. Ten carat or twenty-four carat, gold shines to a bum with a desperate need for a fix," he said, then turned to Sammy, who raised an eyebrow. "Shovel, you try to find an enigma in everyday occurrences, but maybe you're right this time."

"I guess I'm just the suspicious type. But wouldn't it have been easier for the killer to take the victim's wallet rather than bust out his teeth?"

"Three dock workers thought they heard a shot, but traffic is constant around here, so they contributed it to a backfire. However, one worker told me they shouted to see if anyone needed help. If the construction guy hadn't climbed up for his snooze, Soto might have been here for days. We're taking their complete statements now. Do you want to talk to them?"

"No—I've smelled enough reeking odor to last me for days."

"By the way, it's going to be my pleasure relieving you of two-hundred bucks," Bracque said, shooting him a big grin that almost cracked his stern face.

"Why's that?" Sammy asked, thinking he'd just been had.

"The gun's slugs are the most communally used. Gotcha, Shovel." The lieutenant replied, pointed his finger at Sammy, then popped up his thumb.

"Maybe. I'll wait for the lab's report."

"Reinhourse told me he's making progress on the assignment I gave him. You know he's still thrilled that you wanted to know the status of unsolved murdered businessmen. We'll let you know if anything important comes of it."

"Say, Ryan, can you give me a ride back to my office? It's on your way to the Central," Sammy asked.

"Well I—" The sergeant said, then was interrupted.

"Of course," lieutenant Bracque said, "take Mister Shovel along. Now that he's helping us, he's like family to the department, besides he's going to owe me two-hundred big ones."

     TOO BEAUTIFUL FOR WORDS

"Let's go Sammy," the sergeant said grumpily, then stared at the lieutenant, shrugged, turned, and led the way to his police car. "I'm taking the family to Yosemite tonight so we can spend the whole day there Sunday. I don't appreciate being a taxi service."

"Ryan, that's a good idea. I need a break. I think I'll go to Tahoe."

CHAPTER ELEVEN

August 16, 1993—6:45 PM

Sammy's trip back from Tahoe was bumper to bumper. Finally, back in his suite, Sammy headed to his coffee counter and flushed out black grime and grounds, and spotted the donut box he bought Saturday morning. He shook his head, and started another pot of coffee. Entering his office, he flopped down at his computer and began to list the evidence he had garnered into his new Dramatica program. He calculated murder was always wrought with riddles—some were unsolvable. He figured the few clues he had were too lean to start speculating yet.

He returned to the reception area and poured a mug of fresh coffee. He lifted the donut box's lid and took a peek at hard glazed and powdered sugar morsels and thought, maybe later; maybe not. Sammy was always alone, since Harry was murdered. He crunched the right of his cheek, and thought, he lived a rotten life. He hesitated for five seconds, reached in and grabbed a powdered one.

Back at his desk, Sammy considered his own childhood playmates in Ukiah, then turned his attention to Joel and Manny. He rocked his head. Sammy focused on his classmate bullies, the cheaters, the perverts and the budding sexual deviates that needed an occasional spanking. As expected, over the years, he

     TOO BEAUTIFUL FOR WORDS

heard a few of them were incarcerated, but was amazed to find out how many of those toughs turned to be protectors and wondered how did these tormenters change their spots—then it came to him, the bullies could continue to ravage legally with a badge.

He occasionally slurped coffee, and bit through a hard morsel. He spread out the news clippings he retrieved from Joel's sleazy pad, brushed off some powdered sugar, and arranged them by date. The clippings revealed that the killings were one or two per year. Some were a month apart and others more than six months. No set pattern. No set country. No set occupation. Definitely hits by hire. He added them to his growing list of clues.

His stomach called for food and Sammy went back to the counter and grabbed two hard glazed ones from the pink donut box; He didn't want to shower powdered sugar over his papers clues again. He refilled the mug with now lukewarm coffee and returned to his office.

Next Sammy examined the Polaroid photo of a tall lanky black haired model type and a wholesome looking girl sporting very ripe plums on the end of bodacious breasts.

"Where have I seen this gorgeous face before?" He muttered racking his brain. He was positive that he had seen the tall woman before, but where? Then there was the crumpled piece of paper with the strange markings on it.

Sammy worked into the night, struggling to eat three-day-old donuts and drink cold coffee. His eyelids gradually turned into lead weights, defying his efforts to keep them open. His long ride back demanded sleep. He stood up, stretched his arms, snatched the mug, moseyed into the reception area, emptied the cold black stuff, and poured in warm coffee. He figured this would soften the last of the glazed hard morsels.

He sat the mug on the desk, and opened the window, and inhaled several deep breaths, trying to shake off sleep. He conjectured about the comment the lieutenant had said about his new thrift store clothes, and thought, damn that smart ass. Back at his desk, he entered more information into the now revised Dramatica program. His head nodded toward the computer keyboard. When it neared the screen, he jerked back up. The sequence was repeated again and again, until, at last, there was a gentle rhythmic breathing. Our detective, Samuel D. Shovel, pedigree nose and all, was asleep at his computer.

*A*t seven thirty-five in the morning, Sammy was still conked out with his head on the keyboard. His blasting phone startled him. His hand moved like a darting snake after elusive prey, and located the receiver. He tried to shake off his last dream. He wasn't sure where he was, but he believed he was still alive. Good start, his brain sang out. He repeatedly grabbed and dropped the receiver, as he struggled to open his eyes, but finally he firmly clasped a tight grip on the phone.

"Hel—Hello, Sammy—Sammy Shovel."

"Shovel, Inspector Reinhourse here."

"Who?"

"Reinhourse, Inspector Reinhourse."

"Oh, sorry. Your call woke me from a very sound sleep. What—what's up?"

"You know, I've never liked you."

"Man—I don't need this," Sammy said still half asleep. "Do you mean you called just to tell me that? Christ, so does half of the department. Get in line, pal."

    TOO BEAUTIFUL FOR WORDS

"What I'm trying to tell you...well, I've been talking to Sergeant Ryan. He says you're all right, somewhat of a maverick at times, but all right. He said you helped him and the department out by checking on witnesses and snitches. According to him, the only cops that knock you don't like private investigators, because they're always sticking their noses into police business."

"Okay—okay. Look, pal, when I grew up my parents drummed into me the police were my friends and those childhood values remain." Sammy fought to control his stupor. "What in hell has that got to do with your phone call? I'm still half asleep!"

"Let me be the first to tell you, you've won the bet with Lieutenant Bracque."

"Ah ha, the trusted assassin did the deed."

"What?"

"Never trust someone who you thought could be trusted."

"You have a weird take on humanity."

"Really. Ever hear of faithful dogs that turned on their masters and kill them?"

"A few. Maybe your right about this."

Sammy, elated, but disappointed; kill your best friend? Stay focused, pal, there must be more going on here. The hideout and the news clippings put these murders into something much bigger than a simple disagreement between friends.

"All right! You mean Manny's gun killed Joel Ceja?"

"You got it! Now are you ready for the really startling news?"

"Let's have it. Reinhourse, I'm beginning to relish your every word."

"You remember when Lieutenant Bracque gave me the assignment to see if any other businessmen were killed over the past fifteen years? At your urging, I might add."

"I still think it's important. Maybe there's a serial killer out there that hates executives."

"Well, I didn't. But, when I started to search the records, sure enough, within the past three years there were a couple of unsolved murders right here in the city. So I pressed on."

"And?"

"You're going to love this. Within the past fifteen years there have been twenty-five unsolved cases of businesspersons shot to death in the city. So I checked down to Monterey and as far north as Guerneville, then Oakland and most of the other East Bay cities, I even went as far as Sacramento and down to Fresno"

"Did I hear you say persons?"

"Yeah, whoever does this kills women too."

"Anything else?"

"When I was reading through the eleventh homicide file, I noticed a reference to Golden Opportunities. So I went back over the first ten. Sure enough, eight of them had some reference regarding Golden Opportunities performing a marketing survey for their business. Six months to a year later the president or key person is dead or missing."

"Holy shit," Sammy commented detecting the odor of a clever assassin ring. "I think you've stumbled on something big, pal. I mean really big. It's beginning to make sense. I knew there had to be a common denominator, I just knew it."

"Well, you knew something all right. The slug from the last murder victim, an aggressive Walnut Creek realtor, also matches Manny's gun."

     TOO BEAUTIFUL FOR WORDS

"What! When? When was that last victim hit?"

"One week before Joel got it."

"Aha! Manny didn't bother to get rid of the gun and had to use it again. Very careless on his part, but wait, didn't you check the slugs that killed Joel?"

"You won't believe this," Reinhourse said sheepishly.

"Try me."

"Commissioner Darrel Snell figured Joel was the victim of a chance doper looking for immediate cash. So he suggested that Lieutenant Bracque drop having the lab catalog the bullet's imprints and send them out for comparison."

"Who?" Sammy inquired.

"Police Commissioner Snell, Darrel Snell."

"I don't believe it,"

"Well, it's true."

"Who's this Commissioner Snell?"

"Hey, he's a nice guy; a family man. Goes strictly according to procedures. So when he asked the lieutenant to forget trying to search for a match, Bracque agreed."

"I find that hard to believe," retorted Sammy. He weighed what he knew to date. He was beginning to believe Joel and Manny were definitely part of some kind of assassin ring. Was Joel's death the result of him wanting out, and as such, he became a sacrificial lamb? What about his childhood buddy, Manny Soto? Was he gunned down by a judgment error in using an assassin gun twice, closure to a partnership or both? Maybe Bracque needed to call in the FBI—get real, pal, the police and the Bureau distrusted each other.

"Well. I'm going to pass this information onto Lieutenant Bracque as soon as he arrives. I just wanted you to know."

"Hey, thanks, pal. And welcome aboard," Sammy said. "It seems we got a team now. Tell me, did every one of those unsolved murders have a connection with Golden Opportunities?"

"About seventy percent, that's over the possibilities of chance," Reinhourse said.

"Over the possibilities? Christ, pal, to me, it's a perfect match. See yeah."

CHAPTER TWELVE

Important news, good or bad
Is hard to muzzle.

August 17, 1993—8:45 AM

"Sorry to barge in on you unannounced, Donald, but you said to keep you informed if I uncovered any information," Sammy blurted out quite excitedly in the lobby of Golden Opportunities.

"Oh, not at all," Donald responded. He led Sammy through the executive suite and into Joel's office. "In here we won't be disturbed. If you want to talk to an employee, this office is the best place, now that Joel's gone."

As they entered, Sammy gazed at the surroundings and understood what Donald meant when he said," It was in the executive suite where real money was splashed around."

"Has anything been moved or changed since your boss's death?" Sammy asked.

"Nothing will change in this office until Joel's killer is found and brought to justice. That's why I was put in charge of hiring you." Donald eyed Sammy, then added, "You've got another disguise on. Wow, so cleaver having the coat sleeves lengths' different, like you found in a trash can."

"Thanks for the compliment." Sammy stared for a moment, fumed slightly, he said lying outright, "We learned these things in criminology classes." He paused trying to figure out the best way to break the news about Manny.

"I'm here because both the police and I have uncovered the following facts. First, Manny has been found."

"Hooray! Maybe Manny can shed some light on who killed Joel." Donald's eyes lit up and a big smile spread across his face.

"Well, he can't do that. Besides, we know who killed your boss."

"You do? Oh great news! When Manny finds out he's going to tear into whoever did it. I don't know if you knew it or not, but Joel and Manny were best friends. They grew up in the same village. May I call in the executive officers to tell them the good news?"

"Better wait." He suggested, remembering his last encounter with the executive troika. He didn't want to deal with Nancy again. "By the way, did Manny have two front gold teeth?"

"Did you say, 'did have'?"

"To be blunt, pal, yeah, he doesn't have them anymore."

"Have you talked to Manny about his teeth?"

"No—no we couldn't."

"Well, why on earth not?" Donald inquired befuddled.

"It seems he's dead too. That was the second thing I was going to tell you."

"Dead? Really—dead?" Donald was puzzled. "Manny's dead?"

"Fraid so. The last time I saw Manny, they were zipping up his body bag and he was missing his two front gold teeth."

"Was—was he killed by the same person who killed Joel?" Donald asked as the color drained from his face.

"No."

"How can you be so—so sure?" Donald said weakly as his legs began to wobble.

"The third thing I was going to tell you... Manny murdered your boss."

"May, may I sit down?" Donald asked. His knees buckled and he plummeted onto a nearby couch. It was like Sammy had just told him he had incurable cancer and only has days to live. He buried his head in his hands. After some moments, he gazed up, and said, "Sorry, but I don't get it. Why—why would Manny want to kill his best friend?"

"We don't know, pal."

Donald began quivering. He was as white as a mime. Sweat oozed out across his forehead.

"Are you all right? I mean can we continue?" Sammy asked in a soft voice.

"Look, Mister Shovel, what you have just told me is a shocker. But we, and I do mean all of us here at Golden Opportunities, loved Joel. There must be a reason why Manny would want to kill his best friend. We want to know that reason."

"I grant you, it's a mystery. Do you want me to continue investigating?" Sammy softly replied, then thought, oh shit, what am I doing? I could become this gang's target if I pursue this.

"Yes—oh my, yes, an emphatic yes." Donald started to sparkle. "We all want to know what's going on. Money's no object. We're willing to pay, Mister Shovel, no matter what it costs."

Sammy's ears picked up on the money's no object, and like Harry jumped on the words. Natural greed overcame fear and good judgment. "Okay, that's fair enough, but getting that kind of information will be risky—I mean life threatening risky. My hourly fee will be double due to those possible hazards."

"That's not a problem. Mister Ballard mentioned Joel's key-man insurance. It's substantial—multi millions. Now what do you need from us?"

"I'll need additional information. I know this might sound crazy, but can you tell me who did Manny's teeth?"

"Why, I believe it was Joel's dentist." Donald replied as color rushed into his cheeks, and his shoulders straightened up.

"Can you get me a phone number or an address?"

"Both. I'll get them now." Donald said and hurried out of Joel's office.

Sammy scrutinized the office, in awe of its opulence. The safe remained open, so Sammy looked inside and found nothing, it was bare except for black powder. He observed built-in wall cases filled with ancient pottery and other memorabilia. Sammy shook his head. Why weren't these treasures in a museum? In the midst of carefully positioned relicts, he noticed something oddly out of place—a dirty hat, something a boy would wear.

He walked over to the window behind Joel's desk and checked out the view. The fog was off in the distance dissipating fast. Sammy decided the panorama was worthy of solitude. He sat down on Joel's chair, swung it around and stared out into the cityscape. He shut his eyes and thought, all I can see from my window is the downtown streets, humanity thwarting around in every direction and neon signs at night and constant car fumes. This office, this window, this opulent lifestyle—ah, so this is how the rich and famous live.

"Here's the information on Joel's dentist," Donald said interrupting his tranquility.

Sammy turned around, scooted up to the desk and reached for the slip of paper in Donald's hand. He stopped when his eyes fell on the only item, other than the pen and pencil set

     TOO BEAUTIFUL FOR WORDS

that ever graced Joel's desk, a chunk of green stone with a two and one quarter-inch-square base. Sammy picked it up. It was four inches high and it had a flat top, like the Aztec temples Cortez plundered. He held it with both hands. His eyes widened and his bottom jaw dropped slightly when he noticed the same strange markings he saw on the crumpled paper he pilfered from Joel's downtown apartment. He gazed at Donald.

"What—what's this?"

"A paperweight," Donald responded.

"A paperweight? What do all these markings stand for?"

"I have no idea. Joel said it came from a Peruvian temple. He bought it many years ago in a Los Angeles curio shop."

"How long ago?" Sammy said urging him on.

"When he went to college."

"You mean when he was at USC?"

"Why, yes."

"How do you know all this?"

"Joel told us."

"So, pal, if Joel told you, it's true?"

"For the most part, but Herman related the same story."

"Herman? Herman who?"

"Why, Joel's old friend, Herman Zeigler," said Donald. "They were in college together. They were both marksmen for their rifle team."

Sammy's mouth curved up slightly on his right side. It was like the Holy Trinity had been revealed.

"Is there something wrong?"

"No—no, not at all, pal. I understand Joel spent a lot of time in Mazatlan. Is that true?"

"We all did. The company bought a villa there."

"Was this condo mentioned in his will?"

"No, because the company bought it. However, some City Hall aides want us to sell it and turn the money over to the charity trust fund that's being set up in accordance with Joel's stipulations. They're already trying to remove Golden Opportunities from administering the trust. They indicated in a court brief that they know who needs charity dollars in the city. Our attorneys said in the papers they filed they never mentioned the thirty-five percent they'll take off the top."

"When bureaucrats get a whiff of money, they become incorrigible." Sammy informed. He paused for a second. Maybe I've got it all wrong. Could someone in City Hall have orchestrated the killings? He dismissed the thought, of course not, they wouldn't have known about his will.

"Not to worry, our corporate attorneys anticipated this and say they have everything in hand. They're keeping our executor informed of the progress."

"Who's that?"

"Peter Ballard. Peter said we must decide if we want to keep or sell the villa. We're going to take a vote next month at our regular stock holders meeting."

"What if something should happen to Peter Ballard?" Sammy said, taking notice that Peter Ballard didn't tell him everything and also held back information.

"The next senior executive assumes the role of executor. Joel didn't want outsiders deciding what was best for the company."

"He must have heard about the City Hall goon gang. Where is this condo in Mazatlan?"

"Actually it's a home in the El Cid complex. Quite nice and we all got to share time there. You see that's why Joel was so liked by his employees, the senior officers, junior officers, managers and so on, down to even trainees. We all had our turn. It might be once every two or three years, but we knew we could spend a week there. It's fully furnished, has a maid who cooks, a gardener and best of all, no cost. It's like living at a hotel with free room service, but in a swank home. It even has a pool and Jacuzzi. It's a pretty nice perk."

"Say, do you keep records on who stayed there and when?

"Of course. Wait, I know the routine. I'll get you the list."

"Pal, how far back do your records go?" Sammy said laughing.

"From date of purchase."

"Thank you. I'll take it all."

"Mister Shovel, if you had said less I'd been disappointed."

"Did the police know about this paperweight?" Sammy asked, still handling the stone object and thinking - hot damn, more pieces of the puzzle are falling into place.

"Why, yes," Donald said. "They took it to their—er—ah."

"Crime-lab?" Sammy supplied.

"Yes, They had it for weeks, but brought it back."

"Yeah, I think the lieutenant mentioned that. Do you mind if I keep this memento for a few days?"

"I guess not, but we want it back."

"No problem. Actually I'll need it for a week or two. However, do me a big fat favor. If anyone asks for this, tell them you don't know what happened to it and don't know where I am."

He shoved it into his pocket. "I'll meet you in the lobby for the list. Then it's *adiós*. I'm going to visit Joel's dentist and then I'm heading to Mazatlan. Call that maid and tell her I'm on my way. I'll call you when I have news."

"You sure move fast."

CHAPTER THIRTEEN

We're off to see a wizard

August 17, 1993—10:52 AM

---

*A*rmed with two lists and the stone paperweight, Sammy returned to his office. He removed the paperweight from his pocket and examined it for a few seconds, and then fumbled around his desk to find the crumpled note he'd snatched from Joel's hideaway. He noted the markings match. Pulling out his wallet, he checked the amount left on his BART ticket. He pushed the paperweight back into his pocket, folded the note and placed it within his wallet.

He left the two lists from Donald on his desk. He locked his office, then ran down the building's stairs, and waved down a cab. Getting in, he watched two men near his building's entrance glancing at each other, then they rapidly walked away.

He turned to the cabby, "Downtown Oakland," he said. "Fourteenth and Broadway."

The cab wheeled a U-turn, while Sammy watched the two men hop into a white car. The cab was heading down a hill. As it dropped below the sight line, Sammy lost visual contact of the white car.

He wondered if he was being shadowed or maybe the Golden Opportunities' offices had been watched for a prying

---

hawkshaw. He peered through the cab's rear window, trying to make the tail.

The cab traveled along San Francisco's busy streets and approached the Bay bridge, Sammy observed over twenty white automobiles following the same route. However, on the bridge, with cars darting about over five lanes, he could never establish a fix on any one of them.

In Oakland, he calmly walked into various stores, mingled with shoppers, and picked up merchandise suggesting he was shopping. To shake any would-be tags, he went out a different entrance whenever he could and walked away, then he slip into a doorway and paused a minute. He was constantly checking if he was being shadowed.

On 19th Street, he darted down the escalator into the BART station and jumped on the first train to Richmond. He exited the BART in downtown Berkeley, again checking and double-checking for bogeys.

He walked into Café Le Procope and ordered iced-tea and a pastry, and asked the cashier if they had a pay phone. He suspected if he was being followed conversations on his cell phone could be intercepted. He dialed an old acquaintance Andre Pampas, an expert on South American antiquities.

"Andre it's me, Sammy." He said glancing around, no one seemed to be paying him any special attention.

"Sammy! My old friend—where on earth have you been hiding? I haven't heard from you since Harry died. What's a young rascal like you been doing all these years?"

"Trying to get out of the doldrums and make a buck or two. I have something special to talk about—deciphering an old antique. Where can we meet and pass information without being detected."

     TOO BEAUTIFUL FOR WORDS

"Where are you now?"

"Downtown Berkeley, about two blocks from the BART station.

"Do you remember Dwinelle Hall on the campus?"

"Vaguely." Sammy said, thinking hard.

"Go to the second floor and enter room two-forty-two. I'll be waiting."

Sammy left a fiver and started to stroll up University Avenue toward the U. C. campus, stopping occasionally to check for a tail. Instinct told him he was being followed, but the bloodhounds were good, they avoided detection. He didn't want his friend to face danger, if any actually existed.

He reached Dwinelle Hall, a massive building situated on a sloping site. It had two ground floor levels with many side entrances. He smiled. "Damn," he muttered as he walked around to the front steps, that Andre sure knows how to pick them. He entered, waited ten minutes glancing around, smiled at students, then proceeded to the second floor and waited again. He strolled down a corridor and when lingering students finally entered the last classroom, he ducked into the designated room.

"What the hell, this isn't a room, it's an inside hall," he mumbled. Down the hall one-door opened.

Andre waved, gesturing to him to hurry.

Sammy dashed into a small office.

"Sammy!" Andre said, then gave him a swift hug. He noticed Sammy's attire, He grinned for his friend's clothes seemed like he slept in them for weeks. Holding him with arms stretch out, Andre said, "It's been five years and you still look the same, except a few worry lines in your mug. On the phone, you sounded so mysterious. What this all about?"

At Fifty-nine-year-old, Andre looked gaunt, but he could walk and climb like an eighteen-year-old. He always wore tweed sports jackets, colored short-sleeved dress shirts, bow ties and Dockers slacks. When the Dockers displayed holes around the knees he transformed them into shorts. His complexion displayed twenty years of harsh sun at summer digs, yet you couldn't find one strand of gray in his rusty hair.

Sammy shot him a grin, then said, "I don't know if I was tailed, old friend, but I don't want to place you in harm's way." Parking his rump down. He took the crumpled note from his wallet and told Andre where he found it. He removed the stone paperweight from his other pocket. "Andre, I believe this stone holds the key to that note. I just know it."

Andre glanced at the note and paperweight with raised his eyebrows.

"Look how the markings are similar," Sammy persisted. "Several people have recently been killed. Many more were murdered over the past twenty years. None of the killings has ever been solved. I've got a hunch that this stone plays a major role in all these mysterious murders."

"May I?" Andre asked reaching for the stone.

"I was told it came from Peru." Sammy supplied.

Andre's black eyes peered like a microscope as he examines it. He frowned and with his other hand he tugs at his goatee, slightly redder than his hair. "Hmmm. No—no it's not Aztec, more Mayan, but not exactly. I'll tell you this, it's not genuine."

"What do you mean?"

"I mean, it's a fake. It's not an antique. While this may look archaic, I bet it's not older than say twenty or maybe thirty years."

"How in the hell do you know that?" Sammy said glaring at the stone.

"Look closely." Andre picked up a pencil and pointed. "You can barely see a trace of a line—here, here…and here. When this fake curio came out of the cast, the line ran from the bottom to the top on one side. Notice how the line disappears along its path. Let me hold it up to the light. It's hard to see."

"Yeah," Sammy said, "right there. What is it?"

"It's a cast mark. Someone did a sloppy job on this specimen. Of course there are other characteristics that show this supposed antique is a cast resin stone made to look very old, but alas, it's not."

"Does this mean there are more of these?"

"No one knows for sure except the person who made the original mold."

"Andre, can you figure what the symbols mean and tell me what's on this note?"

"I'll try."

"There's a couple of grand in it for you."

Archeologist Andre perked up at the sound of treasure. Showing his Midas demeanor, his left eyebrow raised with the rush of euphoria.

"Make it three. There's a new computer I want. That's all I need to close the deal."

"Done. But don't mention the stone or note to anyone, especially the police. And don't call me. I'll contact you to get the results. Do you remember our code when I was with the Swartz Agency?"

"Vaguely, but I still I have that information at my house. I do remember, "S" stood for Scotts. It was one of Harry's hangouts."

"Andre, you're one of a kind."

"Sammy, I've got to hand it to you, it's been five years. You walk in still dressed as a bum and demand answers, yet you're the same exciting guy I remember. For you, I'll break the code and await your call."

Sammy exited the room quickly, heading down the back hall, cut through an empty lecture hall and slipped out a side entrance. He headed over to College Avenue and caught a bus for San Francisco.

*I*t's a nice sunny afternoon, so Sammy relaxed. On the bus ride to the city, his mind shifted to Mr. Toll and weighed what he grasped so far about an instant vanishing act.

The insurance company's own investigators explored all the usual: morgue, hospitals, amnesia victims, John Does, relatives, area's he frequented, phone calls, incoming and outgoing mail, PO boxes, Driver licenses, credit cards, Passports, IRS and SS numbers, the whole gamut. Like the comatose milk toast duds they were, the otiose sleuths staring into empty sacks.

Sammy figured what they didn't do was investigate why Toll disappeared. Was it the million bucks, was he threatened or did someone want him dead. Sammy also thought about the police investigation: short, no follow-ups and no results. It was as if they were directed to abandon the search. Why didn't the investigators or the police inquire about the phone calls? Sammy found that odd and wanted to ask Toll's Muni chums if they knew whom and why Toll received phone calls before he disappeared.

Sammy stepped from the bus at the San Francisco Terminal. For San Francisco it was a balmy afternoon. His fear of the bloodhounds was gone, so he decided to meander back to his office and perhaps he'd stop for lunch.

His mind spun around Joel, Manny and even Toll. He believed his sleuthing was sprouting spokes, and felt the wheels of justice may soon rotate when that final gear slipped into place. Sammy Strolled along Market Street, and was oblivious to everything as he turned onto Geary walking toward Union Square.

Suddenly, a burly man rushed out of a doorway and bumped him. Jarred, Sammy noticed a scrap of paper drop from the man, but before he could hail him, the hooded figure turned the corner on Kearny. Sammy bent down, picked up the paper and read a scrawled note: You meddling asshole; you're dead.

He turned to confront a man sitting on the far side of the opening, with a small sign in all caps: WHERE DID I GO WRONG?

"Hey, pal, I've seen that sign before. You copied it. Did you see that man who just bumped into me?"

"What man, chump?"

"The guy with the black hoodie."

"Never saw him; you were alone. How about some change, or a buck for food."

Sammy quickly scrutinized the sprawled out man, and noticed his clothes were too clean to be homeless. While he was very light skin, Sammy detected a Spanish heritage, but no gold teeth. The odor of Polo invaded his nostrils. Ah ha, he speculated, a plant to verify I received the message, and he remembered a white car pulled out right after he'd stepped onto Market Street. "How about five bucks for telling me the person who paid you for doing this?"

"Doing what?"

"Pretending to be homeless." Sammy said glaring.

"I don't know what you're talking about."

"You're being deviously honest."

"How's that again?" The man retorted.

"You're not giving me honest answers?"

"They are as honest as the day is long."

"That's not saying much." Sammy said. "The day's length changes constantly. Therefore, you're lying; you're protecting someone. Give that person up, or the police will be informed of your involvement."

"The police don't kill snitches, but they do." The man said laughingly.

"Who are they?"

"If I knew, I wouldn't tell you."

"Why?" Sammy asked his brows rising.

"We'd both be dead before the sun sets tonight."

"You won't help then."

"Retrace the last week, and after you look under rocks for clues smell the ground too—its odor smells death." The man said giving Sammy a brief smile.

CHAPTER FOURTEEN

Camaraderie always wins the day

Sammy entered the Flynn Muni bus barn on Harrison and walked up the ramp to the security guards. He showed his private investigator's license explaining why he was there. When granted permission to enter, he approached a group of drivers and mechanics.

"Do any of you remember a bus driver by the name of Toll—Toll Washington?"

"Sure, mister. He's my supervisor if and when he ever returns. Nice man, a super supervisor," said one bearded middle-aged, dark-skinned, green-turbaned man.

"Anyone else know him?"

"I knows him, mister," a big, burly man said

Sammy eyed him. To say he was an intimidating black man was an understatement. For the long black leather coat gave him a sinister appearance. However, upon closer scrutiny of the coat, it actually was brown leather covered with black stains, grease and dirt. The dangerous bull displayed a ghetto's lifestyle exposing a disfigured face filled with fight-scars and a deformed nose. His huge white eyes protrude slightly. It reminded Sammy

---

of halogen light bulbs that scoured darkness for potential perils that may lie ahead.

"Why's you asking questions around here?" The giant spoke in a monotone still gripping a very large monkey wrench.

Sammy stood in awe, and then quickly displayed his P.I. license. "I've been hired by the Defender Mutual Insurance Company. I'm looking into Toll's disappearance on behalf of his wife, Haddie, Haddie Washington." Sammy said figuring he was no match to tangle with this wrench carrying crusher.

"How does we know dat? The police and other gumshoes have been askin questions around here b'fore."

Sammy understood that he couldn't barge in and demand answers. Most of the drivers appeared friendly so Sammy decided to be tactful with the biggest one and find answers rather than start a fight. "Your name?"

"Jacko." The man responded as he tightened its grip on the wrench.

"Jacko?"

Another man spoke up. "Yeah, Jacko. He's the jack of all trades around this barn." A few chuckles surrounded them and Sammy grinned with them—not at them.

"Jacko, Haddie told me Toll got his name from gobbling down tollhouse cookies as a kid. He has two sons, Charles and Leroy. Leroy goes by Nazr. The daughter's name is—"

"Okay… I, err yeah. What's your name?" He asked as he set down his wrench and searched for a place to park his sizable frame.

"The name's Samuel D. Shovel," Sammy replied smiling in relief.

With no place to sit, the black man motioned Sammy and the other men to move into a corner location, where they could

    TOO BEAUTIFUL FOR WORDS

talk without interference, then asked, "What's you want to know?"

"I want to know the man: his good points and the bad ones. Also, anything you can tell me about phone calls he received the weekend before his disappearance. Has he been gone for long periods before? Has he been absent or late for work?"

One of the drivers retrieved a stool for Sammy to sit on.

"That man was never late," an older man said stepping forward. "The only time he missed work was by doctor's orders, like when, he had walking pneumonia. I can count on one hand—one hand, mind you—the days Toll missed work. I know. I remember him when he worked in the Kirkland Division barn."

Soon more and more men gathered around. Another driver said, "There were no bad points. Hey, this guy was for real. I remember the transit strike back in the seventies. Toll was new to Muni, but kept us together. When that talk radio station, KGO, whipped the public up against us, he knew it was hopeless. He understood our families were suffering like his and we'd never win. The drivers took a straw vote if we should fold. Toll took the information to our union bosses and said we're losing. Toll stood tall and asked them to give in and break the stalemate."

"He was—always look'n out for us—workers," Leo an older Italian man said.

"Yeah, which's why he was considered for a manager's position," another said, "the news came down Thursday evening. Soon everyone knew."

"Manger's job! Was this the Thursday before he disappeared?" Sammy asked in amazement.

"You got it, man. We's ain't seen'm since." Jacko said.

"Did you know he was going to meet someone for breakfast the Monday he disappeared?" Sammy asked throwing out fishing hooks to snag elusive answers.

"He never said a word about it," one-worker remarked, "the police asked many questions about his activities, but they never asked about no breakfast meeting. As far as I knew he ate breakfast at home. Some of us would polish off eggs and bacon down the street at Miss Whestley's from time to time, but never Toll."

"Miss Whestleys?"

"Yeah, a breakfast and lunch joint. Comfort food—lots of it."

"I knows Toll was having trouble with his boy. You know what I mean?" Another black man remarked.

"Not exactly. What are you getting at?"

"He tell me—da boy was hanging around wid some, how do you say it, gang—gangbangers. Maybe, dey did Toll in or something." Leo said trying to shed light on Toll's disappearance.

"Oh for Christ's sakes, Leo, stop with the melodrama shit," a couple of drivers said as they joined in and glared at Leo.

Leo shrugged his shoulders and brought both hands up. "I justa trying—"

"I met and observed Nazr," Sammy interrupted, "he seemed perturbed, like a soldier without a uniform, but I don't believe he would ever hurt his father or let someone else harm him. What do you say, Jacko?"

"How come you don't treat us like criminals?" Jacko asked.

"What!?" Sammy exclaimed, startled.

"Mista Shovel, 'cause that's the ways the cops do it ever time dey come here."

"Maybe it's because I want cooperation instead of just answers." Sammy remarked, feeling the police grunts only investigated the obvious. A missing black Muni worker didn't rank high on their crime-loaded agenda. He knew no one spent any real time sitting with the Washington's and let them provide leads. Toll deserved more from the SFPD, he thought. A man who was well liked by his peers, regardless of his color, deserved a full investigation into his whereabouts.

"None of you had any contact with him from the time he left here on Friday and his disappearance on Monday?"

"That's right. We done told the police that," another commented.

"Nothing else? What about this managerial position you mentioned."

"I called Toll Friday evening to compliment him on getting the job over Artemio Huertes." One driver said.

"Did anyone else phone Toll about getting a new job?" Sammy asked, urging the gathered men to try and recall that calamitous weekend.

Several of them agreed that they called Toll. Sammy's mind bristled with this new revelation. "Artemio Huertes? What kind of manager's job are we talking about?"

"Dis coach division's operations manager." Jacko informed.

"How could you be so sure that Toll would get the job over Huertes?"

"That little Huertes is a weasel. He'd stab anyone in the back to advance," a Mexicano man spoke up.

Others, almost in unison, yell out, "Yeah—yeah."

"Mista Shovel. It'd be befitten for a black man, like Toll to get the advancement. You see dis division was named after the first black man to ever serve on any San Francisco Commission," another black driver said.

"City Hall knew the drivers hated Artemio," someone said.

"Where's this Artemio now?"

"Don't`a know, Mista Shovel?" Jacko asked.

"If I knew I wouldn't have asked," Sammy said giving his best blank look.

"He's the division's new operations manager."

"How come you never told the police or other detectives about this?"

"They never asked," Jacko responded, "all dat they wants to know was the last time we saw him."

Sammy frowned, and suspected Toll hadn't disappeared voluntarily. He passed out his card. "If you ever remember anyone talking about Toll, call this number and leave a message."

Jacko jumped up. "Mista Shovel, you's all right. When we hears some'ng we'll call, you can count on us."

CHAPTER FIFTEEN

When chasing a hot lead
You lie a little and change the subject

August 17, 1993—1:11 PM

Back at his office, Sammy sat down at his computer and booted it up. While double clicking on the Golden Opportunities file, he found Donald's list of Mazatlan vacation visits on his desk. Scrolling down the matrix of the news clippings snatched from Joel's downtown apartment, he compared the dates with Donald's Mazatlan list.

"Bingo!" Sammy exclaimed out loud. "I got you! Ah shit, but who really got you? No, not Manny, he was just a bungling chump."

The phone rang. "Sammy here."

"For Christ sake, Shovel, don't you ever look at your phone messages?" lieutenant Bracque lamented obviously irritated.

"I usually do." Sammy gazed down and noticed that his answering machine was blinking. "What's up?"

"When I called Golden Opportunities, everyone knew who killed Joel. I wonder how that happened?"

"So—okay. I told them earlier."

"Damn you, Mister Shovel, that's my job."

"Good news is hard to keep."

"Don't give me that bullshit. I also was informed that a certain paperweight disappeared. Donald said he didn't know where it was. I don't suppose you know of its whereabouts?"

"What paper weight?" Sammy replied innocently, thinking Donald was a great team player.

"The one on Ceja's desk."

"No."

"No?"

"No, I don't know."

"Look, Shovel, Commissioner Snell just left Golden Opportunities after talking to Peter Ballard. He asked for Joel's stone paperweight. I have no idea what he wants with it, because the crime lab said it was only a cheap souvenir. He was told you were in Joel's office with Donald. No one has seen it since. Now what have you got to say?"

Sammy now confirmed that Snell was more than a bit player in some kind of dangerous role. Could he be part of Joel's gang? Corruption and money are partners. Sammy didn't like to lie, but he had to stall for time. "Nothing."

"Nothing! Shovel, you're putting me into a real bind here. Snell's going crazy over the missing paperweight. He says you're obstructing justice."

"How can this whatever-you-call-it be evidence if it's been lying around for over three months and you had the police lab check it out?"

"Be—because Snell said it, that's why. I know damn well you probably took it."

"Hold on. Since when are you afraid of a police commissioner?"

"I'm not afraid—Dammit, he's part of my three man performance review board."

    TOO BEAUTIFUL FOR WORDS

"Oh, now it comes out. Snell has you stuffed in a cannon and ready to light the fuse."

"Thanks a lot. Snell's talking about having your license revoked. He wants you in jail. I've kept him in check by asking why he wants it, since we determined it had no bearing on the case. He can't or won't answer that, but he still wants your hide."

Sammy decided not to cast suspicions on Commissioner Snell at this time. "You know he can't. Say, Lieutenant, what do you know about a man named Herman Zeigler? And don't tell Commissioner Snell I asked."

"Oh, that's beautiful, change the subject when the heat turns up."

"It's important, very important. If I can book a flight today, I'm going to Mazatlan tomorrow. Don't tell anyone. I have a few errands I've got to complete before I go, so pass any information about Zeigler to Reinhourse. This way I can reach either of you."

"Not so fast, I know—."

"Ta ta, I'll be in touch." Sammy said dropping the phone onto his desk.

CHAPTER SIXTEEN

When your teeth don't hurt,
The dentist's receptionist can be the pain

August 17, 1993—2:40 PM

Sammy called Alaska Airlines to book a direct flight to Mazatlan. Fortunately, a small group of travel guides cancelled the week before, so he was able to get a seat on the first plane out. He wanted to come back the next day, but he was informed he would be on standby.

Because of the suspicious men loitering around his office building's entrance, he copied all of Joel's Dramatica working files onto a floppy. He gathered up the news clippings he found at Joel's hideout, the Polaroid photo of the two women, and stuffed them into his pockets. He copied all the Golden Opportunities computer files onto another floppy, then threw those files into the trash icon, and emptied it. He even went so far as to deleted all the Mac's history files. Exiting his building, he looked both ways, surveying cars parked nearby before hailing a taxi.

He gave the driver the address of Joel's dentist. It was on Sutter two blocks from St. Francis Hospital. When Sammy exited the cab, he wondered why so many medical services bunched together like shoe stores. After all, he conjectured, they were not in competition to see which one offered the shiniest teeth. On the third floor he entered the offices of Terry P. Barns, DDS.

Oh my God, Sammy thought, witnessing an overweight girl seated at the counter, maybe two hundred-fifty pounds, smeared with garish makeup, all bundled up trying to hide her figure.

"Good afternoon," Sammy said to the receptionist in his polite. I-want-a-favor voice. "Is the good doctor in?"

"Yes, but he's with a patient," she answered. "You don't have an appointment, do you?"

"Well—no. I need to ask him some questions about a former patient."

"Are you a cop?" The receptionist asked.

Sammy studied her, she's young, maybe a teenager, but spoke in a guttural tone probably trying to sound more mature. "Well, no. I'm what you call a private investigator. How about it?" Sammy said and wondered, was she real—painted-on freckles, globs of blue eye shadow and frizzed carrot red hair? He decided the gal must have been sired when Divine, in a drunken stupor, mated with Raggedy Ann.

"Well no, too. We already gave to the disadvantage children's fund yesterday. Sorry, you missed the handouts."

Sammy surmised he discovered a plump smart-aleck kid, who, out of spite, resorted to badgering patients. He sweetened his request. "Look, here's a twenty, tell the good doctor someone wants to see him."

"Well, no again. I don't take bribes. However, if that had been a C-Note, well…who knows. How does the saying go, too little; too late?"

"Just who are you?" Sammy asked exasperated.

"And just who are you?"

"I told you, I'm a private investigator."

"I told you, you couldn't see Doctor Barns." She retorted.

"Fraid not, my dear. You never said I couldn't see Doctor Barns."

"I didn't?"

"Fraid not." Sammy replied, now on the attack.

"Okey dokey, I'll tell him. Have a seat," she replied picking up the phone intercom. "Dad, there's a P.I. here to see you."

"Why—why is it, I always have to run into trouble makers," Sammy grumbled, noticing three other patients grinning at his tête-à-tête with doctor Barn's daughter—they had been there before. He located a seat, looked around and wondered if these chairs would spruce up his office. He noticed the chair fabric was new, so he decided not to ask if they're going to be thrown out. After about twenty minutes and an empty waiting room, the doctor entered the reception area and leaned over his daughter. She whispered something and pointed to Sammy.

The dentist loomed above Sammy. He was six feet plus, mid forties, stocky and dressed in a printed medical coat. "I see you met my daughter. She takes classes at the American Conservator Theater." The doctor took a deep breath, then added, "Today she's wearing a body suit, a wig, and weird makeup while practicing improvisational banter with anyone who comes to see me. Most of my patients have learned to ignore her."

Glancing back at the carrot-top, with a forced smile, Sammy asked, "Is there someplace we can talk in private?"

"My office."

"My daughter said you're a detective. Do you have any identification?"

     TOO BEAUTIFUL FOR WORDS

Sammy reached into his upper right hand coat pocket, pulled out his wallet, opened it and showed the doctor his license. "Mister Samuel D. Shovel, Private Investigator. It looks authentic. Tell me, did you know Sam Spade?"

"Doctor, I believe he was fictitious," Sammy retorted, gritting his teeth.

"Aren't we all from time to time? What do you want to know?" The doctor responded and moved behind his desk and motioned to Sammy to also take a seat.

Sammy wondered if all dentists were trained to speak in soothing intonations. He had noticed it before, even in his own dentist.

"I was told you were Joel Ceja's dentist."

"Yes—yes, I was his dentist, it's no secret. I've already told that to the police over three months ago."

"I also was told you made Joel's friend, Manny Soto, his two front gold teeth. Is that true?"

"That's no secret either. Yes, I capped his two front teeth with gold caps."

Sammy got the vibe that dentist was indifferent but pressed on. "How long ago?"

"I don't remember exactly, but it was before my daughter was born. It must have been at least eighteen years ago. I had barely opened my practice when Joel walked in, a very nice young man I might add. A few years later he brought in his friend, Manny Soto."

"Was there anything wrong with Manny's teeth?" Sammy asked.

"No, his teeth were perfect. I remember trying to talk him out of ruining two perfectly good teeth, because Manny wasn't what I would call quick-witted. However, he insisted and Joel asked me to do it."

"Was there anything special about them?"

"No, just two caps. We used a standard ten-carat gold. Why do you ask?"

"Well, someone killed Manny and removed his two gold front teeth."

"What!? I heard Joel was killed, but not Manny. I can't imagine why anyone would hurt Manny, especially for his gold teeth. The gold we use is not high quality and it's only a thin layer. You're sure? The police never said a word about his death."

"It just happened yesterday."

"Darn it all. I always liked Manny. He came in regularly for teeth cleaning. He would always say in his childlike voice, 'Pleeze, Doctor Terry, make'm sparkle.'"

"Think back, was there something special about those caps?"

"Not really—hmmm—except—except... I guess I can tell you now that he is dead. He wanted the backside engraved."

"Engraved?"

"Yes. You talk about the thick-witted asking for the dumbest thing. He wanted the backside of each cap engraved. It was the first and last time I've had a request of this nature. I guess it didn't catch on. I had to send them out to a local jeweler to have the engraving done."

"What was engraved on the caps?"

"Are you working with the police?"

"Phone Lieutenant Bracque at Homicide."

TOO BEAUTIFUL FOR WORDS

"An R and an M. Two initials, Manny said they were his girlfriend's initials. He didn't like tattoos, so he thought of this to satisfy his lady."

"What name did they stand for?"

"I never asked, Maybe that 1940's beauty Ramona Montez."

"It's Maria Montez."

"Thinking back, I believe you right. You really are a detective. Are you sure…?"

"Positive. If you were trying to impress your girlfriend, pal, would you engrave teeth on the backside where no one could see them?"

"Of course I wouldn't—and on the front side they would look funky."

"Who paid for the engraving work?"

"Joel. As I mentioned, he's the one who pressed me to cap Manny's teeth, because at first I refused to do it."

"Doctor, you've been a great help. By the way, did the police ask about the engravings?"

"No, but I told them."

Sammy realizes Bracque held out more information. All that crap about Manny's shiny teeth and a chance doper looking for a fix was staged for his benefit. "I don't want you or you daughter to get hurt, so if a police commissioner by the name of Snell should asked if I stopped by, please, I'm begging you, please say no."

"I'm confused. First you told me you are working with the police. Then you tell me not to tell a Police Commissioner by the name of Snell you were here. What gives?"

"Trust me on this one, pal. It will save your life, and maybe your daughter's as well."

CHAPTER SEVENTEEN

August 17, 1993—5:28 PM

Sammy's last pit stop for the day was the police impound garage. Now flush with greenbacks, he handed the cabby a fifty and told him there was more if he waited. He entered the lot's one-room shed, which served as an office. An older sergeant who looked faintly familiar greeted him. Sammy frowned, no it can't be.

The sergeant stared at Sammy. "Sammy Shovel! I haven't seen you for over twelve years when you used to come up from that L.A. Detective agency. What was it called?"

"I'll be damned. Paul, it is you…. Schwartz, the David L. Schwartz agency."

Sergeant Paul Mackbee threw the papers he was holding on the counter, reached out and grabbed Sammy's hand in a double clasp handshake. "None other. How's life been treating you?"

Sammy noticed ink smeared on the pinky side of Paul's left hand. "The usual—snoop, sneak, question assholes and try to stay alive. Is that why you gave up on homicide? Say, how long have you been keeping track of stolen cars?"

While Paul had aged, his physical stature remained just the way Sammy remembered, a big-boned refrigerator. Paul still

---

   TOO BEAUTIFUL FOR WORDS

stood six-four, two hundred-seventy pounds of lean meat, ready to cuff the likes of King Kong if arrests were necessary.

"Seven years, Sammy. Seven-long-years doing the same drudging job from 11:00 am to 8:00 pm five days a week. I'm a fixture here, but I get a regular paycheck. I'm almost ready to retire with my wife. The best thing though, my children grew up without me always being placed in danger. The wife and kids know I'll be home every evening, late but alive. It means a lot to the family, so I suffer a little."

"Damn, you were one of the best detectives the force had. I wondered what happened to you when Harry and I opened up shop here."

"I heard—sorry about Harry."

"We knew the risks... I thought you might have killed someone important."

"That too."

"Oh no. Not you. Who was it, or should I ask?"

Paul walked over to a coffee counter and poured himself a cup. "How about it Sammy, a cup of black stuff?" Paul continued glancing around for eavesdroppers, "Sorry, we're out of that cream stuff or sugar."

Sammy stared at the glass pot, there was black mud, like bay dredging staring back. "No thanks." He leaned against the counter ready to hear Paul address the pitfalls of being an aggressive cop.

"It was, when my partner and I were transferred to narcotics detail. One of the mayor's top aides, Anthony Keyes, was a clever drug dealer and killer. We could never get anything on him. One night, we tailed him in a rental car."

"Being one of the mayor's aides," Sammy chimed, "Keyes had access to all of the unmarked cars: makes, models, and license numbers. You and your partner used a rental so he wouldn't know you were shadowing him."

"You're good—got the picture," Paul said sipping his coffee. "He went to call on a guy on Lombard near Telegraph Hill, a real prestigious area. While waiting for our suspect to return, my partner called in for a backup to standby because I suspected Keyes was meeting with a criminal in the witness protection plan."

"Witness protection program? Who lived there?" Sammy asked.

"Some guy by the name of Roger Horton. I can't tell you the amount of times the police were there."

"He was a trouble maker then."

"Quite the contrary. A model citizen, who called the department for any violation on his street, especially cars parked near or in his driveway."

"So what made you suspicious?"

He sat down his cup and held up three fingers. "Three things. First, over the years, we arrested several drug dealers in and around Coit Tower. At the time we thought the location, with easy public parking at the base of the tower, made it a dealer's paradise for exchanges. Second, the Mister Horton I talked to had a deep olive complexion, occasionally slipped in east-coast slang that didn't match the born in California Horton image that he professed. Third, he kept calling us about dope trafficking in his neighborhood. The key word—*dopers*—was used twenty years ago, but by now they are called drug dealers."

Sammy gazed in amazement. He worshiped this iron-muscled giant for years. His high forehead was now pronounced and the graying temples showed some aging, but his bull neck still rode low atop his massive shoulders. "Not bad—not bad at all." Mesmerized by his old hero, Sammy lapped up every word and wondered how could the department succumb to a onetime corrupt mayor?

Paul moved opposite Sammy and traced a route on the counter top with one finger. "Armed with a fresh supply of coke, Keyes headed west toward Broadway, then south on Van Ness. To my partner and me it became apparent Keyes was headed for the Cities porn palace—you know the place those two sleaze balls, Arnie and Jim, started. When he turned onto O'Farrell he honked outside the Michell Brothers' joint and headed to the end of the block next to a park. The backup patrol car shot out from a side street corralling him at the corner." At the word corner, Paul moved the coffee cup and placed it down signifying the location of the park as he kept one finger where the O'Farrell Theater stood.

"I bet the Mitchell Brothers' dancers and customers were a little pissed. You made them miss their fix."

"We moved in. Four of us had him surrounded. Keyes got out of his car, appearing confused. One uniformed officer asked him to place his hands on his car and spread his legs. When my partner, Eddie, approached to cuff him, Keyes dropped to his knees, twirled around, and opened fire with an automatic pistol, wounded the two backups and killed Eddie. He missed me and—"

"You nailed him."

His expression incensed, Paul raised his voice. "You don't kill my partner of eight years and get away with it. When he fired his last bullet, I ran right at him empting my revolver into that bastard. Unfortunately, the one through his forehead was at point blank range."

Carefully watching, Sammy realized Paul was reliving a moment in his life that would never go away.

"The mayor was furious. He said we handled the arrest all-wrong and I used too much force. The mayor even went to the press and claimed Keyes was an asset to San Francisco and he never was involved with drugs even though his car was loaded with them.

"That was bullshit, Sammy." Trying to justify his judge, jury and executioner action, he added, "Poor Eddie, he was telling me about his son's first birthday party. After Keyes stopped shooting, I saw Eddie drop dead. It blew my mind and I went crazy. Maybe I did blast Keyes into oblivion, I don't remember much after that. Christ, over the years I wished I helped Keyes up, brushed off the dirt on his clothes and kissed him. All I know is the mayor wanted my hide. Only my clean record saved me and my pension."

"Damn, politics reared it ugly head again. What about the supplier?"

"Arrested. We seized over two million in drugs and money. Then the heartbreaker, the DEA waltzed in and whisked him away. The son-of-a-bitch laughed at us."

"I believe every word, especially the DEA bit. May I ask you a question?"

"I've always liked you, Sammy. It's your nickel. Shoot."

"I couldn't help noticing all the ink on your left hand."

"Oh that. I write left back-handed."

Sammy wondered what on earth was he talking about. "What?"

Paul grabbed a piece of paper and a pen with his callused left hand. "Here, let me show you." He wrote something, and Sammy watched as his left hand was positioned above the line

     TOO BEAUTIFUL FOR WORDS

where the ink flowed. The pinky side of his hand picked up trace amounts of ink as it passed over the lines already written.

Paul handed Sammy the paper. It read: Dear God, I met my old friend, Sammy, today. Please keep him safe. The ink was slightly smeared.

Sammy read the paper and displayed a big grin. "I'll be. Paul, I've never seen writing like this before. All the letters slope to the right in a unique style. How did you learn this?"

Picking up his coffee cup, Paul returned it to the counter. "School. It's better than having your left hand tied down and being forced to write with your right hand."

"Mind if I keep this?"

Paul seemed delighted that he had amused an old friend. "No problem." He returned and put both hands on the counter. Now calmed down, he asked, "So, Sammy, what brings you here? After all these years I know you didn't come by to chat."

"Ah—didn't Lieutenant Bracque tell you that I was coming to look at a black Ferrari?" Sammy informed, still grinning as he folded the note.

"The only message I got was some private dick requested to look at the vehicle. I didn't know it was you. If I did, I wouldn't have let them take the car until you saw it."

"What!?" Sammy blurted out as his grin vanished. "Took it! Who took the car? Who released it?"

"Hold on, Sammy," Paul immediately replied and held up his hands. "This was all done according to the department procedures. Police Commissioner Darrel Snell signed the papers releasing the vehicle. I've got the paperwork here, all the I's were dotted and T's crossed."

"Let me see the paperwork, Sammy asked and conjectured that son of a bitch, Snell had annoyed me again.

When the sergeant went over to the file cabinets and Paul's fingers fiddled through the files, Sammy surveyed the shack and contemplated—from what city dump did they salvage this piece of crap they call an office? It was a blessing that the city didn't generate many hot days. With a metal roof covering the structure, this oven must heat up like a people's bakery without cremation flames.

He saw the western sky was now blazing reddish tones through the shack's only two windows. It made Sammy squint. He spotted a locked key holder next to one of the windows, and a door on the south wall that probably opened directly to the impound yard. He noticed a secondhand desk, some discarded file cabinets and a couple of Playboy nudie pictures thumb-nailed to unpainted plywood walls. The only new object, a white marker board had sprouted numerous sticky notes around its perimeter.

My God, Sammy surmised, if my office looked this bad it's no wonder I can't attract high paying clients. What would Peter Ballard say if he barged into my offices?

Sammy watched Paul stop, start from the beginning and again stop. Paul glanced at Sammy with a sort of I almost have it glance. He began to take out each file and riffled through it, looking for something out of place. "I can't seem to find it, Sammy. I know it's here. I filed it myself."

"Stop looking, Paul, it's gone," Sammy said, who recognized poor acting.

"How do you know that?"

"You said the magic name, pal, Snell."

"You mean this involves one of our Commissioners?"

Paul had just confirmed that he and Snell were a part of the Joel and Manny saga. He wondered what role Paul played.

Maybe he was hired for special assignments. Figuring he had already said more than he should about Snell, Sammy responded, "Ah...no. He's like an pesky gnat, always buzzing around avoiding the swatter."

"Where are you going now, Sammy?"

Sammy deliberated fast, so as not to let on he was leaving for Mazatlan in the morning. He was positive Paul would phone Snell as soon as he left. "Back to my office. I'm going to meet a new lady client tonight. She's promised me dinner. I'll be with her all day tomorrow going over the missing inventory from her business. I'm really excited about this new case."

"Hey, good luck and I'll keep searching for the paperwork."

"Forget it, Paul. I only wanted to see the car." Sammy turned and left.

Outside, Sammy stared straight ahead, opened the cab door and got in, deliberately ignoring the new Mercedes he noticed parked next to the office when he arrived. He gathered his idol had fallen. In the taxi Sammy received that indescribable sickening feeling; the pit of his stomach gnawed as if a nest of treacherous vipers were spewing poisonous condiments throughout his blood stream, making Sammy listless and nauseous.

He concluded Snell had Paul on the take. Jeez, he thought, Paul the solid police investigator was brought down by politics and turned into a criminal. Sammy admired that man, but he betrayed his oath to himself, the public, and the department. What a waste. He wondered what Paul really did for Snell?

CHAPTER EIGHTEEN

Travel is good for your health,
Well, most of the time

August 18, 1993—7:05 AM

"*L*et's see. Here it is, row thirty-nine, seat C. It's right on the aisle. Enjoy your flight," a willowy, delicate faced Alaska Airlines flight attendant said brandishing a three diamond gold wedding band. After everyone was aboard, the usual last-minute checks were completed. Sammy watched the stewardess bolt the door. He felt the plane suddenly jerk, it slowly moved backward, stopped, then shortly a roar of jet engines. The plane taxied to the runway, when he heard a soft voice and watched attendants perform their safety spiel he had heard so many times before. After a short wait and the serious roar of engines, plus a slight G-force, silence, then the rumbling of wheels being tucked away, Sammy was headed for Mazatlan. In the air he took a deep breath that all was well. He finally began to relax, closed his eyes, and thought, ah, the life of a jet setter must be scrumptiously marvelous.

Sammy was told Alaskan's early morning flights served what they called an airline brunch, so when the plane reached its optimum altitude, the fastened seat belt light went blank, the flight attendants started their regular food service routine and went seat by seat taking orders. Sammy decided to hit the bathroom before the service carts blocked the aisle. He unbuckled himself and headed to the rear toilet facilities when an air pocket made the plane dip slightly to one side. He noticed a stewardess, taking orders for drinks, had lost her balance and grabbed an aisle seat, jiggling it slightly. He saw a round-faced man of Mexican descent gazed up and grinned at her. Sammy drew in a startled breath. The man had two front gold teeth that fit the description of Manny's.

Sammy proceeded past the man, totally ignoring him. After he cleared the stewardess, Sammy wondered, what the hell's going on here and how did they know I'd be on this flight? Another Gold Tooth? And who in the hell are they.

Rather than panic, he retired into the toilet, and then made small talk with the attendants serving from the rear section of the plane. When he returned to his seat, he tried to act like he never saw the man with the two gold front teeth.

He took out a small notebook he bought at the airport, at Bracque urging, and spent the next half-hour making entries of everything he remembered since Golden Opportunities hired him.

While lunch was served, Sammy noticed a woman, seven rows in front of him, sitting on the opposite aisle seat. He noted she was constantly fussing with someone or something alongside her. There was an empty aisle seat opposite her. From what he could observe, woman was blonde and fair skinned. He decided she might be a part of his escape from another gold tooth. He started to formulate his plan.

After wolfing down his brunch, he strolled up the aisle and stopped by the woman. He viewed a scrappy little girl was occupying the ladies attention. Sammy beamed and said, "Oh my goodness, what brings you to travel with such a beautiful package."

He saw a woman who appeared to be in her fifties, had a pleasant, but unremarkable face, honey eyebrows, plum mouth accentuated by a slight overbite. He saw she wore little makeup making her skewed nose more pronounced, and a zippered high collar print dress strained to keep her voluminous chest in place. She epitomized Hitler's design of an Aryan Race.

"Oh, thank you," she said, "This is my granddaughter, Heidi."

"I'm five," she said and held up her hand with all five fingers stretched to their limit.

"I can see the resemblance," Sammy remarked. He stepped back about half a step. He glanced at the grandmother, then the child, and back to her. "It's her eyes, and… and her mouth. Yeah, that's it, the mouth and the deep blue eyes, and of course the natural blonde hair. You must be very proud, but grandmother?" Sammy said patronizing her. "That can't be, you look too young."

"Thank you for being so kind." The lady smiled at her granddaughter. "I am her grandmother, and I think she's just darling."

"Trust me, she's more than just a darling. By the way, my name's Shovel, Sammy Shovel. I'm on my way to Mazatlan for some marlin fishing. I have a friend who works at the Shrimp Bucket café. He's going to show me the ropes."

"I'm Katherine Burger. Are you traveling alone?"

Staring down the aisle in the direction of Gold Tooth, distracted, he tried to recover. "Ah…yeah, I am. Do you mind if I join you? The flight becomes rather boring when you're flanked on all sides by serious readers."

　　　　TOO BEAUTIFUL FOR WORDS

"Why don't you sit across from me? I'll save you from those bookworms." Katherine displayed her most sympathetic smile.

Sammy settled in across from Katherine and struck up a congenial conservation. While his plan was partially set, he needed a way to neutralize the Gold Tooth passenger before landing. He kept an eye on his mysterious adversary. Sammy began to notice one attendant continually bringing Gold Tooth a can of root beer to refill his cup, but none had been offered to the other passengers. Sammy wondered if the man brought his own. He excused himself from Katherine and headed toward the toilets cubicles near the rear food station.

"Ah, ma'am," Sammy asked one of the flight attendants. I ate a little too fast and I'm—err—constipated. Do you carry any laxatives?"

"Fast? I remember you," the woman replied slightly nasal toned. "You must have inhaled your food.... We're only allowed to dispense company aspirin."

"I have to go directly from the plane to a meeting. I really need something." Sammy begged, feigning signs of desperation.

She took pity on him and said, "Let me see what I have in here." She reached for her purse from an overhead and scrimmaged around until she found a small container. "Mister, these beauties will move mountains." She handed three capsules to Sammy and cautioned, "Now remember, only take one every three to four hours."

"My dear, you are a life saver and I really mean that." He said, gazing into sweet brown eyes.

Sammy heard a bong noise, saw Gold Tooth's call light was lit, and watched the attendant advance up the aisle. He searched for a root beer can. One was still on the cart; it was open and more than half full. He dumped all three capsules into the can and retired to one of the toilets. He waited for five minutes and re-entered the aisle. He calmly walked past Gold Tooth to his newfound friend, Katherine. He was smiling for he spotted Gold Tooth not only had his cup of root beer, but also the rest of the can.

"Katherine, with you caring for a child and having to deal with your carry on bag, why don't I help you when we disembark, "Sammy suggested. He knew the flight still had over an hour to go before touchdown and wanted as much padding around his planned escape when they reached Mazatlan.

"You're trying to spoil me, Mister Shovel," Katherine agreed. "We'll have to navigate those roll-up stairs to reach the tarmac. Would you mind carrying Heidi down? I'm always afraid I'll tumble head first."

"It will be my pleasure. Katherine, do you know where I can get a map of the area?"

"Yes," she answered, almost laughing. "When we land and clear Customs, like hoards of locus, we'll be plagued by shouting venders trying to sell us timeshares. Ask them; they'll give you anything to entice you."

Sammy learned her husband worked for a company that provided the family a home within the El Cid complex, the same development where Golden Opportunities property was located. Sammy insisted he accompanies her and pay for the taxi.

After about fifty minutes, Sammy observed that Gold Tooth was squirming in obvious pain. Shortly, he saw Gold Tooth head toward the rear toilets moments before the "fasten your seat belt" signs are lit. Excusing himself again, Sammy started to stroll toward the rear of the plane. The stewardess who

      TOO BEAUTIFUL FOR WORDS

gave him the pills stopped him. "Naughty boy, you should be in your seat."

"I know, sweetheart, but the pill you gave me seems to be working."

"Well, make it quick. We're almost in our approach pattern."

Sammy reached the toilets. All of them show a vacancy sign. He checked the aisle to see if anyone was watching, Sammy swung one of the accordion doors open, but the compartment was empty; two to go. The second swing revealed Gold Tooth in agony sitting on a stainless steel throne, splattering his insides out.

When he saw Sammy, he shouted, "I keel you," and from his sitting position lunged at him.

Sammy waited until Gold Tooth's head reached the door, then slammed it with every bit of strength he had. "Not today, pal." Sammy reopened the door quickly, ready to repeat the head-bashing routine. Gold Tooth was out cold, lying on the floor. The stench from Gold Tooth's excrement began to permeate the area. Sammy closed the door and made a hasty retreat back to the seat across from Katherine.

On their departure, the stewardess winked and told Sammy, "I couldn't help but—ah—notice everything came out all right."

"More than you'll ever know." Sammy said, smiled and picked up Heidi.

With Katherine beside him, he carried Heidi down the gateway. Walking across the tarmac toward Customs, he noticed two men looking intently at the plane's passengers coming through the gate. Sammy, Katherine and Heidi appeared to be a family; the men ignored them.

CHAPTER NINETEEN

Mazatlan's people are gentle, caring and attractive
A good combination in any resort town.

August 18, 1993—12:52 AM

*I*nside El Cid's residential complex, Sammy discovered stately, manicured homes, a sharp contrast from those along the roadways from the airport. He said goodbye to Katherine and Heidi, helped them out of the taxi, and carried their luggage to their house. Three blocks farther north and around a bend in the road his cab reached Golden Opportunities' retreat—it was an impressive two stories structure. He noticed the outside was immaculate. Sammy hit the doorknocker several times and soon a cute, short, thirty-ish woman greeted him at the door.

She was dressed in a black midi skirt with a white low-cut blouse, revealing sassy orange sized breasts perfectly proportioned for her slight body. Her ensemble appeared to be a French maids uniform that perhaps Joel had orchestrated. Non-the less, it agreed with her four-eleven frame. Her girlish face flashed a broad smile.

"I'm Sammy Shovel."

"*Buena acogida,* err, velcum, *Señor Shovel.* Donald Anderson, e' colls me. E' tell me you be here soon," the woman responded quite excitedly. *"Por favor, Señor, pase*—O, pleas'a entir."

Sammy waved the cab on and entered what could be Joel's den away from home. He followed the maid into a living room and immediately recognized the same kind of wealth he witnessed in Joel's office.

Barreled ceilings blended into the walls, abruptly terminating at carved stone caps set above massive Mexican cypress timbers, almost glowing with a butterscotch patina. Silver and gemstones were inlaid in three wide bands two feet below the capital. On the ceiling were murals depicting church themes; it was like entering a cloistered sanctuary. The exterior room wall was filled with multi-paned glass. At the center were two pairs of French doors filled with six-inch square colored glass.

Through colored and bubbled glass Sammy glimpsed a pool. He realized Donald was right; it was not a condo.

"Pleas`a, yu sit, mi meik`em brekfess cake." When Sammy parked his rump down on a leather couch, Marita cut and served him a slice. She handed him the plate and informed, "Coffee ridy soon."

He took a bite and his face lit up in surprise. "This is good—real good."

"Donald, he tell me to help yu, *Señor*." Marita said smiling. Wach yu want fram mi?"

"You know my name. What's yours?"

"Marita-Elena Espinosa Lopez."

"Marita-Ellena Espansa Pez?"

The maid giggled and smiled and said, "Mi Marita, pleas."

"Okay, Marita, did you know Joel?"

"*Si, Señor*, yu mean Hoel? Mi bi hem maid fo over fifteen years. Mi bi yon girl when I furs work here. I fiul so empty now dad him ded. I get coffee."

Sammy glanced around. It didn't take him long to figure out that this home couldn't be a hideout. He decided he'll make the effort to search the place anyway.

Marita returned with a coffee and cup tray. She sat it onto a coffee table and poured some coffee for Sammy. "Crema an chugar?"

"Black. How about you, Marita? Don't you want some?"

"Hoel tell mi, mi bi maid. Around gusts mi hav mi place."

"I'm not a guest." Sammy reached over grabbed the pot and poured coffee in a cup. Then he took the cake knife, cut her a slice, placed it on a plate and slid the coffee and cake in front of her. He glanced up at Marita's shocked face. "It's time you enjoyed life."

Marita never said a word; her face expressed euphoria; timidity vanished. She felt like a slave set free. Emancipated, she raised the cup, sipped coffee and beamed.

"Has anyone come here since Joel, er, Hoel, died?"

"No....No won cam. Pleas`a, yu say Joel."

"Did Joel ever come here?"

"O, si. He olwis be so nice. He hansom man. Mi like hem very mach. Mi cry many days."

"Did others come with him when he was here?"

"No. He was olwis alon. No—no, him friend cam two times."

"Do you mean Manny Soto?"

"*Si*. Manny. He and Hoel grow up near Mehico City. Dey be *amigos cercanos*."

     TOO BEAUTIFUL FOR WORDS

"Good friends then?" Sammy said, setting down his cup.

"*Si*.… But Manny be *tonto* and *apestoso*. Mi tell Hoel mi no like hem. He com no more."

"Tonto apesto? What's that?"

Holding her cup in one hand, Marita squeezed her nose. "Dum and stinko."

"So I heard."

Sammy warmed up to Marita and encouraged her. "Have more."

Black pupils in spaniel eyes keep darting at Sammy movements.

He figured Joel kept her on a very short chain. Her speech pattern intrigued him. "Well, when Joel was here, like say for a week, did he spend much time here?"

"No…no. He 'sleep here maybe won or two nites."

"May I ask if the nights were consecutive?"

"*Que*? Con—consequitiv?"

"Did he spend one night and stay for the next night?"

"*Si—si*, he did dad too."

"Ah, ha, you mean he didn't normally do that?"

"*Si*, Hoel cam for vacation end spend his furst nite end den his last nite 'fore he go home."

"Marita, do you know why he did that?"

"He never tell me. When he cam to de villa, Mi ask what meals I should prepare. He always knows. I ask one time, many years ego, where he go. Hoel jest laft end say, '*Chiquita*, 'em here to fish wit *muchos amigos*'."

"He called you *Chiquita*?"

"O, *si*."

"Why and where did Joel hire you?"

"Mi cam from 'small village near Mehico City. Famly a`bi mucho poor. Hoel cam en ask me Papi if he con take me for maid. I be thirteen and I see Hoel pay me Papi. It maka mi feel gud. Hoel treat me very nais, give me mucho pesos, so mi be nice to hem."

Not knowing Mexican family customs, Sammy tried to choose his words carefully. "I don't mean to embarrass you, but do you mean he was intimate with you?" He knew Marita didn't understand the question. He rephrased it. "What I mean is, did the two of you have sex?"

"*Si*—olwes bess when Hoel return fram fish'g."

"You say you never saw him with other men or women when he was here, except Manny?"

"*Si*, es true."

"Do you have sex with any of the other guests that come here?"

"O no! I love Leon. Meivi we marry soon."

"May I look around?"

"*Si*—I show you evrytin. You 'stay tonait?"

"I—I don't think so." Sammy started by prying into every room, closet and drawer he could find. He looked for secret rooms, passages and hiding places by tapping on walls, trim and paneling.

Marita curiously watched his every move. When Sammy left a room, Marita straightened up misplaced curios.

She followed him into another room, and asked, "*Señor*, mi see you bang dey walls. Dey be made of brick; walls bi very tick"

Sammy embarrassed by Marita's comment, asked, "Brick with plaster over?"

"*Si, Señor*. Evertin be built dat way."

    TOO BEAUTIFUL FOR WORDS

He stepped outside. He investigated the pool house, then stood by the pool facing the house, or villa as the maid called it. Sammy started to scratch his head when an enormous shadow bore down on him, holding what appeared to be a huge sickle.

"Leon, dis be señor Shovel. He knew our Hoel," Marita informed.

Sammy turned to ward off potential blows and beheld a huge, paunchy, happy-faced man, who had a partially buttoned blue shirt showing a muscular torso. It was Leon, Marita's lover, holding a rake in his hand.

"*Amigo*," the man boomed out, extending his right hand out in friendship, "Hoel special man. He always play cards with me," He said grinning. "I think Hoel let me win many times.... Do you know him long?"

Marita interrupted, "Leon be our garner." She went to Leon, put her arm on his back and glanced up at him in total admiration.

Sammy witnessed true love in her eyes, something he never experienced in his entire life. Beaming, Leon revealed one partial gold tooth; Sammy immediately noticed Leon's teeth didn't match the ones Joel's dentist described or Gold Tooth's on the plane. The best news—it was a single tooth.

"No, not long," Sammy said, "but I work for his company. They all seem to be pleasant."

"They treat Marita and me like family. Best job I ever have *amigo*. And Hoel, he be so kind. We wonder what will happen to us?"

"I was told the shareholders are holding a meeting next month to decide the issue. I'm betting they'll keep this villa. If they should sell, I'm sure both of you will receive handsome settlements. Marita, will you order me a taxi?"

Marita turned to Leon. "*Voy a cocinar quieres comer?*"

Leon nodded *si*.

Smiling at Sammy, Marita says, "*Si, Señor* Shovel, I make col after lunch. Taxi or pulmonias?"

"Pulmon what?"

"*Amigo*, a pulmonia 's-a open-air buggy. Room for four and hav' a canvas top. They build'm on old Volkvag'n frames. Very popl'r."

"I've seen them on the way here. I'll take it."

"I fix you lunch. Com, you eat now."

After snacking on homemade tortillas, refried beans, spicy nopales salsa, smoked chicken, and queso cheese, Sammy said *adios* to Marita and Leon. He headed for the pulmonia that Marita had called for him. It looked like an oversized golf cart. As he climbed aboard, he observed a car just around the bend with two men in it. He mumbled, "Dammit all; is this trouble again?"

CHAPTER TWENTY

August 18, 1993—3:06 PM

Sammy sat behind the driver and pulled out his map. "I understand there's a tourism office here?" When the driver glanced through his rearview mirror to answer, Sammy caught a better look and estimated the driver must be in his early forties, a tanned Nordic face, cleft chin and denim eyes. He noted the driver was wearing cut-off jeans and a loose light blue shirt over a white T-shirt. To Sammy, it was obvious the man was trying to hide a rock-hard torso; a good candidate for the Marines, regardless of his age. Most importantly—not Mexican in appearance, but Sammy was already mindful of local inter breeding by observing the airport timeshare hustlers.

"Oh sure. It's in the old part of town—at the other end of this city."

The map showed Sammy how Mazatlan stretched along the coast for miles like a perfectly drawn crescent moon.

When they went through the El Cid's security gates, Sammy asked, "Where are we now?"

"On your map, look for the Golden Zone. It's about midway and bulges out."

"I got it. Say, there're seat belts in here. Am I supposed to buckle up?"

"No, not here. I put them in for the few elderly riders to keep them from falling out."

"Nice touch."

"Being from the States, I believe in safety."

"Have you ever heard of the Shrimp Bucket?" Sammy asked, remembering war stories about certain cantinas his partner, Harry, used to fill Sammy's mind with salacious fights.

"Sure. It used to be the in place until Anderson sold it and opened up Senor Frogs."

Sammy noticed miles of hotels and motels hugging the beachfront road along the way. "I like this. Nothing to block your view," Sammy remarked as the pulmonia raced toward Old Town.

"What did you say?"

"Nice view. Does the beach carry on north?"

"Yeah, it passes by tons of timeshares, then swings out at Beach Point Cerritos.

"A Cerritos beach?"

"A hill and a small cove. There's a public fishing marina for small boats at the end. Open-air restaurants and souvenir stands flank both sides of a short dead-end street. Don't eat there, if you value your life. However, you can buy fresh lobsters, clams and oysters right off the boats. An aquatic park's nearby, with water slides for the kids."

"It sounds romantic. I want to check on places to visit while I'm here," Sammy lied, trying to deceive the driver that he was just a wide-eyed tourist.

"Yeah—sure," the driver cracked back sarcastically. "You don't need the tourism office for that. Any hotel has that info. Just ask their concierge. If you want, I can fill you in on my favorite places."

"You speak very good English. I still want to visit the tourism office."

"Tourism office it is. By the way, *amigo*, I was born and raised in Breeze, Illinois. I got tired fighting demigods so I moved on to, how shall I say it, a tranquil life."

Sammy wanted to think, but the driver wanted to talk. Sammy decided to humor him. "What the hell did you do? Christ, you must have really been pissed off at authority to give it all up!"

"Plastics."

"Huh—what did you say?"

"Plastics, you know in the movie, *The Graduate*, the hero was told to go into plastics."

"So?"

"So I went and, boy, did I ever suffer with all of the back-stabbing, corporate ladder climbers who would work ten and twelve hour days just to impress their bosses."

"Well, I heard there's nothing wrong with ambition."

"Ambition my ass, the bastards blamed me for every screw-up they made. What hurts was management knew who did it, but rewarded the assholes for finding a scapegoat. They said it showed initiative. The corporate motto, 'Never admit you're wrong.' It's bullshit, I tell you, bullshit."

Sammy felt the driver needed mental adjustments, but didn't need confrontation, so he stringed him along. "Ah yeah, bullshit. I hear you, pal, I hear you. So, you bailed out, eh?"

"Damn right I did, the bastards. On your left you'll see Senor Frogs. It's the tourist's hot spot now. They flock there like those Capistrano birds in the spring."

Sammy wondered if the white car he spotted when he left Marita was just a coincidence. "Is there a small white car with two men in it following us?"

"We have a tail, if that's what you mean. Do you want me to lose him?"

Who in the hell was this guy that he would refer to the white car as a tail? "No. Besides it wouldn't make any difference. Do you have a name?"

"Tom. Real name, Tommy Thompson."

Sammy leaned toward the driver while trying to glance back at the shadow. "Sounds like a machine gun."

"Well, tourist, we know our weapons. My dad was a distant relative of the man who invented the Thompson submachine gun. Hence the name."

"I've heard of it. It sounds like you know quite a bit about firearms yourself."

"Naw, don't like guns much. Around the corner you'll find the tourism office. A couple of blocks away you'll find Mazatlan's famous cathedral. Look at the upper windows on each side of the entrance. You'll be shocked."

"Why's that?"

"The star of David. The Jewish settlement put up the money to finish it.... We're just passing the Shrimp Bucket on your left."

"Where! Where is it?" Harry's drunken brawls and blustery women flashed throughout Sammy's mind.

"To the left. Right in front of you."

Sammy felt let down. In a rather dull voice he said. "So, that's it." Harry's stories filled with mystique became greater than the fact. "It looks pretty fancy to be a dive."

"It was a real dive, some thirty-five years ago. It's been fixed up to attract the modern tourist. This part of town was Mazatlan, there wasn't much North of here. I understand they had real slugfests in there every night and a couple of killings monthly over prostitutes."

As they pass the Shrimp Bucket, Sammy smiled at the upscale restaurant and imagined a very young Harry in that wharf bar, bashing jaws in the thick of battle, taking on all comers who lusted after his woman of the moment.

"At the end of this road you'll find a world famous lighthouse. Another harbor is over the hill. That's where all of the ocean liners dock. The shrimp fleet located there too. Here we are."

Sammy jumped out and grappled for money, to pay for his ride. He smiled when he spotted Tom was wearing huaraches, trying to convince locals he belonged. "It has been a very interesting excursion, pal. You should be a tour guide. Maybe I'll see you around."

Tom was startled when Sammy shoved a twenty-dollar bill at him. He reached for change.

"Keep it. Consider it payment for the entertainment."

"Hey, thanks," Tom said. "Either you really are a tourist or you're a guy in trouble."

Sammy searched for the white car. Either it had been swallowed up in traffic or was playing the elusive cat and mouse game. "Maybe neither, but if that tag shows up and two men start loitering around, you just confirmed the latter."

Sammy headed up the stairs to the tourism office, which was located in a modest building in the old downtown section. He smiled at a receptionist and asked if there was a restroom. After receiving directions he slowly walked there, but paused just before he reached the door. Pretending to check his shoelaces, he glanced back at the receptionist. She wasn't looking, so he ducked into a side corridor and located a rear exit.

He checked his map again, then strolled north and crossed Angel Flores to enter the City Hall. Inside he sought out the Property Records Department and asked if someone could help him. He watched a thirtyish woman come through door, turned back to hear a man's "Si." Sammy noticed the fair skin on the clerk.

She was about five-seven and lissome. She seemed completely different from the maid, Marita, for her oval face had high cheekbones. She had a sort of aristocratic European appearance, and wore a dark jungle patterned dress with a bright red collar. She spoke perfect English—she was raised in Salinas, California, when her mother and father, itinerate farm workers, worked the lettuce fields in the sixties. "Are you the person who seeks information?" She asked in a throaty voice.

He gave her his best grin and explained that he just came to town and couldn't locate the home of his old friend, Joel Ceja. As in San Francisco, he expected the clerk would take pity on him.

She retreated to large wooden drawers and began her search. She returned and informed, "*Señor,* I searched everywhere, Mister Ceja no own or lease property here."

Watching her every move, he asked, "How about Golden Opportunities?"

The clerk again retreated and hunted through her records. "*Si, Señor,* They lease a villa within the El Cid complex."

Sammy wanted to hurry after being shadowed and started talking faster. "Can an American own property here?"

    TOO BEAUTIFUL FOR WORDS

"*Si.*"

"Where? I mean, anyplace? What about dual citizenship?" Sammy rushed out verbal requests.

"*Señor*, please talk slower."

Ever mindful of being followed, he glanced around for any phantom movement. "Sorry."

"If you were born in Mexico and have dual citizenship, you may buy land anywhere. If you do not have Mexican citizenship, you can buy land fee simple anywhere that's sixty miles from the coast."

"How about here in Mazatlan?"

"You must lease the land. Many banks are set up to do this. The leases are renewable. It is quite common."

Sammy nodded. The clerk had confirmed what he was told years ago. "Are you sure there's no Joel Ceja?"

"It is pronounced Hoel, *Señor*. Let me double check." She looked through the records slowly and returns to the counter. "No Hoel Ceha."

"That's strange," Sammy said scratching his head. It dawned on him—Zeigler. "Maybe he put it in his partner's name."

"What be his partner's name?" the polite clerk asked.

"Zeigler."

Sammy calmly waited as the clerk finished her review. "Sorry, no *Señor* Zeigler. Maybe he only rents property here."

"Are you sure there's no Herman Zeigler that owns property here?"

"No, *Señor*, but there be a Herman Industries who owns and leases *muchos* lands."

Sammy gave her a big shit eaten grin. "Tell me more."

"Oh, *Si, Señor*. They own and lease land all over Mazatlan. Many factories, some homes."

This gang was more than clever, Sammy reckoned. "Show me the homes."

The clerk went to a cabinet and pulled out a folded piece of paper and returned to the counter. "I mark on map, *Señor*."

"*Gracias*" Sammy imagined strolling in San Francisco with this beauty's arm hugging his. He daydreamed they would stop at Macy's window, and he would offer to buy her a new dress. He imagined her leaning over to kiss his cheek. She straightened up and smiled at Sammy.

Startled, he asked, "May I ask your name?"

"Sonia. Sonia Fonseca."

"Sonia. What a beautiful name. Have you ever been to San Francisco?" Sammy gazed down at the map and jerked back to reality. Damn! On her left hand she was sporting the widest wedding ring he had ever seen. He suspected her husband bought it to ward off potential predators. With the Shrimp Bucket still fresh in his mind, he envisioned Harry defying any challenge to reap the covetable rewards for these beauties, and he now knew that Harry's boasts were more than enhanced tales of past triumphs.

"No—only the Monterey Salad Bowl area and Lodi when I was a child."

"Lodi?"

"My parents were migratory farm workers and when Cesar Chavez tried to unionized the grape workers and then the rest of field workers, so my family moved back to Mazatlan," She remarked. Then she glanced up from the map. "The manager of Herman Industries, he be vary nice."

"Oh, do you know him?"

     TOO BEAUTIFUL FOR WORDS

"Oh, *si*, and his wife. She comes by each month to check up on land payments." The clerk finished marking the map and handed it to Sammy. Sonia was all smiles. Her eyebrows curve up at the end rather than down, making her appear even more glamorous.

"How nice. I'll bet she treats you well."

Sammy scanned the map and saw a residence in the El Cid complex and wondered who lived there.

"Oh, *si*, she always tell me to call her by first name, Katherine."

"Well," Sammy continued, studying the map, "she certainly sounds sweet." Suddenly, he froze and regained his senses. "Did—did you say, Katherine?"

"*Si*."

"What's her last name?" Sammy asked, his voice feeble. "Burger, Katherine Burger."

As much as he tried, he couldn't force a smile. He thanked the clerk and hurriedly left the record's office.

Pal, you're in a doused inferno he thought. That babe I used for my escape was their backup. I'm in too deep. Apparently, I know too much, but what in the hell do I know, other than Joel and Manny may be part of an assassin ring? Should I back down or I see this through?

He heading toward the entrance, and a familiar shadow caught his eye. Oh shit, now what?

"*Señor*," a policeman called out. "May I have a word with you?"

"Sure—sure, what is it?" Sammy responded. He stopped and turned.

"*Señor*, we've been looking for a man fitting your description. That man was on a plane from San Francisco that landed here about three hours ago. *Señor,* were you on that plane?"

Sammy turned his head to one side, then rubbed his neck and ear, feigned confusion, and asked, "What plane was that?"

"Alaska Airline, *Senor.*"

"Did you say it was from San Francisco?" He responded, scratching his head as if trying to recollect. Sammy wondered, what do the police need from me?

"*Si Señor.* Alaska flight 262. I see you have airline folder protruding from your coat pocket."

"Well I'll be, 262—you're right." Sammy said checking the ticket.

"The *Jefe de Policia* wants a word with you. Please, come this way, *Señor,* a police car awaits."

CHAPTER TWENTY-ONE

It's fun watching two professionals,
Sparring in a cat and mouse game.
They probe, feint, then lunge for the jugular.

August 18, 1993—3:48 PM

---

*T*he policeman whisked Sammy off to the police station two blocks away. He had orders not to let the suspect escape.

Surrounded by several other policemen, Sammy was escorted into an office. He noted it was bigger than Lieutenant Bracque's and much less cluttered. There was a distinguished tall, thin, man sitting behind a large heavy wooden desk. Sammy glanced down and spotted a plaque printed with the name Don Esparza.

"*Jefe*, the man you seek," the officer reported, his body ram-rod straight.

Jefe Esparza gestured officer, Marcos, to leave, then pointed to one of the two chairs in front of him.

Sammy remained standing while sizing up the situation. He observed both the policeman and the *Jefe de Policia* were fair skinned and had the same slender, aristocratic appearance as the records clerk. I've seen Esparza before, he thought, but where? He rattled his brain until it came to him.

Aha! Gilbert Roland, the silent movie star who kept acting until the nineteen-fifties. All that training I did at the David L. Schwartz agency, sifting through scads of photos and

---

watching old film clips, for copyright infringements finally paid off. The *Jefe* had the same stature, the same look of self-confidence—even the same pencil mustache. Wow, he could almost pass for Roland's twin. His uniform appeared to fit too smartly—probably tailor made.

"Please sit down *Señor*," Esparza said, jarring Sammy thoughts. "*Señor,* a situation took place at the airport this morning. We are contacting all unknown persons who were on early flights for information. I have a few questions for you."

He took a seat on the opposite side of the desk. Sammy learned many years ago not to volunteer information unless asked, so he just stared around the room and waited. He considered the *Jefe* expected any person brought before him would start asking questions, and by doing so would reveal information. He noticed with some amusement that *Jefe* Esparza was pretending to read some papers on his desk. With much delight, Sammy witnessed the *Jefe's* occasional peeking up, trifling momentously for Sammy to make his move, but Sammy kept on smiling. He figured the *Jefe* would finally realize his strategy wasn't working.

"Your name, *Señor*?" The *Jefe* demanded sharply.

"Sammy, Sammy Shovel."

"Where are you from, *Señor* Shovel?"

"San Francisco." Sammy wondered what was this was all about, because nothing happened on his flight, except an injured passenger who the flight crew would have thought hit his head on the toilet room door.

"Do you have a passport or other means of identification?"

Sammy reached in his coat pocket and handed over his passport.

     TOO BEAUTIFUL FOR WORDS

"What brings you to Mazatlan?" *Jefe* Esparza asked, flipping through the blue book.

"Fishing," Sammy said. "I heard the marlin are jumping."

He witnessed the *Jefe's* frowning expression. He guessed it wasn't the answer Esparza expected.

"Señor, unless you're prepared to go many miles out, the marlins are quite scarce this time of year."

"I guess I was misinformed."

"When are you leaving, *Señor*?"

"Since fishing's out, maybe tomorrow." Sammy replied.

"Let us get back to the airport and your morning activities."

Sammy shrugged and sighed, thinking, *Jefe,* it's your turn to fish. "Okay."

"The plane you were on had a passenger of Mexican descent, stocky build with a round face and mustache. Did you see him?"

"See him. Yeah, pal, you couldn't help but notice this oddball. He had two gold front teeth."

Esparza scowled at the word "pal" and raised his voice. "*Señor*, I am not your pal. I am the *Jefe de Policia* and request you give me that respect."

Sammy realized Esparza was all business. He had heard about Mexican jails and its justice system, therefore, he promptly responded, "My apology, *Jefe*. I use the word pal as a colloquialism. I meant no harm or disrespect."

"You say you noticed him?" Esparza asked scowling.

"If we're talking about the same man, you couldn't help noticing him. I mean, he was like a cartoon character, a big head that was out of proportion for his short stature, puffy cheeks, with a—a—uh, pardon my analogy, a Viva Zapata mustache. He was always smiling at the attendants so they could see his polished gold teeth."

"*Señor*, it is Emiliano—Emiliano Zapata. Did you say this man had gold teeth?"

Sammy wondered, what the hell was going on with these questions. Maybe the airline filed a complaint. "Yeah, he had two gold front teeth. I already told you that. Why do you ask?"

Esparza fumbled while opening the passport again, then he gazed down at the name. "Because err, *Señor* Shovel, that man was found dead and his front teeth were smashed out."

"Dead!?" Sammy exclaimed in disbelief. He knew the blow he inflicted on Gold Tooth's head wasn't enough to kill him. First Manny, now this man. What was it with the gold teeth?

"Where did you go after you got off the plane?" Esparza asked almost cracking a smile.

"I helped a woman with her grandchild, paid for her cab and took her directly to her home." Sammy replied. His mind was whirling. Why splatter blood over some cheap gold teeth?

"Why did you do this?"

"We met on the plane. When I found out she was going to the same area I was, I offered to share my cab."

"So you were not around when the deceased was shot to death in the maintenance hangar?"

"Shot to death!" Sammy recovered. "I don't have a gun." Another was killed for low-grade gold? Sammy suspected something big was going on. He wondered if his teeth were engraved like Manny's? He conjectured about those initials, R-M; could they play a role in some kind of organized gang?

"No—no, I do not suppose you do. Do you have any idea why his face was mangled? We didn't find any gold teeth."

     TOO BEAUTIFUL FOR WORDS

If the *Jefe* decided to hold him, Sammy would have to call Lieutenant Bracque for help, and that wasn't a viable option. "I didn't know he was killed." Just like Manny, the golden tooth fairy raised her magic wand and those babies went poof.

"*Señor*, the lady you stated you helped…does she have a name?"

"As a matter of fact she does," Sammy said, seeing his way out. "Her name is Katherine. Katherine Burger. Do you know her?"

"Si, Señor. I know all about her and her husband." Esparza hesitantly replied.

"All good?"

"Who's to say?" The Jefe frowned and glanced at the passport again. *"Señor Shovel."*

"We are about through, wouldn't you say, *Jefe* Esparza?"

Don Esparza gave Sammy a stern stare. "I know what you just did, *Señor*, thinking political pressure will sway my investigation. I went through the Los Angeles Police Academy as part of my training to be *Jefe de Policia*. I'm not the corrupt, taco-eating policeman you Americans believe most of us are."

Sammy leaned over the desk and squarely eyed *Jefe de Policia*. "*Jefe* Esparza," he said. "To be honest, I'd take you over some of the clown-like bullies who call themselves policemen in my city any day."

Don Esparza tightened his lips, his eyes studied his adversary, then his lips curled just a little, as if to smile. "You may go." He said glancing back to the paper he'd been reading?

CHAPTER TWENTY-TWO

August 18, 1993—4:17 PM

---

*O*utside, Sammy hailed a taxi. Before the cab could reach him, Tom's pulmonia pulled up.

"No thanks," Sammy said, "I hailed another."

"I'm trying to keep you alive," Tom responded. "It's my job. Your tail went by here less than two minutes ago. Hop in so we can get the hell out of here."

Sammy jumped into the pulmonia. "Who are you?"

"Like I told you before, I'm Tom. Do you see that white car coming up the street?"

Sammy's heart began to race like the pulmonia. "Oh crap, it's the car that followed us out of the El Cid complex."

"Fastened that seat belt and hang on, *amigo*, I'll shake them."

Tom raced his pulmonia pell-mell in and out of traffic, hitting chuckholes, and swerving down side streets. He hit over a hundred in seconds and turned on a dime. After plummeting down narrow side streets and roaring up others, he swerved between two cars and screeched to a stop. "Duck down!" He yelled.

Sammy's knuckles were white from holding onto the seat and roof supports. Without the seat belt, he would have been tossed from the galloping jalopy at any time.

"Hey," Sammy shouted, "this isn't a normal pulmonia.

"You've been peeking. It was made to look like one, but carries four-hundred horses, dual suspension, wider tires and a few other extras like seat belts and certain stuff—none of which is your business." Tom kept an eye at the cross street, and spotted a white car pass. "We're almost clear of your tenacious ruffians," Tom yelled again. "We'll switch over to *Aquiles Serdan*, it runs parallel to the beachfront highway and will get us back to the Golden Zone. I think we lost them, but keep on looking. You never can be sure."

Sammy's head and body twisted around like a robot machine searching for anything white.

"For whom do you really work for?"

"You might say I work for the Company."

"What company?" Sammy asked. "Don't hand me that Hollywood crap. I'm not that turnip that just fell off the truck."

"The Company, that's all I can tell you. Interpol alerted me that a private eye, named Samuel Shovel, was headed this way on Alaska's morning flight 262 out of San Francisco. I was instructed to check his activities regarding Joel Ceja. They sent me your description. When I saw you disembark with Katherine Burger this morning, I wasn't sure about you. Our ride to the tourism office still hasn't swayed my assessment."

What was going on? This guy, Tom, and everyone else in town knew my every move. "How in the hell did you know I was coming here?" He thought urgently.

"When you inquired about Golden Opportunities in the San Francisco Records Office, it triggered your name to Interpol. We're all just doing our job." Tom added.

"What!? Why Interpol?"

"Interpol has had an eye on Joel Ceja as an international assassin, but has never been able to pin any killings on him."

The words Interpol, international assassin, and Company men put Sammy into his worrywart mode. He felt like a character in of one of Alfred Hitchcock's mysteries, a simple sap thrust into the middle of world intrigue. "I'm confused, pal. Do you work for Interpol?"

"No—I told you, I work for the Company. We exchange and help out with other agencies like—"

"Interpol, I'm getting the picture. How did they know I'm a P.I. and what the hell is the Company?"

"Interpol received your name and description through the clerk in San Francisco's Record's Division."

Sammy thought back to the clerk who helped him. Was *that* why she insisted on giving me a receipt for making copies and made sure my name was spelled correctly? Was *she* the black beauty who was too kind—too kind to be true? Harry, if you're watching all this, you need to give me a swift kick. I'm getting careless.

"They checked with the San Francisco Police Department and found you had a P.I. license. You don't need to concern yourself about clandestine names. So, Mister Shovel, why are you here?"

Sammy was not going to reveal all. "You know I'm here on an investigation regarding Joel Ceja. I'm here gathering information." He raised his voice. "Hey, can you slow down a bit? We lost them and I'm getting cold in this open-air buggy."

     TOO BEAUTIFUL FOR WORDS

"Mister tourist, it's in the eighties."

"With the wind blasting me in the face, it feels like it's in the sixties."

Tom slowed down. "So, you want information? There has got to be more than that feeble answer. Why are you really snooping around here?"

Sammy played it safe. "I'm not sure now that you've mentioned the international sudden death syndrome."

"Nice synonym. Why don't we compare notes?"

"I'm trying to find if Joel Ceja's had a hideout or staging house. Someplace that wouldn't catch the attention of the local police. Have you heard of Herman Industries?"

"That woman's husband who you escorted out of the airport is their manager."

"Just before you picked me up a records-clerk gave me a street map earlier. She circled all the shacks Herman Industries owns. You'd probably know the best ones in which Joel could roost."

"*Amigo*," Tom rebuffed. "This is Mexico. The people live and survive the best they can. What you'd call a modest house in the States the locals would call a mansion. Please don't affix the label 'shacks' to our homes."

"Have you noticed my mouth has a tendency to be two beats ahead of my brain?"

"It's going to be pitch black dark in about two hours. Let's go to the La Playa Hotel, eat and talk. We want to stay in a very busy area. A place where I have other, how shall I delicately put it, Company men. I know this sounds stupid, but trust me on this."

"So all the stuff about Breeze, Illinois, was just fluff."

"Not really. I was born in Breeze."

"What about the rest? Is any of it true?"

"Some. Don't ask."

"Say, are you CIA?"

"No—no—no. For the last time, I work for the Company. You'll have to trust me."

Sammy was tired of the trust me reply and definitely wasn't comfortable about the Interpol revelation. "About Interpol. What on earth are they doing here?"

"They're not here. We work with many agencies on an as-needed basis. But Interpol believes it wants what you want."

"And what's that, or dare I ask?"

"Information on assassinations and who's behind them."

Sammy was confused, I was hired to find out who killed Joel and why. I don't get involved with international intrigue or Interpol. If Joel snuffed out important people on a contract basis, he got it back. Whose dog shit did I step in? These turds are whoppers, bigger than Joel, Manny, Paul or even Darrel Snell. Apparently I've churned someone's pot and the stew's fetidness has scattered its gruesome redolence worldwide. "What do you know so far?"

"First about you. You came on a plane with Katherine Burger and went directly to Joel Ceja's home in the El Cid gated community."

Sammy wondered why did everyone, the good and ugly bastards alike, kept track of me? He felt like a piece of Spam between two pieces of rye bread without mayo—not very tasty.

"Second, one of my men saw two security guards escort a round-faced, mustached man from the plane and left him in a seating area. He got up and started to stagger off when two other Mexican nationals stopped him. My operative videotaped these guys marching the still groggy man behind a repair hangar and

     TOO BEAUTIFUL FOR WORDS

suddenly he heard shots. The operative turned the tape over to the local police after they found the man's body. I'm sure they're looking for the killers."

Sammy gazed straight ahead and offered no comment. Did the police already have this videotape when they questioned him? Sammy suspected he was been played like a fiddle, and everybody wanted his turn with the bow. The good news, Tom didn't know about the gold teeth—yet.

"Third, Interpol had suspicions that Joel knew what's going on. Sometimes a day or two before an international killing took place Joel was spotted here. Interpol found out he switched passports and flew in and out of Mazatlan. It has taken them over three years to get this far. He was extremely clever.

"So you know he was murdered."

"Yes, but not by whom?"

"The San Francisco police just found out who killed him yesterday."

"Who did it?" Tom asked turning when he heard the news.

"His childhood friend." Sammy replied, thinking, *keep your eyes on the road, pal.*

"Why?" Tom asked.

"I don't know. That's why I'm here. I'm gathering pieces to a local puzzle. Joel's company hired me to assist the police. Notice I said local. I never implied international."

"The Company isn't involved in domestic violence. I'm neither CIA nor FBI. We do grunt work for other foreign government agencies. I said, Interpol bribed someone in the San Francisco Recorder's office to let them know if anyone was checking up on Joel's property. I was notified you were coming to Mazatlan today and asked to keep an eye on your activities.

Interpol was sure Joel was an assassin. There are others under scrutiny too, but he was the only one identified working out of Mexico. Interpol says this murderous ring is worldwide."

"Did you know the local police grilled me about the shooting at the airport?"

"Was it Jefe Esparza?"

"Yeah, it was."

"The old boy must have an inkling something's up. He wants to be a part of the kill, so I guess he sounded you out. He already had the videotape. I imagine he thought you were part of the Herman Industries conglomerate when he heard you and the Burger woman shared a cab."

"I wasn't amused." Sammy said. "But I did notice he stopped the interview cold when I mentioned Katherine's name, and you used it as well. How do the Burgers fit in with all of this?"

"We tapped Joel's phone and found he always checked in with whoever lived at the home where the Burgers now reside."

"Isn't wire tapping illegal?"

"Here, in Mexico? When you cross the border, *amigo*, you lose all your American civil and not so civil rights."

"What did you find out?"

"Nothing. If he said anything about a killing it was in code."

"Who lived there before the Burgers?"

"Elsa and Stephen Schmitt.... I understand they lived there for ten years. One day they just disappeared and the Burgers showed up. Interpol tried to find out where the Schmitts went and where the Burgers came from. No records that either ever existed. The Schmitts didn't leave by plane or boat and their car was still parked in front of the house for the Burgers."

     TOO BEAUTIFUL FOR WORDS

"They didn't arrive by plane or ship either?" Sammy interrupted.

"You got it. We know they both acted as managers here for Herman Industries. I say acted, because if I spent as much time in my business as they did, I'd go belly-up pronto. But Herman Industries seems to prosper. We have checked worldwide for just who this Herman could be and his connection with Joel, but we always come up short."

Sammy decided not to reveal Zeigler in the Herman Industries saga. Feeling he was in too deep for a city P.I. and lacked the resources of an agency like Interpol. He stayed with the conversation at hand. "What do they do or make?"

"Clothing. Sports apparel for men, women and children. They sell all over the world. Salesmen come in and out of Mazatlan like bees during a honey run. They were shipping hundreds of containers out of here per week, but they have slowed down the last six months. They're one of Mazatlan's biggest employers. They have factories all over the area."

"Factories? You mean sweatshops, don't you?"

"I try to be nice."

"So, what was the connection between Joel and Herman Industries?" Sammy asked.

"We don't know. Joel only came here once or twice a year. Now, my new friend, you never told me why you're really here. You've cleverly interrogating me. What brought you to Mazatlan?"

"Good question. I'm going to give you a bad answer," Sammy said with a tinge of sarcasm.

"So you're going to hold out on me. If the SFPD wanted information here they would have send their own staff detectives, so why you?"

"Here's the skinny. After it was determined Joel's childhood friend, Manny Soto, killed him, Golden Opportunities asked me to find out why Joel was murdered."

"Didn't you or the police ask this Manny character why?"

"We couldn't do that, for Manny was dead before we put the connection together."

"Great, kill your childhood friend. You've been talking a good story, but again why did you come down here?"

Sammy knew he let it slip out that he had a map of various Herman Industries' properties and homes. Tom was familiar with the area, so why not allow him to advise the best location to find Joel's lair. "In San Francisco, Joel was considered a white knight, wearing strictly platinum armor. He joined all the right clubs, had a home in a nice neighborhood, wasn't married, and was admired by all. However, I found a dark side of Joel. He kept another residence, an apartment in a rough downtown neighborhood, filthy and filled with porn. When I found that Golden Opportunities had a condo—villa in Mazatlan, I came here looking for more information about what he was up to. When the villa was clean, I figured, like in San Francisco, he probably had a diabolical residence here. Will you help me find it? Maybe my answers and even yours are there."

"What answers?"

"Why Joel was murdered in the first place and by his best friend."

"We're almost at the La Playa. We'll look over the map and I'll give you our best take-out dinner."

"Is it possible you could locate a revolver for me? With all these white cars following me everywhere, I may need protection." He realized that he would need a piece in case Katherine's thugs located him again.

     TOO BEAUTIFUL FOR WORDS

"A revolver? Mister, how would you like the ultimate high-tech gun? We're talking about a muzzle velocity so high it will penetrate one-half-inch of steel armor plating, built-in laser sight, silencer, each clip holds fresh batteries and fifteen rounds of armor-piercing bullets. Best of all, it weighs less than two pounds with a full clip."

"You said it would pierce one-half-inch of armor plate?

"Yeah, muzzle velocity. Remington studied how a piece of straw could pierce a tree or fence post during a tornado. Speed, that's what the scientists concluded. They found a way to increase the muzzle velocity of this baby."

"Fifteen rounds? I thought that most automatic handguns held about nine per clip."

"Special ammo. It's like a twenty-two, but the cartridge is munch longer and the bullets are titanium, coated with silicone. They zigzag in each clip. I'll give you twenty loaded clips, but I doubt if you'll need them."

"Sounds like a great toy! I'll take it! How much?"

"I'll show it to you in my office and explain how it works. You may consider it a loan. Remember, I said loan, because it's not for sale and I doubt if you'll need it."

"You mentioned that I probably wouldn't need the gun. Why's that?"

"Other than Joel Ceja's intrigue, there's nothing sinister going on here."

"Then why was I tailed and that Mexican national killed at the airport. He had his teeth knocked out?"

"His teeth were knocked out?"

Sammy clammed up. He had already revealed more than was allowed in the P.I. world. The pulmonia stopped slightly beyond the La Playa's curved main entrance. Sammy and Tom got out. A supposedly sleepy peasant jumped up from a bench in military fashion, acknowledged Tom by a head jounce, climbed into the pulmonia and scooted it away. It was obvious Tom's Company men had been recruited from the armed forces.

"Is that one of your men?"

"He helps out."

"Sure. He almost saluted you…. I'd say Marine."

"You're getting nosy. The Company always assigns a couple of top guns."

"I thought you told me you didn't like firearms of any kind. An arms dealer, selling to the highest bidder couldn't tout that handgun like you did. What gives?"

"I don't like guns of any kind. Some trigger-happy slob, wanting his first kill, shot my uncle on a hunting trip. He's still serving time for manslaughter. I work for the Company. They pay well. The Company needs and uses firearms at a disturbing pace. While I don't approve, it's my job."

"Let's talk, eat, and then plan."

CHAPTER TWENTY-THREE

War is hell—Amen, brother.

August 18, 1993—7:53 PM

---

*I*t was near dusk. Tom pulled away from his hotel compound in a black Ford.

"Why aren't we using the pulmonia?" Sammy asked.

"It's going to be dark, open air buggies are easy targets and they're for in-town use only. Besides, didn't you complain the pulmonia was too cold?"

"Me and my big mouth." Sammy muttered.

On the way to the suspected hideout, Tom turned to Sammy, and said, "By the way, *amigo,* the Company cannot interfere in local politics or police matters. That includes my men and me. The Company's mission is clear. Assist other international agencies in gathering information and/or physical evidence."

"If you can't help, why are you here?"

"It's like I said, we gather information, check on its reliability and inform others who are willing to pay."

"Am I getting naïve down here. Of course, the almighty buck always lurks around. Who's paying for you to check on me?"

The Ford whizzed past the airport. "Interpol. In spite of your sarcasm, I want you to know I'm sticking my neck out by loaning you that prototype gun."

Sammy picked up the gun and examined it again. "Gun. You mean - Mister wonderful. It looks like something out of Star Wars. How come it's a prototype?"

"It jambs occasionally. It's a bug, but they're working on it."

"It jambs! How often? What do you do to clear it?"

"Less than once in a hundred clips. It's the battery connection. Remove the clip and reinstall a new one. That's why I gave you twenty clips."

"I'm not totally stupid. One in a hundred my ass," Sammy remarked while he twiddling with the special gun,

"That's what I was told."

About a mile south of the airport, Tom turned left off the highway onto a dirt road. At the end, sat a lone hovel in a yard infested with weeds and debris. "If your friend, Joel, had a second hideout, this must be it. The house is secluded, worthless yet near the airport."

"He wasn't my friend." Sammy hopped out. "Wait for me while I look around."

Listening to the melodic sound of crickets, he sized up the layout around the house. It was made of plastered adobe brick blocks. He noticed some of the plaster had fallen away, exposing brick and rusty re-bars. Surely, this structure was built from leftovers and hand-me-downs. He skirted the perimeter, climbing over and around discarded parts from cars, tires and rubble. He tried each of the front and rear doors for an easy entry. They were locked. To test each window, he had to climb over demolished car frames pieces and navigates prickly foliage

TOO BEAUTIFUL FOR WORDS

growing against the walls. Although short, Sammy was big boned so he pressed vigorously up at the double hung windows. At the last one, he envisioned the windows laughing at his futile efforts, taunting him 'not today amigo—not today'.

Sammy returned to the car. "I'll have to break in. If an alarm goes off, be ready to hightail it out of here."

Tom nodded, handed him the gun, a bag of twenty clips and started the Ford, turned it around so the getaway was clear. "Give me a high sign once you're inside. Remember the phone number I gave you doesn't work, all you'll get is a busy signal, but we'll know who called for a pickup." Tom pointed above at phone lines and repositioned the vehicle back further under a tree. "We'll keep an eye on the police channel if you're in trouble."

"I welcome that, pal," he said and glanced up. "I see the phone lines. If everything goes well, I'll call the number for a ride back "

"I don't know why I'm doing this," Tom informed his new friend as he reached into the glove compartment, "but here's a glass cutter, should makes less noise."

Sammy grabbed the cutter and quickly forged ahead curving around rubbish. Like any good robber, he made a circle just below the lower pane's latch with he cutter. He gently tapped the pane, managed to secure the glass, and released the latch. With his heart racing he slowly raised the lower window frame, checking for alarm beeps and feeling for alarm magnets. Satisfied, he climbed in. He glanced around for any surprises, finding none, he searched for the living room window, opened it, deposited the bag of clips below, waved Tom off, and threw Mister Wonderful onto a sofa.

Sammy eyeballed a huge moon now hovered above the mountains, while dashing in and out of long narrow clouds and gave him pause. He had the same eerie feeling as a child when he stared at old werewolf movies filled with full moon menaces lurking about. His body reacted in a jerking quiver, suggesting danger was afoot.

Sammy surmised, If Joel was the killer that Interpol and he believed, then special assassin guns should be stored here. Would he be able to find them? His confirmation that Joel was an international hit man could lead who ordered his demise.

He surveyed the interior. A hallway ran straight from the front door to rear door. A dining table and open kitchen were on one side with the living room on the opposite side. His quick scouring through the kitchen cabinets suggested the same lifestyle as Joel's pad back in San Francisco. He pulled back a cloth napkin on the dinning table and revealed a plate of fresh tortillas suggesting others stayed regularly in this den. Down the hallway were other doors on both sides.

Sammy moved to the living room, which contained chairs, side tables, a couch, a coffee table and a large hand-carved hutch. It was filled with religious mementos, surrounded by candles in an assortment of holders attached to the wall. A large crucifix was mounted on the wall to the right of the hutch. As he peered inside the hutch's glass doors, his eyes widened.

"Son-of-a-bitch!" He yelled. Another paperweight! It was just like the one on Joel's desk. He opened the case and pulled it out and realized Andre was right. There were more of these buggers. I'll be damned. This new revelation confirmed that this was indeed Joel's errant nest. Joel's guns must be here. Sammy noticed the crickets outside had become quiet and mumbled,

    TOO BEAUTIFUL FOR WORDS

"Uh, oh. I'm making too much noise." He sat the green stone down onto a side table.

The furniture was too obvious a hiding place, so he methodically began tapping the walls. He soon gave up. The walls were solid brick, just like those of the El Cid villa. Sammy checked the ceilings, then went down the hall and searched the bedrooms and the only bathroom. Nothing. He returned to the living room and plunked down on a soft sofa next to Mister Wonderful, trying to think where the gun cache could be hiding. It must be someplace in plain sight—the superior location to hide anything.

It was almost dark. Armies of crickets were chirping wildly again. Sammy felt the events of the day tug at his body. He picked up Mister Wonderful and removed a flashlight Tom loaned him, then placed them on the coffee table. Slowly his eyelids close and heavy breathing began.

*S*ammy stiffened. Alert for any kind of sound, he realized the lack of sound startled him. The crickets had stopped their mating calls. When he heard a car door slam, he sat motionless, with perspiration budding on his forehead. His stomach gnawed for he reckoned his world may soon cease. He wondered what Harry would do; he slid off the couch. He dropped to his knees, but no time for a prayer. He carefully groped around for Tom's special gun on the coffee table to keep sound from exposing his location. He found Mister Wonderful, and remembered the clips were in a sack below the window. He crawled for the ammo. At the window, he carefully rose up and peeked out near the bottom corner.

In the bright moonlight, he saw eight men were gathered, taking orders from a policeman. Shit, Sammy said to himself it was the cop that hauled me into *Jefe* Esparza's office. But those other guys weren't the police they appeared to be like hatchet men. Did I set off a silent alarm, like the one at Hotel Harald? Damn, I am getting careless; Harry taught me better.

Two of the thugs, casually chatting in Spanish, calmly walked back to their white car and opened the trunk. They were the same ones, that tailed Sammy all day. They pulled out an assortment of automatics, shotguns and revolvers. Two others lifted a pair of iron shields from a pickup. The shields appeared to be about four feet tall and forty-two inches wide with a two inch slot one foot below the top; the sides curved back slightly. The gunmen mounted the shields on carriages with two large wheels taken from another truck. Assembled, they look like Roman chariots without horses. Caesar would have had a field day with this rolling armor. His legionaries could have crouched behind the steel shields, defying any enemy mayhem.

They were crude, Sammy thought, but they seemed effective. On the battlefield, to stay alive you must focus and have firepower. Mister Wonderful high tech gun, you may get to show your stuff tonight.

Sammy remembered the layout. Twelve feet over to the right from the window he would be at the hallway and have a clear shot at both the front and rear doors. The hutch stood near the end of the perpendicular wall. If he could hold out during the first rush, he would knock the hutch over and hide behind it.

Still observing the squad of invaders, he noticed a sleek black Ferrari drive up. I'll be damned, he thought, that must be Joel's car.

A slinky woman got out. She was dressed like a commando, including black ski mask. The policeman and the woman conferred. The commando gal barked out orders like a veteran master sergeant going into battle. Clouds dimmed the moonlight, but Sammy could still see her as she signaled to the men and pointed out their assignments. Three men were to rush from the rear door, two to station themselves from behind the shields and three were to rush from the front. That left her and the policeman as backup.

Sammy wondered if these killers were military trained or just muscle looking for easy money? He clicked on the silencer device and single shot mode. Ever since Harry took a load of lead, he shot first without warning, then questioned any survivors. He unhesitatingly decided to even the odds and create confusion before they could position themselves, but with the moon behind clouds it's too dark, Sammy thought. He would only try to wound them, then he reconsidered, this was combat, kill or be killed.

As the assault team began to move, the moon started to clear the cloud cover, so Sammy started firing Tom's prototype at the thugs' easiest target—the body. All hell broke loose. Several of the hoodlums drop to the ground, yelling and writhing in pain—two bodies never moved.

The woman commando screamed out, *"Pronto, pronto, ve por la puerta de atras."*

Two of the injured thugs hobbled to the rear. Ammo bag in tow, Sammy crawled from the window to the wide archway that led to the hall. He switched Mister Wonderful to automatic, when he heard the fumbling of keys in both the front and rear doors. He fired down the hall toward the rear, dropped the clip and quickly slapped in another. He twirled and fired again when the front door opened emptying the clip in a spread pattern. Dropped his second clip, loaded another and repeated firing again at the rear door.

Sammy dived for the middle of the room, pulled down the hutch and forced it to crash to the floor. The noise alerted the survivors outside to his location. One punk peeked through the open window. Sammy switch to single shot, aimed below the windowsill and another gunman was quickly dispatched. Sammy noticed the bullet went through the brick wall. He quickly surmised, these assassins definitely were not military for their attack wasn't well coordinated. That was the trouble with bullies, he thought, put a gun in their hand and they think they're demi-gods.

It turned quiet—no cricket chirping, no talking, and only an occasional moan. Two minutes went by, maybe more. Intently listening for any sound, Sammy finally heard the wheels of one of the armored shields squeak. He figured the survivors were wheeling it to the front of the house while dragging bodies out of the way. At last, he heard the remaining executioners struggling to lift and position the shield in the open doorway.

Sammy waited to let them make their move. He quietly crawled back to the archway. Traces of moonlight that danced between wispy clouds revealed a figure crawling behind the armored buttress. He was convinced the survivors were going to mount another attack, this time better coordinated. The rear-door thugs will draw his fire, then the person behind the shield could fire at will. He tightened his grip on Mister Wonderful. Well, trusty pal, let's see if you really can pierce armor.

Sammy smirked, knowing at the table of death each gambler must play out their dealt hand. He aimed at the front door shield's silhouette and waited. When the rear door crashed open, he fired two silent rounds at the shield, flipped the gun back to automatic as two stampeding banshees raced toward the living room. Sammy tried to blast the wall between him and the

                    TOO BEAUTIFUL FOR WORDS

hall. Nothing! Jeez, a jamb! As the onrushing thugs near the archway, he dropped the clip, and slapped in another. He saw a black nine-millimeter automatic randomly spitting out lightning at the opening. He stepped back to get a better shot and began to fall over the hutch while blasting across the wall. He heard two thuds, an expiring moan and then, like visiting a cemetery to place flowers at a loved one's grave, utter silence.

In any firefight, soldiers were trained to kill or be killed. Act instinctively, suppress fear and stay focused. Sammy was past the fighting stage, and now he was trembling. He dropping Tom's dispatcher, and felt his hands shake. He concluded he wasn't cut out for this kind of excitement.

After ten minutes of stillness outside, Sammy remained sitting in total silence gradually regained his composure. He his heartbeat has slowed slightly and he began hearing a couple of crickets chirping, then another's. Quickly their love calls invaded the surroundings.

Sammy heeded a moan somewhere in the hall, and heard hints of sirens in the distance. What seemed like an hour-long battle had taken less than twenty minutes. The sirens were wailing louder and closing in on the battlefield.

Sammy detected a fresh commotion outside, footsteps on the porch and a familiar voice.

"Is anyone in here?" *Jefe de Policia*, Don Esparza asked. "You are surrounded. We are going to turn on a light."

"Don't touch that light switch if you want to go on living," Sammy said and picked up Mister Wonderful.

"Señor Shovel?"

"Yeah Pa—p—yeah, me. How do I know you aren't just like your pal who brought me into your office?"

"I do not know what you say."

"Sammy, you all right?" shouted Tom, the Company man, who ran into the house with a flashlight.

"Hey, where were you guys when the action got hot?" He snarled, then added, "Keep that light off me."

"I told you we can't interfere with the Mexican government," Tom replied panting.

"*Señor*, he's correct," Esparza said.

"You guys know each other? Jeez, more great news. I could've been killed here tonight."

Other police cars and ambulances arrived at the scene. More policemen jumped out, searching for survivors.

"Okay, turn on the light, but I'm watching your every move."

The living room was suddenly bright, and Don Esparza exclaimed, "*On dios mio que paso aqui!* There are bodies everywhere! And look! Officer Sanchez! He is here…? So, he is our spy! *Pronto, pronto* get him into an ambulance; post two guards; he will talk to me now."

"You see," Tom said turning to Esparza. "I tried to tell you someone in your command was leaking information."

"*Señor* Shovel, I've been looking for the inside informant for at least five years. I never suspected Officer Sanchez. When I saw you in my office I felt you might be the key to strange happenings in Mazatlan involving Herman Industries. I thought you were on the side of the Burgers."

"Who's behind the shield?" Sammy asked.

The *Jefe* stooped over and removed a ski mask from the floor corpse. It was a woman. "I have never seen her before, *señor*. What a waste; she be beautiful."

"How about you Tom, do you recognize her?" Sammy asked.

                    TOO BEAUTIFUL FOR WORDS

"You got her right in the heart." Tom replied shaking his head. "No. Esparza's right, she was gorgeous."

With his gun in hand, Sammy stood up and went over to the body. "Jeez, this was one of Joel's girls."

"How do you know that?" Tom asked.

"From a photo I found. It's a long story." Sammy glanced back at the hutch. He was shocked; the back had broken open revealing a hollow area. The assassin's arsenal was found and scattered around. "I found them. Joel's assassination equipment was here in the back of this case."

"Holy shit!" Tom said. "Will you look at this stash of professional equipment!"

"*Magnifico!*" *Jefe* Esparza chimed in. "I have never seen *a...tanta armamento de conpacto antes en mi vida.* Look, it—this one packs down to handbag size! Who would know, that you was carrying a lethal rifle."

"You remember our agreement, *Jefe,* we get a dozen slugs from each weapon and we do the testing. Wow! Just look at this stuff," Tom said excitedly.

"Territo, take pictures, dust for prints, gather up the weapons and accompany Tom to their testing lab."

"I'll call an associate. I'm staying with Sammy until he's safely on a plane to San Francisco. I owe him."

Don Esparza examined the homemade shield. He stuck his fingers into two holes below the firing slot. "*Señor* Shovel! Do—do you realize two bullets passed through this armor-plated shield?"

"Really? Did you say two?"

The *Jefe's* eyes spotted the Star Wars device Sammy held. "May I have your gun, please? You will be held for questioning."

Sammy began to hand over Mister Wonderful, but Tom stopped the transfer by putting his hand on Sammy's right arm. "*Jefe*, Mister Shovel's a private investigator in San Francisco. It looks like he's already solved a baffling mystery for Interpol and me. He's exposed your inside leak. As for the gun, it's the property of the U.S. Government, a sort of prototype. I loaned it to Mister Shovel during his stay here. You and I have been cooperating for years. We don't want the existence of this gun known. Do what you can to explain the situation. You know, like some rival banditos."

Jefe thought it over. He knew he would receive recognition for exposing a corrupt policeman, but being slightly greedy he wanted more.

"Do you understand that this prototype gun is the property of the U. S. Government? Do you have a problem with that?"

Don Esparza considered Tom's proposal, then without hesitation, said, "*Señor* Shovel, have a safe trip home."

"*Jefe*," Sammy asked, "will your men look at the teeth on the dead and wounded, and tell me if they have two gold front teeth?"

The *Jefe de Policia* turned to one of the officers. "*Benito, fijate quien tiene dos dientes de oro de enfrente.*"

"Do the initials R-M mean anything to you, *Jefe*?"

Don Esparza paused, frowned, then began to tremble. "Did—did you say R-M?"

"Yeah. The initials R-M." Sammy said, he witnessed Esparza struggling to keep his composure for his face seemed gaunt. "I have a feeling they mean something to you. Am I correct?"

The *Jefe* related. "France had a secret society of assassins during the seventeenth and eighteenth centuries. Their initials were R-M."

"What does the R-M stand for?"

"They were called the Rex Mundi, but no one has heard of them since that time. They were like vicious animals. Brothers would kill each other if just a hint of betrayal occurred. Their code was non-negotiable. Just hearing the initials makes me quiver."

"Why would you know this?"

"Why? Because *Señor*, the Mazatlan area was occupied by the French in 1850. I have traced my family tree back to that time, and discovered I have French blood. I have read their history. I studied their heritage. I embrace many of their customs. For example, our cooking has a few strange twists that are only found here. We don't like our food smothered in hot peppers. Look at the people—most are very fair skinned and attractive."

"Ah yeah, as a matter of fact I met a helpful records clerk, who amply fits your description. But Rex Mundi doesn't sound French to me."

"I like you, *Señor*," Don Esparza smiled. "You are never satisfied with simplistic explanations. During the Thirstiest Century, a group of people known as Cathars had their own code of ethics. They believed there was much corruption in the Catholic Church, so they defied the Pope. The Cathars' morals and ethics were noble and they stood by their code to the death. The Church labeled them heretics.

"In 1208, one Pierre de Gastelnau, a favorite patron of the Church, was murdered. The Cathars were blamed by the Pope and he condemned them. King Louis VIII, a land-hungry ruler, used the murder as an excuse to annihilate Cathars and complete his conquest of Languedoc."

"That's a tragic story but it doesn't explain Rex Mundi, whoever he is."

"*Señor,* it means the king of the world. As French scholars examined older writings in later years, they noticed a hand crafted letter placed randomly on pages in various manuscripts, each letter in a different style. When they put the letters together, from page to page, they always spelled out Rex Mundi. These were known as the writings of the Cathars. Later, the symbol of what the Cathars stood for and their code of honor to the death was adopted by a band of assassins in the seventeenth century."

"Jeez, that's unbelievable."

Officer Benito returned and whispered to the *Jefe de Policia.*

"*Gracia.* Well, *Señor* Shovel, you again surprise me. Yes, most all of the banditos have two front gold teeth."

"I don't want to alarm you, but the Rex Mundi are alive and well and living here in Mazatlan."

The color drained from Esparza's face. The handsome chief tried to remain calm. "How would you know this?"

"The two gold teeth. I bet the backsides are engraved with the initials R-M."

"I do not understand. We have never arrested anyone with initialed gold teeth."

"What about the man you questioned me about this afternoon?" Sammy asked. "You said his front teeth were smashed out. Have you ever found other bodies with their faces smashed in and teeth missing?"

Benito whispers to the *Jefe* again. Don Esparza frowned.

                    TOO BEAUTIFUL FOR WORDS

"*Si,* officer Benito tells me over the years, even before I became *Jefe de Policia,* there have been a few."

"Check the backside of the gold teeth and see if they're engraved with the initials R-M."

"Sammy, do you know what you might have just stumbled onto here?" Tom said surprised.

"When the Germans waltzed into Paris during World War Two, maybe some of them stumbled onto the history of this Rex Mundi bunch and later applied it. I've got a hunch that names like Herman, Elsa and Stephen Schmitt, and Katherine Burger suggests a new clique of assassins. What's Katherine's husband's first name?" Sammy asked.

"Karl, spelled with a K," Tom said.

"The Katherine Burger I met would be the right age to be the daughter of a German soldier."

"Damn, that's one hell of a speculation, but you could be right on target. I have a nagging hunch you've uncovered a huge iceberg, but you only chipped a protruding tip. What about it *Jefe*?"

"*Senor* Shovel, you have created more mayhem in one day than I witness in months. However, the results be *fantastico.* I'll worm what I can out of deputy Marcos and pass it onto Tom.

"Do you have an Interpol name I can call when back in San Francisco?" Sammy asked Tom.

"You bet, an Englishman, Bill Johns. He's in London and he was the one who tipped me off about your arrival today. I'll call and tell him to contact you."

"Not by phone. I believe mine are tapped."

"Oh no, he won't call. One day when you least expect it he will be standing alongside you and say, 'I'm Bill.'"

"How will I know him?"

"He's a black man in his early sixties, with graying temples and wears a black Bowler. Very distinguished, I might add."

"I can see a beautiful friendship in my future," Sammy said. "*Jefe*, you said earlier you thought I was connected to the Burgers. What's their hold here?"

"Employment, *Señor*, employment. Herman Industries has a financial influence on much of Mazatlan. And they never let the public officials forget it. If you confront them, killings and strange disappearances occur. Nothing can be proved. They have people in many other successful businesses. Anderson fought them but, alas, he was killed in 1989 in a mysterious plane crash."

"Anderson?"

"The founder of the Shrimp Bucket and Señor Frogs," Tom explained.

"Are you going to question the Burgers, since Herman Industries leases this property and they represent them?"

"I already had a car dispatched to their villa when I arrived here, *Señor*. I expect to confront them shortly."

"You can do me a real favor, *Jefe,* by telling anyone who should ask, that some snooping San Francisco P.I. was killed in the, err, bandito melee. If you have any pictures of the Burgers or Schmitt's, will you send them to the San Francisco Police Department care of Lieutenant Bracque?"

"*Señor* Shovel, you are welcome anytime in Mazatlan, by whatever name you choose to use." Don Esparza said grinning.

Sammy turned to walk away with Tom, but he stopped and went over to the coffee table. "May I take this, ah, paperweight with me?"

The *Jefe de Policia* nodded and waved him on.

CHAPTER TWENTY-FOUR

There's no place like home,
When sharing adventures with friends.

August 19, 1993—1:04 PM

---

*O*n the three-hour trip back to San Francisco, Sammy had plenty of time to reflect on the previous day's events and the information Tom revealed when they had met for brunch at the La Playa that morning. Like before, as soon as the plane reached cruising altitude lunch service began. Since he was on standby in the boarding gate's waiting room, he discreetly checked each passenger for any sign of gold teeth. Therefore, he knew he was out of danger, relaxed, and almost enjoyed Alaska Air food.

He reclined back his seat a little and thought of the information Tom had given him, and it was an earful, the discovery of the Rex Mundi had so ruffled *Jefe* Esparza that he didn't trust anyone anymore. "And yes," Tom said, "the Burgers were nowhere to be found; they went poof just like the Schmitt's."

Sammy was again seated on an outside row seat. A very plump middle-aged woman was situated next to him, and at the window seat, Sammy was informed, was the lady's fourteen-year-old daughter, who was what he'd call a potty licker—constantly going to the toilet.

Shuffling to let the young miss out, Sammy quickly gulped his watered-downed bourbon and soda. Since he was standing in the isle he asked the stewardess to bring him a double when the girl was reseated.

As he stood there, his thoughts went back to his and Tom's conversation. Tom told Sammy the bad news. "Deputy Marcos had died during the night of the attack." He then added, "*Jefe* Esparza went raving mad and immediately had his men check the entire hospital staff for gold teeth." Tom glanced around to catch eavesdroppers, then added. "Esparza learned from the ambulance drivers that the deputy's wounds hadn't been life threatening when they carted him away.

The stewardess noticed the girl had returned. She brought over two bottles of Wild Turkey and a bottle of soda, instead of Jim Beam and whispered, "It's on the house—I'd go crazy by now."

Sammy shot her a huge grin and remembered Tom laughing when he told him Esparza wanted a full autopsy completed on the body with another doctor in attendance and two other private toxicology reports of his choice. Sammy figured the *Jefe* assumed Mazatlan was now overrun with the Rex Mundi's running amuck everywhere.

A half hour before touchdown, the airline crew handed out a sugary snack and gave two to Sammy's row. The teenager was thrilled when her mother gave her another one.

Sammy ate one and also gave the teenager one. Then the girl leaned around her mother, and said, "Thank you sir."

He shook his head at the girl's happy face and raised eyebrows because she had more goodies than anyone else on the plane. Sammy thought, yeah girl, but don't you know that sugar can be a killer. Then noticed her mother didn't eat the sugar infested treat—hmmm, perhaps too much pasta. He went back over Tom's information. The police had raided the El Cid

Burger's home and all offices and buildings tied to Herman Industries properties.

The plane was getting close to SFO, and the Flight Attendants made debris sweeps.

He pulled out his notebook, carefully reviewed his previous entries, then added more data. The bourbon and sugar treat was tugging at his eyelids. He adjusted his seat all the way back and closed his eyes. He began to mull over Mister Wonderful and his harrowing battle yesterday evening. A disturbing sleep took over. Wavering black blobs appeared each engraved with Karl, Herman, Stephen, Katherine and Elsa in a slimy green muck that tumbled around as if they were in a bingo cage. Each time the spastic turmoil stopped, it began again and again. But strands of the green slime dribble broke loose and slid more and more toward a huge murky gray "Z" image that had a mouth at its center surrounded by vicious red tiny teeth—it was a monstrous black holed octopus that swallowed everything. "Was this behind the murder for hire syndicate? Be wary mister detective," he told himself still in his slumber, "don't mix dreams with reality."

*T*he captain's voice shook him from his daydreams. "Attendants, prepare for landing."

Still groggy, Sammy tried to put his mind back into its running gear. He knew this information was far too complicated for a P.I. without resources. He decided to turn all the information over to lieutenant Bracque including the green paperweights.

The white bird's cluster of rubber wheels squealed upon touchdown, spitting out smoke-puffs, when its braking wheels rolled along the tarmac. The roar of jet engines reversing their thrust, twitched the enshrined cargo of gaiety. Most passengers clapped; they arrived safely knowing most crashes occur at takeoffs and landings.

"Welcome to San Francisco." the steward announced. "It's four-o-four and the temperature is sixty-two degrees," he eyed the sea of faces, then added. "Please remain seated until the fasten seat belt sign goes off and we come to a complete stop. Have your custom's card ready for inspection."

At the custom's station, Sammy showed his passport and had nothing to claim, no luggage, so he waltzed right through.

After a wiz, and locker search, he clutched his retrieved disk and newspaper clippings. Noticing it is 4:50 PM, he called Lieutenant Bracque at the Hall, "I have intriguing news. Bring Inspector Reinhourse with you to my office around six." He said, then abruptly hung up.

*H*e noticed approaching his office door that one of his plants leaned against his corridor window wall. Unless there was a major earthquake within the last forty-eight hours, somebody moved the plant. Not knowing if the door had been rigged to set off a charge, Sammy decided to proceed with caution.

He thought for a minute then dashed to the janitor's closet, grabbed paper towels, a mop and bucket. He filled the bucket half-full with water and positioned it four feet from the door. He stuck his key in the lock, but didn't open the door. Instead he packed wet paper towels between the doorknob and frame to hold the handle open. He wet down the mop for weight, placed the handle inside the bucket, aimed the mop head for the door edge, pushed the soaked dirty cotton strands and ran for cover. Around a corner, Sammy heard the mop hit the door. With no explosion or shotgun blast, he peeked, and saw the door had

                    TOO BEAUTIFUL FOR WORDS

opened about one foot. Slowly he went to the opening, and without removing the bucket or mop peered in.

"Ahhhhhhh! Shit," he exclaimed disgusted, "my office has been thrashed."

He heard voices in the elevator, so he ducked around the corner again to catch any returning robbers. When the elevator doors opened Lieutenant Bracque, Inspector Reinhourse stepped out, then to Sammy's surprise, he saw Sergeant Ryan. "You're just in time for the cleanup party," Sammy announced in a whisper.

The three of them stood before his door, noticed the mop, soaked paper towel rolls and bucket. They gave Sammy bewildered stares.

Still whispering, "Look inside and see what greeted me," Sammy said sarcastically. "Be careful, I'm not sure whether the place has been booby trapped. And don't call out my name when you go in. The place may be bugged.

"I would suggest we enter slowly and check for booby-traps," Sammy advised.

"Wow—totally trashed," Reinhourse blurted out.

"Jesus, what a mess," the lieutenant said. "Is there any thing in here that's not torn apart?"

"What were they looking for?" Sergeant Ryan asked.

Sammy disguised his voice and spoke with a crackling fake Italian accent. "I's` Janitor. I fine`a some baddies a`break` in dis office, so I say I betta call da police and have 'em, howd` ya say—dust`a dis place."

"Goddammit, we are the police!" Lieutenant Bracque exclaimed.

Sammy was irked. He put his finger to his lips and mouthed the word "bug"—over and over. "How soon`a would dey be here?" He said and waved his hands to get out.

"Oh, of course, the latent print team, I forgot to make the call." The lieutenant said, "Ryan, get a forensic team over here."

"I'm calling it in now, Lieutenant," Ryan adlibbed. "They should be here in about five minutes. What would you say, Inspector?"

"Oh, definitely five minutes, maybe less," Reinhourse agreed, while hunching his shoulders and bring his arms up in a what-is-going–on gesture.

Sammy shook his head. "Should`a I wait for dem?"

"No, that won't be necessary. You may leave," The lieutenant said.

"You go too, lik`a da police station?" Now Sammy nodded his head.

"Well, I guess we've done all we can here." the lieutenant said. "Why don't we go back to the Hall of Justice?"

Once outside the building, Reinhourse yelled, "What the hell was that all about?"

"Inspector, if you tore a place up looking for an item you were sure was there but didn't find it, why not leave a bug or two so when the owner returned, he might reveal its hiding place."

"But what the hell were they looking for?" Reinhourse asked.

Sammy mind flashed back a couple of days. Did this gang know I found Joel's hideout? Do they know I have the photo, news clippings, the crumbled note or maybe…the paperweight? And who told Gold Tooth two and Katherine Burger I was going to be on yesterday's morning flight to Mazatlan?

Sammy pulled out the Mazatlan duplicate of the stone paperweight he took from Joel's office. "Maybe this!"

The lieutenant's heavy eyebrows congregate at the nose, making his eyes even fiercer. "God dammit, Shovel, you said you never knew the whereabouts of that paperweight. You've had it all along. Commissioner Snell's going to be really upset and I might add, I'm disappointed too. I thought you were going to cooperate, not impede this investigation."

"Lieutenant, who did you tell I was going to Mazatlan?"

"No one except Reinhourse—you told me to tell him."

"Reinhourse, did you tell anyone?"

"No, the lieutenant told me it was confidential. I told no one."

"Hey Sammy," Ryan added, "I didn't even know you were gone until I received the Lieutenant's call to meet at your office tonight. That was over a half-hour ago."

"Lieutenant, are you sure you told no one else? Try to remember."

"What difference does it make?"

"For Christ's sake, it's important."

"Damn you, Shovel, I told no one on the force, but I did mention it to Commissioner Snell, when he asked where you were. He wanted your butt for taking that paperweight."

"Lieutenant, that slip almost cost me my life in Mazatlan."

"What!? What on earth are you talking about? Are you implying Commissioner Snell's dirty?"

"I see filthy muck all over him. This little stone paperweight, which you claim I took from Joel's office, was given to me by the *Jefe de Policia* in Mazatlan."

"What! You're lying. And what the hell's a *hay-fay?*"

"The chief of police in Mazatlan, Don Esparza. Now, according to our agreement, I'm going to fill you in on a sinister assassination ring. I'm in over my head. I'm turning it over to you to finish the investigation with the manpower it will take. Even your own police department will be in over their heads, but some of the answers are here in the city. I want to be part of the solution and help capture these killers. Do you agree to be the lead and tell no one? If Snell gets wind of this we're all dead."

"Dammit, Shovel, I don't even know what you're asking me to agree to," Bracque said eyeing him intently. "I can't act alone. There are police procedures and protocols that must be adhered to. The department doesn't expect loose cannons rattling around, bringing pandemonium to the establishment. I've known Snell for years, he's a good family man. You better have some damn good reasons before I'll stick my neck out."

Sammy wondered what he must do to convince Bracque to go it alone. "I suggest we go out for dinner and I'll explain all. Don't trust anyone. Don't tell anyone what you are about to hear. It will save lives—maybe even your own. The only other players who know for sure that there are murders for hire are the assassins themselves, an archeologist and Interpol."

"Wow." Reinhourse jerked his head. "You lost me. Are you paranoid? Interpol? What's this all about? What are you doing talking to Interpol? They deal with international crimes."

"Yeah, Shovel, what have you been drinking?" The lieutenant joined in.

"Hold it," Sergeant Ryan advised, "I see a couple of squad cars coming."

Uniformed officers jumped out and Sergeant Ryan greeted them. He motioned to the building and gave out instructions, then returned to Sammy's group. "I told them to call in the electronics team to sweep your office for bugs."

"Thanks, Ryan," Sammy asked still glancing around for white cars, "Where's your car parked, Lieutenant?"

"Down at the Hall, we got a ride from another inspector."

Sammy hailed a cab. "Climb in, folks," he said as he opened the cab doors. "After all, you announced we were going down to the Hall. Let's not disappoint them."

"Who's them, for Christ's sake?" Reinhourse asked disgustedly.

"If I knew, I'd ask you to make an arrest."

Once inside the sanctity of the Hall, Sammy asked Bracque, "Where can I find a secure phone line?"

The lieutenant pointed to a bank of phone booths. "Take your pick. It's your choice."

Sammy made his call while the lieutenant listened. "Good evening, Professor.

"I'm listening."

"The information we discussed about the dig in Peru has been finalized.

"Good. I'm ready for it."

"It will be delivered to your office before tomorrow morning. It will be labeled S-845. Thank you for your patience."

"And thank you."

Sammy hung up.

"Should I ask what that was all about? In fact, maybe I shouldn't ask anything? You're acting weird, Shovel, very weird."

"What time is it?"

"Six-thirty."

"Let's get your car and go eat dinner."

"Hey, the department's not going to pay for this."

"Lieutenant, I will pay and sing into your ears. Let's go."

"Where're we going?"

"Jack London Square in Oakland. You're going to meet a friend of mine."

CHAPTER TWENTY-FIVE

A relaxing dinner always sets the tone,
For a spirited conversation,
And plans for resolution.

August 19, 1993—8:15 PM

Seated at the restaurant, Lieutenant Bracque asked, "Why are we eating at Scotts in Oakland? We have plenty of excellent seafood restaurants in the city, including the original Scotts."

"Because I told my friend we would meet him here."

"Oh! May I ask when you talked to him?"

"You heard me talking to him back at the hall."

"I heard mumbo jumbo. What in the hell were you talking about?"

"I said good evening. That means we meet tonight. I mentioned the information about the dig in Peru. That means bring all of the information I gave him to date, including the stone paperweight I left with him."

"So, you did take the paperweight!" Bracque said, shaking his head in disgust.

"Of course I did. It is an important clue. That's why Commissioner Snell wanted it, but that will be revealed later. When I said it would be delivered to your office before tomorrow morning I was telling him the meeting would be over before midnight. And finally, when I said it will be labeled S-845, it means he's to meet us here at Scotts at 8:45."

"You expect me to believe that?" Reinhourse said totally exasperated. "You know, Shovel, sometimes you're too clever for your own good. How in the hell would anyone know that?"

"That's the whole idea. If anyone listens, they will not have enough time to break down the information. I've known this gentleman for years. We've worked out our own code when I worked in L.A. I hoped he scrutinized his notes after I left him."

The waiter arrived for drink orders. He glanced at the lieutenant and smiled as his eyes sweep the other faces. In a soft melodic voice, he asked, "Something to drink this evening, gentlemen?"

"Bring me a Bud," Reinhourse said. The lieutenant asked for the same. Ryan asked for a Heineken.

"Ryan, you're going to force our friend into bankruptcy if you keep ordering like that." Bracque said quickly, yet laughing.

Sammy ignored Bracque and winked at Ryan. "Wild Turkey with soda in a tall glass."

Bracque can't hold back. "You order fine Bourbon and we drink beer. I thought you said you were living a hand-to-mouth existence."

"Why, Lieutenant, I believe you're jealous."

"Okay—okay—enough of all this small talk. Shovel, you said you were going to let us in on what you know to date. Remember, you agreed to share information if we let you become involved with this case. That's the only reason I haven't thrown you in jail. Talk!"

The busboy brought water, sourdough French bread and a lot of butter. Ryan pulled off of a piece of bread and started buttering it. Soon Reinhourse and Bracque followed.

Sammy studied Sergeant Ryan slapping butter on the sourdough, raised his eyebrow. He wanted to go slow and to make sure Professor Andre Pampas arrived with the crumpled paper he took from Joel's apartment. He was optimistic that Andre decoded it, therefore, he glanced at the busboy, "Keep it filled," and nodded toward the breadbasket. He then produced a three by five notebook that immediately caught the lieutenant by surprise.

I don't suppose that's what I think it is," Bracque asked in astonishment. "Let me see that."

"No can do. It's written in code. You wouldn't understand all the nuances.

"You mean no one can read your writing."

"Know it all. Let me start by reviewing what we know about the participants. First, there's Joel Ceja, supposedly a model citizen in San Francisco, but he's been known to Interpol for years and tagged a probable international assassin."

"What—international assassin?" Bracque responded.

"Wow," Reinhourse added in unison. "You keep mentioning Interpol. What gives?"

"I'm getting to it. I don't believe Joel snuffed out anyone in this country."

"Boy, is that great news," Reinhourse cracked right back.

"He ran a successful business, Golden Opportunities, that does marketing for business owners. The owners would spill their guts out to Joel's employees. Whenever a client represented a threat to a well-heeled company that had hired Joel's boss to protect it, the owner or a key employee of the rival firm would be murdered or made to mysteriously disappear. The local murderer was none other than Joel's best friend, Manny Soto. Reinhourse has alluded to the connection during his investigation of unsolved murders. Isn't that right, Reinhourse?"

"So far he's correct, Lieutenant."

"Are you sure?"

The waiter brought the drinks and noticed the bread was almost gone. Sammy advised him that they were waiting for another person and would wait until he arrived before ordering dinner. Reinhourse took his beer bottle and took a deep drink, ignoring the glass.

"Do you mean, can I prove it? Not yet, but together we will. The second player is Manny Soto. When you found his remains he had his front teeth knocked out. I understand Commissioner Snell told you someone was looking to hock his gold teeth yet left his wallet and other valuable possessions."

"I told you I didn't believe that," Bracque said, then poured his beer in a glass. "I'm getting mighty disturbed by you blaming one of our commissioners for all of your questionable actions. You better have some answers, or I'm going to end this charade and have Reinhourse arrest you."

"For what reason?"

"Hundreds."

The busboy returned with more bread and butter, glanced at the untouched water glasses and then left for another table. Ryan immediately reached for the breadbasket.

"I believe Snell didn't want you to know about the engraving on Manny Soto's gold teeth."

"There you go mentioning Snell again. I already knew about the initials R-M." Bracque said.

"But I bet Snell didn't know that."

"Come to think about it, I don't believe I did mention that to him."

"How did you know they were engraved?" Sergeant Ryan said as he pointed his bread at Sammy.

"I talked to his dentist." Sammy came back with a smirk, and twirled his highball between his fingers.

"Well so did we. That's how we found out. That dentist said the initials were the name of Manny's Soto's girl friend," Reinhourse said intently.

"If you want to impress a girl by engraving two gold teeth you don't put the initials on the backside where no one can see them."

"We thought so too," Bracque said, "but we couldn't find anything else that matched R and M.

"Don't be shocked, but in Mazatlan I discovered the initials R-M stand for Rex Mundi, an Old French secret society specializing in, get this, assassinations. That's the third piece in this puzzle."

"You're getting closer to the deep end. Are you sure?" Ryan said.

"The society supposedly hasn't been heard of for over one hundred fifty years. I now suspect that during World War Two some Nazis stationed in France not only found out about the old society, but also resurrected it. Reinhourse, do you know who Herman Zeigler's father was and where he came from?"

"No, but I'll check."

"Don't bother," Lieutenant Bracque said. "His father was Garth Zeigler, an immigrant from Germany. A few people who traveled to France shortly after the war said he was part of the SS in Paris, but nothing was ever proved. The rumors were dismissed as envious gossip. That was what I was going to tell you when you hung up on me."

"Did you know Herman Zeigler and Joel were classmates at USC?"

"No—no we didn't," the lieutenant answered.

"Well, they were. I figure Joel was an opportunist. He demonstrated that when he hitched a ride to Mexico City. He probably conned the Perez family into feeling sorry for him, so they sponsored him into the States. Later, he meets Zeigler. Herman recognized ambition. I imagine he told Joel when the time was right he would send for him. One day, Golden Opportunities opened with Joel as the owner. Everything was to be legit. By the way, they were both marksmen on the college rifle team."

"Wow—It's coming together." Reinhourse said over a mouth full of bread.

"Go on. Finally you're getting my attention," the lieutenant shot back.

"Lieutenant, who asked you not to run a ballistic test on the slugs taken from Joel?"

"Commissioner Snell," Bracque responded in a dull voice.

"The fourth piece isn't a person, it's this stone paperweight, like the one that adorned Joel's desk. But it isn't really a paperweight. I believe it's a decoder," Sammy said as he pulled the stone from his pocket.

"You keep alluding to more than one of these stones. Yet, I only see the one you took from Joel's office."

"I told you, this didn't come from his office. I'm betting there must be more than the two I know about. They could be scattered worldwide. They decode messages like the one I retrieved from Joel's hideout."

     TOO BEAUTIFUL FOR WORDS

"Hold it. What hideout?" Bracque said angrily raising his voice

"The one on Eddy Street. I thought Burglary would have notified you by now?" Sammy immediately suspected Snell's tentacles engulfed Burglary and kept Bracque from discovering Joel's flophouse.

"Well they haven't, God dammit," the lieutenant exploded, almost breaking his beer glass when he slammed it down. "You took evidence? Are you crazy? This time I can have your license!"

"Lieutenant, I took it to the man we are about to meet in fifteen minutes. He will give it back to you. I needed a quick analysis. If you had either the paperweight or the crumbled-up note, Snell would have gotten one or both, and you'd have nothing."

"So, that's why Commissioner Snell was so excited about the missing paperweight," Bracque said and relaxed a little.

"Bingo. And why he or his boss tried to have me killed in Mazatlan."

"You mentioned boss. Do you have anyone in mind?" Reinhourse commented.

"Don't know for sure, but while I was in Mazatlan I discovered Herman Industries has a significant influence there."

"Herman Industries? Are you implying Herman Zeigler again?" The lieutenant said. "You know, you keep indicating that Zeigler's involved in all this. Actually, he's a nice guy. His daughter's a little wild, but he's done a lot for the community."

"Aha, they all sound nice, but the plot thickens," Ryan said comprehending the complexity of the case. He finished his bread and snatched another piece of sourdough, then proceeded to pile butter on it.

"More than you know. Joel also had a hideout in Mazatlan. I went to Mazatlan to visit a villa owned by Golden Opportunities, but they only lease it. I was looking for weapons, assassination weapons. I didn't find any. I went to the registrar at the city hall and, with the help of Tom, discovered the real hideout slightly out of town near the airport. There's where Joel kept his arsenal of assassination weapons. You should have seen them. And this is where yours truly almost got nailed again."

"Again?" Bracque asked.

"Yeah, pal, again. The first time was on the airplane. The second was at Joel's hideout. By the way, as far as anyone knows I was killed in the ensuing gun battle there. And I would have been if it weren't for a prototype gun loaned to me by Tom."

"Who—who gave you this gun?"

"Tom," Sammy answered and got the feeling Bracque wanted more information than he was capable of giving.

"Tom? You mentioned him before."

"Yeah, Tom, he's a Company man."

"What company?"

"I don't know. When the Feds have some secret operation going on, they seem to use the name Company. But he works for some clandestine part of our government."

"That's Hollywood bullshit. If you're making this up, so help me I will have your license. What's so special about this revolver that he gave you?"

"He didn't give it to me. He loaned it and it's not a revolver. It's built on the principle of a Gatling gun. The chamber has a barrel that holds five cartridges, free wheels and is controlled by a computer chip. On automatic it will fire up to fifteen rounds in four seconds. It has a built-in laser sight, a silencer, and it will pierce a half-inch of armor plate. It was very

    TOO BEAUTIFUL FOR WORDS

special for there was no extension to muffle sound, but the end it's a little wider to hide any flash. A small hole on bottom of barrel, half and inch from the end, absorbs sound and directs gases into an asbestos chamber that loops back to the base giving the bullet added speed. Each clip holds a built-in battery. You can change the automatic firing rate from four to twelve seconds in increments of four."

"Dammit," Bracque said. "How do you know it will pierce a half inch of armor plate?"

"That's what saved my life. I'm ashamed to admit it, but I killed a woman with that gun. I was in a lethal firefight. There were no negotiations; the assassin gang wanted me dead at any cost. I have her picture." Sammy said and pulled out the photo of the two women having sex that he absconded from Joel's San Francisco hideout. He placed it on the table and Bracque immediately picked it up.

"Ah! Christ! One of these women is Herman Zeigler's daughter. I can't believe what I'm seeing. It's disgusting," the lieutenant said sickened. "Where did you get the photo?"

"At Joel's city hideout."

"Which one did you shoot?"

Sammy pointed to one of the girls as Bracque passed the photo around.

"Wow—I know that one," Reinhourse chimed in. "Her name is Anita Lopez. She loved men with power and cops in uniform. She is—was a model for Laura Beckman Fashions. Wow, was she ever hot stuff."

"On the back of the picture you'll find the license number of the car used by the two hoodlums who came trying to catch me ransacking Joel's hideout."

"Reinhourse, check it out," the lieutenant ordered. "I'm going to call burglary tomorrow and find out why they've kept Joel's apartment a secret."

"Better yet, why don't you ask Commissioner Snell." Sammy grinned.

"Dammit, Shovel, I beginning to believe you're right about all of this," the lieutenant said.

The waiter cozily moved over to their table.

Sammy signaled for another round by twirling his index finger. Reinhourse pointed to the breadbasket.

"When I saw Anita in Mazatlan, she was the one in charge of annihilating me. I knew I'd seen her someplace before, but I just couldn't remember. Now I know. It was in the newspaper ads for Beckman's clothing line. By the way, several other names came up when I was there. Reinhourse, can you do a check on Karl and Katherine Burger and Stephen and Elsa Schmitt? It seems they ran Herman Industries in Mazatlan."

"They all have German names," Ryan remarked as the busboy delivered more bread.

"Ryan, I know that. I'm not stupid you know," Reinhourse retorted somewhat irritated as he reached for more bread.

Bracque watched Ryan and Reinhourse. "How can the two of you eat so much bread and pile on gobs of butter and stay so thin?"

Ryan smiled and Reinhourse shrugged.

"The Schmitt's were there first," Sammy continued. "At the first sign of trouble they disappeared. Tom informed me the next morning the Burgers quietly slipped away during the night. As far as the Mazatlan police can ascertain, neither husband nor wife left by plane, ship, train or car—just like the Schmitt's, they vanished without a trace. Interpol has no record of either family. But guess who checked in with the Burgers whenever he arrived in Mazatlan?"

"Joel Ceja," Bracque confirmed.

"Right again."

"But why did Manny kill Joel?"

"I'm not sure, but it may have something to do with the gold teeth. Don Esparza told me the code of the Mundi assassins was to obey without question. The society would pit brother against brother, no mercy. If Joel was a part of this gang then he had to conform. Maybe Joel knew the next victim and someone in the organization, like Snell, found out. The leaders might think Joel would want to warn him. If Joel hesitated to notify Manny to make the hit, it would signal betrayal. Manny had the gold teeth with the engraved initials. I believe the gold teeth denote an elite soldier in their gang. Manny would obey the society without question."

"Hell, kill your best friend without question?" Reinhourse asked.

"Until a better scenario comes forth, I guess so. You understand, I'm not sure if there ever was a target or if Joel leaked the plot to a friend."

"I guess we'll never know." Ryan said and reached for more butter.

"At least not yet." Sammy said grinning.

The waiter brought more drinks and passed them around—Sammy spotted a familiar face and jumped up.

"Here comes my friend, Andre," he said. "I'm hoping the crumpled paper and paperweight I loaned him will give us new clues."

CHAPTER TWENTY-SIX

August 19, 1993—8:48 PM

"Gentlemen, may I present Professor Andre Pampas, archeologist extraordinaire."

"Good evening, gentlemen," Andre said softly, as he sat down. "Ah, ha! I see you have another one."

"Another what?" The lieutenant asked.

The professor removed a stone paperweight from his pocket and placed it on the table next to the Mazatlan copy.

"God dammit, Shovel, you were telling the truth," Lieutenant Bracque said surprised.

"May I, Sammy." Andre picked up the other stone and examined it. "No question about it, they both came from the same mold. This one has been finished better, but they're both fakes."

"Our lab told us that, but how do they do that?" Reinhourse asked.

"Quite simple," Andre added. "They have been made up from stone materials found in Mayan ruins. They grind the stolen rubble from sites like *Chichen Itza* into powder, add resin paste and pour the mixture into a mold. The markings may seem

---

similar to those seen in Mayan temples, but they have no relation - except to look like an old Mayan fragment."

"Professor," Sergeant Ryan asked, "what's this stone, really?"

"I believe it's like an Enigma machine used in world war two. An enigma is a puzzle. These so called paperweights decipher coded messages."

Sammy beamed with satisfaction. The two stones were passed around.

"Don't even think about saying it," the lieutenant reminded Sammy. An upset Bracque knew his lying nemesis had spoke truthfully.

"Yes," Andre continued, "it decodes messages like the one Sammy brought to me."

"Well?" Reinhourse and the lieutenant say in unison.

"Sammy gave me this stone and a crumpled piece of paper and asked me to decipher the message. I must admit that at first I couldn't find a common denominator. But, as in all riddles, when one piece falls into place, the balance will surely tumble. So it was for the stone and paper."

Sammy was still smiling.

Reinhourse couldn't restraint himself any longer. "What's on the paper?"

"Gentlemen, I see all of you are now seated, may I take your orders?" The waiter asked as he approached the table.

"Ah shit," Reinhourse muttered.

The waiter glared at Reinhourse. "I beg your pardon?"

"A New York steak, rare, and a baked potato," Reinhourse said and slumped back.

"It comes with a salad; house dressing?"

"Yeah, sure."

"I'll have the same thing," the lieutenant said.

"Is the salmon fresh?" Ryan asked.

"Always. It comes with rice and sautéed mixed vegetables. You can have the salmon either poached or grilled."

"Grilled."

The professor glanced up from scrutinizing the menu. "Do you have any quenelles?"

"Very light and fluffy, with a beautiful lobster sauce for an exquisite appetizer."

"I'll take an order of the quenelles, no salad please. For the main course I'd like *petrale sole meuniere*, but prepared with only a batter of milk, a little flour and some breadcrumbs seasoned with fresh parsley and thyme, preferably panko. Add a little extra pepper to the coating. No egg; fresh lemon on the side. Did I hear you say the fish is served with rice?"

"Of course, sir."

"Have the chef take a little cooked rice and add minced shallots and heat it quickly in a hot frying pan with a smidgen of olive oil, and a dash of sweet butter at the finish. What is your vegetable tonight?"

"I don't believe this," Reinhourse mumbled quite agitated.

"Tonight, for the fish dinners we have a medley of summer and gooseneck squashes sautéed in butter, garlic, a little white port for sweetness, with a dash of raspberry vinegar and prepared red peppers, or you can have creamed spinach with or without garlic, topped with fresh grated nutmeg."

"I'll have the squash but hold the garlic."

"Of course, sir."

"Do you have BV's Carnero Chardonnay Reserve?"

"Yes. An excellent pairing that holds up to the sole and finishes well."

"Bring the wine right away.

The waiter turned to Sammy.

"Give me the same as the professor, but don't hold the garlic."

When the waiter took the menus and left, Bracque, Reinhourse and Ryan glanced at each other. Finally Reinhourse asked, "What are quenelles?"

"Fish dumplings," Andre said somewhat surprised and pulled some papers from his pocket and laid them on the table. "Gentlemen, this paper contains the message Sammy gave me. Note the markings are similar to those on the stones. As it turns out, they are more than just similar. They stand for letters of the alphabet, not English but German."

"Wow—son of a bitch," Reinhourse exclaimed.

"German!" Bracque snapped back.

"The note reads, 'Manny to free Ralph Brydges.'"

"Free? That's a strange word for kill," Lieutenant Bracque said.

"True," Ryan said, "but in a courtroom, any decent attorney could show no hint of a death threat."

"Ever hear of Ralph Brydges?" Sammy asked the police entourage.

"Never heard of him," the lieutenant answered.

"Sammy, I've got no clue," Sergeant Ryan said.

Reinhourse shrugged his shoulders. "Maybe the message's wrong. How about it, Professor?"

"I don't make mistakes. That's what was written on this crumpled piece of paper."

"By the way folks," Sammy cut in. "I found this note behind a wastepaper basket next to Joel's bed on Eddy Street. He obviously didn't like what he read, so he crumpled it up and threw it at the basket. We've got to find out if a Ralph Brydges exists."

"You keep saying 'we.' This is a police matter, dammit," Bracque said in a most official voice, indicating he was now in charge.

"Hey, isn't that what I said. I told you when I got back. It's over my head, and in your court now. I just want to be there when you pop the assassin chief's noggin."

"Reinhourse."

"I know the drill, Lieutenant. If he exists, I'll find him."

"I'd like to get back to one of the department's own commissioners, Darrell Snell. When I went to look at Joel's impounded Ferrari, it was gone. Sergeant Paul Mackbee said it was picked up. He claims you never told him that I was coming in to look at it."

"Reinhourse, you were there when I made the call. Didn't I tell Mackbee that Shovel was coming to look at the Ferrari?"

"That's what you told him."

"In fact, Mackbee said he knows you, Shovel, from your Los Angeles days," Bracque said.

"When I asked who released it, he said it was Commissioner Snell. I asked to see the paperwork. Mackbee fumbled around pretending to search for the file, but it was obvious he was on the take."

"Christ, he's got less than a year to retire with full pension," Sergeant Ryan said.

"I still don't know why you wanted to see the Ferrari," the Lieutenant said. "I told you we went over that car with a fine-

    TOO BEAUTIFUL FOR WORDS

tooth comb. There was nothing out of the ordinary. In fact the car was almost too clean, if you know what I mean."

"I just wanted to look at it, that's all. However, to put your mind to rest, I know where the Ferrari's located."

"What the hell," Bracque remarked.

"You found it in a chop shop?" Reinhourse asked.

"Anita drove up in it when she tried to annihilate me. It's probably still impounded in Mazatlan unless one of the local officials laid claim to it. And there's Herman Zeigler. Could he be the top man who decides the fate of others? And last, where's Joel's gun? My vitals say Manny was killed by Joel's gun."

"The slugs were from a .38," Bracque informed.

"When I first heard of Manny's death, I wondered if it was ordered as sort of retribution in Joel's honor or because Manny used a previous throwaway gun to commit the deed. Then again, it may be closure to the San Francisco team of assassins. We may never know."

"God dammit, Shovel, I've got to hand it to you. It's all making sense," Lieutenant Bracque declared.

When the waiter returned with three salads and two orders of quenelles, Sammy said, "Amen, and please don't tell me 'we'll take it from here.' Since I've been shot at and almost killed, I want to witness the finale."

"We'll take it under advisement, Shovel," Lieutenant said grinning. "By the way, where are you going to stay now that your office has been ransacked and probably your condo too?"

Sammy watched Andre poured him some wine. He picked up his glass, and they toasted each other for a job well done. Sammy winked at Andre, then smirked. "It's for me to know. I don't dare show up at my digs. Let's just say, I'll keep you informed. However, pal, you owe me for the bet you made on Manny's gun."

"You're not really going to hold me to that—are you?"

Sammy knew he had Bracque in an awkward position, because Ryan witnessed the bet. "I'll tell you what. Instead of the four hundred…."

"That was two hundred."

"Instead of the two hundred, why don't you pick up the tab for dinner. Anyone for dessert?" Sammy asked, forcing Bracque to duke it out with words.

"You always have to have the last word, don't you?"

"But of course, *mon ami*."

"If you hadn't brought us this information, I'd—I'd."

"Well, thanks."

"Zet tah-LOR!"

"Ah, can't pronounce our French?"

"Damn you."

"You're welcome."

Bracque sat fuming until Reinhourse remarked, "Gee those fish dumplings sure look good."

"What!" Bracque exclaimed, he turned glaring at Reinhourse.

CHAPTER TWENTY-SEVEN

A nice man is about to walk into your life,
He may have all the answers you seek.

Sammy checked into Kensington Park Hotel on Post the night before. He liked it because it's less than a block from Union Square. He knew the hotel was also an Elk's Lodge and many from the SFPD were members. It kept the riff raff away. He didn't want to be seen around his office or condo, but still wanted to be in the downtown area.

This next morning he was on the phone, "I want to leave a message for Donald Anderson. Tell him that his uncle is back in town and wants to meet him for lunch today, around one, at his favorite restaurant."

Sammy took a sip of the complimentary coffee while he sat on the edge of his hotel bed. He rooted around in his wallet, and found Haddie Washington's number and casually threw his notebook on the bed. He decided to tell her about his meeting with several of Toll's workers. That way she would know he was working on the case.

When Haddie answered, she said, "Mist'r Shovel, a man that goes by the name of Jacko said he's been calling your office for two days. Now I don't wants to upset you, Mist'r Shovel, but

Leroy say you's just like the others. You know what I'm saying?"

"I was out of town on assignment, Haddie. Did Jacko leave a number where I can reach him?"

While talking to Haddie, he thrashed about trying to find his notebook, saying under his breath, "I just had it—where did it go? Oh here it is. I hate these damn things."

Haddie gave Sammy the number of the Flynn Division garage.

He wrote the number down, then he reassured her that he was working on finding Toll. He immediately called Jacko.

"Muni."

"I'd like to speak with Jacko."

"He's busy. Call him at home."

"Wait—don't hang up." Sammy said, thinking fast. "This is Doctor Mayer, at the San Francisco Free Clinic. I have some important test results I need to discuss with him."

"You mean that damn Jacko's got clap again?"

"No. It's something different and confidential."

"God dammit. He's always sticking his pecker in someplace where it doesn't belong. Hold on, I'll transfer you."

"Maintenance."

"This is Doctor Mayer. May I speak with Jacko?"

"Yeah, wait a minute." Sammy heard someone yell, "Jacko—Jacko. Get your ass over here…. You got a phone call."

Sammy waited, hoping he didn't get cut off. "Yeah? Dis' Jacko."

"Jacko, this is Sammy. I understand you were trying to reach me."

"Who?"

"Sammy, Sammy Shovel, Toll's detective."

     TOO BEAUTIFUL FOR WORDS

"You's hard ta get, man. Say, can you meet around seven tonight? Got a guy who wants to spin a little."

Sammy thought it over, and said, "Sure, but it's got to be in a public place."

"Da bowling alley in Japan Centa."

"I'll be there at seven."

*L*eaving the hotel, he meandered down Powell Street to Market to buy another cellular phone in one of the electronic shops. He phoned Lieutenant Bracque and gave him his new phone number, and explained it will be harder for someone to trace. He didn't reveal where he was staying, but asked the lieutenant if he could ask Ryan to send a team over to his condo to check if it was thrashed like his office. As usual the lieutenant immediately reprimanded him. "Shovel, we're not a janitorial service. I suggest you look in the yellow pages under the heading—"

"Hold up. I only want to know if my digs are bugged.

"I'll talk to Sergeant Ryan, but don't get your hopes up."

"Thanks for all the help. Have you located—"

"No. Do you want to hear more swell news?"

"Sure, since I have turned this mess over to SFPD."

"The Mazatlan police sent us a teletype. They found another green trinket at the Burger house. It was located next to their phone. Imagine that. I guess when Joel arrived he contacted that house for further instruction. Begrudgingly, I've got to tip my hat to you. If I hear more news I might tell you, then again, probably not. I'm not forgetting nor is my chief about how you stuck the department for a $378.45 dinner the other night. Since the restaurant isn't in the city, he threatened to take it of my paycheck because I didn't ask for prior authorization. You made me look like a fool, and I'm not forgetting it."

Sammy pressed the *end* button and mumbled, "I hope he isn't trying to shut me out."

In every man's life, when the rush of immediate excitement subsides and the pangs of hunger rear up, it reminds us we are mortal beings, born of flesh and blood. Our stomachs howl, *"Feed the pig."*

Sammy sensed the urgent need of nutrition. He decided to stay clear of his regular haunts and found a little coffee shop on Geary. Sitting at the counter, he dug into his eggs and hash browns, and crunched down the bacon. Chewing away, he pulled out his notebook and started reviewing evidence that he shared with the police last night. As he concentrated on Andre Pampas' revelations, he heard a voice say, in a very British accent, "Hot tea please, cream and sugar. I'll take wheat toast with orange marmalade."

"We don't have marmalade," a shrill voice said almost emanating from the nostrils of a very skinny waitress. Her years and actions suggested that she had worked the feed-trough most her life. "Will strawberry jam be okay?"

"Oh—quite!"

Sammy looked up at the mirror behind the counter. Sitting next to him was a middle aged black man, slightly plump, wearing a black suit, white shirt, wild colored tie, and a black bowler hat slightly cocked to one side. "Son of a bitch, you're good, pal, really good. How on earth did you find me?"

"Inspector Bill Johns at your service, old man."

"Inspector Johns, it's a pleasure." Sammy said smiling as he shook Bill Johns' hand. "Our mutual friend, Tom, said you'd find me. I didn't believe him."

"Mister Shovel, having been trained in Scotland Yard, I usually find my man. And a man as exceptional as you deserves finding."

"Call me Sammy, Bill. Exceptional, me exceptional?" Sammy said with a nasal snort.

"Oh don't be so modest, old man. You hold the key to solve an international assassination ring. You've found out more information the past few days than Interpol has in years." Bill chuckled slightly. "But, you must admit, it almost got you exterminated. Enlighten me, how on earth did one man manage to dispatch all those bloody hoodlums?"

The waitress placed a small pot of tea, a cup and saucer, and cream and sugar in front of Johns.

"You know, pal, uh Bill, I'm going to tell you just how I did that, indeed, but a little later. We've got this caper almost figured out and believe me, we know who's the ringleader behind all of the assassinations."

"We?"

"Yeah, the San Francisco Police Department and me."

"I see…. So the local police are involved?"

"Of course," Sammy responded. "I work with the local authorities. By doing so I keep my license in good stead with the State Board."

"Quite! Well, go on, old man, I want to hear all of the delicious details."

"Here's a synopsis of what we've discovered. First, we believe Joel Ceja was killed because his boss thought he might try to warn a victim. It seems Joel received a message that a friend of his was to be the next hit." Sammy paused when he saw Johns remove a black-leathered notebook from inside his left side suite pocket. He noticed an imbedded crest and when Johns opened it was a like mini desk. Sammy thought, I want one of those. "Second, the messages were transferred among the gunmen by a code using identical cast copies of stone paperweights with strange markings on them. The markings were on the decoder device." Sammy took his biscuit, and sopped up the remaining egg dregs while he watched Johns quickly write down information on the right side, then added the date to the upper left side mini calendar. A packet of post-it-notes was placed below the calendar. Dang, he realized, these Interpol guys are well disciplined. "Third, local killings were done out of San Francisco by a man named Manny Soto. Joel whacked the international targets. Joel's staging hideout was in Mazatlan, where, as you heard, I almost got killed."

"My head's whirling. Slow down."

"Fourth, Herman Industries, the industrial giant in Mazatlan, fronts for Herman Zeigler, who lives here in San Francisco. I believe Herman's behind the whole murder-for-hire operation. It seems his father was a Nazi during World War Two. The Nazis discovered a centuries-old society of French assassins, alive and well and, best of all, living in Paris. Herman's father adopted their name and most importantly their code of ethics. Hence, the killing of Joel."

"I sit here in total amazement, old man. Go on."

"Fifth, the next man to be assassinated is Ralph Brydges."

"How on earth do you know that?" Bill asked rather shocked.

"We broke the code and decoded the message, Joel crumpled up the message in his apartment. The message reads, 'Manny to free Ralph Brydges'."

"I say, rather clever wording for a murder message. But, how should I word it, ah…very negligent on Joel's part."

"Neither the police nor I have any clue as to just who Ralph Brydges is. The police are working on that lead as we speak. As soon as they find out they're going to call."

"What makes you think they will call you?"

"On this case we established mutual trust. It wasn't easy to get, but, as it's turns out, we're like the three musketeers."

"Oh! I see, old man. So, you are one of the musketeers?"

"No, I'm the outsider, D'Artagnan. And sixth, a police commissioner seems to be one of Herman Zeigler's men." Sammy watched the waitress bring Johns his toast and jelly. "Last, I can't go to my office because it's been ransacked and I believe bugged. I'm supposed to be dead, killed in the shootout in Mazatlan. So I can't go to my apartment either. The police are checking if it was broken into."

"How long have you been working on this?"

"I don't know for sure, maybe a little over a week."

"A week! We could use a man like you."

"I like it here."

"Where are you staying?"

"At a hotel in town. I'm going to walk there now. Care to join me?"

"When I finish my tea and toast, lead on, old man."

Sammy was so happy to have met an Interpol agent he threw down a twenty for the bill. Say, I thought Tom said you were with Interpol, but you told me you were trained at Scotland Yard?"

"Precisely. I was with the Yard for years, but let's say I was approached with a very generous offer to transfer to Interpol. You might say, once it was offered I couldn't resist."

Sammy and Bill head up Geary and cut across Union Square when Sammy's cellular phone rings. "Speak," Sammy answered.

"Sergeant Ryan here. Boy, were you right. We found eight listening devices in your office. Some were obvious, to divert us away from looking further. We found one that was tied to your phone line above the ceiling, besides the one in the receiver. Your office is clear now."

"What about the mess?"

"Sammy, you know we don't clean—"

"Has the lieutenant called you about my condo?"

"I thought I'd tell you that we found two bugs there."

"You what? Your men debugged my condo?"

"Yeah, when we left the Hall last night the lieutenant asked me to check your apartment too."

"Why that bathetic asshole. You found two bugs, everything else okay?"

"Ugh, Sammy, why did you have to ask that?"

"How bad, Sergeant."

"The worst you can imagine is not bad enough."

Sammy had a conniption fit right there in front of God and everyone. His feet left the ground and his arms thrashed around into the air like some demented fool. "God dammit—God dammit, someone's going to pay!" He screamed snarling. "Wait—Did they cut open any of my leather upholstered furniture?"

"It was like following a horde of machete wielding natives blazing a trail in a jungle."

"Damn—And I live in a secure apartment building; a lot of good that did."

Passersby's stop, stared at his more intense antics of jumping, turning, and stomping his feet. They begin to throw down coins and a couple greenbacks for the show. He calmed down and asked, "By the way, has the lieutenant received any pictures from Jefe de Policia Esparza?"

"I have no idea. When I see him I'll ask. Sorry, Sammy."

"What happened, old man?" Bill inquired.

"Those Rex Mundi bastards ransacked my apartment too. I'm really pissed now."

Sammy slinked onto a Union Square bench and thought about how he'd gotten himself into this mess, then noticed money strewn around. He glanced up at Bill and mouths, "What gives?"

Johns only shrugged, for he had no notion of American customs.

At Bill's urging, Sammy gave him a blow-by-blow account of his gun battle with Mazatlan's elite banditos. He decided to not mention the gun from Tom until the very last. A sort of boy, you gotta see this beauty. He was about to explain to Bill what the gun did when his cell phone rang again. "Speak," Sammy said into it.

"God dammit Shovel, this is Lieutenant Bracque. Who in the hell told you to answer a phone like that?"

"Lieutenant, I don't want to announce that I'm alive and well, when I'm supposed to be dead in Mazatlan."

"Oh—I forgot."

"Why did you call?"

"Reinhourse, er—ah—oh yeah—Reinhourse thinks he located Ralph Brydges. He lives in an apartment, somewhere in the hilly part of San Carlos. I still don't believe we have the right man."

"Why's that?"

"This guy's a fashion designer. He has made Sports Attire, the hottest summer attire in the world. I don't see any connection to Zeigler."

"Lieutenant, it's a perfect match. May I meet with him?"

"Well, I don't know."

"Lieutenant!"

"Okay—okay, I'll call when we reach him. The complex manager says he's gone for the weekend. We'll try to set it up for Tuesday morning, at a halfway point." Bracque decided to feed Sammy some more information, because he was aware he did have a pedigree nose for sniffing out clues. "I'm really pissed about you breaking into Hotel Harald. I talked to Burglary this morning. The two men the officers caught ransacking Joel's hideout were released within an hour of being booked by some misplaced paperwork. There's an APB out for their return. Can you believe that?"

"Yeah. Any ideas?"

"After our conversation last night, you're damn right I have an idea who engineered the fiasco. Three hours after they were out of the door, Burglary was notified the robbers were parole violators. Since they both carried guns we could have held them."

"Well, doesn't that beat all?"

"May I add something even more intriguing that even you don't know—each had gold teeth."

"Were they Mexican?"

"That would be too easy. There were from some Slavic country."

"Oh jeez. The plot thickens." Sammy said, glancing at Bill.

                TOO BEAUTIFUL FOR WORDS

"We'll be in touch, but one more lapse in judgment, and you're going into the slammer. Got that?"

Bracque's new revelations made Sammy forget to tell Bill Johns about Mister Wonderful. Sammy learned Bill was staying at the British consulate, and they trade phone numbers before departing.

*I*n a forest of color, Sammy careened his way through tightly grouped umbrella tables. Chatter from patrons flooded the ears of diners and passersby's alike along Belden Street's outdoor seating. Nearing Post Street, he noticed Donald nervously glancing around as he sipped iced tea. Getting closer, Sammy spotted below the umbrella's rim glitz and trash, Nancy and Mack. Sammy grabbed a chair opposite Donald, frowned and nodded to Nancy and Mack.

"Meeting like this is making me jumpy. Are we being watched?" Donald revealed,

"Who knows, could be—hope not. I counted on you remembering you're favorite restaurant. Nancy—Mack; what brings you here?"

"Actually, it's my favorite luncheon spot." Donald said.

"We wanted to join Donald for lunch, isn't that so, Mack?" Nancy remarked, forcing a smile.

"If we're being watched, should our staff ask for police protection?" Mack asked.

Sammy grinned at the tagalongs. "It's me they'd be tailing, not you. Besides, if they wanted me dead it would have happened by now. Are you going to just stand there or join us for lunch?"

Nancy glanced around, then shot him a smirk. "There are no chairs left."

"What a shame. Another time?"

Nancy and Mack understood they were not welcomed. "Another time then, Donald—Mister Shovel, ciao," Nancy said and whisked Mack away saying, "There's an Italian place down there and I see empty chairs—hurry before they're grabbed too."

After Nancy and Mack meandered away, Donald asked, "So you don't believe we're targets?"

"No. I do believe they have a surprise in store for me."

"So that's why you keep dressing in disguises. Who are they?"

"Donald, a good question that I can't answer—but I may know soon. I want to pass on information to you without anyone listening and that includes Nancy and Mack. How did they know you were going to meet me today?"

"They just showed up and said how about lunch."

"Do you find that strange?"

"Kind of. They rarely join anyone for lunch."

"From now on when I call I'll use a pass word."

"You mean using code words and stuff like that."

"Sort of. First, I want to thank you for letting Marita know I was coming."

"Was Marita a help?"

"Yeah and no. I can tell you I found some of the information I was seeking. Until all of the pieces are sorted, facts verified and arrested made, I'm not going to reveal what I know."

"I think I understand. What do you want me to do?"

"Nothing. If Nancy and Mack should ask about our meeting, tell them I've run into dead ends. Do you understand what I'm saying?"

"Yes."

"Remember, tell no one, not even your wife. When you receive a call from Uncle Bob, it will be me."

"Why Bob?"

"Doesn't everyone have a Bob somewhere in their family tree?"

CHAPTER TWENTY-EIGHT

August 21, 1993—7:07 PM

Sammy drove Peggy, a Volvo, he bought second hand, and named it after the only girl he took to a prom. He parked Peggy in front of Japan Town's bowling alley. He found Jacko with a man dressed like a lumberjack including skullcap. They were in a booth, intently watching the alley action. Sammy slipped in beside Jacko.

Without turning Jacko shouted, "Hey, what ya doing, man. You knows, you can get killed doing dat."

"Why, Jacko, I thought we were friends."

"Oh. It's you, Mista Shovel. Sorry.... This be my ole buddy, Raymond. We's go way back."

"Does he work for Muni too?"

"Ole Raymond? Hell no. He cleans up at Walt's."

"Walt's? What's a walt's?" Sammy asked, knowing it wasn't dancing.

"A used appliance emporium up the street from the Flynn bus building." Raymond's gotta cushy job der."

Sammy noticed how Jacko gazed protectively at the elderly man of Spanish descent sitting across from him, and

---

　　　　　　　　TOO BEAUTIFUL FOR WORDS

knew Jacko was his true friend. "How about a round of beer? My treat."

"Whata say, Raymond?" Jacko asked.

Sammy watched Raymond's shriveled frame sit and stare straight ahead, and figured Raymond's brain was trying to sort out Jacko's request. Faltering slightly, he smiled at Sammy. "Okay, if you wish."

Sammy signaled the drink gal over. "Three Coronas, please."

Surprised, Raymond glanced at Jacko and grinned. "I never drunk Corona a'fore."

"What do you have for me, Jacko?" Sammy asked, noticing there are some bowlers, but not many and figured that was why he found a parking spot so easily. He had heard the owners wanted to turn the place into retail. That would mean more tourist traps and restaurants. He wondered why owners were so quick to throw in the towel when their take on the percentage slowed. Christ, he acknowledged, it's greed. Glancing around at the lack of dazzle, he had to admit most of the magnetism was gone and the locals didn't find bowling the hot commodity it once was.

After listening to Jacko, Sammy understood Raymond worked weird hours cleaning up the front of Walt's..

He sized up Raymond's description of Walt's and figured the Emporium was a showcase of recycled dreams for the less fortunate

Trying to help out his friend, Jacko explained that Raymond made a deal with Walt. He can work anytime before nine and for as many hours he wanted as long as the stoves, washing machines and other appliances sparkled. Walt expected a clean front every day, including Sundays for his nine-to-nine operation. In inclement weather Walt expected the used appliances to be covered and supplied the tarps. For this, Jacko complained to Sammy, Walt only paid Raymond a measly hundred a week.

"You tell em, Raymond. You know, tell Mista Shovel what you told me."

The waitress returned with three beers and three glasses. Raymond's frail hand grabbed the bottle and he took a sip of the Corona. Jacko followed suit. Raymond's paunchy cheeks showed a smile, "It tastes jus like beer, good beer." He lifted the bottle to his lips again and downed three long gulps that half emptied the bottle. He then looked up from the Corona and asked, "Can I calls you Sir Shovel?"

"Of course you can, Raymond." Sammy said as he poured his beer into a glass. He realized Raymond had lost quite a few brain cells over the years—or worse maybe they never existed. "I'm pleased you like it, Raymond." He watched Raymond cradle the bottle of Corona between his gnarled fingers as if it was a treasure. Taking it slow, so Raymond could gather all of his wits, Sammy asked, "Now, what do you have for me?"

"It's about that Toll fellah you was ask'n about. I seen him, I did."

"When—when did you see him, Raymond?"

"I guess it was the day he disappeared. I used to see Toll and some of the other boys every day getting ready for their regular runs. After that morning, when he left with another man, I never sees Toll again."

"Did the police ask you about this?" Sammy said quite shocked.

"No..." Raymond reflected, "no one ever asks me anyting. Why do ya sup—supo.... Why's dat?"

"I don't know, Raymond, I don't know. What did you actually see that morning? You mentioned a man?"

"Well, Sir Shovel, I sees Toll coming to work real early, I did. It still dark. It—it wasn't even light out. He went into the bus building. You see, I was clean'g up Walt's. To see Toll der dat early surprises me. Awhile later he crosses Harrison. His jacket his over his shoulder. I never sees Toll go into Miss Whestley's ever, but he did. Yes sir, he did."

"Miss Whestley's?" Sammy interjected.

"Miss Whestley's a diner down about a half block from da drivers' entrance to the Flynn building" Jacko explained.

"Oh yeah, I remember now. This was unusual then?" Sammy asked.

"If someone bought Toll breakfast or lunch, he a'bliged." Jacko spoke up again,

"So, Toll was going to get a free breakfast."

"Yes Sir Shovel. I thinks he was. I stops what I was doing. Heck, Walt never checked up on me anyway."

"And?"

"What? Where was I?" Raymond queried wondering were he was.

"Raymond, tell Mista Shovel what you done toll me." Seeing that Raymond's confused, Jacko repeated. "The white dude. Tells em about the big white guy."

"Oh, de man who went into Miss Whestley's. I don't know why; Toll never ate there regular; It's' nice place; plenty of good food. Miss Whestley, she never held back on portions."

"Raymond! Don't ya stray none," Jacko urged,

"Huh…? Oh. What was I saying?"

Jacko raised his voice slightly. "The big white guy. Tells Mista Shovel about the white guy."

"Yes—the white guy. After a spell da both comes out."

"Who?" Sammy asked.

"The white guy—his chest's like a fifty-gallon barrel sett'n on piano legs shaped like dem grizzlies; big, big man, kind of like` hulk. He done leads Toll away from Miss Whestley's, puts him into the back seat of a car and drives off."

To Sammy the actions sound too familiar. "You said he put him in the back seat?"

"Yes Sir Shovel. Da big man puts him in da back seat."

"Did the car have markings on the side?"

"No, Sir Shovel. It was green. I done notice Toll didn't have his jacket. I goes inside Miss Whestley's and sees it wadded up in a booth. I grab it for Toll. There was only one cup of coffee on the table and a couple of dollars."

"Did anyone see you take Toll's jacket?"

Raymond fussed with his bulky plaid jacket, slugged down the rest of the beer, bent down below the seat, brought up a shopping bag, and sat it on the table. "No, Sir Shovel, Miss Whestley never pays attention to me. It's still here in this sack."

Sammy straightened up. He felt like he just swallowed Tweety Bird. He reached for the bag. "Did you search the pockets?"

"I sure did—after about a week. He had some change and a couple of dollars. I took em for holding his jacket."

"May I?" Sammy said, as he examined the Muni issue coat. He checked all of the pockets. Nothing, they were all empty. He noticed the upper left-hand pocket was buttoned shut, he pushed the button through the cloth eye, looked inside, reached in with two fingers and carefully guided out a folded paper with the tip of his fingers. He grabbed a cocktail napkin so

TOO BEAUTIFUL FOR WORDS

any prints would not be disturbed. It was on Muni stationery, handwritten. Sammy read to himself:

> **Dear Mr. Thomas Washington, Supervisor:**
> **Please meet with me to discuss your new position, Monday morning, at Miss Whestley's, at 5:00 AM, for breakfast. I will discuss the transition procedures with you.**
>
> **Harry Callahan, Aide to the Mayor.**

The handwriting caught Sammy's attention. "Gentlemen, promise me that you'll never say anything about this conversation, the coat or this note I just found. Do I have your word?"

Jacko and Raymond glanced at each other. "Sure man, but why?" Jacko asked.

"Do you want to keep on living? There are ruthless killers out there who will kill for this information. They don't take prisoners."

Jacko spoke right up. "Hey man, you gots my attention, I hears what's you saying."

"Yes sir, Sir Shovel." Raymond added.

"I'm taking the coat and note for evidence. Tell no one about our meeting, especially any Muni personnel. You never saw Toll's coat or the message—do you understand?"

On his way out, Sammy paid for the beers and for two more rounds for Jacko and Raymond.

Sammy climbed into Peggy. "What the hell's going on?" He wondered. "I've never seen handwriting—written left backhanded—in my life. Now I have two in my possession in less than five days. It can't be a coincidence."

*B*ack in his hotel room, Sammy found Paul Mackbee's amusing scribble and compared it to Toll's note. He almost prayed that Toll's note would be different from Paul's, but the letters had the same ink smears. The pit of his stomach felt queasy and his pulse was racing on high octane. He nervously checked the *Dear God* against the *Dear Toll*, then Sammy mumbled, "Dammit, no it can't be. They're identical."

He picked up the phone and dialed for Sergeant Ryan at Central Station.

"Central Station."

"Is Sergeant Ryan there?"

"This must be Mister Shovel."

"Cindy, how'd you know it was me?"

"You call here so often it was easy. What can I do for you this evening?"

"I need to talk to Ryan—er, Sergeant Ryan."

"He's off this weekend. Let me check his schedule... He'll be here at eight, Monday morning."

"He's gone all weekend?" Sammy asked.

"It's the easy life of a sergeant."

"Thanks, Cindy. Don't leave a message, I'm not at home."

"At home? That's a laugh, I heard you're on the run."

"Funny, your not."

*A*round nine Monday morning, Sammy dialed SFPD Central. "Has Sergeant Ryan arrived yet?"

     TOO BEAUTIFUL FOR WORDS

"May I ask who's calling," a screening voice answered.

Sammy didn't recognize the female deputy. "This is Samuel Shovel. I need to talk to him pronto."

"I'm not an Indian, Kemo Sabe. Is he expecting you?"

"No, but we go way back."

"If you're talking about cattle drives and tumble weeds, you've reached wrong jurisdiction. You should have called the U.S. marshal, or maybe Wyatt Earp.

"You're not funny. Who put you up to this nonsense? Sammy said exasperated.

"What ever do you mean? Maybe you should have asked instead of demanding."

"You win. May I please speak with Sergeant Ryan?"

"Yes. Cindy left him a note that you'd call this morning and that we weren't to take any lip from you—so watch your tongue, Kemo Sabe. I'll connect you."

A few minutes later, Sammy heard, "Sammy, Ryan here."

"Ryan, I don't like to ask favors."

"What? You're always asking for confidential information. The only reason I do what I can for you is because you give us clues that we don't have the manpower to check out ourselves."

"Okay, your right. However could you verify if Paul Mackbee took any vacation dates last October."

"You're up to something. Why do you want to know? And those are personnel records.

"It has to do with Joel's missing Ferrari," Sammy fibbed a little. "Find out the exact dates. And, Ryan, I need the information quick—real quick. I'll call this afternoon."

"That's too quick. Why can't I call you on your cell phone?"

"Because every time you call me it cost money. Since I'm still locked out of my office and apartment, so to speak, I'll call you."

"Oh yeah. The man who made his own city a prison."

CHAPTER TWENTY-NINE

A nice chap being
groomed for slaughter

August 24, 1993—9:12 AM

Sammy and Bill entered a Denny's restaurant in Redwood City. He spotted Lieutenant Bracque because of his large frame. Reinhourse was there as well. There was also a young man sitting between them.

Bracque was surprised to see Sammy's friend.

Reinhourse spouted off, "Who told you to bring an unwelcome guest?"

"This is Bill, Bill Johns. He's working with me." Sammy replied, and couldn't help but notice when Bracque and Reinhourse glanced at each other and mouthed a word that looked like "shit." He figured they were upset that he brought Bill with him to meet Ralph Brydges.

The lieutenant shook his head. "Sit down, you're blowing our cover...Shovel. This is our Ralph Brydges."

Sammy reached out and grabbed Ralph's hand. "Pleased to meet you, Ralph." He turned to Bracque. "Tell me, lieutenant, what have you learned so far?"

Bracque's bushy eyebrows collided together, upper and lower lips smashed together, and his cheeks puffed slightly in disgust, and belted out, "We've learned nothing, because we haven't asked him anything, except what he wants to eat and drink some coffee."

"Well, by all means proceed." Sammy said, sitting down next to Reinhourse.

Bracque gave him his 'damn you' glare.

Sammy paused as the waitress arrived at their table with a fresh coffee pot. She gave him and Bill her morning happy smile. "Coffee?"

"Black," Sammy said. "I'll have eggs over, hash browns, sausage and sourdough toast. How about you, Bill?"

"Hot tea, with rye toast. Any marmalade?"

The waitress poured Sammy's coffee. "Orange."

"Splendid." Bill Johns said, as he pulled out his black-leathered note pad.

As he sipped his coffee, Sammy peered over the cup's rim trying to size up Ralph. The young man had a sleight build, dirty blond hair, pretty boy face. He dressed like a fashion model in a loose off-white turtleneck and a multicolored, long-sleeved, V-necked pullover that was bought from one of those men's expensive boutique, probably at Pebble Beach. Sammy could see Ralph took care of himself. The young man's hands were pampered; the nails manicured. Sammy would bet that his toenails were also pedicured causing young babes to chase after him. He wondered if he was married.

Bracque put down his cup. He turned to Ralph, and asked, "Tell me, Ralph, did you ever meet or know Joel Ceja?"

"Oh sure. We worked out at the same health club on Market Street."

"Does the club have a name?" Reinhouse asked.

"Pinnacle Health Club. Too bad about Joel. I mean the murder. He was a real great guy. We occasionally tossed back some suds together after a workout."

Bill whispered to Sammy, "Suds?"

"Beer," Sammy explained.

Bill cocked his head, slightly befuddled.

"How often did you see him?" Bracque asked.

Sammy watched Reinhourse take notes and reluctantly brought out his spiral notebook and fumbled for a pen. He sensed Bracque was scrutinizing his latest attempt to take notes.

"Oh, let me see…. At least two, maybe three times a week."

"How long did you know him?" Bracque inquired.

"I met him about three months after I came to California. Membership in the health club was free to all employees where I worked. So I signed up. I think I noticed Joel there about a month later. We became pals by spotting each other with the heavy weights. Gradually we became workout partners." Ralph's eyes opened wide. "Say, I was out of town the night he got killed. I've got witnesses."

Sammy suspected that Ralph thought he was going to be arrested. He decided to wait and test Ralph's story.

"Hold on, Ralph," Bracque said, "no one has even the remotest idea you were involved with Joel's murder. In fact, quite the contrary."

In a tremulous voice, Ralph said, "Sorry, sir, you were making me feel guilty."

The waitress brought more coffee, Bill's tea, and the breakfasts. "Will there be anything else?"

Bracque gazed around. "No, everything's satisfactory." He turned back to Ralph. "Did Joel warn you that someone might try to kill you?"

Ralph dropped his fork. "What! Kill me. Why? I wouldn't hurt a fly.... Well, maybe real flies..." He glanced around. Four pairs of eyes were glaring at him. "Hey, what's going on?"

"Mister Shovel is a private investigator," Bracque said. "He thinks your life may be in danger. Shovel, why don't you explain why to Ralph, and maybe you can enlighten all of us."

Sammy put his knife and fork down, took a swig of coffee, then said, "Call me Sammy, Ralph."

"Okay, Sammy, shoot.... Oh heck. Poor choice of words."

"Are you married?"

"For Christ's sake, Shovel, we know he's a bachelor."

"Well, I didn't. Ralph, you just told us you came to California. How long ago?"

"About a year and a half ago, maybe a couple of months longer."

"And from where?" Sammy asked.

"New York. I was an assistant clothes designer at Bill Blass Designs."

"Why did you leave?"

"I saw an ad in one of the trade magazines for a sports clothes designer. Since I had some ideas about a fresh look, I answered it."

"Who placed the ad?" Sammy replied.

"Why, Sports Attire. I'm proud to say were doing quite well since our new line came out. Some really hot stuff."

"And you designed it?"

"Well, yeah." Ralph's demeanor changed to excitement. He bubbled when telling the enclave how rapped up he was in his work. "I became chief designer after about six months. The previous line sucked. Nothing but bland colors, cut lines made for men and women over forty and the materials costs were excessive. With the connections I knew overseas, I revamped the entire collections and reduced cost by more than twenty percent. Right now I'm riding high and couldn't be happier. But there's been no animosity within the firm. We all share in the profits by seniority. So the better I do, the more the veterans make. I think that fair and square—don't you?"

Bracque and Reinhourse stared in disbelief.

Bill Johns nodded his approval. He understood the American 'dog eat dog' way.

"You see, Sammy," Reinhourse interrupted. "I told you your professor was wrong. This man isn't a threat."

"Shovel, are you finished?" The Lieutenant added.

Sammy knew Ralph was the target. He wanted to be careful and not scare Ralph away from helping the police. "Almost. Tell me, Ralph. Now that Sports Attire has hit the big time, are you shipping worldwide?"

"You bet we are. The orders just keep pouring in. We're on a roll!"

"Any foreign competition?" Sammy asked.

"Of course. Germany, Japan, Italy, and some upstart company in Mexico."

"Where in Mexico?"

"I don't know. Maybe, if I heard the name."

Bracque and Reinhourse spoke in unison, "Mazatlan?"

"Yeah, yeah that's the place."

"Son," Lieutenant Bracque said, "are you sure Joel didn't contact you that your life may be in danger?"

"He never said anything to me. And I saw him the day before he was murdered."

"Did you receive any strange messages or phone calls?" Reinhourse asked.

"Funny you should ask. A strange fax did come to our offices about me leaving town immediately and going back to New York. The staff all laughed."

"It was from Joel, trying to save your life, Ralph. He must have really liked you, because he gave his life trying to save yours," Sammy said, trying to enlighten him.

"You—you really mean someone's going to try to kill me too?" His voice quivered.

"It looks that way," Reinhourse said.

"Ralph," Sammy said, "has anything out of the ordinary happened to you?"

"Like what?" Ralph replied hesitantly, his face quivered.

"Like being followed, strange phone calls or hang-ups, people watching your house." Sammy asked. He took a bite of sausage, picked up his pen and waited.

"Nothing like that. I take the Caltrain to work. I live in an apartment. The only thing that's happened to me lately, I received an invitation to Laura Beckman's fashion party. I understand it's one of the city's swankiest bashes each year. Tickets are by invitation only, strictly formal. I felt very fortunate to have gotten one."

Sammy grinned at Bill Johns.

"I say, what a perfect opportunity to commit murder," Johns said.

"Oh no," Ralph exclaimed. "I'm not going."

   TOO BEAUTIFUL FOR WORDS

"Oh yes, you are," Bracque interrupted. "And you're not going to tell anyone about our conversation. Your life depends on it."

"But—but—I'll be all alone."

"Don't worry, Ralph, we'll be there with plenty of muscle." Bracque announced quite confidently.

Sammy glanced at Ralph, and recognized a coward when he saw one. He explained, "Ralph, your friend sacrificed his life for you. You owe it to Joel to see this through."

Lieutenant Bracque cleared his throat, and put on his forceful, take-charge manner. "Now, when and where's this party? What time does it start?"

"Will I be safe until then?"

"I believe so," Bracque quickly assured.

"Saturday night. This Saturday, August twenty-eight, at old St. Matthew's Hotel. It starts at seven-thirty."

"At the party, we'll have men dressed as waiters, hotel personnel and guests. They'll all have their eyes on you, Ralph." Reinhourse assured.

"Don't show up until after eight-thirty." Bracque said. "You can go now. We'll see you in four days. Don't contact us. We never met."

The four of them watched Ralph leave, but Reinhourse was still mad about Sammy bringing an uninvited guest. "Who's your friend?"

"Inspector Bill Johns from Interpol. He has an office in London."

Reinhourse and Bracque stared at each other, then the lieutenant said, "Oh."

Gentlemen your friend, Mister Shovel, has almost broken open an assassination ring that we've been trying to uncover for years. You might say, I'm here for the kill. An American agent notified me about what happened in Mazatlan. He explained I should meet Mister Shovel with the idea that together we might solve who is the bigwig," Bill Johns added.

"We now know who's behind all of the murders," the lieutenant said. "It's Herman Zeigler. We've just got to catch him doing something wrong. This Saturday night I bet he's planning to murder one Ralph Brydges. We're going to be there to catch him." Reinhourse triumphantly said.

"It sounds like you lads have everything under control. May I be a witness?"

"Yeah, Lieutenant, I need an invite too," Sammy said.

"I'll do what I can. But just don't get in the way. It's a police matter now. We do it our way. Do you understand, Shovel?"

"I don't have a problem with that. Do you, Bill?"

"When you give Herman Zeigler a go, I jolly well want to be there. I can inform Interpol and report all about the cracking details," Bill said, and folded his leather note pad and tucked it back into his coat locket.

"I'll submit your request to the Chief and let you know."

"Hey. I thought you agreed not to tell anyone," Sammy admonished.

"How am I going to ask for the kind of operational help we're talking about without involving the Chief? However, I told him what you said. While disturbed he vowed to keep it confidential."

"Say, that was a very impressive gadget you used for taking notes," Reinhourse said.

　　　　　　　TOO BEAUTIFUL FOR WORDS

"Yeah, Shovel, you should have one of those instead of that stupid blue colored spiral notebook you pretend to write down information in." Bracque added.

Bill seized an opportunity to secure his relationship with the blokes before him. "I say, I'll order one of these notebooks for each of you, compliments of Interpol. I'll even add some boxes of refills that should last a couple of years."

"You're kidding us?" Bracque said.

"I never bamboozle. Write down your address and give it to me," Bill replied, then got up. "I'm afraid the tea's twitching my bladder. I'm going to pop off for a whiz."

Sammy watched Bill leave for the restroom. "Say, Lieutenant, did you get some pictures from Jefe de Policia Esparza?"

"Yeah, I got them. No, we've never seen either couple. Why don't you come by and point out the woman you claimed was part of the Herman Industries operation. I'll pass them around to other departments for a lead."

"Lieutenant, could you also send them to other jurisdictions?" Sammy asked somewhat disappointed,

"Like where?"

"Like major cities."

"Do you know how many major cities there are?"

"Okay—how about Los Angeles, Chicago, New York, Detroit, Las Vegas, Miami and Jersey City for starters."

"My, we know our crime centers, don't we," Bracque said.

Sammy watched Bracque write down his address, then Reinhourse. He wondered why the SFPD believed the world revolved around them. He guessed it was that way with all police departments, no matter how big or small. They rarely checked with agencies outside their jurisdiction. That was how criminals got away with so much crime The Feds were the worst they would only share bits and pieces of misinformation.

"I only asked," Sammy said, as Bill returns to his seat.

"Did I miss something?" Bill asked.

"No, I guess not," Sammy answered.

"I'll see what I can do," Bracque said. "I don't suppose you're willing to pick up the check?"

"Not really. You set up the meeting."

"Just like the one at Scott's? The division chief is now scrutinizing every petty cash receipt I submit." He threw down two twenties for the breakfasts, then handed Bill his home address—he wanted to make sure the package wasn't confiscated by some curious chief when they saw the word 'Interpol' on the package. "Come on, Reinhourse, we don't have the rest of the day to relax. We have the public to answer to."

Bill watched Lieutenant Bracque and Reinhourse departed, and said, "That Bracque is a bit rough."

"Yeah, but a good cop."

CHAPTER THIRTY

August 25, 1993—10:30 AM

---

*T*he next morning Sammy phoned the Kristy Lipp agency to ask about the report on Nancy Foster and Mack Dirverson. The receptionist informed him that the report was complete. She asked if he wants it mailed or couriered.

"I'll be right over."

"Wait! Kristy has to sign it. She won't be back until after two."

"I'll be there at two."

Sammy strolled into the Kristy Lipp Agency a little after two, nodded at the receptionist and headed for the coffee area.

The strapping young woman said, "Wait! Kristy told me if you want coffee I'm to get it. Black?"

Sammy gazed down and thought, Kristy sure knew how to pick them. A dimpled face surrounded by maple sugar hair; sweet—very sweet. "Yeah—yeah. You have a name?"

"Deborah."

"Debbie what?"

She stood up. "It's Deborah, Deborah Carrick. I don't answer to nick names."

"Oh, so you're one of those. Where's Kristy?" Sammy asked, and watched a mini-skirted booty wiggle as each curvaceous gam took a step.

"She's not here yet. I told you Kristy would return after two. If you want to continue our conversation, I respond when hailed by my given name." Deborah disappeared into a snack alcove.

Sammy gazed up and saw several of Kristy's part time operatives staring. He searched for Pepi then shrugged. He began working on Deborah's emotionless demeanor. "Deborah. Hmmm—Deborah—I remember exposing a Deborah about two years ago. She was your age and height, and built like a brick…"

Deborah came around the corner, with a mug of coffee in tow. "Do you want me to hand this to you or shall I splash it in your face.

"You're good—held your temper—all business. How long did Kristy interview you before the hire?" Sammy laughed and took a slurp of coffee.

"Less than ten seconds and I'd watch your words of exposing women. People might take you for a pervert."

Sammy sprayed coffee, like a high-pressure nozzle, all over the counter.

Deborah cracked a smile, winked, retrieved a file from her desk, and handed it to him, then retreated for paper towels.

"Touché." Sammy said. He found a chair and started to peruse the report.

Kristy and Pepi walked in laughing, ignoring Sammy sitting quietly with his head buried in a folder. Kristy saw Deborah, who moved her eyes and head to the left. "Mister Shovel, what a pleas—what a surprise."

"It's about time. I've been waiting for hours. Hi Pepi—nice job you did on those motorcycle thugs." He couldn't help noticing the colorful Spanish peasant dress and remembered her remark about a *Contessa.*

Pepi looked at Kristy and raised her eyebrow slightly. "What thugs are you talking about?"

"The ones at Hotel Harald."

"Come again."

"Okay, have it your way. How about a big kudo from me for delivering Joel's hideout."

"Joel who?" Kristy asked.

Realizing he's tipping his hand, he said, "I just started to read your report. Want to clue me in?"

"I'll have Pepi go over the particulars—she did most of the legwork. Deborah, coffee all around."

Sammy noticed that Kristy was a little curt. After the receptionist sorted out the polluted mugs laced with cream and sugar from his unadulterated black, she left.

"Deborah told me you hired her right away."

"She's my niece and forget the nepotism crap. Deborah is well qualified. Head for my office, you know the way. Come on, Pepi, mister Shovel wants his ears scorched."

Kristy sat behind her desk and nodded at Pepi. "Tell Sammy what you discovered about Nancy, the golden girl."

A harassed rhino expressed less annoyance than Sammy did when he glimpsed Pepi taking out a spiral notebook. "Born outside of Yreka, near the Oregon Border, in 1965, and lived in squalor. She did well enough in school to receive a scholarship to Chico State. She majored in business administration and minored in human resources. Upon graduating, Nancy applied to Cal State in Hayward to get her Master's Degree because of their reputation as a progressive business school. Golden Opportunities' president, Peter Ballard, had a job fair booth at Cal State in the spring of eighty-seven and hired her on the spot."

Kristy jumped in. "I wonder who was, err—is their CEO? Any ideas, Sammy?"

"Smart ass. Who told you?"

"For God's sake, Sammy, we're in the same prying profession. There's an ugly rumor that a local P.I. was paid big bucks to find Golden Opportunities CEO's killer. Any comments on that speculation?"

Sammy didn't want confrontation. "Can we continue with Pepi?"

"Every time you come in here you spout poor mouth. What gives?"

"I thought we were friends. I offered you a job and we negotiated a fee."

"I beg your pardon—you chiseled down my fee."

"Did you loose any money on Pepi's assignment?"

Kristy shot Sammy the I could kill you look. "Pepi, continue with the report."

Sammy thought, I gotcha. "So far that's general information. Where does this gal—woman get the money for all her jewelry and clothes?"

"Joining Golden Opportunities, Nancy was put in charge of personnel at the tender age of twenty-three. She's been there ever since."

"I still don't hear money," Sammy said.

"If you keep interrupting you'll never find out," Kristy informed.

Sammy took a gulp of lukewarm coffee, cradled it in his hands and glared at Kristy.

        TOO BEAUTIFUL FOR WORDS

"A middle aged man," Pepi continued, "Walter B. Comeaux" comes to Golden Opportunities with a plan to open French bread boutiques in suburban shopping malls and high traffic locations in the city and down the peninsula—strictly fresh, high quality artisan breads including croissants and breakfast pastries."

"You don't mean the ones that the lunch-crowd now lines up for sandwiches, do you?"

"The very ones. He had millions to invest because he sold his RV Company after his wife died. During a Golden Opportunites' strategy session with him, guess who walked in?"

"Nancy Foster."

"Love at first sight; they married within two months. But get this: Walter's fixings only occasionally smolder—little smoke; little heat; no flames. So he agrees to let Nancy enjoy an open marriage. He bought her a three thousand square foot flat in downtown San Francisco. We tailed her and found she leaves her Alamo hills mansion, her horses, and her husband around nine on Monday mornings, stays all week at her apartment with some young stud and returns on Friday afternoon to her Alamo ranch. She puts on jeans, a western shirt and frolics around the horse barns with Walter and fusses in her garden."

"What? She's promiscuous?"

"Like a pyromaniac on the forth of July. She resented being poor; teenager boys ignored her; she had no one to kiss or cuddle; she became sexually frustrated. While she idolizes Walter, she now lives in a breezy world that allows her to swing and flash money. Some say she's a borderline nymph. All bedmates arrive from Monday to Thursday, then it's *adios*. They're quickly dispatched like bedbugs—she turns up the heat to over 100° for any bug kill from Friday to Monday once a month. Sometimes they're gorgeous women, even two. She then brings them home to Alamo—trying to jump start Walter. In a police report two years ago, Walter had to fast talk and grease palms when she tangled with a boy going on sixteen. In San Francisco she is known as Nancy Foster; in Alamo, Mrs. Nancy F. Comeaux."

"Jeez, who would've thought? Say, how does Walter manage Nancy, his horses and the bread boutiques?"

"He sold the bread company a couple of years ago for more multi millions. I did hear an unsubstantiated rumor that something is going on between her and that Mack fellow we checked, but it isn't an affair."

"How do you know that?"

"Nancy likes them young. He's older than her husband. However, a neighbor reported seeing Walter, Nancy and a man with a Hawaiian shirt riding together a few months back at Comeaux ranch."

Looking at the file folder, Deborah handed him, Sammy asked, "Is it all in here?"

"Plus details and some pictures."

Sammy glanced down at the cold coffee mug he had been nestling in his hands and sat it on the desk. "Pepi, will you give me the short version for Mack?"

"Born 1938, raised in the Corn Belt and graduated from University of Nebraska. Got a job with a CPA firm, married, had two boys and hated ever second of his miserable life. Divorced a domineering wife, and enrolled in the University of Hawaii's graduate school."

"Ah ha, the Hawaiian shirts—but why the gold chains?"

     TOO BEAUTIFUL FOR WORDS

"When he realized his wife believed intercourse was for making babies and she made it clear that two boys was enough he was shut out of her bedroom."

"You mean they weren't that sexually active."

"She shut him out completely and made him sleep in another bedroom. He was humiliated. Being in the mid sixties, he heard San Francisco's Haight Ashbery and dreamt about free love and flower children. He moved to Hawaii, went to school, acted like he was made of money, hence the gold chains. It worked. Mack attracted bevies of party girls willing to be trained by an experienced, rich, older man."

"Two sexually deprived soul mates. No wonder Nancy and Mack bonded," Sammy mused.

"After grad school, jobs were hard to get in Hawaii. He worked as a tour guide during the day and played beach bum for the vacationing romantic damsels until he clicked with the IRS. They transferred him to their San Francisco office in seventy-four. Two years later Golden Opportunities beckoned."

"That's it?"

"Not quite. There is a rumor he's been buying up Golden Opportunities stock when an employee terminates, selling it for a profit and investing the money in some land scheme with Walter Comeaux. We don't have access to his books so it remains scuttlebutt, but as I mentioned, we know he's been around Walter's and Nancy's ranch."

"Did he remarry?"

"I guess you'd call her a common law wife; thirty something. In your file is her photo with Mack when they went shopping last week."

"Pepi, you did it again. How on earth did you get all this information about Mack's activities in Hawaii?"

"I don't know what world you live in, Sammy," Kristy said," but detective work relies on networking. Mister gumshoe, didn't you hire us?" She picked an envelope from her desk and passed it to Sammy. "Here's our bill. I don't want any arguments this time."

Outside, Sammy's head felt like ice-cold mush, without sweetener and he wondered if Joel was getting wise to Mack. Did Walter promise Manny a big nest egg if he would pop Joel. Did I stumble onto the assassin gang by default? Grabbing his cell phone, he punched in some numbers. "Donald, I want to talk to Donald. Tell him it's Uncle Bob. It's urgent."

"Uncle Bob?" Donald answered very surprised.

"We must meet—now, and alone. Name a place."

"Err—the—the Justin Herman Plaza, by the water fountain."

"Fifteen minutes?"

"I guess so."

Sammy's voice sharpened and he bellowed, "No so's. Be there." He cleared the phone while his pace hastened, heading towards the meet, while gobbling down a couple of hot dogs

"Over here Donald. Sit down."

When he sat next to Sammy, Donald said, "You seem angry."

"Not angry, confused. What do you know of Nancy and Mack?"

"Are we being watched?" Donald said glancing around.

"Right now I don't give a damn. What's with Nancy and Mack? You said they didn't fraternize with the other employees. Explain."

"Just that—loners. They attend all of the parties, you know social gathering, in-house get together, birthday

    TOO BEAUTIFUL FOR WORDS

celebrations, but they never fraternize. They are strictly business like."

"How often did Nancy use the Mazatlan villa?"

"Never, neither did Mack."

"Do you find that strange?"

"No. Nancy went to Europe with her husband; Mack to Australia with his present girl friend."

"Where does Nancy live?"

Donald caught on. "She lives with her husband, Walter, on weekends and stays in the city during the week. She's like a bitch in heat if that's what you're driving at, but, as I tried to intimate, she's never compromised a Golden Opportunity's employee."

"Do you know that Mack has been buying other employees stock?"

Donald gazed at him surprised and little shocked. "No, I didn't, but that's not in my area of expertise."

"Can you check his records and find out what's going on? Also check if Nancy's name or her husband is mentioned in any documents."

"Mister Shovel, you're the detective. We told you everything in the office is open for scrutiny by any employee. There are no locked file drawers; no hidden agendas, no secretes. A few employees work Saturday mornings. Meet me in the Lobby, this Saturday, around 3:00 PM. You can examine whatever you want."

CHAPTER THIRTY-ONE

August 26, 1993—11:33 AM

"*H*ey, Bill. It's a few days before the Laura Beckman bash, so how would you like to explore California's wine county?" Sammy asked over the phone. "Imagine touching and squeezing ripe red morsels between your fingers as you fittingly sip its older cousin's fermentation. Basking on a balcony overlooking a sea of grapes enjoying its fulfillment right at the source."

"I have no clue what you said, but splendid, old man. We English are quite taken by California whites, and the reds too. I am in a state of titter, when do we go?"

"Not we, only you. I'm still running a PI operation out of a hotel room. Take your rental and go through St. Helena about two and one half miles. Take a right on Lodi Lane. It's on the left. I know you won't believe this, but brace yourself for the Wine Country Inn, they look like a scene on an English post card. I've arranged for you to stay in room twenty. Don't drink too much wine. I'll see you Saturday at St. Matthews, around eight."

"My god old man, how splendid. You've done this for me?"

"I've got work to do, enjoy."

"Cheers. Room twenty?"

"The inn's very best. It's my treat from one colleague to another."

"Jolly well done, but the expense."

"I'll write it off—Bill, for God's sake leave Interpol behind and relish the wine. The owners will be waiting for you and they'll send you to the best wineries.

"The devil you say. I'm on my way, old man."

Back in his hotel room, alone and impatient, Sammy grabbed the phone, and punched in Ryan's cell phone number. "Sergeant Ryan, come on, what's the skinny on Paul Mackbee?"

"Sammy, I have to be careful about this," Ryan said being ever cautious. "Paul took sick leave starting October eleventh, for three days. He was back at work on the evening of the fourteenth. I peeked in his file-jacket and saw a doctor's certificate stating Paul had a severe case of laryngitis."

"Can you get the name of the doctor?"

"Sammy, I don't know. It took me a day to compile that information. I'm sticking my neck out. Even official police business of this nature would require authorization to go into anyone's record."

"After what I told you about the Ferrari and my suspicions about Paul, can't you get Bracque to make a call?"

"When we ate at Scott's, I thought we agreed not to tip our hand."

"I forgot," Sammy said. "Why don't you ask Cindy to do the snooping? She told me she's in tight with some gal in Records. Also, have her ask if she knows where Paul usually vacations."

"You're on to something, Sammy." He glanced around checking on eavesdropping. He didn't want Central's staff to know he was speaking with a P.I. "Don't lie to me, because this has nothing to do with the Joel Ceja killing. If you don't want to tell me, I'll understand, however I'm not at your beck and call. You're not part of the department and, contrary to the public's perception, I have regular duties I'm expected to perform when on watch."

"I can't tell you, but it may have something to do with the assassination gang," Sammy admitted.

"I'll talk to Cindy, but don't call me about getting this kind of information again. I'd say our slate is even Steven."

*B*ack in his hotel room, Sammy perused some potential new clients in his spiral notebook. He picks up the phone and punched in Mark Grossnell's number.

"Is Mister Grossnell there?"

"I'll page," says a flat female voice. After a pause, Sammy heard, "Barry here."

"Barry Grossnell, this is Sammy Shovel calling. You contacted me about some warehouse thefts. How may I help you?"

"Are you the private detective I called last week?"

"Yeah. I've been out of town on an assignment."

"It's a good thing you called, I was just about to give up on you."

"Sorry."

"Sometime ago I joined a nationwide Merchandise Wholesalers' Association and they required a big name accounting firm, like Ernst and Ernst, to go over my books. They went way back and found sundry items have been missing, year after year. I never noticed because the dollar amount was minuscule. Do you think you can help me with something like this?"

                    TOO BEAUTIFUL FOR WORDS

"Of course, that's what I do. I'll be over this afternoon and we can discuss the details and my fee. What's your address?" Sammy wrote it down. "Gather up the audit that triggered the discovery of the thefts, a list of the types of missing merchandise, personnel records and any alarm systems, cameras or other security measures you have already installed for my examination. A small amount usually suggests an inside job."

Sammy stretched out on the bed. The turmoil of the last few days and his brush with death in Mazatlan had caught up with him. He questioned the killings he had caused in the universal name of justice. He knew he had to live with crying children longing to be held by strong arms and be comforted with gentle kisses? His heart went out to wailing mothers and blubbering children who saw their patriarchs as heroes, giants among men. He shut his eyes and tried to comprehend how devoted fathers mutated into primeval butchers?

Dammit, all he could visualize were children running around waiting for their Papa's to come home. Nearing slumber, his looping images of gold tooth desperados bouncing children on their laps rained down on his subconscious. By taking one's life, he knew his job sucks.... Sammy was conked-out on the bed.

The hotel phone's piercing ring startled him from a deep sleep. Instinctively, with head buried in a pillow, he reached out and searched with his hand for the receiver. He grabbed something and pulled it to his ear. "Hel—hello."

"Mister Shovel?"

"I—I think so…Jeez, what a dream."

"This is Cindy…. Officer Cindy Basset."

"Oh…Cindy!" Sammy muttered, and sat upright as if he had been hit with a full bucket of ice water.

"Sergeant Ryan said I should call you regarding what I found out about Paul Mackbee. Paper and a pencil handy?"

"Hold on, Cindy." Sammy untangled the phone cord from around his neck, then found his notebook. "Shoot."

"Kuldoop Atil, he's the doctor who unwittingly signed Paul's health certificate."

"Could dupe a till?"

"Sounds strange, doesn't it. Write it down, first name, K-U-L-D-O-O-P, last A-T-I-L."

Sammy hurriedly wrote down the information. "Kuldoop Atil? Where do they find these foreign quacksters?"

"He was born and raised right here in San Francisco. He worked at one of those free clinics."

"I can't imagine Paul going to a free clinic."

"Oh he went, according to Doctor Atil, but not for treatment. He used to help out once a month to protect AIDS patients as part of the city's reach-out program until the money ran out."

"In other words, Paul was paid by Joe Public."

"You got it."

"Were you able to find out anything about his vacation habits?"

"A gal friend of mine, Rita Howe, a cute bean-counter in accounting, told me Paul invited her to stay at a campsite he owns at Lake Davis. When she discovered Paul wasn't bringing his wife and kids, she declined."

"Campsite?"

"Rita said Paul told her it would be all right because he has a trailer permanently parked there and that he would sleep in his truck. Rita still declined his offer."

"When was that?"

"About five years ago. Rita now's married and has two girls."

"Where's Lake Davis?"

"In Plumas County, about five hours from here. Turn off somewhere around Truckee and go north."

"Anything else?"

"Actually, no. Except for some altercation with Mayor Holtsmark about eight years ago, he's been clean."

Hiding that Paul was mired deep in stenchy-waste, Sammy said, "Thanks, Cindy."

*H*e bought a California map, rented a four-wheel drive and would meet with Barry Grossnell before he left to find Toll's grave. He figured he would be on his way to Lake Davis before six. He called information and asked for the Plumas County Sheriff's Department. He opted for a direct connection, and heard it ring only once before he slammed down the receiver. Idiot, he said to himself, Mackbee would probably be in tight with the local sheriff. He visualized him trading war stories with the local floggers while slugging down boilermakers. He guessed if he talked with them, Paul would know in less than two hours that I was planning to snoop around his property. Paul would have the sheriff arrest me for trespassing.

He called information again. This time he asked for the Plumas County Assessor's Office. He found that Paul did own property around Lake Davis. The clerk on the phone gave him general directions on how to get there. Sammy perked up when he was told about the one horse town of Portola that had lodging and eats.

He took the rented Cherokee and went to his meeting with Mark Grossnell. Sammy discovered the existing warehouse security measures consisted of three outside lights activated by motion detector. Sammy wondered why more merchandise wasn't missing. He explained that an operative will contact him next week to set up an electronic surveillance system that will trap the burglars.

Sammy assertively, quoted a high fee while giving Grossnell a take-it-or-leave-it façade. Grossnell didn't hesitate and agreed to Sammy's fee. For the first time in his life Sammy felt he belonged in the P.I. World.

At six-twenty he headed across the Bay Bridge, on his way to Lake Davis. He stopped in Auburn for a steak dinner with an hour-long catnap. Then drove for hours toward Portola. He felt fresh like a hunter wanting action. He was anxious to snare a corrupt crony.

CHAPTER THIRTY-TWO

August 27, 1993—1:18 AM

Sammy arrived in Portola a little after one, and noticed a red neon sign sputtering VAC_ NCY at the edge of town—the A was missing. Tired, he was thankful the inn had a room and forked out fifty bucks to flop for one night.

At seven in the morning, he gazed out the window. Surveying the street he thought, "Yep, a one-horse town, but a hunter's Shangri-La." He smiled at the parade of old buildings housing coffee shops, a grocery store, a hardware store, clothing and antiques. A newer sportsman's store touting tackle, bait, and an assortment of hunting rifles. Sammy bet that this store had enough lethal gear to stave off any whims the local bears might fancy.

After a shave and shower, he attended to urgent body functions, compliments of eating hot dogs. Gathering last night's shabby clothes, he hurriedly dressed and trotted out into Portola's leisure domain.

He crossed the town's only thoroughfare for breakfast. He salivated with each step at the thought of scooping up runny egg yokes and golden hash browns with a toasted English muffin. Sammy entered Katy's Hog Paradise and found an empty booth.

"Coffee?" The waitress inquired and proceeded to fill Sammy's cup.

Sammy glanced up from the menu and saw a huge curly mop of hair, dyed flaming red, parted down one side so that sixty percent hung from the other—so much for the do-it-yourself coiffure. He noticed the waitress appeared to be five-nine, wasp-waisted with spindly legs. Sammy figured she was around thirty-eight turning forty-eight and wore very little makeup. It reminded Sammy of those starving Ethiopian's bodies: plenty of protruding bones devoid of charm. He saw she had deep-socket eyes that set along side a thin pointed nose that terminates over sweet full lips. Sammy read her name tab—Ruth Stoggs. He then noted her bare left ring finger.

"Black, eggs over on your number six. Can you have the cook make the bacon crispy?"

"Sure, hon. Carl bakes the bacon so it's brown and crispy. He says it gets the grease out of that gooey fat stuff."

"Good lad. How about an English muffin too."

"Sure hon.... Say, you kinda talk cute," Ruth said as she winked and walked away.

"Jeez," Sammy mumbled, "one day with Bill Johns and I'm mimicking him."

Sammy watched Ruth work the restaurant's floor and overheard men laugh and women giggle at each table. He promptly came to the conclusion that Ruth wasn't much to look at, but she could charm a death row inmate into ordering maggots over brown rice for his last meal, eating every wiggling morsel and giving her a generous tip.

Ruth brought more coffee. "Passing through?"

"Sort of," Sammy lied, "but I'm stopping to visit with a friend of mine. He said I should look him up if I ever went to Reno. I took these back roads on the chance we might connect."

"What's his name, hon?"

"Paul. Paul Mackbee. He said he lives in a trailer somewhere near Lake Davis."

"Never heard of him. What does he look like?"

"Beefy, about six-four, going on fifty."

"That describes half of the town folks and seventy percent of the hunters."

"Let's see, he has dark hair with a spray of gray around the temples. It surrounds a square-jawed face with a skewed nose, the result from wrestling a—a person down some stairs. His complexion is light, he's left handed and recently someone described him as being barrel-chested."

"The only man who lives around here that answers to that description is Bulldog Bill. I haven't seen him in six to seven months. The four months 'fore that he'd been a regular every weekend. He does that, comes and goes, you know. He owns a piece of land about seven miles from here. Does a lot of fish'n and deer hunt'n. Smokes the fish and sundries the deer kills for jerky. Actually, it's not bad in fact the last batch was quite tasty. He told me he sells it in Frisco."

Inside, Sammy bristled when he heard San Francisco's name defamed. Feigning a smile, he asked, "Does he come with his family?"

"You must be talking about someone else. Bulldog doesn't have family.

"I noticed everyone seems to know you. Were you raised here?"

"Naw. I shook Arkansas in my teens. After waiting on tables here and there for years, I discovered Portola. The town and me clicked. I got a nice place just before you come into town." Ruth heard the cook's ring. "I'll get your eggs."

Finishing his breakfast, he motioned to Ruth for another refill. She bounced over and topped off his cup. "How was everything, hon?"

"Ruth—perfect. Have you known Bulldog long?"

"Over ten years. He's a regular here, at Hog Paradise."

"May I ask how you and Bulldog get along?"

"Well, hon, it's no secret, when Bulldog's in town, I'm his faithful bitch."

"In other words, the two of you are an item from time to time."

"Well, we've been known to grind the nasty's. Except for a few one-night stands, I haven't got a lot to look forward to. But when Bulldog comes to town, we splash liquor around Harry's Saloon, and just make total asses out of ourselves. It's kinda like busting out moonshine at a Saturday night Ozark's stomp, everybody joins in, sweating like hogs in heat, and we all gets silly stupid."

Sammy bit his lip to keep from busting out laughing at Ruth's metaphor. "Sounds like loads of fun."

"Say, what's you got going on tonight, hon?"

"Don't know yet."

"Well, with all this talk, I'm getting a relentless twitch down south and the flames need dousing. I gets off at three; keep me in mind." Ruth scribbles on her order pad. "Here's your check. My phone number's on the back." With that she gave Sammy a wink and strutted off.

Sammy threw down a twenty onto his table for a bargain breakfast. If he wanted more information, she would remember him.

Sammy entered the only grocery store and picked up some chips and a readymade turkey sandwich for lunch. He figured it was going to get hot and dusty, he searched and found a small Styrofoam chest, loaded it with soft drinks and ice and put the sandwich on top. He headed for the hardware store. On the way he spotted Harry's Saloon up the street. He shook his head imagining Ruth stirring up the locals into lunatic exploits, and remembered his own Harry's antics. He grinned feeling the name was appropriate.

"Yes sir, may I help you?" The hardware clerk asked in a bass voice.

"Shovels, where are they?"

"About the middle of the right wall. We've got a good selection for up here."

"May I set these groceries on the counter while I pick one out?"

"Sure. I'll keep an eye on them. You're not from around here, are you?"

"Alas, no, beautiful country though. I'm visiting a friend, if I can find him. He lives here on weekends during the hunting season. I was told his trailer is about seven miles from here. He's a big man, six-four, dark hair with—"

"Oh, you must mean Bulldog Bill."

Picking up on Paul's alias, Sammy said, "Yeah, ole Bulldog. Does he come in here often?"

"Varies. He can be here every weekend for months and then we won't see him for almost half a year."

Sammy began to lie big time. "Sounds like Bulldog, all right. He's supposed to come up this weekend. I'm going to surprise him…. Ah…what does he usually get? Maybe I can replenish some supplies."

"Nothing special. Usually items to repair his trailer. The only thing he buys regular is the lime he uses when he guts deer."

"What does he do with the bones?"

"Uses the lime pit to eat the remaining flesh away, then I understand he sells the skeletons for bone meal. In fact, he sells everything, including the hides."

"How much lime does he usually get? Maybe I should buy some for the next hunting season."

"Heck, that starts next month—you're not a hunter are you?"

"No, just a friend. How long is deer season?"

"Here in Plumas County—third week of September to the fourth week in October."

"Maybe that's why he asked me to come by—to sort of help him get ready for his big day. Does he need more lime?"

"Bulldog bought more than hundred sacks about eleven months ago. I guess he was stocking up then. I haven't seen him for months, but, rain, shine or snow, Bulldog's never missed an opening day."

"Are the sacks large?"

"Fifty-five pounders."

"Well, let me get my shovel, I told him I would help plant some azaleas. Can you give me directions to his trailer?"

"Azaleas up here?"

"Maybe I misunderstood. I'm not a horticulturist."

CHAPTER THIRTY-THREE

You're not a forensic investigator,
But you know the knee bone,
Is connected to the thighbone.

August 27, 1993—10:47 AM

Sammy arrived at Paul Mackbee's property and calculated it was about ten acres, situated in a forest of tall trees. He parked behind some clustered trees, his head giddy with the scent of towering spruce, the fresh air, and total quiet—a combination hard to beat. He walked over to a stump, sat down, and thought, I'm alone and could be lost if it weren't for the dirt road and Paul's trailer sitting atop a slight knoll. If you were an outdoorsman this could be your utopia ticket.

He appreciated why Mackbee purchased the land, but didn't understand why he left his family out of enjoying such beauty; no city noise, no neighbors in any direction. Total isolation. He examined land's natural terrain sloped to the road and the lake, with huge boulders rising above clumps of Manzanita everywhere. Sammy figured if Paul took Toll for his final ride, it would have been up here.

Paul was too good a cop to make stupid mistakes, and would never take the chance that some hunter might stumble on a skeleton by sheer accident. If Paul dispatched Toll, he buried the body here and kept tabs on it until the lime did its deed.

"Why didn't I bring some of my old duds?" He asked himself. "I'm going to get my new slacks all messed up and where should I start?" Sammy added as he went to fetch his new shovel from the Cherokee, and began to explore the property. He ignored the trailer and the deck that had been added—too close he reckoned. He walked around the lower area, trying to find the lime pit used to render deer innards and bits of meat from bones. He attempted to get the lay of the land and determine the direction of the prevailing wind. He knew the area around a smoke pit would still have the smell of deer death, even with the use of lime. Wait, his brain warned, I haven't smelled anything, yet, but fresh, invigorating air. "No, it wouldn't be in a location where someone would come upon it by accident." He surveyed the area again. "Up there," he muttered. "Up that slight grade."

Sammy kept the search organized. He moved three hundred yards to his right, stopped, and turned left ninety degrees. He checked the landmarks again, then plodded along another twenty-five paces forward, turned another ninety degrees left, then returned another seven hundred yards, going past the stump in the opposite direction. He kept the search organized by skirting Manzanita and rock cropping.

Almost an hour later, he stepped up the hill another ten paces. His nose detected the faint odor of death. "It's here," he mumbled.

Following the all too familiar scent, he found a fence, an open gate, and beyond the gate, two large open pits, separated by thirty-feet. But there was no body, no obvious grave, no bones, just ashes and pieces of burnt wood in one pit and the remnants of lime in the other.

At one end of the fire pit, he noticed a metal contraption about twenty feet long with hooks stretching up about six feet.

     TOO BEAUTIFUL FOR WORDS

Remembering what Ruth said, he figured Paul set it over the wood-burning pit to smoke fish like they do in Mexico.

Sixty feet away, down a steep embankment. He went through the thick underbrush, to what appeared to be a level area. When he followed along a path that snaked around some boulders, he came upon groups of canvas tarps. He removed them. Sammy found a huge wooden drying rack and a ten-foot long bench with overturned galvanized washtubs beneath. Beyond the drying rack were two huge old refrigerators set onto a Joe McGee steel frame. Ashes were below and the doors were covered with smoke debris. Nearby was a third of a cord of cherry wood. Mounted on an angle-iron frame were two fifty-gallon drums, with half-inch hoses dangling down. Upon further inspection, he spotted traces of oil soaked into the soil, and realized an emergency generator sat there.

He spotted another gravel road beyond. He continued along the path to another gate and saw it carried through until the brush hid its source. Heavy electrical lines, ready for reconnection to the generator, lead to the fence. He noticed poles for lights.

Of course, he thought, Paul had to keep natural predators from enjoying a free lunch. He inspected the fence; he saw it would be electrified.

For the next two hours, Sammy scoured the area trying to find disturbed soil and a potential grave. It was getting hot so he removed his coat. He checked the area just inside the fence perimeter and finally he spent another hour outside. No disturbed soil or signs of digging. The thought of making jerky in the winter made Sammy shiver and he tried to think of something else.

The memory of the golden hash browns at breakfast begins to gnaw in his stomach, making his mouth salivate—yeah it was time to feed the pig. He returned to the Cherokee. He grabbed a bag of Sunchips, the turkey sandwich and a diet root beer and headed back to the stump. As he nibbled on the sandwich, he mumbled, "Am I an idiot, or what? I'm sitting on a stump while I'm stumped. How could Paul come up here all these years without his family's knowledge and bring back deer jerky to sell in the city?"

Sammy pictured Paul, probably in a four-wheel-drive truck, firing at anything that moved, be it buck or doe. He envisioned a man on a mission, unloading his catch at the pits, gutting and skinning the deer, slicing it into strips, seasoning it in the tubs, gave it its first smoke cure, then carefully laying out the meat on the rack for an initial set. Then the strips went into the drying ovens to complete the process. He didn't go deer hunting just during the season, he slaughtered deer probably all year around if he needed cash. Sammy wondered how much booze it would take to have the local game warden look the other way? This wasn't a vacation spot, but a business operation. It wasn't deer season then, so why was Paul up here so many days after Toll disappeared. Then too, Ruth was of little help talking about how they splashed booze around, and her casual remark, "The last batch was quite 'tas-t-y'...."

"No! Oh my God, no!" Sammy shrieked with every ounce of breath he could muster, then threw-up his lunch and retched once more. With a napkin, he wiped his mouth. "Please Paul, you didn't turn into a cannibal or did you?"

Sammy grabbed the shovel, then ran back up the hill, while his mind conjured up Toll's grim death. Murdered, brought up here, cut into pieces, seasoned, put out on the rack, then into the ovens to dry and be sold in San Francisco as deer jerky. Christ, wait until San Francisco locals find out they're also— cannibals.

He guessed the bones were broken into pieces, limed to rid them of any clinging meat, and sold for bone meal. "Teeth with fillings had to be knocked out," he said aloud. "I'm betting any gold or silver amalgam was melted together with lead for fish weights. No corpse; no Toll; no nothing. Paul, you bastard think you're so slick; yet soooo sick."

Sammy arrived back at the pits panting from the climb. Paul had to burn the clothes, he surmised. "I'm sure Paul raked the pit clean, but I owe it to Haddie to find the needle in the haystack—if one ever existed."

He gabbed his shovel and started digging spade's full of ash and debris out of the pit. His breath became a pant, which in turn forced him to gag slightly—he needed a vapor mask. He carefully sifted through the ashes and fouled dirt, before heaving out the next shovel full.

He didn't hear the quiet tread of paws that were sneaking up on him, until it growled; Sammy froze, fear icing his blood. He turned slowly, and beheld his new adversary twenty feet away—a huge black bear, standing erect, exhibiting a you— could—be—my—lunch attitude.

With its mouth open as wide as the Grand Canyon, the bear shook his head back and forth. It growled again. Saliva drooled from its jowls.

Sammy knew if he ran for the Cherokee, the bear would easily overtake him. He remembered the advice given on a public television wildlife program: Appear bigger than your attacker. Sammy grabbed the shovel and raised the blade above his head, rocking it slightly from side to side. "Wait...think!" He told himself. "Did they say move or remain stationary?"

He held the blade high and doesn't budge. He thought if he stepped back the bear will detect fear, but if he moved forward the bear will assume an attack.

The bear continued an uneven roar, like wailing echoes emanating from inside ancient Indian burial caves, but the bear held staunch.

By the same token, Sammy stance remained firm.

The bear began to exhibit doubts about his prey. Its head bobbed up and down, making more slobber plummet to the ground. It's forelegs slowed down and one paw began touching its head.

Sammy waved the shovel again, occasionally darting it forward in a menacing gesture. It was still a standoff.

Finally, the bear decided not to tangle with something it didn't comprehend. It dropped to all fours and lumbered off.

Shaken and angry at being so careless, Sammy grabbed the shovel and smote it as hard as he could, blade first, deep into the pit's damp soil. He heard a clink.

He rushed to the pit's rim, fell to his knees then stretched his hands. Frantically, he cautiously scooped out ash and soil. When he reached the damp dirt, his fingers moved against the shovel trying to find what the blade had hit. His nails were caked up with foul muck, and his sleeves were covered with ash and grime; there went his new togs.

Sammy stretched farther down gently wiggling his hand until he touched a piece of metal. He grabbed something small and round with his thumb and index finger, he drew it out of the pit slowly.

It was a burnt metal button.

　　　　　TOO BEAUTIFUL FOR WORDS

He wiped it with his shirt and recognized the letters M-U-N-I across the face. Sammy jumped up and shouted, "I got you; you careless cannibal!"

CHAPTER THIRTY-FOUR

Does anyone truly know how to tell you,

That your loved one is dead?

August 28, 1993—9:05 AM

Haddie excitedly welcomed Sammy into her home.

Struggling to put on a smile, which he was sure had all the charm of a bank loan officer. "Good morning, Haddie." Sammy said. "I'm not too early, am I?"

He'd phoned Haddie Washington upon returning from Portola the night before, hinting that he had some news regarding his investigation into Toll's disappearance. Being a Saturday, he asked that the whole family be present to hear his report.

Sitting with Haddie and her children, he was at a loss for words. How could he explain that the man they loved was being sold throughout their city in corner liquor stores? He wondered how to wade through Toll's death and enlighten them that their loved one had been cut up, seasoned and sun-dried into jerky. Better simply to say he was cremated, he decided.

Sammy sat for another moment with his head bowed, until Haddie asked if he would like some coffee and some breakfast sticky rolls. He glanced up, and said, "No, thank you, Haddie."

"Why, Mist'r Shovel, you seem tired." Haddie said analyzing him.

"I was out of town, near Reno. I had a long drive back last night."

"See, mom," Nazr lashed out. "I told you he's like all the others, you know what I'm saying. What' ya do? Lose all the insurance retainer money at a dice table?"

"Now, Leroy, let the man speak." Haddie said, giving her son a firm stare. "He asked 't talk to us."

"Nazr, shut up. I feel something's wrong, very wrong," Charles said, eyeing Sammy. "It seems like you have been strapped into the electric chair and are waiting for the warden to pull the switch. Why are you so down?"

Celina started to shake. She grabbed her mother's arm in a vise-like grip. "Mommy, I'm scared."

Sammy figured he would rather take on ten firefights like the one in Mazatlan than face Haddie and her children. Oh, God, he silently pleaded, help me get through this ordeal. "Leroy, I wasn't in Reno gambling. Gambling is for suckers."

Leroy jumped up and shook his fist at Sammy. "My name is Nazr. Don't ever call me Leroy."

Sammy shot to his feet as his meek attitude changed. "I'll call you Leroy until you show some respect to me, your mother, Charles and Celina. And if you don't sit down, I'll put you down." He said, his nose a mere inch from the younger man.

"I thinks he means it, Leroy," Charles said, "I've put up with this Nazr crap long enough myself."

"What?" Leroy exclaimed knowing he had to make a choice, either his homeboys or family.

"You heard me," Charles said, "Sorry. Please, go on."

"Haddie, I was in Portola. It's a little town outside of Lake Davis, about an hour from Reno. That's where Toll was taken when he was kidnapped."

"Oh my God!" Haddie exclaimed. "Kidnapped?"

"We don't have that kind of money," Charles said.

"He wasn't taken for money." Sammy blurted out, "He was murdered and cremated. Probably the same day he disappeared."

The room went deathly silent.

Haddie leaped to her feet, screamed, and tore around the room, wailing, "Toll, Toll, where is you, my God, Toll." She grabbed his picture from a side table and thrust it to her bosom.

"Daddy, Daddy. Oh lordy—lordy, I want my Daddy." Celina whimpered.

Leroy sat, his lower lip trembled. "I thought... you know what I'm saying...I thought you was going to bring us good news."

Sammy tried desperately to find the right comforting words, but said, "I can't lie. I speak the truth."

"Are you sure?" Charles asked.

Sammy reached into his top pocket and pulled out a small plastic sack containing the button he found. "What are the chances of this burnt Muni button ending up in a remote mountain campsite belonging to anyone other than Toll? A campsite owned and operated by the man whom I believe is the perpetrator." Sammy passed the button to Haddie.

Haddie stopped weeping and dried her eyes with tissue, her face reddish and puffy. She dropped down onto the couch.

Sammy motioned to Leroy to get a cold wet washcloth and bring it to his mother.

Haddie examined the button as Celina hugged her. "Oh Toll. Why you... I don't know what to say. What's to become of us? Mist'r Shovel, can you help us?"

Sammy watched Haddie treasure the button. "I can't help spiritually,' he said. "I'm not good at that sort of thing, but I'll make sure your family gets the million dollars."

"What happens now?" Charles asked.

"It's a police matter. I'll have to give the button to them. Even though it's been compromised, they should be able to match residue from the button to the pit ashes where I found it, or confront the killer when they try to worm a confession out of him. I'll ask the authorities if the family can have it back after the trial."

"Then you know who did it?" Leroy said dejected when he returned with the wet washcloth. Sammy watched him put it gently on his mother's forehead.

"I have a strong suspicion." Sammy said. "This button and other information will be turned over to the police. They will conduct an investigation on my findings and make appropriate arrests. I'm sorry I yelled at you, Nazr, but I knew this was going to be difficult for me to explain. You know, none of you will ever see, talk to, or be hugged by your dad again." Instantly, Sammy regretted those words. In his usual fashion of speaking before shifting his brain in drive, he spit out an uncaring remark and worsened a traumatic situation."

Haddie and Celina started bawling again. Charles slumped over holding his head between his hands.

"I got to hand it to you man," Leroy said. "You's better than Shaft, you know what I mean. How'd you find all this out so quick?"

"Nazr, in spite of computers and high-tech gimmicks, you ask questions, listen carefully, take notes and have a lot of blind luck."

"Call me Leroy. What 'ja say it meant before?"

"In French it means - *The King*."

"If I straightens up, do you think I could become a police officer? I think—because of what happened—I think my dad would like that."

"Leroy. There's no doubt. How would you like me to arrange for an SFPD officer to come by here give you a ride-along, then take you to the Hall of Justice and show you around? They can tell you what you'll need to know to get into the police academy. I will tell you this, they're looking for college men."

"You'd do that for me, after all the shit I flung at you?"

"Yeah, Leroy. I knew this was a special family when I first stepped into your home. There's love and respect here. You tried to show some arrogance, but I could see it wasn't in your heart."

"You think I've got a chance?"

"Of course, but I'd work on losing the phrase 'you know what I mean.' It's unbecoming an officer."

Leroy strained a smile, and the chip on his shoulder vanished. "Would it be possible for you to come by again?"

"I would be honored, Leroy. I truly see a young man who has found purpose in his life."

Sammy left a family shattered by the loss of their patriarch. Time, money and friends may heal a little, but they would never forget the man, the father, and their hero who loved tollhouse cookies.

   TOO BEAUTIFUL FOR WORDS

CHAPTER THIRTY-FIVE

To get your act together,
It's best if you clear the air.

August 28, 1993—11:10 AM

Back in his hotel room, Sammy dialed Sergeant Ryan. "Want to meet me for a beer?" Sammy asked, then suggested they meet at Maltese Tavern at noon. "I'll buy you lunch as well."

"Maltese Tavern? Where do you find joints like that?" Ryan responded Cynically.

"It's not a joint." Sammy said. "They keep changing owners and names. It's in the plaza across from the rear of the Palace Hotel."

"If you're going to spring for lunch, you must want something extraordinary." Ryan retorted. "Does it have anything to do with Paul? Never mind, I'll be there."

Sammy called the Selix store to rent a tux for the Beckman bash. Perfect, he thought, Selix and the Maltese Tavern were a few blocks from each other.

Next, he dialed George Stanton of Defender Mutual. "George, Sammy here. Sammy Shovel. I have news about your missing person, Toll Washington."

"All right! Where did you find him?"

"In the mountains above Pertola."

About time he turned up, we're going to cancel his policy. The lady who wrote the insurance has been fired. Other heads will roll too. She was young and seductive. After only three months on our payroll she went after older clients and talked them into large term insurance policies always dangling a hint of sexual indulgences. The poor saps fell for her scheme. Her bankroll swelled beyond our seasoned salesmen.

"Did you take photos of the hiding Bastard?" Stanton demanded.

"Hiding, hell. He's dead." Sammy retorted.

"What! Oh Christ, tell me you're kidding—please."

"He was murdered, the day he disappeared."

"Do you know what this means?" Stanton said pleadingly.

"You're going to hand Toll's widow a check with a lot of zeros, and pay me eighty- thousand."

"Can you prove this? I could have sworn the family was scamming us."

"The police are involved. You'll get their report. Toll was a respectable man. Since the Washington's desperately need money, will you do me a favor, don't hold their check too long. Take a thousand out of my fee and hire an investment counselor for them. I don't want the money to go poof. I want the investment counselor to set up a program that's administered by a bank and make sure his two younger children to go to college, and the money's not spent on stupid cars"

"Are you sure he's dead?"

"Positive. Did you write down what I asked?"

"Vaguely."

"Damn it George, this is important. Get some paper and write in down. Have the counselor talk to Charles, Tolls oldest son and a very sensible college graduate.

"Okay. I never met this Toll guy… You're positive he's dead."

"Do you chew on jerky?" Sammy asked.

"Sure, all the time."

"Then you've probably met Toll Washington."

"Huh?" Stanton muttered perplexed.

"Where do I send my bill?"

"Same as last time. Corporate—say, didn't we agree on two percent?"

"Sorry pal, I have your fax and signed memo that says eight. We'll talk later."

*S*ammy called Golden Opportunities, but the phone rang and rang. Finally a man answered.

The janitor was out of breath from his sprint down the hall, he slid to a stop before the desk, and seized the phone. "Golden Opportunities," he paused as he drawing in air, then added, "The offices are closed."

"Wait. I'm looking for Donald, Donald Anderson," Sammy said.

"Is he working today?" The janitor asked

"He—his wife said he was at the office."

"What's his extension?"

"I don't know, but he's a vice president," Sammy said getting flustered

"So are thirty others. There are about twelve bodies around here. Hold on while I look around," the janitor said, trying to be helpful.

Sammy heard the phone click and was about yell out, Oh Shit, when Donald came on the line, "This is Donald Anderson. How may I help you?"

"Donald, this is uncle Bob. Are we still on for our fishing expedition this afternoon?" Sammy asked covertly.

"Yes, just as we discussed." Donald said.

"Same time?"

"Same time." Donald replied.

*H*e never understood the phrase, "Clothes makes the Man." At Selix he haggled over everything and left with a real monkey suit. The manager told Sammy, "Don't tell anyone where you picked up this suit. In fact burn it when you're done; I don't want to see it again—thank you, and proceeded to cut out any references to Selix."

It was almost noon and Sammy reclined back in a chair at the Maltese Tavern's bar. He was relieved that the morning's ordeal was over. He never wanted a repeat with a family like Haddie and her children again. To him that was worse than challenging King Kong's brother into a bare-knuckles fight in a back alley fight.

He asked the bartender to bring something foreign and cold, with a foamy head and a lot of alcohol. Sammy knew Ryan loved exotic beer on tap. He would spoil Ryan today.

The bartender delivered a glass of Guinness Stout. He guzzled it halfway down and saw Ryan enter in plain clothes and waved. "Over here, Ryan. Where's your uniform? You don't look dressed."

"I can't come in here and have a beer if the public thinks I'm on duty."

"That's what I like about you. You never lose sight of your obligation to the decrees of deportment issued by the department. What about the night we had dinner in Oakland."

"I wasn't in the city. What's that black stuff you're drinking?"

"Good and cold." Sammy signaled the barkeep to take care of Ryan with the same brew.

"I try to act professional and play by the rules, if that's what you mean."

"That's why I'm going to have you make an arrest early this evening."

"What time? I'm on duty later tonight thanks to you.… When are we going to eat, I'm famished." The barkeep delivered Ryan his drink.

"Finish your beer. Now what did I do wrong?" Sammy asked.

"Remember that little matter with Ralph Brydges?" Ryan said, then took a sip of his beer. "That Beckman's party is in a downtown hotel, which just happens to be in Central's jurisdiction. Lieutenant Bracque requested I bring a squad of officers."

"How well I remember. I'm going to be there too. Do you have five or six officers who are as clean as you and can keep their mouths shut?"

"I'd like to think all my men are that way."

"Forget what you'd like, Ryan, do you have six?"

"Yes. Very professional men; what are you up to now?"

Pulling out the paper sack from his pocket, Sammy reached in and removed Toll's button. "Ever see one of these before?"

Ryan takes another sip of his beer and examines the button. "It's a burnt, metal, discolored, right now a dirty Muni button."

"Come on, Ryan, take a last gulp and let's have lunch." Sammy picked up Raymond's bag containing Toll's Muni coat and letter supposedly from Harry Callahan and guided the way into the dinning room. "I'm going to tell you a story that will make Manny's knocked-out teeth seem pale."

After they were seated, Sammy said, "They have a clam fettuccine in here that will make your palate burst with excitement."

The busboy delivered water, bread and butter. Sammy watched Ryan dig in and remembered Bracque's comment at Scott's about piling on the butter and not gaining weight. After the waiter took their lunch order, Sammy filled Ryan in on the two days. He mentioned the phone call from George Stanton and the million-dollar term insurance policy. "When Toll disappeared," Sammy said, "he was in competition with one Artemio Huertes for a nice promotion.

Ryan got the liquidate signal right away. "Artemio hired Manny to get rid of Toll?"

"I—I don't think so. I don't believe Manny or Joel knew Artemio or anything about him. Besides, I'm having troubles with another scenario."

"What do you mean, another scenario? I thought you had this all worked out."

Sammy growled under his breath, "when will you learn to keep your mouth shut?" He asked himself. "Nothing's changed, but the killings may be more complicated."

"Does Bracque know about this?"

    TOO BEAUTIFUL FOR WORDS

"Not yet. I'll know more this afternoon. If anything changes, Bracque will be informed. Now getting back to Artemio. He's a rising star in the city's Mexican community. A man of importance attracts women who are drawn to power."

"Say, didn't Reinhourse say something like that about the woman you killed in Mazatlan? What was her name?"

"Anita. Reinhourse said she was hot stuff. I bet she was playing all three of them."

"Three? What three?" Ryan asked.

"Add Snell to the top of the list along with Paul Mackbee. The way I see this, Artemio tells Anita that Toll was in the way of his getting the Muni's promotion. During one of Anita's show-and-go episodes with Snell, she convinces him to help Artemio, by promising Snell more regular goodies. Snell tells Anita to give Paul a couple of good rides and in return Paul will do the honors."

"How can you be so sure of all this?"

"I admit it's speculation, but take the Ferrari. Anita was driving it in Mazatlan. I'm positive Snell promised it to her and Paul gave Anita the keys. I'm betting they took their reward out in sex."

"I don't know, Sammy," Ryan said, shaking his head. "I'm sure Missing Persons tried to find this Toll guy. Why didn't they discover all this?"

"They probably did a superficial investigation. I'm sure Snell convinced them Toll schemed up the whole thing to collect the insurance money. I'm betting that he told the investigators to concentrate on Toll's home town, Detroit."

Sammy went on and explained how he stumbled onto Paul and Artemio through a Muni mechanic named Jacko and other Muni workers. He said Jacko's friend, Raymond, held the key and it came together.

The waiter brought their lunch. Sammy watched Ryan take a bite of the clam fettuccine.

"Damn, you were right," Ryan said. " It's outstanding."

Sammy smiled, then he proceeded to spatter the Portola saga to Ryan. "It was a fifty-fifty chance how I met Ruth Stoggs." He told him, then he enlightened Ryan on Katy's Hog Paradise. "It took some time, but Ruth finally revealed Paul's identity, Bulldog Bill, and she said Bulldog wasn't married. Ruth gave me a description of bulldog's deer jerky operation. The hardware clerk confirmed this as well." Sammy said, then he dropped the bomb on Ryan. "Ruth said the last jerky batch was quite tasty." He paused at Ryan's confused stare. "I found the Muni button in the fire pit." He watched Ryan freeze, drop his fork, and saw his jaw drop. Sammy knew how he was feeling as Ryan turned pale and gagged over his plate.

"You expect me to finish my lunch now?" Ryan said, "Christ, that's the most sickening thing I've ever heard. Damn that Paul, he's made San Franciscans unwitting cannibals."

"I'm betting Paul thinks this is his finest caper. I'm hoping Paul's wife doesn't know about his extras curricular activities with Snell and murdering Toll for sex."

"It will be the least of her problems." Ryan returned to acting like a police sergeant. "You say you've checked and Paul is on duty until eight."

"That's what I was told," Sammy said, "I want to face him down about the Ferrari and the Muni button around six tonight."

I'm off today, but right now I will be there for the takedown."

   TOO BEAUTIFUL FOR WORDS

"I want to face him down tonight. Can you and your men keep me from getting blown away?"

"Yes and I'm keeping this button."

"Good idea. I'll get another one from Jacko and his buddies."

Ryan now had a take-charge attitude. "First, I'll confer with Lieutenant Bracque, then get a search warrant and send two officers to Paul's and Snell's houses at the same time. The officers will ask Paul's wife for a list of places where he sells his jerky. I'm sure we'll find some for DNA testing."

"While the lieutenant talks to the brass, I suggest—"

Ryan interrupted. "What you mean is, you want to tell us how to do police business."

"I'm only suggesting. Is that a crime?"

"With you, I'm never sure."

"Why don't you have Bracque send a team up to Portola? They can interview Ruth Stoggs and rope off Paul's property as a crime scene. Since I don't know what relationship the local sheriff has with Bulldog Bill, I wouldn't alert them until after your team arrives. The sheriff may destroy evidence, by accident or deliberately."

"Gee whiz, that never entered my mind. Are you positive missing persons didn't try to find Toll?"

"The insurance company gave me a copy of the police report and those of two other detective agencies they hired to find him. I told you what Raymond said. I've made copies of everything; they're in the jacket bag along with the letter and note Paul wrote me. This would have been a perfect murder, but what Artemio, Snell and Paul didn't know was that Toll took out an insurance policy a year before; the insurance company would be out one million bucks if Toll died or disappeared. That,

Sergeant, was too much for Defender Mutual to just walk away from. I'm the third detective they hired to find Toll."

"What a stupid blunder."

"You got that right. Aren't you going to finish your lunch?

"I'm not hungry," Ryan said as he narrowed his eyelids.

"How about a wire and vest?" Sammy asked.

"I think I can get it cleared, but why?"

"Around six tonight we..."

*R*etrieving another Muni button took longer than Sammy expected. Entering Golden Opportunities' around 3:20, Sammy saw Donald, the eager executive who was willing to pay, sitting on one of the lobby's sofas. Sammy thought, if only Donald knew all the casualties the 'willing to pay" claimed so far. "Donald, sorry, I'm late."

"It's okay. I didn't have anything else planned. Where do we start?"

"Is—is anyone else around?"

"We're all alone. I had to reactivate the elevators so you could get up here." Donald went to the central fire control elevator panel, put in a key and turned it clockwise. He turned, and noticed Sammy watching him. "That prevents other occupants from entering our offices."

"That's good news. I want to see Mack's files—the ones that deal with the company's stock."

Unlike before, Sammy ignored all the glitter as Donald lead the way to Mack's office. Inside, he pressed Donald to point out where the stock transactions were kept. Opening a file cabinet drawer, Donald said, "They're all in here."

"Start bringing them to me. I know what I'm looking for."

Donald grabbed some of the files, sat them down, and said casually, "The police spent days going over all of the files, especially these. Don't you think they would have noticed anything out of the ordinary?"

Sammy sat quietly for a moment, glared at Donald, and realized, of course they would. He imagined Harry laughing and pointing out to friends another dumb dick who failed to ask questions or even perused police reports. Embarrassed, he said, "They might have overlooked something. I want to check to see if there's any connection between Nancy's husband, Walter, and Mack."

"You asked me that Thursday, so I asked Nancy."

"You didn't—now they know they're being investigated."

"Not necessarily. I said I heard rumors of an investment opportunity."

"Okay—I still believe you blew it. What was her answer."

"She said Walter was committed to Golden Opportunities. He told her he was willing to share in a long-term land deal if anyone wanted to invest. She asked Mack, who asked his fiancée, and she put up ten million dollars."

"What! Where did she get that kind of money?"

"Her father's a big-time contractor in Sidney."

"How come I never heard about these things?"

"I don't know—maybe you never asked."

Sammy sat fuming at himself, acknowledging that he was an even bigger asshole now. "Let me glance at this stuff." He went over stock transactions and within twenty-five minutes discovered that Mack immediately offered to buy stock from terminated employees on behalf of the company. The stock remained with the company. Everything was in order, no fraud, no embezzlement, and no nothing. Sammy tried to cover up another of his blunders. "Everything seems to be in order, Donald."

"What's next?" Donald asked as he put back the files.

As they walk out to the lobby elevators, Sammy said, "We're getting close. You'll receive a full report shortly—and my bill."

Donald pushed the call button and an elevator door opens. "Mister-er—ah. I told you, we're willing to pay."

Sammy stepped into the elevator. "Yeah—yeah you did say that; everyone says it." As the car descended, his mind conjures up all the bodies strewn in and around a hovel outside the airport in Mazatlan. He mumbled, "Yeah, pal, if you only knew the misery those words 'willing to pay' caused."

CHAPTER THIRTY-SIX

Got a date with cannibal Bill.

August 28, 1993—6:20 PM

Sammy paid the cabby and walked into the Impound Garage.

"Well, I'll be damned," Paul Mackbee said with a warm smile. "Sammy, I haven't seen you for seven years and now twice in less than two weeks. And what's with the monkey suit?"

"I'm going to a shindig tonight."

"Good to see you again. What car are you in pursuit of tonight?"

"I'm not looking for a car at all. I just wanted to tell you I found the Ferrari."

Sammy watched Paul's facial expression change to that of a kid who was just about to get spanked for eating most of his mother's baked cookies for the church social. Recovering, Paul forced his smile to return. "You say you—you found Joel Ceja's car?"

"I said I found the Ferrari; I never mentioned anyone by the name of Joel."

Paul still flaunted a smile and had both his hands on the countertop trying to worm his way out of his tongue slip. "When you came hunting the car, you must have mentioned it was Joel's."

"No, pal, I never referenced the late Joel Ceja, who also was banging Anita. You poor sap, you thought she was your and Snell's girlfriend."

Getting riled, Paul's unfaltering spin on everything started to wobble, and like a twirling top, that ran out of vigor. Snared, Paul shifted to the attack mode. "God dammit, quit calling me pal. You've got a very nasty habit with that pal shit. Look at you. You're short, stocky, with a receding hairline, like that Webber guy. You know," Paul started to laugh, "that English bloke that writes all those musicals."

"You mean, Andrew Lloyd Webber? While he's my size, I find him handsome and whom, I might add, Sara Brightman married."

"Whomever, she probably married him for his money. Mirrors lie to the repulsive and lure you to believe you're normal. You have a borderline gorilla face. You couldn't attract a Miss Ugly if you tried…. See that door over there? I'm going in to take a wiz. When I come out I'll expect you and your sorry ass to be out of here."

Sammy watched Paul go through the door. He went to the entrance, opened the door checking if Ryan and his officers were in place, and then slammed it shut. Hearing the toilet flush he waited for Paul to antagonize him further.

"Damn you!" Paul wailed "I told you to get the hell out of here."

"We haven't finished, just yet."

"What do you mean, just yet?"

"What about Anita and the Ferrari?"

"Leave Anita out of this. Since you've never had a girlfriend, what business is it of yours who I fuck and why?"

"Then you admit the two of you were seeing Anita."

"And just what the hell are you insinuating?"

"That you and Snell gave Anita the Ferrari."

"You can't prove that." Paul snarled like a trapped mountain lion trying to protect its kittens. "You—you nasty snoops are all alike. Can't make it in a real police force. Hucksters, all of you, shaking down clients and pursue tiny indiscretions for what I'd call pocket change. You get your jollies by sneaking around taking photos of harmless infidelities. When I think of you guys getting off by filming people cheating, it makes me sick."

"Sorry you feel that way, but to use your own atrocious vocabulary, you won't be fucking Anita again."

"Whatever you did, asshole, Snell will have her released. What did she do? Bring the car back into the States?"

"There's nothing in the world that Snell can do now. You'll never see Anita again."

"Why's that, or should I dare ask?"

"I killed her rotten ass in Mazatlan."

"What! You son-of-a-bitch! Anita's dead…? Oh, I get it. Since no girl in her right mind would ever date you, you killed my gratuitous pussy because you couldn't inspect an overpriced sports car?"

"You've got it all wrong, pal. It was kill or be killed. I chose the former."

"Quite calling me pal, God damn you!"

"Okay, do you like the sound of Bulldog Bill better?"

Sammy saw fear in Paul's eyes. The relentless fox trapped him. Paul moved to one side. Sammy was sure he has his service revolver just below the countertop. "I don't know anyone named Bulldog."

"How about Ruth Stoggs, Toll Washington and Artemio Huertes?"

"Never heard of them."

"Is that so?" Tapping the handkerchief's pocket of his tux jacket, Sammy said, "Then you tell me how I could find a button from a Muni uniform in your jerky operation pit near Lake Davis."

Paul grabbed his revolver. "I don't know how you did it or even why, but you're good, Sammy. I've got to hand it to you. Of all the P.I.'s around the city, I always considered you one of the best. You're even better than Harry."

"I thought you said we were all hucksters."

"A few. I thought I raked that pit clean."

"You raked, but missed the only button he had."

"Shit—which one was that?"

"His pants waistband. You've been cooped up in this hellhole for so many years, and slipped up on basic procedures. Examine before you burn."

"I hate it when you're right. Put your hands up where I can see them."

Sammy carefully unbuttoned his coat, and swung it open. "Paul, I'm not carrying my revolver. Gunplay would only attract attention."

Paul laughed slightly. "For Christ's sake, you're wearing suspenders. You're getting fat. You're a pasta victim… and the coat doesn't match the trousers…what cut rate cleaners did you rent that from…? Say, why in the hell were you even involved with the Toll Washington case?"

"Insurance. Toll had a term policy for a million dollars in case of death or disappearance."

"Crap! Why didn't Snell check that out?"

     TOO BEAUTIFUL FOR WORDS

"Lazy, I guess. But why did you turn on what you believed in?"

"After Mayor Holtsmark was booted out of office, I asked for a review. The bastard chiefs' said I was lucky to still have a job and to quit whining. About that time Commissioner Snell walked into my life. He promised me good clean money for a few favors. He delivered, the department didn't."

"So you're part of the Rex Mudi."

"Rex who? What are you talking about?"

Sammy's now knew Snell only used Paul for simple local jobs, and was never part of the organization and probably figured the less Paul knew, and perhaps others, meant less leaks to a world wide assassination ring.

Paul moved back from the counter and waved his revolver, signaling Sammy to do the same. "I don't trust you."

"Paul, you've turned into human feces."

"Well, screw you too!"

"You've got the drop on me; what now?"

"If you're like most dick-shits, you want all the glory for yourself." Paul picked up the counter phone with his free hand and punches in seven numbers. Sammy knew he was waiting for someone to answer. "Snell, this is Paul. I've got a situation here that demands your immediate attention. I'll be here until eight— hurry up and call me back… better yet, get over here." Paul hung up and turned his attention back to Sammy. "Now, where's that button?"

"I have it right here, along with the letter you wrote to Toll. I was amused by your reference to *Dirty Harry's* fictional character, Harry Callahan."

"I thought it was a nice touch. Pass over the button, the letter and any other shit you confiscated from my property. I guess I have the right to kill you for trespassing."

Sammy shifts his weight, while moving his arms down.

"Don't make any sudden moves or I'll blast you right now."

Sammy reached into his top pocket and pulled out an old Muni button that he obtained from Jacko and the Muni drivers earlier. He stepped toward the counter to pass the button to Paul, but dropped it and the button rolls. Sammy bent down below the counter to pick it up.

In two seconds, Paul realized he had lost sight of Sammy and empties his gun at where he should be.

But Sammy had rolled over towards the far end, and pulls out the department service revolver, which Ryan's men have strapped to the back of his suspenders. He fires across the bottom of the counter.

Paul screams, "Auuuh, I'm hit! You bastard, I trusted you. You said you weren't armed."

"I said I didn't have my revolver. Paul, you really have been cooped up here too long. Do you think I'd come in here and confront you, and not be wired or armed?"

Sergeant Ryan and his men rushed in and took over.

"Did you get it all?" Sammy asked.

"The whole thing, Sammy, the wire worked perfectly," Ryan responded. "I thought you were a goner when Paul opened fire. Why didn't you give him the button? That was our signal. Now I've got to answer to the chief why you shot Paul, and worse yet with a department revolver."

Paul was brought to his feet, bleeding from one calf. Handcuffed, he yelled at Sammy, "You dumb little asshole you don't play by the rules."

"Rules? There're no rules in a shoot-out."

"Read him his rights and lock him up." Ryan said to Officer Skip Knoll. "Wrap something around his calf and get a medic there too. I don't want one drop of his blood disgracing our vehicles. Do you hear me," he snarled, "not one drop!"

"What about Snell?" Sammy asked.

At the mention of Snell, Paul's face went white; his head dropped in dejection.

"Gone. The entire family was gone. They left everything, their cars, clothes, and even half-eaten dinners. Snell's coffee cup was still warm," Ryan explained. He was furious that one of his trusted officers betrayed him.

"I'm familiar with that trick. Any ideas?"

"I only told two officers that he was dirty, five minutes before they were sent to arrest him. Snell and his whole family vanished. It's either one or both. We'll find the culprits…we have an APB out for the family.

"Sammy we've got to talk. Every time you have a gun in your hand you use it. Why did you shoot Paul?"

"Toll's wife, Haddie. She suffered for nearly ten months because of that jerk. He has to suffer too."

Ryan shook his head. "Sammy, you can't pop people and claim they deserve it. Give me back our revolver. Do me a favor, don't shoot unless you're returning fire."

"Didn't Paul empty his gun at me?" Sammy asked.

"Yeah—after you provoked him."

"You're getting a little particular in your definition."

"We go by what the DA says."

"Great. May I keep the vest until after the Beckman party?"

"You keep shooting people! The lieutenant's not going to be happy about this. I'll see if it can be arranged, but don't count on it. I'm betting he's going to lock you up. Come on before one of the arriving investigators has you arrested. Bracque can't protect your trigger finger forever."

Following Ryan out to a squad car, Sammy asked, "Are you still going to take me to the party?"

"I don't know. I'm going to get Bracque on the radio now. He's going to be furious about you discharging a departmental gun. You'll probably end up in a cell down at the hall. Everyone in the department is getting tired of you shooting at people, including me. Even the department's police chief has heard that the real *Dirty Harry* is likely a shoofly."

"Thanks again, pal."

"Bracque, this is Ryan. We got Paul Mackbee and the wire worked perfectly. Sammy wormed everything out from our dirty officer, but shot him in the leg with a departmental 38." The sergeant said into his car's radio.

Bracque screamed so loud over the radio that Sammy had no problem hearing him "He what! Not again!" Lock that loose canon up. I still haven't explained his shooting Guido in the leg to my chief."

"Wait!" Sammy said loudly, "Paul shot at me first and emptied his service revolver"

"Ryan, is that true?"

"Yes. Paul tried to kill Sammy."

"Dammit, Shovel always has a plausible excuse."

"I want to be at this shindig tonight. Bracque, you said I could be there."

"Ryan, make sure our trigger happy detective doesn't have a gun and bring him along. If I lose my promotion, I'll be gunning for you myself—did you hear that Mr. Shovel?"

"Affirmative." Sammy retorted, smiling at Ryan.

CHAPTER THIRTY-SEVEN

Hobnobbing and rubbing noses with the swells?
Naw, it's just the hoi polloi.

August 28, 1993—8:30 PM

Sammy read the sign at the St. Matthew's entrance; it was built after the 1906 earthquake. In the grand ballroom of the Hotel, the party's ambience overwhelmed Sammy's senses. He examined tracks in the thirty feet high ceiling. He figured the ballroom could be divided into six smaller rooms, for there were six huge crystal chandeliers, one in the center of each bay with a stage at one end.

Sammy envisioned the Phantom of the Opera and shuddered at the thought the chandeliers could drop. He thought he had seen the room in an old movie. The flick *San Francisco* with Clark Gable and Jeanette McDonald flashed across his mind. He appreciated the ballroom embodied old San Francisco; extravagant gilded cast moldings and polished brass define its elegance.

He was relieved that Bracque's wrath had worn off. He heard the low drone of aimless chatter interrupted by sudden outbursts of laughter. He grinned at the spectacle of beautiful people provocatively attired in every imaginable color showing off their best attributes surrounded him. His nostrils detected commingled scents of perfume, men's cologne, liquor, and haute cuisine. He watched women daintily holding exquisite crystal,

---

     TOO BEAUTIFUL FOR WORDS

while sipping fine wine. He knew how Godzilla would have felt shopping in Tiffany's.

Sammy analyzed the men closely, then mimicked their movements, he was determined to look like he belonged. He turned and was splashed with champagne.

"Sorry, little man," a burly galoot muttered, then continued with what Sammy considered an idiotic conversation with another man.

Sammy bit down on his lower lip, but suddenly eyed a familiar face. It was Edie LeFan. Wondering how she was surviving after he'd nailed her husband for a phony home-repair scam, he weaved his way through clusters of gorgeous creatures and received two more splashes. A part-time model in her late thirties, Edie was still attractive, despite what Sammy put her through.

He watched her elusively moving about, then slowly made his way in her direction; the odor of a familiar perfume flooded his nostrils. It was strong and floated around her like a cloud. Evening of Paris; it was all Edie. Getting closer, Sammy noticed she was really playing dress-up, apparently sporting her finest makeup for the soiree; however, she was sprouting canary claws around her eyes. Sammy hailed her. "Edie! How's that husband of yours?"

Being a model, Edie was tall. She peered down at Sammy's receding hairline. "Why, Mister Shovel, what on earth are you doing here? And I can't believe you own a tux, if you call that rented one a tuxedo. Only the black bowtie looks new, but alas it's a clip on."

"Hey, I'm just mingling with San Francisco's finest."

"I've news for you, dearie," Edie retorted. "This charade may appear genteel, but don't ever cross these people—say, you're wet with champagne, and there's dirt on the right side of your pants leg. Oh, I get it, you dropped a case of Mums to sneak in when the caters went to investigate."

"What on earth do you mean?" Sammy prodded.

"Oh, get off it! You probably bribed your way in. I know Laura Beckman wouldn't have sent you an invite. By the way, I'd watch my backside if I were you. Some of guests at this shindig are pals of guys you helped put away, or worse yet, killed…. Say, the way you indiscriminately splatter lead around town, how come you don't end up in the poky, too?"

"After my partner, Harry, took-it in the slats, you fire at me, I fire back—now it's double coming back. The department remembers Harry and is playing it soft, but lately they're getting frustrated."

"Say, what bus did you think I just off of?"

"Hell, I don't know. I'm just trying to earn a living. I've got to eat too." Sammy took a step back. "Edie, you look very sassy tonight, like you're ready for a photo shoot."

"Thank you, dearie. I'm modeling some of Laura Beckman's fall line."

"You're being paid to be here?" Sammy asked, but Edie was staring over his head. After about fifteen seconds he said, "What the heck are you looking at?"

"Oh my God." Her lips trembled. "Oh God—Oh!"

"What is it?"

"The most gorgeous Woman I've ever seen just appeared through the ballroom doors."

Sammy started to turn he had to see this for himself, but Edie grabbed his shoulder. "Don't turn. She's looking this way."

"Well, just how good-looking is this broad?"

                    TOO BEAUTIFUL FOR WORDS

"She's not a broad, she carries herself like a well-groomed lady. I'm a broad. In fact, she's so gorgeous, I'd want to boink her."

"Boink?"

"Have sex, silly!"

"Hey, I thought you were straight. What about Stan? You said you'd wait for him."

"Dearie, I've been a switch hitter all my life. If Stan were here, he'd say, 'go for it' and with that gorgeous woman he'd beg to join in. Beside, why do you think Stan trusts me while he rots in stir?"

"Is she still looking this way?" Sammy turned. "I've got to see this.... Oh—jeez." Sammy stared at a coal-black-haired beauty, wearing a lemon-toned silk gown. A vibrant deep purple scarf surrounded her waist. Silky strips hinted of lemon, blush and violet streamed down from the waistband and kissed her purple shoes. Her complexion was unblemished and shimmering pale; it was almost like finely polished alabaster without the sheen.

"I've got to keep moving," Edie whispered. Or some of the boys will get the right idea. They never figured out how Stan got such a light sentence."

"I convinced the police that Stan was coerced by your shady friends." Sammy said.

"I know, don't remind me. Say, I still have, well—never really—uh, thanked you."

"Please, you don't owe me a thing. I came to like Stan and I want to keep it that way."

"You know, dear—Mister Shovel, I'm betting that lady is the reason you're here."

"I'm not sure, but it's strange that one so beautiful would be here without an escort."

"Gee! Thanks for the compliment. But, I admit, she's splendiferous."

"Whoa, where in the heck did…?"

"Crosswords, dearie, crosswords. It helps pass the time. I'll keep my ears open for dirt."

Sammy wandered over to the buffet table and picked up some hors d'oeuvres and scanned the room for Herman Zeigler. He spotted Zeigler's daughter from the Polaroid picture. His eyes followed her every move. Sammy noticed a commotion at the ballroom's foyer, and watched her run over and throw her arms around a middle-aged man who epitomized the image of the Gray Fox: debonair, trimmed mustache and dressed in a tailored tuxedo. The distinguished gentleman constantly smiled, exuding a jovial personality. Zeigler's daughter escorted the man to a woman who Sammy presumed must be Laura Beckman.

He saw Edie again, now dressed in a red leather suit, with a white blouse that had tiny red dots scattered about. He muscled through the gathering crowd to confirm his suspicions. "Edie, is that Laura Beckman?"

"Oh, we don't know our hostess, do we?"

Flustered, Sammy said, "Jeez, I'm just checking." He then asked for another conformation, "And whom is she talking to?"

"Herman Zeigler, one of the sweetest men around San Francisco. Isn't he a doll? When he talks he sounds like a Shakespearean actor. I don't know what he's doing here."

"What do you mean?"

"Look around you, dearie. This crowd's loaded with misfits. That's what makes up the fashion world. People on

     TOO BEAUTIFUL FOR WORDS

drugs, gays and lesbians, wannabe fashion designers, super models and has-beens, like me. Then there are *players* and young toughs, all seeking excitement.

"On the other hand, Mister Zeigler's a real gentleman. He has his hands full with his daughter, though. She's trouble. I understand her father has had her in rehab twice already. She feels her father's life approaches boring, so she hangs around with people I knew, and still know, all too well."

"Thanks," Sammy said, totally stunned. He was numb; did the man Edie just describe sound like a ruthless killer? He wondered if he had been wearing blinders, because all of a sudden, he realized clues have come too easily. Was Lieutenant Bracque's original assessment about Zeigler correct? Crap, do I have this all wrong? Harry, help me out here. Sammy felt like he took a sucker punch in the stomach. All his blood began to drain from his head. He was ready to hit the canvas, when his body was jostled.

Sammy turned to see who bumped him. Before him stood the Woman. Up close he saw lightly applied makeup, with that certain professional touch that only Hollywood stars and the best models could afford. Sammy stared at coiffured black curls, that delicately cuddling her oval face. The Woman had high cheekbones, soft violet eyes, a dimpled chin, and a mouth always slightly open demanding someone's lips caress its perfection.

"Sorry, little man—I didn't see you."

"I'm delighted to meet you." Sammy replied, seized, and kisses her hand while scrutinizing the rest of the package.

"Yikes!" She quickly pulled her arm back. "For gods sake—quit slobbering on me! And—just who are you?"

"Sammy, Sammy Shovel.... You're beautiful—too beautiful."

<hr>

"I know, weird one. I saw you watching me earlier. What hiding place did you crawl out of? Let me guess. I get it—prison?"

Stepping back, Sammy admitted to himself, that he had never seen a woman so exquisitely proportioned—tall, yet not too tall. Her gown had multiple slits exposing shapely legs. "When I said too beautiful, I mean look around the room. Haven't you noticed other woman won't look at you? Even most of the men turn away. You're—you're too beautiful for words."

"For a dumpy guy, you seem to have all the answers."

"It's my business to observe."

"Ah ha, not prison then—a gumshoe maybe?"

"I like the term detective."

"A private dick!"

"Will you keep it down." Sammy said, hushing her.

The Woman went along with the gag, and spoke softly. "So—we're on assignment are we?"

"Maybe. I've got to mingle—see you around."

"I'm sure you will. Ciao!"

After regaining his composure, Sammy spotted Bill Johns at the bar, beckoning to him. He made his way over to where Bill stood. "What's up, Bill? Hey, are you drinking?"

Bill took a sip from his glass. "Just a sherry, old man. Quite-a-smashing-good-party. Have you tried one of these spanking good little crab cakes." Bill gobbled one down and smiled. "Quite tasty. Ah, look over there. Our target, Ralph, has just arrived."

Sammy frowned for a second, turned, and watched Ralph glad-handing anybody and everybody. "For a guy who's afraid of killers, he's playing cozy-up real well. Bill, will you keep a vigilant eye on Ralph? I've got an uneasy feeling about Herman Zeigler."

"What do you mean, uneasy, old man?"

"I don't know, but something's amiss. Have you seen any police or Lieutenant Bracque?"

"Two of the waiters, three guests, and four dressed as hotel personnel. The lieutenant's in the command center, room two-twelve, along with the inspector we met at breakfast, and several other officers."

"You must mean Reinhourse. If anyone in this room is a policemen, I certainly don't recognize him."

"Oh, quite. The lieutenant told me they're on loan from a city called San Jose. He intimated that he's worked with them before."

"Why that old devil." Sammy moved away, but kept an eye on the Woman. He noticed her wandering about, but she never struck up a conversation. He witnessed more and more guests arriving. Technicians were testing the stage microphones. The place was buzzing with titillation. He turned to gaze at the entrance one more time, and was hit with a glass of bourbon in the face. Sammy shook the liquor out of his eyes, stunned, but not by the liquid running down his face. He couldn't believe Peter Ballard just walked through the door flanked by Nancy Foster and Mack Dirverson.

Sammy felt like he was being slapped around like a ping pong ball—the champagne, a beautiful woman, bourbon and now suspects. He smelled as if he just emerged from a liquor vat.

Sammy pushed his way over to them. "Mister Ballard, we meet again. May I ask what brings you here?"

Peter's eyes widened, startled at the sight of Sammy. "Mister Shovel…my…you do get around. I think you remember Nancy and Mack."

Mack had forgone the bohemian look and was wearing a tux like Ballard. Nancy, to Sammy's surprise, sported a simple black gown, with ribbon-like black ruffles from the waist down. For contrast, she showed off a sixty-inch pearl necklace tied in a knot about halfway down. Only her wedding ring graced her fingers.

"Pleasure to meet you again". Sammy said, then quickly shook their hands trying to get at the chase. "Why are you here?"

"You remember, Mister Shovel, the detective we hired," Ballard said.

"How can I forget; we almost had lunch this week." Nancy remarked sardonically

"He and the police discovered Manny killed our Joel."

"Oh, that was terrible news, learning Teddy Bear shot Joel." Nancy said.

"Teddy bear?" Sammy asked.

"The ladies called Manny, *Teddy Bear*, because he was round and jolly," Ballard said.

Sammy staid focused. "Yeah, he was jolly all right… What brings you here?"

Ballard's impressive voice replied, "Why Laura Beckman called me this afternoon. She asked if I would bring our controller and personnel manager with me to meet a relative of Joel's. She intimated it was Golden Opportunities' new owner. Laura engaged a suite for us on the fifth floor. She and this new owner wanted to go over the personnel records and our last quarterly financial details around midnight."

"Did Laura mention a name? Who is this person?"

    TOO BEAUTIFUL FOR WORDS

"She told me Joel's cousin was a very nice lady by the name of—of—."

"Phoebe Goold," Mack threw it out.

"Never heard of a Phoebe Goold. Did you say she was related like a cousin or something?"

"That's what we were told, but she doesn't know or is ignoring the fact that Joel changed Golden Opportunities to a stock company about seven years ago," Mack explained. "The employees now own seventy-five percent of the stock. Joel's will states any yearly proceeds from his twenty-five percent are to go to children's charities."

"I heard that from the police," Sammy advised.

"I tried to tell her, but she hung up," Peter said.

Sammy wondered, if Joel's relatives were going to try a hostile takeover by making an offer they couldn't refuse—like death "Have you talked to Donald lately?"

"Every day," Ballard responded.

"Has he said anything about my continuing investigation?"

"He told me in strictest confidence we should expect a report soon." Peter glanced around; in a flat voice, he asked. "Are you under someone's obligation now?"

"Something like that. You say you were asked by Laura Beckman to be here. Is that right?"

"Yes. Is something amiss, Mister Shovel?"

"No. It's been a pleasure—meeting all of you again." Elbowing through tuxedo bliss, Sammy wondered if all this malarkey about Nancy, Walter and Mack being partners, the buying and selling of stocks and some broad named Phoebe rang true. Jeez, maybe Bracque's intuition about Peter Ballard was correct, but is it even bigger than the lieutenant imagined. Did Golden Opportunities hire me to play patsy?

He decided to seek out the Woman. Maybe she held answers about Ballard. "We meet again."

"So, you're going to be my antagonist tonight. I noticed you've swung around the ballroom—tumble onto anything suspicious?"

"Yeah and no."

"I noticed your shirt has a large stain on it and I smell bourbon. I thought you said you were on assignment."

"I've been splashed repeatedly."

"All alkies say the same thing."

"Stop it, this is serious. I'm sober and frustrated."

"Okay, what's the verdict, detective?"

"I don't know for sure, but you're beautiful and unescorted. Outside of being discreetly greeted by Laura Beckman, with a cheek peck and wheezing a few words into your ear, everyone has ignored you. Or were they told to ignore you? I saw a couple of decent-looking gents approach, but they were quickly rebuffed."

"For a short guy you observe a lot. This isn't a social call if you're wondering."

"Since you look like a model, employment then?"

"Maybe an opportunity—maybe not. You keep asking me questions. What gives?"

"I believe your life may be in danger."

"Little man, for an ice breaker, that's a terrible line. Do you use it often? I mean, being in the business and all."

"This is for real. I believe you're part of something going down tonight. Does the name Ralph ring a bell?"

"Not yet, but who knows, he might get lucky."

"Who invited you, Herman Zeigler or Peter Ballard?"

"I don't kiss and tell, shamus, but I will tell you this, I never heard of Herman what's-his-face or Peter Rabbit."

Sammy spotted Laura Beckman and others gathering on the stage. "Uh oh! I don't believe it."

"Hey, you've got a lot of nerve, treating me like that. After all, dick, I thought we bonded."

"No—not you, and the name's Sammy. I just saw Katherine Burger. Damn, she's spotted me. What the hell is she doing here? She supposedly vanished from the face of the earth."

"Another one of your girl friends? Sam, shame on you. You men are all alike, just players."

"Hey, it's Sammy…. I don't play with—damn, now she talking to some elderly gentleman. Ahhhh! Shit, she's pointing me out."

"If we're going to be friends, I'm going to have to wash your mouth out with soap."

"Now he's talking to a big tough-looking mugs. Damn— Dammit, he's headed this way. Look, sweetheart, I'm telling you, your life may be in danger, if you somehow get involved with a young man by the name of Ralph. I want the both of you to take the far right stairway when you leave this ballroom and go to the roof. Don't go down, people are watching the exits and you don't want to meet them. I'll join you on the roof."

"That's the sweetest thing you've ever said."

A big man approached them with two back-ups. "Hey you, shovel-off, dick, and don't come back."

"I thought you said your name was Sam?" The Woman said.

He turned to the Woman before they could escort him out. "Remember what I said." Sammy said hurriedly.

The Woman watched the two mugs march Sammy out. "I will, sweetie."

CHAPTER THIRTY-EIGHT

The best-laid plans often go astray.

---

*O*utside, in the ballroom's pre-function space, Sammy saw tipsy revelers milling about and noticed a man dressed in black with an earplug, then another one. Were they security, San Jose policemen or the bad guys?

He strolled over to one with a smile and asked, "Excuse me, pal. Do you have the time?"

The man glanced at his watch. "Almost ten." He flashed two gold front teeth. By his demeanor, Sammy figured he could be one of the Slavic men who rushed to Joel's downtown hideout.

Sammy wandered off, mumbling, "The bad guys, confirmed."

He headed for the main lobby, then stopped in the gift shop for the evening Examiner. As he paid the cashier, he checked to see if he was tailed. Sammy grinned when he spotted not one but two determined wolves stalking their prey; one stocky the other tall and wiry. "Well, well, well," he said to himself, "I must really have pissed Katherine or her old friend off."

Sammy handed the cashier a quarter, and then ten spot. He asked for a roll of quarters. He used the newspaper to shield

---

the transaction. "I think I'm ready now," he said to himself as he fisted the roll of quarters.

Sammy headed for the elevators. The deadly wolf pack tracked him at what they believed was an undetectable distance. Sammy entered an elevator and pushed the button for the sixth-floor. He wanted to rendezvous with Lieutenant Bracque on the second floor, but used the six as a diversion.

The center opening doors started to crack open. Sammy glanced both ways, then dashed out into the corridor and crossed the hall. Then presses for another elevator, as he tightened his grip on the roll of quarters in his right hand. Another set of elevator doors opened. Inside stood a fiery eyed, snarling, gold-toothed wolf. The burly killer went for his gun, but Sammy barreled in like a tornado and punched the thug's firm-chin with his quarter leaded hand. Like a cartoon character, the man's body went ridged, then slid down the wall into a heap.

In the elevator cab, Sammy fished a handkerchief from his pocket, and relieved husky Gold Tooth of his gun. "A nine millimeter fitted with a silencer." Sammy mumbled to himself. "That's why he couldn't quickly get it out of his shoulder holster." Sammy pressed the second-floor button.

He lifted the half-unconscious man to his feet. When doors open he shoved him out the door, and immediately he heard muffled popping noises. He lost his grip on Gold Tooth when bullets thrust the semiconscious man to the right. Sammy took a firm hold on the confiscated gun; dived out of the elevator; fired to the left and missed. But so did his new adversary, the second wolf sent to dispatch Sammy.

The toothpick turned to flee, and Sammy fired off two rounds. He hit the gunman's rump and leg. The goon went down, and his weapon skidded across the floor. Sammy jumped up and

                    TOO BEAUTIFUL FOR WORDS

approached thug, holding Gold Tooth assassin's gun with both hands.

Bill Johns emerged from a cross-corridor, exclaiming, "Well done old man." He rushed over to the wounded man and grabbed his weapon. Sammy observed determination in Bill's face. Bill started pointing the gun when Bracque's men arrived.

The first officer said, "Freeze and drop the gun." When he noticed Sammy, he repeated his command, "You over by the elevator, drop that gun."

Doors along the corridor had been flung open and cautious heads were peering out. Soon curious guests in various stages of dress started to straggle out. One of the policemen greeted them. "Please, folks, we have everything under control. Go back to your rooms." He waved his hands, telling all the prying eyes to go away.

Another officer tried to shush one stubborn onlooker, who kept insisting. "That man over there looks dead." Still trying to peek around the towering blue figure, she started to step back.

"That's right, ma'am, the shows over," the officer said. "Go back to your rooms, we have everything under control."

Sammy returned to the elevator where the first Gold Tooth's body was sprawled out, and knelt down. "Better get Sergeant Ryan out here. This guy's been hit real bad." He turned to Bill Johns, "Hey, pal, I thought I asked you to watch Ralph."

"I was, old man, but there are too many cooks. So I came looking for you. And, may I be so bold as to ask, what became of you at the gala?"

"I was asked to leave, and not too politely. Here comes Sergeant Ryan now. You know you shouldn't have touched that gun with your hand. Now your prints are on it." Sammy said, eyeing him.

The sergeant arrived running.

"Ryan, this one might not make it," Sammy advised. "His pal, moaning over there, thought he was shooting me when the elevator door opened."

In no time at all, three more policemen head toward the elevators. "Move the wounded immediately," the sergeant barked. "I don't want to alarm more of the hotel guests." Ryan grabbed his shoulder intercom. "Call the hotel manager and advise there's blood to clean up."

"Good work, Sergeant." Sammy said.

Ryan glared at Sammy. "Didn't you have enough excitement earlier this evening? Didn't you listen to what I told you at the impound garage? Don't you ever think first and shoot second? Now you've really got the department into the pickle jar." Ryan turned to an officer. "Remove that gun on the floor to keep this loose cannon from more damage."

Sammy slouched as if ready to be handcuffed.

"Only our friendship keeps me from arresting you," Ryan said.

Inspector Johns looked over the situation. "Quite!" He said.

"And who are you?" Ryan asked.

Sammy started to say, "He's from…"

"One more word and you're handcuffed," Ryan said.

"I'm inspector Bill Johns from Interpol, London office. I'm working with Mr. Shovel and Lieutenant Bracque."

"You should have stayed in London. You've picked up some bad habits hanging around with Shovel. Why on earth did you pick up that gun?"

     TOO BEAUTIFUL FOR WORDS

"To keep that moaning thug over there," he motioned to beyond the elevator Sammy dove from, "from trying to fire at my friend again."

Hotel management and the cleaning ladies stepped from an elevator.

Ryan snapped at the other officers, "Take them around the corner to the command center. Sammy, if Bracque doesn't send you to the Hall I'll be surprised."

*I*nside the command center, Bracque lectured Sammy. "God dammit, Shovel, you can't start shooting people in this hotel. Are you crazy," Lieutenant Bracque roared angrily. "We could hear your gunplay all over this floor. I'll have to answer to the Chief about this. Give me your goddamn revolver. I'm putting you under arrest."

"I didn't bring my revolver. I took the gun off of a thug that wanted to shorten my lifespan. Ryan's has it with my handkerchief wrapped around it. If it's any consolation, they tried to kill me first. I only wounded them."

"Where is that gun again?" Bracque demanded.

"I told you, Sergeant Ryan has it."

During Bracque's' admonition of Sammy, Bill Johns walked around, observed the officers doing their work, took notes, then sat on a sofa never saying a word.

An officer, with an earplug, motions to the lieutenant and then takes his finger and runs it across his throat.

"Wounded? Why did one of them just die? Bracque exclaimed.

"I didn't do it! It was the other gunman trying to kill me. Why do you always try to pin every homicide in the city on me?"

The lieutenant's lips pinched, but didn't smile. "Because of your record," he roared. "You're an easy target. I heard what happened, but not the details. You're lucky I don't handcuff and book you. I want to know every minute what you were doing. Give your statement to the officer seated at the table. You know the routine. I'm sick and tired of you shooting people." His eyes narrowed. "For Christ's sake, Shovel, when are you going to realize it's against the law? Even for the department. If we discharge our weapon, we're put on administration leave and then there's an investigation by internal affairs.

"Since Harry died, you've become obsessed with revenge," Bracque said so loud, guests could hear him from two floors up. "Get over it! The days of shooting people when they don't stop are gone."

"Okay, Okay, but first look at the front teeth on both of those thugs. I'm betting they're are a matched pairs of gold teeth with the initials R-M on the backside."

"I'll have Ryan check. Now—sit down and start talking to Officer Moran."

As Sammy located a chair, away from Moran, he meekly asked Bracque, "Did you know that Nancy Foster, her husband, Walter, and Mack Diverson were in some land speculation deal?"

"What has that got to do with this investigation? And yes, we knew."

"Why didn't you tell me?" Sammy asked accusingly.

"Did you ask?"

"You said we would share."

"What—what was there to share? Everything they did was above board and proved to be true. You talk about Golden Opportunities. There were lots of deals going on within that firm, because the employees knew a gold mine when they saw it staring them in the face. They invested their pension funds with Ceja's approval. Do you know how many files folders we have on this investigation?"

"Not really."

"Shovel, contrary to what Harry might have told you, we aren't stumbling Keystone Cops. We check and double-check information and follow-up on leads. Your only flaw, outside of shooting people and jumping to conclusions, you think about minute details too much and muddy the big picture."

Belittled, Sammy sat dejected and wondered what happened, I had the one-arm bandits just where I wanted them, everything was spinning towards four cherries across and the big payoff, then a lemon showed up.

"Reinhourse, tell Mister Shovel about the car and license plate that he had us look up."

"After Burglary arrested the guys ransacking Joel's apartment at the Hotel Harald, they recorded the license and engine number, then sent it over to the impound garage."

"I'm betting it's gone." Sammy retorted.

"Oh, the vehicle's there, if you call melted metal a car," Bracque said.

"Sammy, both the license and car were stolen," Reinhourse said. "The car came from LA, the license somewhere above Redding."

"As you suggested again, the San Francisco Police Department sent the photos of Mazatlan's Herman Industry managers to other cities. Bracque commented.

"The photos led us to a married couple with grandchildren. They live in Orange County. The other man and woman live in Los Angeles, but they're not husband and wife.

The names you gave us don't match their present handle, except the unmarried lady called Elsa Schmit, she's really Elsa Hofherr. Save your breath, we already asked. There's no known connection between them. Nothing, nada."

"Did you know I got kicked out of the party," Sammy said.

"No!"

"Remember the woman I told you about in Mazatlan, Katherine Burger, you know, the one that vanished. She's at the party and pointed me out to some elderly gentleman who promptly had me removed."

"Who said Laura Beckman doesn't have good taste."

"Very funny."

"These are photos I received from Mazatlan. All of the surveillance officers have copies. Look them over and tell me which one's your—friend." Bracque said, pushing the photos towards him.

Sammy handed one back to Bracque. "This one, and she's not my friend."

"According to the LAPD, your Katherine now goes by the name Phoebe Goold."

Sammy perked up, like someone just staked him with a fresh bankroll. "What! I'll be damned. Remember Peter Ballard?"

"The heavyset president of Golden Opportunities. Yes and he checked out clean."

"Well, he's here with part of his staff to meet, get this, Joel's cousin, Phoebe Goold. Laura Beckman said she's here to take control of his firm."

"What's she wearing?" Bracque asked.

"A turquoise gown with red and green flecks scattered about. It looks like it was sprayed on."

"Reinhourse, get on that. Check with all operatives in the ballroom and locate her. By the way, Shovel, we've been checking on our plain Jane, Ralph. He's quite the ladies' man; borders on being a *player*."

"A *player*? That's it—keep an eye on the most beautiful *Woman* at the party. She's tall, about five-eleven, black haired, wearing a yellow gown with pastel colors streaming through it. Her complexion's pale, almost white. Say, why don't you have a video camera set up in the ballroom?"

Bracque put his elbows on the table and his face into his hands, as if totally disgusted. Finally he glared up at Sammy and said, "Are you running this investigation? Dammit, Shovel, we're lucky we got this room without tipping our hand. So what do you do? Shoot up the place and blow our cover. That's what you always do. Now, get out of my hair and let the department and me do real police work. I'd like to remind you that you're lucky you're not under arrest and I'm not hauling you down to the Hall to be booked right now."

"Lieutenant, if my good friend here agrees to keep quiet, may he stay?" Bill Johns asked.

"Ryan, turn on the speakers so our friends can hear what's going on. And Shovel, don't question me again."

Reinhourse pressed the mike button and asked, "Is anyone listening?"

"Ten-four. Steven here. I've located the Goold women dressed in blue. What other name did you say?"

"Burger."

"Whatever. Now she is walking over to Herman Zeigler and grabbing his arm. She's pointing out Ralph as they talk. Now she's turning him around and pointing out a tall black-haired lady. Jesus, what an exquisite specimen of womanhood."

"Tell Steven's to keep his mind on his job." Bracque yelled.

"She's still holding onto this Zeigler guy and walking over to Laura Beckman. The three of them are just standing and talking. Out."

"Jimmy, report."

"Ten-four. I'm on the other side of the Ballroom. I can see everything that Steven is reporting. The three of them have broken up their conclave and are now approaching the gorgeous tall black-haired model. Laura Beckman introduces Herman Zeigler to her. He's shaking her hand. Now he's turned and pointing toward Ralph. The four of them are making their way toward me where Ralph's situated. Out."

"Jimmy, get closer and stay with them."

"Ten-four. Okay. Herman leading the way, the four of them are surrounding Ralph. I'll leave the mike open as I pick up empty glasses. Over."

Herman just placed his hand on Ralph's shoulder, and said, "Ralph Brydges?"

"Ralph just turned around."

"I'm Herman Zeigler." They heard Herman say through the mike.

"Oh-uh?" Ralph muttered.

"I'd like to introduce you to your hostess, Laura Beckman." Herman said.

"Young man. I've heard nothing but praises for your fashion designs. I've wanted to meet you. That's why I invited you to my party." Laura said.

"Ah—thank you. Ah—gee what a super party—ah—lovely models. Ah." Ralph replied.

"Steven, can you still see them?" Reinhourse asked.

"Yeah—Herman's acting like cupid. His eyes are mirthful and he's almost giddy. I'm going to get closer."

"Laura, the young man's speechless." Herman said. "I promise, Ralph, she's not trying to woo you away from Sports Attire. May I also introduce, Kate Maclaren. She's Laura's sales rep in L.A."

Steven cut in. "Did you hear that? That dame's got another name. Three aliases in one night? I think she's going for a record."

"I'm very pleased to meet you, Ralph." Kate said. "Laura told me how you single-handedly turned Sports Attire around. You must be rewarded for your efforts. Maybe we can talk later."

"Ah—yeah—ah—later." Ralph stammered.

"Steven, did you get all of that? Jimmy can't talk. What are they doing?" The Lieutenant inquired.

"Herman Zeigler's radiating success. He's taken Ralph by the arm and now he's turning to that beautiful Woman. Over."

"It's my great pleasure to introduce you to one of the most gorgeous European models I've ever seen," Herman said. "Ralph, may I present Zondair?"

"Ah—you're—you're beautiful." Zeigler chuckled as Ralph stumbled over his tongue.

Kate's belly laugh came through the mic. "At last!" She said. "He does speak!"

Zondair's voice sounded more like a purr to Sammy, who was listening.

<hr>

"Come with me, Ralph, you're mine now. Let's sit over there and chat," she graciously murmured.

They heard clapping, then Herman said, "Well, ladies, how did we do?"

"Herman, better than you'll ever know." Laura replied.

"Steven here. Herman Zeigler is scanning the crowd. He's spotted his daughter. He's going over to her. He's giving her a hug and now a kiss on the cheek. He's leaving the ballroom. Out."

"Matt, are you and Bennett in a position to intercept him in the lobby?' Bracque asked.

"Sure thing, Lieutenant. Ten-four."

"Be careful, he might be carrying a gun. I understand he's dangerous," Bill Johns cautioned.

Sammy frowned, then said, "Yeah, be careful, Matt. We want him alive, don't we, Bill?"

"Why, of course, old man."

The lieutenant glared at Sammy and snarled.

"Ten-four. Don't worry, we've got two men behind him and one closing in on either side. Here he comes. We've got him. Out."

"Bring him to our control room," Bracque barked out.

CHAPTER THIRTY-NINE

August 28, 1993—10:52 PM

B*racque* waved Herman to take the seat between him and Inspector Reinhourse. They, however, remained standing.

"What's the meaning of this?" Herman Zeigler shouted rather indignantly, but still stood.

"The meaning is," Bracque shouted back. "We want to question you about the late Joel Ceja for starters. Sit down," Bracque added insistently.

"What? Joel? What on earth are you talking about?"

"I'm talking about the murder of Joel Ceja," Bracque pressed.

"I didn't murder Joel. I don't even own a gun."

"How did you know he was shot?" Reinhourse inquired.

"Are you crazy. It was on the news, in the paper and on the radio. In fact, sometime last week, you announced who the killer was."

The two police officers roared questions in rapid fire, dallying an old police-badgering trick, that made Herman turn his head from side to side.

"Did you know Joel Ceja?" Lieutenant Bracque inquired.

"Of course, I knew him. We went to USC together. We were on the rifle team."

"I thought you said you don't own a gun," Reinhourse reminded him.

"I don't. My father was in the war and made me believe guns were evil. He made me believe we should talk out our differences. Never resort to violence. I've tried to keep his message alive. I'm not much of an athlete, but I liked competition. At SC we used rifles to score points, like in any other sport."

"Why did you talk to Katherine Burger this evening?" Bracque asked.

"Katherine who? I don't know anyone by that name."

"Okay, what about Phoebe Goold?" Reinhourse pumped a way.

"What's going on here? I've never heard the name."

"You introduced Kate Maclaren to Ralph Brydges, didn't you?" Bracque demanded.

"Yes, I did."

"Well," Bracque stated exasperated. "Kate Maclaren, Phoebe Goold and Katherine Burger are one in the same. She concocts aliases."

"I didn't know that. I met this Kate person about an hour ago."

"What did she say to you?" Reinhourse coerced further.

"She told me she was Laura Beckman's sales rep in the LA area. She wanted me to introduce two young people whom she said were made for each other. Now, this really charges me up. Playing cupid makes me feel good all over. If I can play a part in making two young people's future, it would make me proud."

"Quite stalling." Bracque yelled.

"Do you know Laura Beckman?" Reinhourse demanded.

        TOO BEAUTIFUL FOR WORDS

"Yes. We serve together on the Union Square redevelopment committee."

"How many times have you been to Mexico?" Bracque inquired.

"Mexico? I haven't been there for years. Joel and I used to go to Tijuana when we were at SC, but I haven't been there since."

Bracque leaned forward getting in his face. "Are you trying to tell us you don't lease property in Mazatlan?"

"I'm not trying to tell you anything, it's a fact, I haven't been to Mexico in over twenty years. Check my current passport for any entries."

Bracque's directed his fierce eyes toward Herman. "Where's your passport?"

"At home."

"Did you stay pals with Joel?" Reinhourse asked.

"As a matter of fact, when he moved here I was delighted, but we just sort of drifted apart over the years."

"Do you know an Edie LaFan?" Sammy asked, trying to save Herman from further hounding.

"Shovel! I told you to stay out of this," Bracque said.

"Yes, poor woman," Herman enlightened, "because of her age, she has a tough time finding modeling jobs. She receives the leftovers, but Laura hired her tonight to show off her fall collection. All in all though, she's had nothing but bad breaks. Her husband's in jail, but I believe when he gets out, they're going to turn their lives around. She occasionally works for me as a temp."

"Please, Lieutenant, may we have a side conference, with Inspector Reinhourse and Sergeant Ryan, before we all lose our cool?" Sammy asked.

"Okay!" Bracque shot the other officers a warning glare to keep them quiet. "Okay—let's step outside, but it better be good."

Once outside the command center, Sammy asked, "Lieutenant, did you or any of you see Inspector Bill Johns leave?"

They glanced at each other, then shook their heads 'no'.

"Well, he's gone." Sammy said.

"I checked out your inspector through the department." Bracque said. "He works for Interpol, and has an office in London. Now, don't tell me you're going to make something about his leaving the interrogation. Maybe he went to take a piss."

"Okay, let's say he did. I know you're going to tell me I'm crazy, but I'm beginning to believe Herman Zeigler."

"What! Oh great. You're the one who had this all figured out. You've explained it so many times you've convinced all of us. Now you say, you've got the wrong man? What gives?"

"Hold on, I'm not sure. I said I believe we have the wrong man. Can we have your operatives sweep the ballroom one more time to see who's with whom and what's going on?"

"Shovel, you're trying my patience," Lieutenant Bracque lamented. "So help me, if you've screwed this up, the entire San Francisco Police Department will be off limits to you forever."

"Come on," Reinhourse interrupted, "it'll only take a moment. Remember what you told me weeks ago in your office?"

"Yeah—okay. It got a little heavy in there. Maybe I've overreacted."

Back inside, Reinhourse called Steven. "Whatcha see, ole buddy?"

     TOO BEAUTIFUL FOR WORDS

"The party's going on fine. Oh, oh, the blue-gown lady, the one with all the aliases, she's approaching Ralph and Zondair. She's waving a key in front of them. She's pushing them together, places the key into Ralph's hand, and points to the door. I'm trying to read her lips. It looked like she said, 'Have fun'. Ralph and Zondair are leaving the ballroom…Laura Beckman is approaching our many-named mystery woman. Over."

"Arrest them." Sammy said to Reinhourse,

"Arrest who?"

"The two women. Bring them here."

"Lieutenant?" Reinhourse said.

"Do it!" Bracque said,

"Steven, did you copy that?"

"Ten-four. Got it. Out."

"Have Jimmy follow Ralph and Zondair. They should be headed for the roof." Sammy said.

"How do you know that?" Reinhourse glanced at Bracque, who nodded *it's okay*. Reinhourse told Steven, "Bracque confirms."

"Is there anyone else in the ballroom with an intercom to us?" Sammy asked.

Reinhourse hit the button on the mike. "Ken. Are you there?"

"Ten-four. I've been listening."

"Sammy Shovel, a private investigator, wants to ask you something. He's working with us."

"Is there a distinguished gray-haired black gentleman wandering about?" Sammy asked.

"That's a negative. No one here now fits that description. An old man left with a group of men about ten minutes ago."

Suddenly the door bursts open, and Laura Beckman and Katherine Burger were marched in, handcuffed, and spitting mad. "What's the meaning of this," Laura protested.

"Sit down," the lieutenant said forcefully. "Consider yourselves arrested."

Katherine spotted Herman Zeigler. "I thought you were—"

"Being detained by your friends," Sammy interjected. "Is it still Katherine Burger, or maybe Phoebe Goold or Kate Maclaren."

"I want my lawyer. I'm not saying another thing."

"You got it, buster," Laura Beckman chimed in. "Buzz off."

Sammy smiled at Katherine and said, "I bet you were surprised to see me this evening." He turned to Laura. "Where in England were you born?"

"None of your bloody business." She retorted looking down her nose at him.

Gazing down at his mystery bitch with the many names, Sammy says, "I'm tickled to inform you Golden Opportunities is a stock company. Joel must've had a notion about his future and wanted to protect his employees. They own most of the stock. When the workers find out what really happened to Joel, they won't give you the time of day, let alone hire you as their new CEO. I knew you'd be thrilled. The Mexican authorities will want to talk to you, also, and your husband—"

Bracque shook his head as he watched the ladies go from confusion, to hate with venomous glares shooting at Sammy. .

Herman Zeigler remains silent. He acknowledges the ladies by a glance, but never uttered a word.

     TOO BEAUTIFUL FOR WORDS

"Lieutenant, I spoke with that good-looking women to meet me—" Sammy said,

"Zondair." Bracque advised.

"Yeah, her, to meet me on the roof. I promised to save that damsel if she was in distress. Reinhourse, will you and Ryan follow me to the roof…? Ryan, may I have a shoulder radio?" Sammy asked.

Reinhourse again turned to the Lieutenant, with dismay written all over his face. Bracque shrugged, and turned to Ryan, "Get a shoulder radio and give it to Mister Shovel, but try to hide the damn thing under his coat."

"Why?" Reinhourse asked.

"I don't want anyone thinking this loose cannon represents the SFPD. I'm giving Shovel all the rope he needs to hang himself or become a hero. It's in his hands now."

"Oh, can I have a gun?" Sammy asked, trying to maintain a serious expression.

"No! No—no—no. I don't want to hear of you even touching one—do I make myself clear?" Bracque said emphatically.

An armed man with helmet, resembling a soldier, arrived at the door.

"I believe the SWAT Team's here." Bracque said to Reinhourse and Ryan. "Have a few of them follow our master sleuth before he finds a way to shoot up the entire downtown area. Have the rest find another way to the roof."

CHAPTER FORTY

Ugly little man,
Even an uglier disposition.

Sammy started up the stairway, he'd advised Zondair to take.

Near the last floor, he found officer Jimmy slumped on a landing. He checked him out. The policeman had been hit over the head, but he was still alive.

Fumbled with the shoulder radio, he finally managed to press the talk button through his shirt. "Jimmy's down on the tenth floor. Hurt, call an ambulance. I'm going to the roof." Before setting off, he relieved Jimmy of his handcuffs.

Sammy climbed the stairs to the roof level and cracked-open the door. He peered around.

The hotel was built shortly after the 1906 earthquake, it was crowded with added mechanical equipment, ducts and fans, in addition to the original skylights and chimneys.

He spotted a man guarding the stairway structure. The thug had a gun in his hand. Sammy grabbed his roll of quarters, pulled out his wallet with his left hand and threw it so the man would have to pass in front of the door opening to investigate.

The man turned at the sound, then cautiously walked toward the noise. After the thug cleared the door, Sammy hurtled out of the doorway. He hit him from behind. The man dropped

---

his gun. Sammy grabbed his coat, turned him slightly, then with quarters clinched in fist delivered a right cross to the man's jaw.

Sammy picked up the goon's gun, another 9mm with silencer. Then dragged him into and down the stairwell to the mid-landing. He cuffed him to the stair railing, ripped off some of the man's shirt and fashioned a gag. He spotted two SWAT team members on the landing below and brought his index finger to his mouth. They nodded.

He returned to get his wallet, then heard, "Mister Shovel, over here."

Sammy recognized Ralph's voice. He crouched down and proceeded to the direction from where he'd heard the call. His eyes widened as he recognized what Ralph holding, a quivering Zondair.

"My God—I'm glad to see you, Mister Shovel." Ralph said relived.

"You took my advice." Sammy said.

"I'm sorry about the way I acted, but I knew something wasn't kosher as soon as I walked into that ballroom. I had to find out what was going on, so I acted dumb. Please, forgive me," the distraught woman said.

"It's okay—I like—" Sammy said.

"Mister Shovel," Ralph interrupted, "I believe we're not alone!"

"I'm frightened." Zondair said trembling.

"You're probably right. I've already encountered one thug." Sammy said to Ralph, as he searched the area for something to shield Zondair and Ralph if the action started before more help arrived. He spotted a large fan unit, over to his left. "Come on," he said, pointing. "Crawl over to that big tin box and stay low."

"What about my gown?" Zondair asked.

Ralph put a hand on her shoulder and started pushing her toward the fan. "Trading a gown for your life is a no brainer. Crawl, sweetheart." Ralph said.

Just before the trio reached the fan unit, a shadow moved ahead of them. "Stop," Sammy whispered, "trouble ahead. Stay on this side of the fan, then dive behind it when I say 'Now'."

Still crouching, the three of them halt their advance.

"You can come out, Bill, we know you're there." Sammy said.

Inspector Bill Johns emerged from behind the other side of the fan unit. "Good show. Tom said you had a bloody way about you when it came to this sort of thing. You didn't disappoint. Tell me, old man, what made you suspicious?"

"From the time I first saw you, pal, you never offered any advice until the police were about to arrest Herman Zeigler. You wanted him kidnapped or killed by some gunplay you planned in the lobby, but when police officers came from all sides, it thwarted your plan."

"Mister Shovel, why on earth would I want this Herman person shot?"

"Why? So he couldn't talk. That way the police would believe he was behind all of the murders. How did you manage all of this from London?"

"I hate to disappoint you, old man, but I had nothing to do with any of those unfortunate mishaps. Now, as we have been talking, two of our associates have positioned themselves to your right. You will now drop the peashooter you retrieved from our associate. Lay the gun down and out very carefully, Mister Shovel. Good lad. That's it. Stand up. Now, kick it towards your

   TOO BEAUTIFUL FOR WORDS

right. Good show, old man, I think we have it." His voice changed to a forceful tone "You two also stand!"

Sammy helped Zondair to her feet. He made sure she was next to him. "Pardon me, pal, but did I hear you say 'our associates'?"

"Of course, old man, I'm just, what you might say, an expense to a very highly organized murder-for-hire syndicate."

"An expense?" Sammy asked confused.

"I keep my employer informed if Interpol has any idea who's behind the international hits."

"For a price, Bill, for a price. What does it take to buy an Interpol inspector's services?" Sammy replied.

"I'm not cheap if that's what you are driving at. I have no idea who takes care of local blokes or how."

"Local blokes? How local?" Sammy asked his eyebrows raised.

"Oh, I'd say New York, Chicago, Washington DC, Los Angeles, and, of course, here in your own San Francisco. In four years the syndicate will expand worldwide." Bill puffs out his chest, and added, "I'll be in charge of the London eradications."

"I just love your capricious attitude about all this. You left out Vegas and Miami." Sammy informed him.

"Business is business, old man. Miami has too much undesirable drug traffic. Vegas, too much surveillance."

"Undesirables? That's so sweet. So Herman Zeigler's not the ring leader?" Sammy asked.

"Quite. He was used as a foil. And very successfully I might add. We fooled you."

"I don't fool easy, pal, but I've got to admit, it's been brilliant. I mean using German characters on the stone decoders really had me convinced. And by befriending me, you knew every move we were making. I don't know why I'm asking, but what about Peter Ballard?"

"Who?"

"Never mind, you answered my question.... Tell me, is Tom part of the syndicate team?"

"Please, old man, Tom is a pompous gullible bureaucratic twit. We don't have men standing behind every door, every tree, or every pole. We employ just enough to eliminate problems. Each member is a spoke on the wheel and only knows what affects him directly."

"I like Tom. I'm glad he's clean. I now suspect you tried to kill me on the second floor, but Sergeant Ryan's men foiled your plan."

"Please, to kill is rather harsh. Why don't we say neutralize."

"You English have such an odd way of defining words." Sammy said with a shake to his head.

"The best news is we're going to complete our assignment tonight, by rubbing out Ralph, who is a major thorn in my employers' side, depose of an unfortunate lady and exterminate an extremely pesky detective, who damaged our elite Mazatlan partners. We are so powerful and confident we want to show the whole world we can accomplish all this right in front of the San Francisco police's noses."

"Is this where I'm suppose to beg for my life?"

"Well, old man, it's been a real pleasure meeting the individual who annihilated one of our best-trained teams. But, now it's time to meet your host. By the way, he wants to kill you. Being the gracious henchman you believe I am, I'll let him tell you why."

An old man stepped out from the shadow of the fan unit.

    TOO BEAUTIFUL FOR WORDS

"Mister Shovel, may I present Francisco Perez. Sammy—
as I said, he's going to kill you—personally."

There, before Sammy and his friends, stood a rickety old
man with drooping shoulders somewhere around eighty-five, but
looked two hundred. Sammy recognized him as the one who
instructed the thugs to remove him from the ballroom. Stooped
over, he seemed to be about five-two. His face showed deep-set
black eyes, postulated face and through a cruel mouth gaped
tobacco-stained teeth.

"You—you meddling punk." The man's raspy voice
quavered. "You killed Anita, my granddaughter. I'm going to
make you suffer, you miserable fucker, while your friends watch.
Their deaths will be quick, but not yours. I'm going to make you
beg for death."

"Well, well, well," Sammy taunted. "Are we a little
pissed off that I got that bitch of a granddaughter before she got
me?"

"You—you no good fucker! I know what you're trying to
do! Make me kill you quickly…. No—no, I want this to be
painful—very painful."

Sammy stared at the small snub-nose .38, then to the
man's gnarled fingers. He thought he glimpsed a shadow. "Say,"
he said, "do you have permit for that concealed weapon? You
could get into a lot of trouble carrying a Saturday-night-special
in this city."

"Keep it up! I'm beginning to hate you even more." The
man sneered.

"Tell me, asshole, how did you manage to wrestle the
Rex Mundi society from the Nazis?" Sammy said.

"I tell you, mister, it's going to be such a pleasure—a real
pleasure when I kill you. I mean really total satisfaction." The

old man noticed Bill Johns shuffling his feet. "Stand still, you big black oaf—you're annoying me." He turned back to threesome, and stuttered, "I—I—ah, what was, ah," turning back to Bill, "what was I saying?"

"Something about the Nazis." Bill replied.

"Ah—oh yes, don't give those Nazis credit for anything but their own self-regard. They wouldn't recognize gold unless it was rubbed in their noses." He paused trying to catch his breath. "I was a first class sergeant stationed in Paris for about a month. In the service, everyone called me Frankie. I had lots of buddies. I had what you Americans refer to as a—a—a cha—cha—"

Bill helped, "Cushy?"

"Cushy job. I was a translator. Yes, I know, how can a man of Mexican background speak German?" Perez raised his voice, "I'm not Mexican!" He retorted firmly, then coughed and wheezed repeatedly. Wind-gusts unexpectedly hit him from behind and Sammy received a face full of his rancid breath, as did Zondair. She jerked her head back, almost heaving up some hors d'oeuvres.

"I came from a very large family in Northern Spain. My grandmother made us speak and read French and German and English. We were very poor and had nothing. At eighteen, without a job... I—I, let me think, ah, I

"Immigrated?" Bill suggested.

"I immigrated to this country just before the Nazis invaded Poland." The cold air was taking its toll on Perez, he suddenly wheezed. He pulled out his inhaler, took two deep whiffs, then continued. "During World War Two, I was invaluable to the U.S. Army as a translator. While in France, most of the enlisted men were only interested in screwing

     TOO BEAUTIFUL FOR WORDS

women and drinking French wine. But my grandmother always told me to adopt opportunity, so I went to the Paris library."

Sammy shot a glance at Bill Johns, then thought, "What a sweet boss. He's so deadly wholesome." Frowning, he swept the roof behind vulgar mouth and detected more hints of shadows. He raised his voice to cover any rustling or vibrations. "What happened then, old man?"

"Don't call me an old man!" Perez paused for a moment to catch his breath. "I found some books on their sordid history and lo and behold I read about the greatest assassin's ring France has ever known. I wrote down the information. Ca, cu, er,…curiosity, I imagine. But, I used it in the late fifties, when war heroes were forgotten and jobs where hard to get. Yes." He thundered, pointing to his chest. "Me, Frankie Perez, found a new niche."

Sammy wondered if the old man only knew vulgar words without help from Bill Johns. He leaned in Zondair so she would get ready to run for the fan housing about four feet away. "How on earth did you know Herman Zeigler?"

Perez snickers. "I—I—in—I, interred—I—"

"Interrogated." Bill supplied.

Perez snarled at Bill Johns. "I interrogated his father after he was captured. I found out he was stationed in Paris for over two years. Actually, he was a nice man, not the typical Nazi. He hated the war and the killing. At the time, I agreed with him, so I always remembered him. But in time, I forgot his name." Parez's eyes grew misty as he recalled happier times. "In the sixties I found the waif, Joel, in Mexico. With his cute little dirty hat, we all came to love him. Since we only had one older boy, Dorlisa and I adopted him as our son. He was a smart kid and a whiz at math. Later we sent him to USC. In his second year, I discovered

Joel's roommate was Herman Zeigler. The name clicked. A little investigation revealed he was the son of that same man I'd interrogated so many years before. All of my pieces for riches fell into place. Enough of all this chatter. It's time for you to start dying."

Sammy was sure others were on the roof. The question was - friend or foe? "Wait, asshole, you've only told half of the story here." He gave Zondair harder push.

She squeezed his hand, finally catching on that it was time to run.

"Please, old man. Don't upset Frankie more, it'll only make your death worse." Bill interrupted.

"Why should I tell you, why—tell me, why?" The rapid movement of his vocal cords makes Perez cough again.

"Well, pal, you don't want the three of us to go to our graves not knowing all the gory details, do you?"

"Please, mister," Zondair begged, "why did you send for me?"

The old man stared at Zondair. "You are beautiful beyond words. It's a shame you must die. I had no idea just how beautiful you were. You see, my dear, we planned to have you meet Ralph at the party. We knew he had an eye for the ladies. I told my niece, Laura, to engage a woman whom Ralph couldn't resist, and set them up in a hotel room. The next morning, the maid would find you both dead, the result of a lovers' quarrel. Cost was no object. I see my niece didn't let me down. You are that woman and more. Don't you agree, Ralph?"

"Yeah, she's a beauty all right, but what did I do to you?"

"You—you son of a bitch are destroying my clothing line in Mazatlan."

"You'd murder me for some lousy clothing sales?"

"You little shithead. You've already cost me over fourteen million in sales!" Perez said. Convulsions immediately overtook him. His time in the cold air and his tale had taken too long.

"So, pal, Laura Beckman's your niece," Sammy interrupted.

"I'm not your pal, mister! Didn't I tell you, I'm going to kill you."

"Yeah, with you it's turned into rote, you've mentioned it repeatedly. But Laura's has a British accent."

"For a detective you don't know much, do you?"

"What?" Sammy asked, trying to confuse the old vulgar man.

"I said—ah…," He turning toward Bill again, "What did I say?"

"You don't know much for a detective."

"You're try to mix me up, Listen, flatfoot, I told you, I came from a very large family. We scattered after the war."

"Who's Phoebe Goold?"

"You mean Jane Phoebe Perez Goold? You stupid sneak, she's my daughter," Perez bellowed, then stared coughing violently, due to San Francisco's foggy nights.

"Jane?" Sammy asked?

"She despised being called a *plain Jane*, if it's any of your business."

"Elsa? Of course she's the other one." Sammy said, suddenly understanding.

"Oh, you're so smart."

"Why did you take on Joel, was your son, killed?"

So much chatter forced Perez to breath even more heavily. "I loved that boy, but he lacked the heart for killing. He wanted out. I was willing, but the code of the Rex Mundi's hardnosed bastards became more than I could control. But, you should know that Joel's gun, the one I bought for him when he graduated from USC, is going to kill you!" He started waving it in a menacing gesture.

"How in the hell did you get Joel's gun?" Sammy asked staring at the .38.

"In the military, you learn, always try to have a back-up. Commissioner Snell was there to witness Joel's killing and to relieve Joel of his revolver." He said, he held Joel's gun steady and glanced at it. "This was Joel's first gun, I still cherish it." Perez paused coughing again. He has been out in the cold too long, and hacked up some vile-looking green stuff.

Sammy gazed at him in disgust, this bitter foul-mouthed little old man stood before him shaking a tiny revolver he could barely hold.

Sammy turned to Bill and said, "Bill, I think gonorrhea mouth is about to croak without having a chance to kill us."

Bill Johns seemed bewildered and was about to speak, but Perez interrupted him, "Don't you wish? That moron, Manny, became a liability. By my direct order, Snell took care of him and used Joel's gun. I don't like it when some dim-witted fucker kills my family. That's why I'm going to kill you—you son of a bitch. I'm going to start with your right knee cap, then your left shoulder beginning right now."

"Now!" Sammy bellowed, and pushed Zondiar and pulled Ralph to the ground behind the fan. He threw his body over Zondair.

"Everyone freeze!" Reinhourse roared through a bullhorn, as the police burst from the stairway door. Gunshots were heard all over the roof. SWAT Team members advanced from all sides of the perimeter and spread out.

During the sudden commotion, Bill Johns grabbed Perez and scooted him to the other side of the fan unit, as more gunfire erupted, then everything went quiet, except for few moans.

"I'm hit—I'm hit." Ralph yelled over and over.

The police proceeded in an orderly fashion, and checked out each thug and the criminals behind the fan.

"The black man's dead; an old man is still alive, but barely." One officer reported.

Getting off Zondair, Sammy asked, "Are you hurt?"

Jumping up, Ralph yelled, "I'm hit; I'm bleeding. I thought you were suppose to take care of me, not shield someone else."

Sammy held his hand out to Zondair.

"Oh Ralph, I thought he was just trying to get friendly." She said as she sat up.

Sammy squinted and gave her a half smile. Then he tightened his lips, as he inspected Ralph. "For God's sake Ralph," he said disgustedly. "it's only a Band-Aid wound on your left arm. Relax, you tore a little bit of skin on fan's frame."

"But you said the police were going to protect me."

"Not now Ralph—there are dead men here; some are dying; others wounded."

Ryan arrived clutching his shoulder radio. "Get some ambulances and the coroner, a few are still alive. Ten-four."

"Sammy," Reinhourse said, "are you and the others hit?"

"No, except, Ralph skinned his arm. Thanks, Reinhourse. That was great timing."

"Timing hell, we've been listening to the entire conversation. You didn't turn off the mike. That's why we couldn't let you know the SWAT Team were on the roof."

Sammy shrugged, then shook his head. "I saw two of them in the stairwell. I never did know how to work one of these damn things."

CHAPTER FORTY-ONE

There are women in this world.
Then there's the Woman.
I'll take the latter.

August 28, 1993—1:15 AM

---

*W*ith Reinhourse leading the way, Sammy, Ralph, and Zondair were finally brought into the second-floor command center. Lieutenant Bracque turned and eyed the trio. "Mister Shovel," he said. "This has got to be one of the most screwed-up investigations I've ever been on."

"Don't remind me," Sammy said. Then turned to Zondair, and said, "Perhaps you should sit down until I get things sorted out with the police? Ralph, clean up that scratch with some soap and water in the bathroom, and have one of the officers look at it. A simple band aid should do the trick"

When Zondair removed the blanket the police provided while she was still on the roof, she began brushing dirt and gravel from her gown, then sat down.

Sammy poured some coffee for the both of them. He brought two Styrofoam cups over to the woman and handed her one.

Zondair gazed up at her savior, cradled the cup, then mouthed, "Thank you!"

Ralph returned. "You were right, it's more of a scratch, but it hurt like hell." He sat next to Zondair examining every exquisite feature she possessed.

Sammy forked over the second cup of coffee to Ralph. "I thought you might need this. He turned to the Woman. "Is there anything else you might want like a donut, ah, err—"

"Zondair. The name's Zondair." She said.

"I couldn't remember, sorry," Sammy said. "What's you last name?"

Zondair crossed her legs, slowly, so Sammy could get a glimpse of her shapely gams, and purred. "Who needs two when one will do?"

"I—I was just—er—one name's fine with me." Sammy stammered.

"You saved our lives tonight. Thank you." She thrusts her elbow into Ralph's side.

Ralph still in a daze, his face drawn and listless, but picked up on Zondair's jab. "Yeah, er—thanks. But I don't get it. Why would someone try to kill me because of some tops and shorts? I thought being a clothing designer was the safest job in the world."

"Pal, in today's world, nothing is safe." Sammy replied, then gazed at Ryan, and asked. "Any word on Snell?"

"Not yet. We've posted an APB. I have two officers picking up Artemio Huertus. Mackbee's been booked—completely."

Bracque's eyes light up as if Christmas had come early, and said, "I wish I could have see their faces in Booking, when they escorted in a cuffed Mackbee and made him dance the dance."

Ryan winked.

"No, you didn't? Not the rubber gloves too?" Sammy asked startled.

Bracque grinned like he just hit the Lotto.

   TOO BEAUTIFUL FOR WORDS

"You mean they made him spread his cheeks apart and they started digging?" Sammy said surprised.

"I told booking he deserved our best." Ryan informed.

"I think the both of you are enjoying this. Why didn't they take him to the hospital?" Sammy chuckled.

"When one of our own betrays the department's trust, we go out of our way to accommodate them. Since you only grazed him, they patched him up during the booking process." Ryan informed them.

"I guess it's tit-for-doing dat." Sammy said.

Raising hedgerow eyebrows, Bracque flashed contentment. "We contacted the Chief and he's sending a contingent to Portola. Now, for some good news. My Chief wanted to know how all this came down. I want you to know, I didn't hold back. He wants to see you in his office. I believe he's thinking about a Citation of Merit. That's not bad for a civilian. Don't mention all of the shooting incidents."

"I was only doing the job Golden Opportunities hire me for. In fact, for once in my life I'm handsomely paid."

The lieutenant squirmed, for he knew Sammy wasn't even mentioned when Bracque laid claim to a big drug bust. "I agree. I—I—Look, Shovel, I'm sorry about that Knuckles Malloy caper. I admit you deserved the credit."

A pompous Sammy had completely forgotten about his old partner, Harry, and started to strut around ready to address a throng of admirers. Sammy cracked a smile, hinting to Bracque the slate is clean—but he wanted more. He observed policemen running around like bees who had found their hive was invaded—unorganized order.

"You seem to have a happy contingent. Which reminds me, I must call Donald, so he can share what happened with the Golden Opportunities' clan. I don't want to deal with Peter Ballard right now. Er—would you ring the Golden Opportunities' room on the fifth floor and tell Ballard—."

"That Phoebe Goold's detained?" Bracque said, smiling.

"That would be nice."

Bracque leaned back. "When things go well, we bask in the little glory that comes our way. The press is on the way. Your name will be mentioned. Laura Beckman and Phoebe Goold, or whatever name she claims to be, were taken to the Hall and are being booked as we speak. Things are jumping all over this world. The FBI has been alerted and the LAPD was contacted to round up members of the Perez family. We've already informed the Mazatlan Chief—Don—ah, Don—"

"Esparza." Sammy supplied.

"We got him out of bed, but he was very happy. He said you should visit Mazatlan again as his personal guest. We are alerting other major cities about the assassination ring. And we are in communication with Interpol about their Inspector Bill Johns and the situation."

"He's dead."

"Not Esparza. I just talked with him."

"No, Bill Johns. How does a man go sour like that? I liked the sucker." Sammy said.

"Sorry, I have no idea other than greed. He's no different than Mackbee. When a renegade smells money loyalty evaporates," Bracque said.

"Lieutenant, phone call from the CHP has been forwarded here."

"Put it on speaker phone," Bracque said.

"Done—go ahead."

Bracque here."

"This is Sergeant Norman Franks from the Highway Patrol. We have a family in custody that was driving a stolen white Mercedes. They seem to fit the description of the APB you folks put out about one Darrel Snell and family, but his drivers' license says his name is Julian Perez and claims they got into the wrong car after dinner."

"Perez? You got the right desperado. Describe him."

"Five-nine. Black hair, stocky build and a tattoo on his left shoulder that says, "Welcome to San Francisco, under an image of the Golden Gate Bridge,"

"Blond wife, and three kids, two boys and a girl?" Bracque asked.

"Affirmative."

"You have detained our most wanted criminal for this evening, officer. Nice work. Don't let them out of your sight. I'll inform the Chief and we'll arrange for their transportation back here. By the way, where did you locate them?"

"Fifty miles south of Salinas on highway 101. Wouldn't have noticed them, except the car was reported stolen in San Mateo. The owner saw them drive away and gave your police the license number. They mentioned to the police that it was a family that climbed in. Very unusual for car thieves, so we figured there had to be more to it. When the car was spotted, we stationed three cruisers in front and two in the back as we closed in. Strange though, the wife was clinging to a cell phone in her left hand, and in her right was a small paper weight."

"Green, pyramid and has hieroglyphic symbols on it?"

"Yeah! How did you know?"

"Oh we know all about those green paperweights now," he said, turning towards Sammy and winked. Officer Franks, you have made our day. Again, thanks for the great work." Bracque hung up. "Did you here that? The CHP picked up Snell and his brood."

"I'm glad you got that SOB. He tried to have me killed three times—maybe more." Sammy turned to his companions. "We want to get out of here. Can we give you our statement now?"

Bracque grinned at him, and said, "No need to, we have it all on tape. I'm not going to say anything about your gunplay this evening. We'll talk about it later with my Captain, but I would learn to keep your piece at your office. Both Sergeant Ryan and myself still have problems with your quick trigger finger, like the wounding of Guido last Christmas. However, I will admit you solved a forty-year old drug problem. However, even in self-defense you still have to answer why you shot Paul Mackbee when Ryan's men were bursting into the shack, and a Mexican National on the second floor tonight.

"I was hoping you forgot."

"Get real. You're not in Mexico. By the way, Herman Zeigler heard the whole thing, as did the two women. I must admit you really pulled out the information from that foulmouthed Perez."

"I was only holding out for the troops to arrive."

"Mister Zeigler is indeed a very gallant man. He holds no grudge. In fact, to show what kind of man Zeigler is, he's down in the ballroom and will be giving his views about the outcome to the press. He told me he was particularly impressed with a certain local private investigator. A police car is escorting his wife to be with him. He wants her and his daughter on each side of him when he gives the interview."

"What about Zondair and Ralph?"

"They can go, as soon as we find out how we can reach them. Go on, get out of here and take Ralph and his lady with you." Bracque stared at him and then down at the table and waves him off, but abruptly turns back. "If you don't want to answer questions by the press, I'd disappear for a few days. Who ever you rented that tux from won't take it back—it's soaked in blood, smells fowl, and has gaping holes in it from your encounter on the roof."

"You win. In fact I was told to burn it." Sammy said glancing at Zondair.

*O*utside the hotel, Sammy, Zondair and Ralph stood together. "That was close—too close." Ralph said, "I thought the police said they were going to protect me." He stared Sammy in the eyes. "Didn't you know your friend was part of that assassin gang? I could have been killed."

"It's not a perfect world—no I didn't. Things happen, even in the best of regulated stakeouts. The assassination ring knew all of the police plans. And were always one step ahead of the department thanks to my Interpol friend."

"That's no excuse. You're used to getting shot at. I'm not!" Ralph said fixedly.

"I'm grateful for the heads-up in the ballroom.... I enjoyed our rapport," Zondair interrupted,

"Say, that tête-à-tête was amusing," Sammy said watching Zondair finally smile. He asked, "How about some pie and a cup of hot chocolate? I know a spot near here—my treat."

Ralph's sea legs returned. He glanced at Zondair with renewed interest. "Hey, that was quite an ordeal. I guess they won't be killing me now. The pie sounds good. How about you, doll?"

"Sorry, I don't eat sweets, only sweet things."

"Oh wow." Ralph muttered, staring at Zondair like a lion ready to pounce on a baby wildebeest for a quick hors d'oeuvre. "I'm as sweet as they come. Do you want to finish our date? After all, it's paid for and I want to devour you."

Zondair gave Ralph a smile that could melt baker's chocolate a hundred yards away. "Why, Ralph, aren't you afraid I might consume you? Rumor has it that some of the men who escorted me were never heard of again. But if you're willing to be tied, gagged, and humiliated... and—er.... perhaps, in my moment of extreme passion, I may lose total control, and my nibbling could turn into gorging. I might absorb your very soul." She peered into Ralph's eyes. "If all that suits you, then by all means, I'm ready."

Ralph's' excitement dimed rapidly, like hard stems of spaghetti when it hit boiling water. "Whoa—hey, I don't know what you have planned, but after what I just went through I'm not up to experiencing any kind of physical violence. Besides, I just remembered I have to get up early tomorrow, to meet—ah—yeah, I'm going surfing with a couple of buddies. Wow, look at the time. Oh gosh, it's one forty-five. Sammy, ah—Zondair, it's been—ah—a, ah, pleasure. Oh my God, you're unbelievably beautiful. I—I—Maybe—we—ah maybe next time. Rain check?"

"We'll see, won't we?" Zondair remarked.

Ralph scurried away.

When he's out of sight, Zondair said, "Poor Ralph is still a sniffing, snorting boy."

"Yeah, but talented."

She gazed down at Sammy and purred sweetly, "You know," turning her head back and forth to fluff her hair, "you look just like that English Actor, Bob Hoskins, except he's a smart dresser. You're wearing a tux that has rental written all over it, and not a good one at that."

"Really!"

"Yes Really. The coat material doesn't match the trousers, and the pants are a sort of one-size fits all—baggy. Look at your cummerbund. I see black threads sprouting where it's been sewn onto the back strap—a hasty repair job.

"Oh, I get it, you're the fashion editor for the New York Times."

"No, Esquire."

"Funny."

"Well, my amusing little shamus, what now?"

"What now, what?"

"Your gesture of throwing yourself over me was very noble. You were in control all evening—actually quite magnificent. I want to thank you for saving my life. I mean—I really want to thank you."

"Okay, I hear you. You were an innocent victim; Ralph was informed there could be danger. So, what's your suggestion, as if I didn't know?"

"Do you know what I am?"

"A hooker?"

"Your words—simple and to the point of hurting."

"I didn't mean to offend you," Sammy said apologetically, realizing that maybe he went too far in his snide comment.

"Ease up, you haven't. In fact, I'm beginning to like your style. No, I'm not a hooker, *per se*. I'm a courtesan, a very high priced, and, I can honestly say, high-class. My clients are men of rank and wealth who will pay over ten thousand dollars for me to be their evening's consort."

"Whoa, I'm just a poor P.I. Moreover, that kind of activity didn't cross my mind. Besides, I don't mess with the local stuff."

"I'm not local and I know it did."

"Did what?" Sammy questioned.

"Cross your mind. I could feel it when we first met. Your eyes gave you away. I saw your eyes shamelessly undressing me.... What are your plans for the next couple of weeks?"

"Weeks? I don't know—I have some routine investigations, some warehouse thefts—nothing major."

"It's almost two in the morning. Let's go to the airport and take the first plane out to wherever it goes. Do you have a passport?"

"Sure, but I don't carry it with me, and I'm wearing a smelly booze and blood infested rented tux."

"Well, get it, bundle up that rented rag and burn it, and we're off. When we arrive in our paradise, we'll buy the necessities."

"Off? Off to where?"

"Who cares; first plane out. Mexico, New Zealand, the Riviera, Paris—you'll love it there—New Delhi, the unknown."

"I don't have that kind of money!" Sammy responded exasperated.

    TOO BEAUTIFUL FOR WORDS

"Listen, you unromantic flatfoot, it'll be my treat for two weeks and I'll pay for your trip home and reimburse the tux." Stepping back, she added, "I'll even buy you a decent wardrobe. I told you, I'm a high-class courtesan, proud of it and, I might add, very well healed. This little gig that was planned tonight cost someone over three hundred thousand dollars because I had to break off a previous big payday commitment in Europe. Ms. Beckman paid in advance. I have villas and places to stay in almost every part of the European Continent. I own a few; I stay at some. I promise you, I'll be yours, body and soul for two weeks. What do you say…? Sammy?"

Shovel just stood there. He didn't blink nor stare at the beauty before him. His eyes glazed over. For once, he was speechless.

With a devilish grin on her face, Zondair leaned down and whispered, "Cat got your tongue?"

Sammy took a deep breath as he stepped to the curb and raised his hand. "Taxi!"

ABOUT THE AUTHOR

Ronald M. James was born during the great depression, and as a toddler watched WPA men build a new street, from his home's big front window. His playmates were a red rider wagon, a small black satchel and rocks. By using his imagination he had conversations with mythical street workers that bloomed into fashioned fantasies by age four. He used cardboard boxes to create fun spaces for his neighborhood playmates to enjoy and he kept telling stories all through high school. In college he abandoned writing and studied architecture. James had a successful architectural career and retired, however he wanted to keep his creative juices fluent, so he returned to his childhood story telling days and joined a writers group. Like architecture, each day he couldn't wait to create, finish, and start new stories—like this one, *Too Beautiful For Words*.

Author Website: **www.ronaldjamesbooks.com**

Other books by Ronald M. James:

The Two Jacks (Adult)
Harrington Manor
An Adventurous Night—The beginning

The Samuel D. Shovel, private investigator series, continues with another new novel,

WAIF

CHAPTER ONE

Fire a warning salvo at a disinterested
Private eye and he'll dog it to resolution.

March 7, 1994—10:50 AM

"**Y**ou've reached the offices of Samuel D. Shovel, Private Investigator. How may I direct your call?" a soft voice asked. More than a secretary, Zondair and Shovel were playing footsies. To please Sammy, she tailored her role of a hardboiled attorney's secretary, snuggling in an out of a miss placed contemporary chair and desk, yet still surrounded by Mr. Ugly interiors. Even the city's garbage dump, reeked better with its sweet sour odor, instead of stale rotting fumes from ancient Easter eggs hunts that crept into office finishes long ago. She glanced at the dark trail around the coffee bar, shuttered, then smiled sinisterly for this was to be the last day she would ever smell such filthy cluttered gas of rancid bouquet again.

"Who is this?" San Francisco Police Department homicide detective, Lieutenant Bracque demanded.

"Why Lieutenant, you've hurt my feelings. This is Zondair." Wondering why was he so upset.

"What!" Bracque exclaimed. "What the heck are you doing there? I have important information, and my chief demands that I inform Mr. Shovel at once. This could be life or death. Get him on the line; I haven't got all day."

"Calm down, dearie, I'm just helping out my new lover buddy."

"What do you see in him? He's short, dumpy and dresses in sleaze. Is he in for Christ's sake?" Bracque said, thinking why did his nemesis get so lucky.

Zondair flexed the fingers of her right hand and admiring her recently pedicure design. "I think he's cute. Besides, where it counts — he's all man and then some."

"He must have something... if a beauty like you takes him on an all expense vacation for a month. Well, is he or isn't he there?" Bracque barked, still envious of his hated P.I.

Zondair's chatter alerted Sammy. He was trying to suffer through all the noise Home Depot's Expo's remodelers were changing below. Both he and the lessor beneath him were told two days tops. The Expo gang were planning to arouse the ordinary to the extraordinarily by removing the stale 1948 trappings. Sammy's new and only love engaged and paid for a complete renovation of Sammy's offices. She advised him he had to change his image to attract more wealthy clients like Golden Opportunities — this time he listened.

He thought it had to be Lieutenant Bracque. He jumped up and swiftly entered the reception room, stopping at the coffee bar. He wanted to eavesdrop while pouring a mug of coffee. He glanced toward Zondair, and brought his right index finger to his mouth. He rummaged through dirty mismatched mugs and selected the one with the least caked-on mold growing on the bottom. He gave its contents a couple of watery swirls; he dumped it out, looked at the bottom and did it again. He poured in hot Java. Then ferried himself toward the reception desk, and seized an opportunity. He set his mug down and approached his newfound love. He stood behind Zondair, gently massaging her shoulder.

Zondair twisted her head with the phone still firmly pressed next to her left ear, glanced up, then puckered her lips together and released them, throwing a phantom kiss Sammy's way; bringing a gesture of satisfaction. Whiffs of *Poison* perfume drifted from Zondair's earlobes, flooding Sammy's nostrils.

Warm sensations gripped his groin. Moving to the front of the desk, he sat on one end so he could relish her face. He eyed her assesses and every facial feature, but he couldn't help thinking, enjoy your moment of bliss, she could evaporate like donuts in a police station, just like she's done in the months before, but she always comes back. *"Why?"* He asked himself.

"What can I say, except I like it and didn't want it to end," Zondair added, quite content.

"Oh, that's just great," Bracque said exasperated, then continued, "Enough of this. I need to talk to Shovel. I told you this is important, dammit!"

"It's been a pleasure, Lieutenant. I'll tell him you're on the line." Zondair said, then punched a button putting Bracque on hold and turned to Sammy. "The Lieutenant seems a little frustrated that I'm with you again."

"He'll get over it. It's hard for his unromantic mind to comprehend," Sammy grinned.

"Sweetie, must I remind you that you were in the same category before you met me."

Hurt, like a puppy when he was around Zondair, his tail snapped between his legs. "So, you've reminded me. I'll take the call in my office," Sammy said, verbally abused.

"You're not going to drink out of that mug, are you?" Zondair scolded, spying stuck on mold spores now floating to the surface.

"Coffee's coffee. A little mold never hurt anyone," Sammy replied, shooting her a half smirk.

"Au courant," Zondair snapped back, "give me that mug, it has death written all over it. I'll clean it properly, then make a fresh pot. I bought some of Pete's coffee yesterday. I understand it's quit tasty.

Scurrying back into his office, Sammy reached over, grabbed the phone, and plunked his stocky, muscular frame onto his chair. "Why, Lieutenant Bracque, what a pleasant surprise."

"Shovel, what the hell is Zondair doing there? I thought the two of you just had a fling and she was history."

"She likes me. Why are you calling?"

"Oh brother. You—you both make me sick carrying on the way you do."

"Look Lieutenant, I know it's hard for you to understand how someone so beautiful could like a middle-aged bachelor like me, but it happened. So, get over it! What's with the call?"

"I've been asked to advise you to lay off getting involved with your new client, Zoë Humerstein."

"Sorry, pal, I don't know or ever heard of Zoë... Are you sure you got the name right?"

"That was the name I was given. I wrote it down and read it back. Hey, I'm only the messenger here. I volunteered because I know you."

Sammy glared at the phone, at a complete loss listening to Bracque. No one, from any police department, had ever told him to drop a client. These kinds of events were puzzling.

"Here's a fresh mug of coffee," Zondair announced, then marched back to her desk, smarting.

"I hate to disappoint you, but seriously, I've never met, nor can ever remember meeting, anyone named Zoë. It's a lovely name though," Sammy said.

"All I can tell you is this came from somewhere at the top, maybe even higher. I... I respect you and don't want you to get hurt," Bracque lied, "That's the only reason I offered to make the call. When the word came down, everyone here in Homicide seemed startled."

"I hear what you're telling me, but if this Zoë calls, I'll hear her out."

"I wouldn't expect anything less of you." Bracque retorted, and dropped the phone back to its cradle.

Sammy sat for a moment in a daze, then took a slurp of coffee and smiled, for Pete's was indeed, quite tasty. His mind went over the conversation. What was Bracque really trying to tell me? On his way back to the reception area, he remembered movies where someone was warned before the fact, but never heard it actually happening.

"Zondy, I'm sorry. I acted like a clumsy child about the coffee mug. Please forgive me," Sammy said, doing his best to appease. "That new coffee, what's the name again, was wonderful?"

"Pete's. I accept you apologies."

"Did I receive a phone call from a woman named Zoë?" Sammy said, getting a tad antsy.

"I don't think so. I'd remember anyone whose name started with a 'Z'."

"You're sure?" Sammy said.

"Yes, sweetie, but several others called. Let me see," She started going through her phone message log. "Yes, here they are. While you were out this morning a Barry Grossnell called again about the warehouse thefts. A Jay Mathew of Computer World wanted to know if you're ready to upgrade your computer. And a Mrs. Humerstein wants an appointment to meet you."

"When did Humerstein call?" Sammy asked hurriedly, his body stiffening.

"About 9:30 A.M.; that's what I've listed here."

"I don't get it. Bracque called to tell me to lay off the Zoë Humerstein case. It's now 11:10. If her call came in at 9:30 this morning someone had to know she was going to call me, or my office is bugged again. I know Lieutenant Bracque and his men; they wouldn't place a listening device in my office."

"You mean Mrs. Humerstein is Zoë?"

"Yeah. In less than an hour and a half someone telephones the top brass down at the Hall, clues them in on Humerstein; they check around the departments to find someone who knows me. Bingo, they find the good Lieutenant and ask him to call me."

"What if they're listening now?"

CPSIA information can be obtained
at www.ICGtesting.com
Printed in the USA
FSOW04n1043270817
37903FS